"A gem of a novel set in the E[...] *Manor* immerses you in a worl[...] and expectations in 1920s Ireland. With a dash of danger and a soul-satisfying romance, Jennifer Deibel shines through the characters of Annabeth and Stephen, drawing them together through a faith forged and tested amid a backdrop of war. Well done!"

Laura Frantz, Christy Award–winning author
of *A Heart Adrift*

"An immersive read that left me feeling as though I had actually traveled to Ireland. Deibel is proving herself a master at taking readers from all over the world and throwing them into the culture and time of her stories. Pick up this book and be transported to 1920s Ireland, where folklore abounds, conflict is brimming, and love is in the air."

Rachel Fordham, author of *A Lady in Attendance*

"What a superb visit to Ireland! Authentic, lively characters are spun to life in this tale based on the captivating legend of the Claddagh ring. Set during the Irish War of Independence, *The Lady of Galway Manor* showcases a fascinating piece of Irish history alongside the raw, internal struggles of two characters who are destined to be enemies—and a remarkable source of healing for each other. Deibel brings the tension to a heady climax like a seasoned pro, weaving in and out of danger and high stakes until the very end. Anyone wishing to visit Ireland needs to experience a book by this author. I could almost taste the sea air, and I didn't want to leave!"

Joanna Davidson Politano, award-winning author
of *A Midnight Dance*

the
LADY *of*
GALWAY
MANOR

Books by Jennifer Deibel

A Dance in Donegal

The Lady of Galway Manor

the

LADY *of* GALWAY MANOR

Jennifer Deibel

Revell

a division of Baker Publishing Group
Grand Rapids, Michigan

© 2022 by Jennifer Deibel

Published by Revell
a division of Baker Publishing Group
PO Box 6287, Grand Rapids, MI 49516-6287
www.revellbooks.com

Printed in the United States of America

Library of Congress Cataloging-in-Publication Data
Names: Deibel, Jennifer, 1978– author.
Title: The lady of Galway Manor / Jennifer Deibel.
Description: Grand Rapids : Revell, a division of Baker Publishing Group, [2022]
Identifiers: LCCN 2021023645 | ISBN 9780800738426 (paperback) | ISBN 9780800741112 (hardcover) | ISBN 9781493434213 (ebook)
Subjects: LCSH: Ireland—History—War of Independence, 1919–1921—Fiction. | LCGFT: Romance fiction. | Historical fiction. | Novels.
Classification: LCC PS3604.E3478 L33 2022 | DDC 813/.6—dc23
LC record available at https://lccn.loc.gov/2021023645

This is a work of historical reconstruction; the appearances of certain historical figures are therefore inevitable. All other characters, however, are products of the author's imagination, and any resemblance to actual persons, living or dead, is coincidental.

Scripture used in this book, whether quoted or paraphrased by the characters, is taken from the King James Version of the Bible.

Published in association with Books & Such Literary Management, www.booksandsuch.com.

Baker Publishing Group publications use paper produced from sustainable forestry practices and post-consumer waste whenever possible.

22   23   24   25   26   27   28   7   6   5   4   3   2   1

For the Ultimate Author of Life:
MAY YOU BE HONORED
AND GLORIFIED
THROUGH THESE WORDS

For Hannah, Cailyn, and Isaac:
MAY YOU EACH KNOW, EXPERIENCE,
AND OFFER TRUE LOVE, LOYALTY,
AND FRIENDSHIP

CHAPTER
1

No one ever tells the truth about love.

The stories and fables paint a glowing portrait of valiant acts and enduring romance. Love, it is said, is the most powerful force in the world.

Stephen Jennings knew better.

He watched the pair from behind the polished-glass case as they huddled together, giggling and fawning over one another. Stifling a groan, Stephen slid his hands into his pockets and leaned on the stool behind him. His fingers curled around the worn paper in his right pocket, its presence both a comfort and an annoyance.

"This one here, lad." The gangly man gestured to the top shelf of the glass case. "We'll take it."

The rusty-haired lass swooned. "Oh, Charlie, do ya mean it? In earnest? Oh!" She squealed and threw her arms around her beau's neck.

"Very good, sir." Stephen removed the silver ring from the case and buffed it carefully with a polishing cloth. He started with the hands that encircled a heart, then moved to the crown that topped it. How many times had he recounted the tale of the Claddagh? More than he cared to tally. With any luck, the lovebirds wouldn't ask him to regale them with the legend today. When the ring was sufficiently shined, he handed it to the gentleman.

Fingers trembling, the man took the ring. A foolish school-boy grin spread across his face. His lass clapped incessantly, still giggling. The man glanced at Stephen out of the corner of his eye, the all-too-familiar twinkle of delight mixed with mischief gleaming in it.

Oh no. No. Not here.

The man sank to one knee. "Maggie, you know I love you."

Maggie erupted into hysterics. Stephen gritted his teeth, jaw aching from the movement, and pasted on his best smile—though he feared it came across more as a grimace.

"You know I love you," Charlie repeated. "And I couldn't wait another second before askin' ye . . . will you marry me?"

Unintelligible sounds gurgled from Maggie's lips as she yanked him off the floor and kissed him hard, then held out a trembling hand.

"Is that . . . is that a yes?" The man's puppy dog expression rivaled that of any canine begging in the alleys.

Good heavens, man, are ye daft? Stephen fought the urge to roll his eyes, while ignoring his own painful memory that surfaced unbidden. *Not now.*

"Oh, aye, Charles! Yes! Yes! A thousand times, yes!"

"I love you!" they declared in unison.

Stephen had seen what "love" could do. Not even a mother's love—which is said to be the most powerful—could protect his own beloved mammy from leaving this world while bring-ing Stephen into it. And the glassy-eyed, giddy type of love the couple before him now displayed had certainly not served any grander purpose than deluded self-fulfillment. How could they be so blind?

Charles slipped the ring on Maggie's finger and presented her hand to Stephen. "Is it on properly?"

Stephen cleared his throat. "Aye, that's right. The tip of the heart points in, toward her own heart, if she's spoken for." He looked between the two, who only had eyes for one another. "And it seems she is most certainly spoken for." Though he tried to avoid it, his voice sounded flatter than it should have. After all, the store needed this sale. He pasted another smile on his face. "*Comhghairdeas.*"

Charles looked at him now. "*Go raibh míle maith agat.* A million thanks." He handed the payment to Stephen and guided his bride-to-be out of the shop.

Stephen watched them leave, resisting the urge to rush and slam the door behind them. Bolt it. *Fools.*

"I can't do this anymore." He dropped his head. His knuckles were white, and the edges of the case dug into the heels of his hands. He slapped his palm onto the wood beam acting as the side of the case, anchoring it to the wall.

It was bad enough he was the only one who seemed to understand the truth of this ruse the world called love. But his family made their living peddling the idea and legend of it. It was salt in an ever-open wound. How could no one else see? Love was a myth. A crutch. And he couldn't be part of flogging the lie any longer. He rubbed his hand over his head, down his face, then pulled the worn piece of paper from his trouser pocket, unfolding it.

He read the words he already knew by heart.

Dear Mr. Jennings,
    We are delighted to accept you as an apprentice at Sánchez Iron and Masonry Works. Your family's skill with design and

craftsmanship is well known. We look forward to adding your expertise to our repertoire. Once you have acquired the necessary funds to relocate, please let us know and we will make your lodgings ready.

Sincerely,
Roman Sánchez

Eyeing the door to the shop, Stephen could no longer deny the inevitable. *It's time.* His father would be devastated. But the thought of staying here, hocking jewelry, and reliving his family's legacy day in and day out was enough to bolster his courage to tell his father of his plans to leave. Any shards of regret that remained melted away like the wax in their jewelry molds, leaving only white-hot frustration to solidify in his heart.

Replacing the letter in his pocket, he turned to search for Seamus Jennings. But before he could take a step, his father entered from the back door of the showroom, the faint scent of lavender wafting in his wake. And he wasn't alone.

"Ah, Stephen, there's a good lad. I've someone I want you to meet." Seamus's eyes carried more spark than usual, and there was a bounce in his step Stephen hadn't seen in ages.

Stephen turned his attention to his father's guest. Standing arm in arm with his father was a strikingly beautiful woman. Her golden hair twisted on top of her head in an intricate weave of braids and coils before falling around her shoulders in soft curls. Blue eyes pinned Stephen where he stood, and soft dimples accented her rosy cheeks as she smiled at him. She was beautiful, aye, but something about her seemed . . . amiss. Her dress, too fine. Her posture, too straight. He'd been around long enough to know a beautiful face and beguiling smile meant nothing. The most striking face can hide the blackest heart. What was this lass's secret? Still, Stephen's heart thudded unnaturally against his chest. He told himself it was due to the uncertainty of her presence in the shop and not her allure.

"Stephen, my boy, this is Lady Annabeth De Lacy." Seamus beamed.

Stephen shook himself from his thoughts and turned his eyes sharply to his father. "Lady? De Lacy?" Stephen's voice rose an octave. "As in—"

"How do you do?" Annabeth interrupted him and extended her left hand, fingers daintily dangling down.

Stephen looked from Annabeth to his father and back. "De Lacy?" He practically spat the name out.

"That's right," she continued, hand still extended, and lifted her chin. "My father, Lord De Lacy, is the new landlord for this parish." She cleared her throat and gave her hand a slight twitch, her unblinking eyes boring into Stephen's with expectation. Nae, demand.

Seamus continued to beam. When Stephen failed to respond, Seamus frowned and jerked his head slightly in the direction of the woman. "Where're your manners, lad?"

Making no attempt to mask his irritation at his father bringing a British courtier into the shop, Stephen stepped forward, grasped her fingertips, and waggled her hand briefly before dropping his arm back to his side. "Miss." He nodded curtly. "Father? A word?"

"*Lady* Annabeth is to be your apprentice," Seamus announced, so proud the buttons practically popped off his waistcoat.

"Appren— My what?"

"Just what I said, lad. Lady Annabeth here is to be your apprentice. You're to teach her the way of things. Ensure she knows the legend of the Claddagh, show her how to make the rings. She's quite an accomplished artist." He winked at Annabeth, and she rewarded him with a pearly white grin.

Nodding at Seamus, the woman said, "Please, call me Anna."

Oh, now *she wants to be informal? Not likely.* Stephen glanced at her from the corner of his eye but kept his attention fixed on his father.

An apprentice? What was the old man thinking? Sure, it could work to Stephen's advantage if there were someone capable of staying on when he left. But a woman? And a *British* woman no less? Had his father forgotten they were in Galway? Having a woman like this in the shop could only serve to hurt business, not help it. Unless they wished to cater only to the blow-ins and invaders from across the Channel. Despite his own frustrations, Stephen would sooner die than see that happen. He crossed his arms over his chest, cleared his throat, and repeated himself, this time through gritted teeth. "Father. A word!"

"Och!" Seamus waved a dismissive hand then patted Anna-beth's arm. "I'll only be a wee minute, lass. Take a look around the shop, so."

She offered him a polite, but tight-lipped smile and took a half step back.

Father and son stepped to the front of the shop, as out of earshot of their new guest as possible. "What's the meaning of this?" Stephen hissed.

"Now, now. It's not as bad as all that." A hint of resignation flickered in the old man's eye.

"Is that so?" Stephen's jaw ached.

Seamus pressed his lips into a thin line and shrugged.

Stephen scoffed. "And what about Tommy, huh? After what they—"

Seamus lifted a silent hand. He stared hard into his son's eyes for a long moment before answering. "No matter what has happened in the past, this is our present right now. You're going to do this." He paused. "I need you to do this."

Stephen's heart hitched at the look in his auld man's eye. But then he glanced back at the woman invading their shop and ire burned anew in his chest. "A British lady?" He ran his hand down his face. "The landlord's *daughter*? Father, have you gone mad?"

"Mad? Have you seen the lass?" He chuckled and winked at Stephen.

Oh, no you don't. Stephen wasn't going to let his father use humor to diffuse this situation. Not this time. Not with this. "Be serious, man!"

Seamus's smile faded again, and he closed the small distance between them. Lowering his voice further, he said, "Serious, ye say? How's this for serious? The British government has sent us lowly Irishmen a new landlord." Seamus glanced over his shoulder then continued, "I don't know if ye'd noticed, but the last one they sent us was a real saint." Sarcasm laced the old man's voice.

Stephen released a puffed laugh. He couldn't deny the previous landlord had been a tyrant. "True."

"Well, that shiny new landlord—who we have no idea whether he will be benevolent or worse than the last fella— has requested we apprentice his daughter. It's a mite out of the ordinary, I'll grant you, but I'm not quite in the mood to cross the Brits at this stage." Footsteps punctuated his point as a unit of soldiers marched past the shop. Whether Irish or British troops was impossible to tell.

Stephen sighed as an unwelcome shiver traversed his spine. He crossed his arms over his chest to stave it. The auld codger had a point, much as he hated to admit it. "Fine, I'll grant you, we need to stay in their good graces, if they even have any. But why me? The pair of ye seem to get on just fine. Why can't ya teach her yerself?"

"In case ya haven't noticed, lad, I'm no spring chicken." He stretched his arms out to accentuate his point. "I'm gettin' too auld to even be running the shop, let alone teachin' another wee one. I was going to talk to ya about it anyway, but when Lord

De Lacy approached me last week, it was mere confirmation. It's time."

"Time?" Stephen's brow furrowed. "For what?"

Seamus's hand worked the back of his neck, and he stared at the ground for an uncomfortable stretch of minutes. Finally, he cleared his throat and said, "For you to take over. You're a better jewelry smith than I ever was, and you've a smart head for business on yer shoulders. That last bout with the fever I had over the winter is what clinched it. The shop . . . she's yours." Seamus pulled a handkerchief from his waistcoat pocket and swiped at his eyes. "Come now, lad, and properly meet your apprentice."

CHAPTER
2

nnabeth pulled her eyes from the scene of father and son in heated debate. It truly was none of her concern. And yet, there was something about the way the pair engaged that drew her. Whether it was Seamus's charm or Stephen's brooding stare, she couldn't say. But so far, Ireland was turning out to be far different than she'd expected—different than she'd been told.

Attempting to ignore their argument, she scanned the store. Two large glass cases flanked an aisle at the front of the room. The till sat on top of one case, while a smaller display unit topped the other. Behind the cases, a counter lined the back wall with cupboards filling the space above and below. Heat radiated from a stove in the corner, adding to the shop's cozy feel. As the men's hushed voices continued near the front door, Anna forced her attention to the jewelry on a shelf near the window. Lines of rings shone in the late-morning sunlight, and she lifted one from its crevice. She ran her finger over the cool, smooth silver. She'd never seen anything like it. From below, it looked like any other silver ring, but on the face, instead of a gemstone or smooth band, was a strange design. A heart—gently rounded on top to create the illusion of fullness—held on either side by a hand.

On top of the heart stood a crown, not unlike the images and sketches she'd seen of the Crown Jewels.

"—teach her yerself?" Stephen's voice drifted from the front of the shop.

Anna glanced over her shoulder to see Seamus shaking his head, replying with adamancy.

Stephen's shoulders softened slightly before the stoic rigidity returned. When Seamus fetched a handkerchief and wiped his face, Anna turned away and replaced the ring. Then, curiosity getting the best of her, she kept her back toward the men but strained to catch any other bits of the conversation that might make their way to her ears. After all, she told herself, if they were discussing the landlord's daughter, surely it could be a matter of concern for the Crown.

Footsteps approached.

"Now, m'dear," Seamus said, his voice thick. "Stephen will take good care o' ye."

Anna met the older man's gaze. While his eyes still held their spark, there was a definite hint of sadness behind them.

The smile faded from Seamus's face before he called over his shoulder, "Won't he?"

A pregnant pause filled the air before a sigh sounded from behind Seamus. "Aye, Da."

"*Anois.*" Seamus took Anna's hand, giving it another pat, then returned his flatcap to his head and quit the room.

Anna turned and watched until Seamus was beyond her sight. The back of her neck tingled, and she got the distinct feeling Stephen's stare was pinned to her back. Straightening her posture, she turned to face him.

He studied her, but his face remained like stone except for his jaw muscle that worked back and forth. His eyes, the same pale green as the Connemara marble statue in her family's foyer, reflected complete disdain.

What could cause him to be so perturbed at her presence? Could apprenticing a woman really be so terrible? If the Irish were truly as unorthodox as she'd been taught, would they not relish the breaking of a socially entrenched gender belief? And what of Anna's station? Was it not an honor to have a lady of the court under his roof? Nevertheless, perhaps the mood would soften if she were to extend an olive branch. "Thank you." She cleared her throat and took half a step toward him. "For being willing to teach me."

Stephen's eyebrows knotted for a fleeting second, and his head bobbed once.

"I know it's a bit unconventional to have a female apprentice." She chuckled. "'Tis unheard of in England, in truth. However, it seems my father could only take so much of my—eh—presence at home all day long." She lifted the corner of her mouth and let her shoulder rise and fall.

Was that a start of a smile on his lips? Encouraged, she continued, "My sister is content with all the trappings of the homelife of a courtier. And she's already found ways to entertain herself. But for me it can be so dull rattling around that manor house. After all, what's a lady to do to occupy herself when there is no court?" She laughed.

All hint of levity fell from his face, and he cleared his throat. "Yes, well, we'll make do." Stephen shifted his feet and looked around the shop. "You'll need to get acquainted with things. Let's start here—with the showroom."

As he took her around the room, she listened attentively and tried to ask all the questions she could muster. One case held more Claddagh rings than she could count. Another held necklaces and bracelets. Additional display units around the shop boasted an assortment of jewelry types, ranging from brooches to hair pieces and more rings. Nearly all had some form of the Claddagh symbol. Some had gemstones embedded in them, some used only silver or gold. Yet others held intricate designs woven with multiple metals and colors.

Anna marveled at all the nuances that could exist in one single design. While each piece of jewelry included the same elements—the hands, the heart, the crown—no two were exactly alike.

She stepped up next to Stephen. The scent of musk and heather wafted off him. He busied himself adjusting one of the countertop displays. "And you make all these here? By hand?"

Stephen's brows lifted. "Aye. This shop has been in our family for more than seven generations. Each jewelry smith has put his own stamp on the design, adding a flourish or a gem." He gestured to a door along the western wall. "The design room's just there."

Anna followed him into the room. The pungent aroma of metal, dust, and smoke filled her lungs. A large cauldron with fire in its belly and sand filling its bowl radiated heat in one corner. Two walls were lined with wooden counters, blackened and chipped from time and use. Hammers, chisels, and other tools she didn't recognize littered the room—yet everything was tidy and in place. Organized chaos.

Anna walked along one counter, running her fingers over the rough edge. She shook her head and puffed out a breath. "Incredible. 'Tis truly breathtaking work you do." She came to a velvet-lined tray and brushed her fingers over a particularly intricate brooch in which a series of Celtic knots surrounded the Claddagh symbol. Stephen came up and stood behind her.

The warmth of his presence so near unnerved her. She turned to meet his eyes, and he simply stood staring at her, brow furrowed.

"T'anks," he said at length.

The intensity in his gaze shook her. It wasn't the gaze of desire. Nor was it curiosity. No, this . . . this was something altogether different. She turned her focus back to the brooch. "Seven generations, you say?" She lifted the piece from its place and inspected it more closely.

"Aye."

"That's such a long time. There are families in the court who would kill for that kind of longevity."

A sour laugh escaped his lips, puffing the hair on the back of Anna's neck. "I don't doubt that." He snatched the brooch from her hand and set it back in its place.

Anna froze except for a slight shake of her head. Spinning around, she hurried to correct her misstep. "What I mean to say is, it's utterly fascinating to learn all the beauty and creativity that has been going on here. And for so long."

Stephen lifted his brows. "Oh?"

She nodded. "I had no idea."

Stephen wagged his head. "I'm sure you didn't," he muttered.

"Pardon?"

Stephen pinned Anna with his stare once again, leaving her wondering what he could be thinking. After a long pause, he sighed, shrugged, and leaned against the back counter. "I don't know what ye've been told, but we aren't barbarians. The Irish are a highly creative and passionate people." He pushed off the counter and paced in front of her, waving his hand in a circle as he spoke. "Song. Dance. Story. Art. It all has a deep, abiding place in our history, culture, and . . . well . . . in us. It's how we share our past, ourselves. It's how we remember." He stopped pacing and looked out the small window at the front of the room.

Anna scanned the area once more. "Yes, I'm beginning to see that." She joined Stephen at the window. "I myself have long held an interest in design. I've enjoyed learning various arts over the years, much to my parents' chagrin. Alas, in the court, it isn't proper for a lady to extend herself beyond needlepoint and court dances." Anna pressed her lips together and shrugged.

"But once I heard about these rings, I knew I had to come and learn. And Father seemed just as eager to have me out of his hair for a while." She laughed.

Now Stephen chuckled for real and bobbled his head as if to say, "I know how he feels."

Anna chose to take it as jest, while trying to ignore the dimple that appeared along with his all-too-brief smile. A tray of Claddagh rings caught her attention. "So, are you going to tell me?"

His eyebrows resumed their seemingly customary position. "Tell ye? Tell ye what?"

"The story. What it all means—the hands, the crown. What's this legend I keep hearing about?"

Though sunlight streamed through the window, a shadow darkened his face. "I think we've had enough tutelage for today. Get some rest, and we'll start in earnest on Monday." He gestured toward the door. "After you, Lady Annabeth."

Anna regarded him for a long moment then swept past him, welcoming the icy blast of wind from the open door. Under her breath she whispered, "It's Anna."

CHAPTER

3

Paddy McGinnty ground his molars as he eyed the passing carriage. Tossing his cigar to the ground, he mashed it with the toe of his shoe and allowed a curse to escape his lips.

Confound it all. Those Brits'll have us bowin' down to them 'til the rapture. Wagging his head, he glanced up to see Molloy eyeing him from a doorway across the street.

Something had to be done. With the new landlord's arrival, the time was ripe for action. Nodding briefly, Paddy inclined his head in the direction of the pub. Molloy bobbed his head in agreement and sauntered off, whistling the tune of "*Óró Sé Do Bheatha Bhaile,*" signaling the rest of the lads to the impromptu meeting.

"Nora," Paddy called into the open doorway. "I'm goin' down the pub." Not waiting for her reply, he set off for Tigh Hughes.

Once all had arrived and settled around the table in the back room, Paddy cleared his throat. "Right." He rubbed his fingers along his stubbled jaw. "As ye know, the new landlord's arrived from *Sasana* to keep us in our 'rightful places.'"

Murmurs rumbled through the group, and young Ciaran spit into the fireplace.

"Has anyone actually seen the man?" Molloy asked.

Paddy nodded. "I saw his royal carriage rollin' through town not ten minutes ago. A right dandy of a contraption." He raised his brows, pursed his lips, and sat as straight as an arrow, a look of mock piety painted on his face. The group rewarded him with a laugh.

Ciaran snorted. "Figures." Next to him, Mickey snickered, earning an elbow in the side from his older brother.

"'Tis high time they leave us be," Paddy continued. "We declared independence ages ago, yet they still think they have the right to come and keep us under their pasty, white thumbs." He wagged his head and crossed his arms over his chest.

Another rumble of distaste.

"What'll we do? Ambush? Kidnap?" Old Man Burke asked.

"We have to be smart about this, lads," Paddy answered. "If we want to make changes that last, we have to make sure we're wise in what we do." The lads didn't look convinced. Most of them were itching for a fight. They just didn't understand it would come to them one way or another eventually. But in order to win, they had to do it right.

He leaned forward and rested his elbows on the table. "Look. We can't shoot first and ask questions later. Ye've seen how that's gone down in the past."

Nods and more mutterings rippled around the table.

"Alright, then," Molloy said and drained his drink. "What do you suggest?"

"First," Paddy said, "we need to do some reconnaissance. Some of ye stake out the manor house and see what we're dealin' with as far as the grand lord himself. The rest of ye, keep an eye and ear out around town. Who are they socializing with? Which other landlords they get snug with will tell us almost more than an'thing. But until we know more, ye all know what to do. Nitpick. Annoy. Use yer wiles and ways to make him question everything. And spread the word—quietlike, though—to the rest of the lads."

Heads bobbed and pints lifted in acknowledgment.

"Mickey 'n I can skulk around the house. We hunt in those woods anyhow." Ciaran eyed his brother. "*Ceart go leor?*"

Mickey grinned. "Aye."

"*Iontach.*" Paddy slapped his knees. "Excellent. You lot report back what ye find, and we'll go from there. Now, I must get back to the chipper. It's comin' on lunchtime."

The group dispersed and scattered in as many directions as there were men. As Paddy headed back to his shop, he turned things over in his mind. Indeed, if the Brits were daft enough to think the Irish would all just roll over and allow their homeland to continue to be invaded, they had another think coming.

As the carriage rumbled over the cobbled street, cutting through the heart of Galway City, Anna struggled to reconcile the morning's events in her mind. Seamus had been an absolute delight. Nothing at all like the "scoundrelous dogs" she'd heard about from her father and others in England. His joy was contagious, and though lacking in health, Seamus lit up the room. Many times throughout the morning Anna found herself laughing in spite of herself at his delight with life. Stephen, conversely, while entirely handsome, seemed angry at the world. No, at *her*.

"These Irish need our help," Father had told her when he first announced his new position as the landlord of Galway Parish. "They don't know any better than to cheat, steal, drink, and fight. It's up to us to show them the cultured and sophisticated way of life. God's way."

To hear Father tell it, the Irish were barely civilized and practically begging them to come and help—to save them. So for

Stephen to show such disdain for her upon first meeting con-
founded Anna greatly. Never mind the fact that what she saw
in that shop was some of the finest, most intricate artistry she'd
ever seen. Surely an uncivilized people would be unable to create
things of that caliber. Wouldn't they?

When the grind of the wheels on cobblestone changed to a
hollow whir, Anna pushed the scarlet curtain aside and peered
out the carriage window. They'd passed beyond the medieval
stone wall that still surrounded parts of the city and were headed
west on a rutted dirt road. To the south, rock walls sliced the
land into haphazard squares that ambled down to the shores of
Galway Bay. To the north, a thick wood bordered the road as
far as the eye could see. Mesmerized by the rolling waves and
gulls dancing in the sky, Anna let her body match the rhythm
of her conveyance as it wound its way along the snaking path
into the west.

At length, after one final sharp turn north, Galway Manor
came into view. Two pairs of tall, rectangular windows flanked
either side of the grand front door. Double columns on the portico drew the eye to the second floor and an arch that stretched
over the central window. Even though it was no grander than the
estates that housed the courtier families in England, the mansion
still stole her breath each time she arrived. There was something
about this house, this place. Something foreign. Haunting. Altogether intoxicating.

But more than the ornate furnishings and impressive architecture, the land itself called to her. The air held an almost magical
quality, along with the mist that seemed ever suspended between
earth and heaven. This land practically hummed with vibrant
life, and she couldn't help but feel more and more alive the
longer she was here.

As the coach rattled to a stop in front of the expansive main
entry, Mother stepped out to meet her.

"Good morning, dear." She placed a weak kiss on Anna's cheek. "I trust things went well?"

Anna twisted her mouth to the side and drew her shoulder up. "Yes," she answered slowly.

Fire flashed behind Mother's eyes. "The brigand didn't harm you, did he?" She'd protested this apprenticeship from the start. One evening early on in the discussion, she'd said, "They can't be trusted—Irishmen. Who knows what they're capable of?"

Now Anna rolled her eyes. "No, Mother. He was perfectly courteous. Well . . . a mite cranky, but courteous." She hooked her arm in Mother's elbow and pulled her toward the kitchen. "The elder Mister Jennings was absolutely delightful. I can't remember the last time I laughed so much."

Mother's lips slid into a half smile and she nodded.

"But Stephen—er—the younger Mister Jennings seemed completely surprised at my arrival. I don't believe his father had informed him of the arrangement until today."

"Well, dear, you never know with these people. Perhaps he'd already heard and is just disagreeable." She tucked a stray piece of hair behind Anna's ear. "Never mind the fact the ruffians are disrupting the world with their so-called war for independence." She practically spat the last word. "You can't expect these people to welcome us with open arms. Though they should be grateful we're here at all. To help them."

Anna inwardly cringed. She didn't like the way Mother referred to the Irish as *these people*. Granted, Anna didn't know the Irish from Adam, but what she'd seen so far was vastly different from the pictures painted prior to their move across the Channel.

"Anyhow," Anna continued as they entered the warmth of the kitchen, wanting to shift the tone of the conversation, "the jewelry they make is absolutely stunning. I've never seen the like of it." She fetched two teacups from the shelf and poured them some tea.

"Grand, is it?" Mother took her cup. "Thank you."

Anna lowered herself onto the bench seat of the large wooden table that served as food preparation area, tea table, and breakfast table for Katy, their cook. "Not grand, per se. It's not like the Crown Jewels. It's not flashy or gaudy. It's simply"—she lifted her eyes to the ceiling as if just the right word could be found floating among the wooden beams—"intricate."

Mother's brows arched. "Intricate? Hmm." She sipped her tea. "It sounds . . . lovely." The flat tone in her voice grated on Anna's nerves.

"Yes, Mother, intricate. You really should see it. This particular jeweler specializes in one specific design—the clah-dawg, I think it's called."

Mother grimaced. "The name leaves a little something to be desired."

Anna shrugged, trying to remember how Stephen had pronounced the word. "I'm not saying it right. When he said it, it was lovely."

Mother cocked a single brow and took another sip. "He?"

Anna's cheeks warmed, and she hid them with a long draw from her cup. Yes, Stephen was uncomfortably handsome, but there was no reason to ruffle Mother's feathers with misconstrued meaning. Better to keep things vague. "Mister Jennings. He told me the name of it, but I just can't seem to make my mouth work right to say it the way he did."

Mother set her teacup down and fastened her gaze on Anna. "Indeed."

Clearly, things were not going to shift the way Anna had hoped. At least not with any speed. Anna suppressed a sigh and drained her cup instead. The tea gone, she retrieved their empty cups and placed them in the basin for Katy to wash later. "I think it's going to be quite the adventure."

Mother rose and a chuckle lifted her voice and her countenance. "Then it should be just your cup of tea." Smiling, she kissed the top of Anna's head. As she quit the room, she called over her shoulder, "Just remember—you're a lady."

Anna chewed her lip. A lady. What did that even mean, truly? In England, it simply meant lots of rules and no fun. Here, though, she wasn't at all certain what a lady looked like. Acted like. And she suspected for a British woman in Ireland it meant a very isolated, lonely existence hiding away from the realities of life. Perhaps this was her chance to re-create it in her own way.

"Like being a jeweler's apprentice," she whispered. In truth, Father allowed her a much wider sphere than was typical of most courtiers—much to Mother's dismay. It seemed Lady De Lacy was always on the brink of swooning over yet another of Anna's social faux pas. But the distance this new opportunity afforded them from prying eyes—which at first seemed a curse as it pulled Anna away from her friends and everything she'd known—was already proving to be a blessing in disguise. While certain artistic pursuits were socially accepted back home in England, the truth of the matter was that this apprenticeship would never happen there, especially not with the match that had been proposed just prior to their leaving England. The magnitude of this opportunity wasn't lost on her. And she vowed to make the most of absolutely every moment. Even if it meant dealing with a cantankerous host.

CHAPTER

4

Anna stared at the tower jutting high into the slate sky as she headed to the Jenningses' shop the following Monday. The air, tinged with salt and a whiff of fish, tickled her senses. She was still getting used to living so near the sea. Arched windows spanned the sides of the medieval church building. And, was that a mermaid? She squinted to better decipher the image.

"Now that, Lady Annabeth, is what we here in Ireland call 'a church.'"

Anna spun on her heel and nearly bumped into Stephen's chest.

She fell back a step. "Beg pardon?" She absently patted her hair.

Stephen tipped his chin toward the building. "Ye looked a wee bit confused, so I was tellin' ya that's what we here in the land o' heathens call 'a church.'" A hint of a smile played on his lips.

Anna feigned surprised recognition. "Oh, thank you, grand sir. I would've been lost without you." She dipped a curtsy and laughed. "Now that you mention it, I do believe I've seen one of these before."

Stephen's gaze lifted to the ancient arches, his smile deepening briefly before retreating again.

Anna noticed his eyes held a spark of levity.

"What was it ye were studying so intently?" he asked.

Blinking, Anna forced her thoughts away from his chiseled features and back to reality. "Oh." Heat flushed her cheeks. "I was just trying to determine . . . is that a mermaid?"

"Aye." His reply held no hint of jest.

Her mouth fell open. "Truly?"

Stephen nodded, then looked at her directly for the first time that morning, sending her stomach dancing.

Why did his gaze unsettle her so? She pulled her mind back to their conversation and turned to look at the figure on the church building again.

"How odd. Why would a mermaid adorn a house of worship?"

"This is St. Nicolas' Collegiate Church." Stephen's tone suggested that information in itself should clear her confusion.

Anna stared at him blankly.

He looked from her to the church and back. "He's the patron saint of children . . . and mariners." His brows arched higher, and he inclined his head toward her.

Goodness, he truly thought her daft. "Ah. I'm a bit unfamiliar with all the patron saints." Her lips sank together into a line, and her gaze returned to the church. "Well, it's lovely. And whimsical."

Stephen laughed—but it was completely devoid of mirth. He looked around and then frowned. "You're a long way off from the shop. Did you come to pray before reporting to work?"

A breeze rushed down the street. Suddenly chilled, Anna pulled her cloak tighter around her shoulders. "No, I haven't been able to see much of the town yet, so I asked the driver to let me off here at the top of Church Street so I could take in some sights on my way."

Stephen nodded. "I see. Well, it's getting close on to nine. Shall we?" He gestured a hand in the direction of High Street.

"Yes, of course."

They walked in awkward silence past St. Nicolas'. Though people bustled about the city, things were eerily quiet, other than birds singing in the trees overhead.

"I thought I'd show ye our most common method of making the rings today," Stephen said. His voice held resignation. And restraint. Anna wasn't sure which she preferred—the silence or the chill of his tone. What modicum of cordiality their encounter held a mere moment ago was replaced with this hint of indifference as soon as the conversation turned toward the shop.

Anna infused as much delight in her voice as she could. "Brilliant, I can't wait!"

He only crooked his mouth into a forced smile and nodded.

They turned right on High Street. The charm of the cobblestone and two- and three-story buildings lining the streets immediately endeared Anna. Irish architecture was so different from British. The Irish had so much more character. Though the buildings were stone just like in Britain, they were less harsh somehow. They held both strength and grace. Beautiful.

She slowly turned in a full circle to take it all in. Brightly colored window trims and doors infused life into the gray buildings—their vibrant shades of red, white, black, and yellow greeted the cobbled street and passersby. Colorful bunting hung in the windows of several shops, and the aroma of bread and sausage rolls floated faintly on the breeze.

Movement from the corner of her eye jolted Anna from her admiration. Stephen stared at her intently. However, when she met his gaze, his eyes were softer. Not quite tender, but he seemed surprised at her reaction to his city. Pleasantly surprised, she hoped.

"Pardon me." She dipped her head briefly, then lifted her eyes to the skyline once more. "I can't get enough of the style here. I never would have dreamed it would be so vastly different from Camberwick. It's like I'm in a whole new world."

"That's because you are." His voice was barely audible.

Before Anna could respond, lilting notes wafted toward them, followed by a pure, young voice that beckoned her. Anna strained to find its source, finally attaching it to a small lad, no more than twelve, standing atop an old fruit crate. Next to him, a younger boy played the concertina. The older boy sang a wistful melody. Anna was mesmerized. She didn't know if it was the clarity of his voice, the moving lyrics—a love song to the city of Galway—or the light yet mournful melody, but tears sprang to her eyes. She knelt down until she was eye level with the younger lad and listened, all the while her heart stirring more with each note.

When the song ended, Anna offered a boisterous round of applause. "Well done, gentlemen. Well done, indeed!" She reached into her reticule, pulled out an Irish pound, and dropped it in the upturned flatcap in front of the performers.

The boys' eyes grew wide. "Gee, t'anks, miss! T'ank ye ever so much!"

"Thank you both for the captivating song." She nodded and smiled warmly at the boys, then turned back toward Stephen. The softness in his eyes remained, but something about the way he regarded her gave her pause. Doubt knifed at her that she would ever be able to earn his favor—nae, his trust.

They resumed their journey to the shop, while behind them a lively reel kicked up, and the older lad now sang with exuberance in Gaelic.

"You'll often find buskers all along Shop Street and High Street. It's more active on Saturdays and market days, of course, but the day there's nary a busker in Galway City is the day the world ends."

Anna smiled at the sentiment and found herself lifting a prayer that there would always be buskers in the city. She never dreamed Galway would be so endearing and exciting. A city teeming with music, architecture, and art—the very last thing she'd expected. And it seemed God had created the moment as a gift to her very soul. A sense of contentment settled deep in her belly. Anna savored it—allowing the brisk sea air, the melodious tunes, and even the salty flavor on her lips to sink into the special place in her memory reserved for only the most significant of moments. In the distance, the Claddagh Shop came into view.

Stephen glanced sidelong at Annabeth as they approached the shop. She had been so captivated by the busker boys. The music seemed to truly move her. If only he could trust that she was genuine. Every other encounter he'd had with a Brit had been laced with disdain and deceit. How could he be sure she wasn't just playing him for a fool?

It wouldn't be the first time, boyo. The unwelcome thought rushed in like a winter gale and anchored itself in his consciousness. Stephen shook his head to dislodge the idea, but there it remained. An image of Marie's face sailed across his mind's eye. A reminder of just how foolish his heart had been.

"What's the name of this method?" Annabeth's voice broke through Stephen's reverie.

He studied her face as he ushered her inside the shop. Her eyes alight with curiosity and brows raised awaiting his answer, she seemed genuine enough. Then again, the most deceitful often did. He mustn't let himself be taken in by whatever agenda she might be harboring. *Business. It's just business. Get through this apprenticeship, find a way to ensure Seamus is taken care of, and get out of here.*

He cleared his throat. "It's called the lost-wax process." He began setting the needed elements on the workbench.

"Sounds mysterious." Annabeth giggled. "Like a Sherlock Holmes tale. *Sherlock Holmes and the Case of the Lost Wax.*" A wide grin spread across her face, deep dimples bookending her smile.

If she were anyone but Lady Annabeth De Lacy, he would have appreciated the humor. But her joke fell flat. At least he pretended it did. Cocking a brow, he simply muttered, "Indeed."

Her smile faltered and the light in her eyes flickered. Guilt pricked Stephen's gut, but he suppressed it. "Nothing mysterious, 'tall, m'lady. It's to do with the wax that melts away from the mold."

Annabeth rolled her lips between her teeth. "Yes. Yes, of course."

Stephen pulled one of the stools out from beneath the workbench and sat it next to Annabeth before retrieving the second for himself. He gestured for her to sit.

She eyed the stool for a moment then gathered her skirts and awkwardly positioned herself on it. Stephen watched, perplexed, as she struggled to get situated. Whatever shiny, beaded fabric her dress was made of rustled loudly each time Annabeth moved. And there was so very much fabric. The train of the garment billowed so fully around the stool, Stephen could hardly move without getting caught in it. What in the heavens had possessed her to wear such a thing to smith jewelry?

Stephen ran his hand over his head and face, released a deep breath, and began the lesson. "This," he began, holding up a bit of beeswax, "is where we carve the design." He took a probe and began etching the basic outline of the Claddagh design.

Annabeth strained to see the intricate details he carved. She leaned farther over, her hair brushing his shoulder. A whiff of lavender and some other floral scent floated in the air between them as she moved. This woman smelled unwelcomingly good. Stephen's hand faltered and he dropped the instrument.

"Are ye alright there, Lady Annabeth?" he murmured but kept his eyes focused on the beeswax. Her face was far too close for comfort to concentrate, let alone to look at.

"Hmm?" Her eyes remained fixed on the beeswax, brows knitted in concentration.

Stephen cleared his throat. "'Tis delicate work, miss."

"Mmhmm." She nodded, but remained pressed toward him, gaze trained on his hands.

Stephen shifted, then forced himself to look at her. "It's a wee bit tricky to work it right without proper room to move." He rolled his shoulder slightly.

Annabeth's cheeks reddened, and her lips formed a perfect circle before she mashed them together. "Oh, yes. Of course. My apologies." She repositioned herself on the stool and straightened her posture.

"Brilliant." Stephen nodded and returned to the task of carving the detailed design.

A few moments passed and Annabeth slowly leaned into him again. Their shoulders touched, and a lock of her hair tickled his ear.

His hands stilled, and Stephen cleared his throat. "M'lady?"

"Oh, dear me. I beg your pardon. And, please, call me Anna." She plopped back down on the stool, but her foot caught in the train of her dress and she missed the seat, dropping onto the floor. Sitting there in a mound of peach-colored dress, she looked like an immense fairy cake, her hair serving as a golden cherry.

A guffaw burst from Stephen like water from a weakened dam. As he fought to control his laughter, he reached a hand to help her up.

Annabeth merely stared at him in shocked silence for a moment until she began to chuckle herself. Her chuckle built into a giggle before finally erupting into hearty laughter. She placed her hand in his and allowed him to help her to her feet. They stood laughing like eejits for a few moments until Stephen realized he was still holding her hand.

The hilarity of the moment began to fade, and he released her fingers from his grip. "Now, are ye alright, there?"

"Good gracious me." Annabeth brushed her hands over her skirts and patted at her eyes. "If only Mother could see me now." She shook her head. "Quite the lady, I am."

"*Tá.*" Stephen bobbed his head. "So, ye're not hurt, then?" He pushed his brows upward.

"No, no. Not at all. A hidden blessing of such full skirts—lots of padding. Just a bit of a bruised ego, I'm afraid." A sheepish grin settled on her face.

"What . . . what, may I ask, were ya doin'?" he said.

"I couldn't see." She gestured to the forgotten beeswax on the workbench. "I was trying to get a better look at your carving."

"Ah," he replied. Was he relieved or disappointed? "Well, I'll try to make it easier for ya to follow what I'm doin'. But some things ya just won't be able to truly suss out until ye're tryin' for yerself."

"Of course," Annabeth replied while righting her stool. She settled herself on it once more. "Please, continue."

Stephen returned to his own seat and retrieved the wax. "See here, I've carved the hands and the crown. Why don't ya have a go at the heart."

Annabeth's eyes grew wide. "Truly? Are you sure I won't get it wrong?"

"No, I'm not sure." He shrugged.

Her mouth opened and closed twice before she raised her hands in mock surrender. "Maybe you'd best do it. I'll just watch the first few times."

Stephen extended the wax toward Annabeth. "I didn't mean

anything by it. Just that we won't know yer skill 'til ya give it a bash." He waggled the wax and probe in his hands.

Grimacing slightly, Annabeth took the implements from Stephen's hands. She adjusted her elbows to rest on the workbench and set to work carving the heart between the hands in the wax.

Stephen watched as closely as he could while keeping proper distance between them. Occasionally, he let his attention drift to Annabeth's face. Her blue eyes focused intently on the task at hand, while the tip of her tongue poked out of the corner of her mouth. She reminded Stephen of a wee kitten learning to hunt. He chuckled at the mental image.

Annabeth's gaze shot to his, her eyes wide. "I'm doing it wrong, aren't I? I've ruined it."

Stephen waved his hands in front of him. "No, no, not at all. It's only . . ." His voice trailed off.

"What is it, then? If I'm doing something improperly, please tell me. I want to learn." She rested a hand on his forearm. "I truly do."

"Ye're doin' just fine." He turned his palm upward and moved it toward the wax. "Let's have a look."

Annabeth cringed and placed the carved wax into Stephen's hand. He lifted it close to his face to inspect her handiwork. His mouth fell open and his eyes widened. "This is"—he cleared his throat—"this is quite good."

She clasped her hands under her chin and grimaced. "Are you certain? You're not just saying so to . . . to be nice?"

As much as he'd love to put her in her place, he couldn't deny skill when he saw it. "No, I'm being honest." He tipped the carving so she could see and pointed with his pinky finger. "See here, where the heart, hand, and crown all meet? That's very tricky to do—especially when two different artists are working on it. Each person has their own style, y'know?"

Annabeth nodded.

"At any rate," Stephen continued, "this is not at all bad for yer first go."

Annabeth smiled, her dimples returning in earnest. "What's next?"

Stephen spent the next hour or so showing Annabeth how to create a clay ring mold, transfer the design, and pour the liquid metal into it.

"The molten silver," he said, "melts the wax and takes the shape of the mold. Once it's cooled fully, you break off the clay and ya have yer ring."

Annabeth patted the back of her hand across her forehead and returned to her seat on the stool. "Astonishing," she said. "Simply astonishing." A grin spread across her face. "Let's do it again."

Stephen chuckled in spite of himself. As much as he hated to admit it, Annabeth's eagerness to learn made it easy to want to teach her. She wasn't too hard to look at either. *Keep your wits about you, man.*

"I think that's enough for the moment," he said. In the distance, the church bells rang. "Are ya hungry?"

Annabeth beamed. "Famished. Who knew jewelry making worked up such an appetite?"

CHAPTER

5

Anna wiped her hands on a clean cloth and fetched her cloak from the rack near the door, desperately hoping the rumbling in her stomach wasn't audible.

"Where do you typically take your lunch?" she called over her shoulder while fastening her cloak at her neck.

Stephen came around the corner sporting a tweed flatcap and jacket. The jewel and earth tones in the cap accentuated the green in his eyes. Goodness, they were lovely. Yet full of sadness . . . and anger. Anna dropped her gaze to her hands as she pulled on a thin pair of gloves. But the image of Stephen's eyes remained firm in her mind. What was his story? What could have hardened him so?

"It depends on the day, really."

Heat crept up Anna's neck. Had she voiced the question aloud? "Beg pardon?"

He opened the door and waited for her to exit first. "Lunch. I don't patronize the cafes and pubs every day, but I try to regularly."

Anna released a breath she hadn't realized she'd been holding. "Right, of course. Seems sensible."

"Some days," he continued, "I eat upstairs in the flat, and others I pack a lunch to the Claddagh and eat there."

Anna stopped walking and turned to face him. "You . . . take a lunch to eat . . . at the Claddagh? You mean you eat in the shop?"

"I—" His brows pressed together. "I take my food to the Claddagh. And eat it there."

Anna brought her thumb up to chew at her nail but tasted glove instead. She clasped her hands in front of her and pressed her lips together. "Forgive me. Clearly I have much to learn. The Claddagh is the name of the ring design we made today, correct?"

Stephen nodded.

"But it also sounds like the Claddagh"—she bit the side of her lip—"is a place?"

Shifting his weight, Stephen crossed his arms over his chest and heaved a sigh. He studied her for a long moment. Something like irritation, frustration, and yet somehow also compassion warred in his eyes. "Come wi' me."

Anna followed as he led them south down Shop Street. A grocer swept the entrance to his store. On the opposite side of the road, a robust man with rosy cheeks covered in silver stubble sat in a chair, resting his head against the wall of a pub, snoring loudly. An empty whiskey bottle sat on a barrel next to him. The air was comfortably warm, but the breeze brisk. Anna pulled her cloak tighter and drank in every detail as they walked.

Stephen's voice broke into her thoughts. "Do ye like fish 'n chips?"

Of course, Anna had dined on fish many a time. And Katy routinely prepared delicious potatoes roasted in duck fat for supper. But how could she tell Stephen she'd never partaken of this favorite street food of Britain and Ireland? Families of the court were above such fare, she'd been taught. *Peasant food*, Father called it. Anna glanced at Stephen from the corner of her eye, only to find him looking squarely at her.

"Well?" He twisted his lips to the side and raised his brows in question. "Do ye or don't ye?"

"Well," she began, "I like fish." She shrugged her shoulders with a sheepish grimace on her face.

Stephen's jaw dropped. "Don't tell me ye've never had fish 'n chips?" He lifted his cap and ran his hand across the top of his head. "'Tis a favorite staple of the Irish . . . and British, so I'm told."

"It is, you're right!" Anna couldn't bring herself to admit that, though it was the favorite food of the commoner, courtiers wouldn't deign to partake of such things. Of course, those things had never really mattered to Anna. The court and all its rules and social graces always sat ill with her. She longed for adventure. Fun. Deep, meaningful relationships. And while those things did sometimes occur within royal circles, it had not been her own experience. "I *have* always wanted to try it," she admitted. But how to explain why? "I just haven't had the pleasure yet. I . . . was waiting until I could . . . have the very best."

He stopped walking and studied her again. His face was like stone, yet something in his eyes betrayed the hardened exterior he tried so hard to keep in place. He seemed to be warring within himself. What about, Anna couldn't begin to guess. Whatever it was, each moment brought more and more clarity that her arrival had awoken something new for him to fight.

At length, his shoulders softened, though only slightly, and the faintest hint of a smile played on his lips. "Then ye've come to the right place." He lifted his hand and gestured to something behind Anna.

Turning, she read the sign above her head. "McGinnty's Fish and Chips." A pair of painted fish frolicked on the sign, bookending the name. Windows framed in bright red covered the whole front of the establishment, aside from the door. Lively voices called back and forth from within, and the most enticing aroma wafted out of the open door.

"And that"—he pointed farther south, where glistening water danced just beyond the next row of shops—"that is the Claddagh. It's the part of town where the original creator of the ring lived."

Anna shielded her eyes, straining to see the area. The sun on the water that rushed from the river into the bay summoned her like a siren. Across the mouth of the river, squat rows of thatched, whitewashed homes gleamed in the midday light. Intense curiosity welled up in Anna's chest, overwhelming her. She had to see more. To know more. She started to move in that direction when a hand caught her elbow.

"Ye'll get to explore to yer heart's content. That's where we'll take our meal. But first, if ya don't mind . . ." Stephen nodded toward the door. "I'm famished." He smiled, and Anna turned toward McGinnty's.

"Anna?" A woman's voice stopped them just short of the entrance. "Anna, is that you?"

Anna turned and couldn't help the grin that stretched across her face. "Hello!" The two women embraced briefly and bussed one another on each cheek before turning their attention toward Stephen. "Stephen, this is my sister, Emmaline."

Surprise danced in his eyes. He stared at Anna for a moment, then removed his cap and offered a shallow bow from the waist in Emmaline's direction. "M'lady. 'Tis a pleasure."

Emmaline waved a dismissive hand. "None of that 'lady' business for me. Anna here is the lady of the family." She wove her arm around Anna's elbow and offered a weak smile at her sister.

Anna's heart clenched. The poor girl. She adored the whole notion of a courtier's life. Alas, while her sister was technically still a lady, Anna, as the eldest, was the one being groomed for a life in the court and to take over things when her father was gone. Much to the girl's heartbreak.

"Miss De Lacy suits me just fine," Emmaline finally added. Anna patted her sister's hand.

Stephen, seemingly unaware of the tug-of-war in the two sisters' hearts, inclined his head before replacing his cap. "As you wish." He smiled politely. "Lady Annabeth and I were just about to have a bit of lunch. Care to join us?"

"No." Emmaline smiled. "Thank you. I must meet Owen back at the carriage. I came to have tea with a friend and must be off home now. But it's a beautiful day. You two go enjoy it." She winked at Anna.

Heat flashed to Anna's face, and she gritted her teeth. The cheek of her! "My dear sister, 'tis only a quick break before we return to work at the shop."

Emmaline lifted a gloved hand to her chest. "Of course, of course. I meant nothing by it." She gave Anna a quick hug before straightening her bonnet. "'Twas a pleasure to meet you, Mister Jennings."

Stephen tipped his cap. "Good day, Miss De Lacy." Then he turned his attention to Anna. "After you, Lady Annabeth."

Anna headed toward the door. "It's Ann—oh, never mind."

CHAPTER

6

The scent of hot oil, fish, and indeterminate spices washed over Anna as they entered McGinnty's fish shop. The air inside was thick and damp, and a layer of moisture seemed to appear instantly on Anna's skin.

"*A Stíofán! Cén chaoi a bhfuil tú?*" A giant of a man in a smeared apron with wiry hair, a round nose, and twinkling brown eyes greeted them.

Stephen grinned. A deep dimple appeared in the stubble on his left cheek. So that's what he looked like when he genuinely smiled. He should do it more often.

"*Go maith.*" The men shook hands. "I'm well, Paddy, thanks. You?"

"I can't complain now, so I can't." Paddy placed his hands on the counter. "The usual?"

"Aye." Stephen nodded. "Two, if you please. And this is someone you should know, Paddy. This is Lady Annabeth De Lacy."

Paddy's brows arched. "De Lacy, you say? As in—" The light in his eyes dimmed, and a shadow of something Anna couldn't place flitted across his face.

"Her father's the new landlord, and she's been apprenticed to me." The dimple retreated, and Stephen's jaw muscle tensed.

Paddy's face darkened and he opened his mouth to reply, but Stephen gave such a slight shake of the head it would've been imperceptible had Anna not been looking right at him.

"Right, so." Paddy wiped his hands on his apron and shouted to the kitchen. "*Dhá phláta. Anois!*" He smiled stiffly at Anna before turning his attention back to Stephen and informing him of the price.

Anna opened her reticule. "Please, allow me."

Both men stared at her, mouths agape.

Her throat grew suddenly as dry as cotton wool. Had she committed another egregious faux pas? "It's the least I can do. You're being so generous in allowing me to interrupt your schedule, to take the time out of your days to teach me. Please, I'd like to pay for this." She looked back and forth between the men. "If that's alright."

Once again, Stephen's jaw tensed, and he chewed his lip. He stood quiet far longer than was comfortable before he put his hands in his pockets and nodded. "Yes, of course. By all means." He took two steps back and kept his gaze on the floor.

Paddy opened and closed his mouth and Anna couldn't help but think he must look like his own catch of the day before it's fried up. At last, he smiled, clapped his meaty hands together, and repeated the price for Anna.

She jumped at the impact of his clap and with shaky steps, moved toward the counter and removed the amount from her purse, handing it to the man. "Thank you very much." She forced a pleasant smile. Paddy—though he regarded Anna with polite distance, and a look in his eye she couldn't quite discern—genuinely seemed a delightful, jovial gentleman. But she couldn't ignore the sinking feeling she'd misstepped somehow, and neither man was going to enlighten her.

A voice called from the kitchen and two steaming portions appeared before them. "Here ye are, lads—" Paddy's face reddened, and he flashed a look to Stephen, who appeared to be trying not to laugh. "Beggin' yer pardon, miss. One fish and chips for the lad, and one for the lady." He wagged his head once swiftly to the side, the twinkle returning to his eye.

Anna, however, was focused on the food. It smelled divine, but she'd never seen anything like it. Two large slabs of golden-fried fish lay atop a bed of thick-cut strips of potatoes, also a beautiful golden brown. What caught her, however, was the cone of newsprint in which it was all wrapped. She looked at Stephen, who cradled his as if it were a priceless treasure.

As though he felt her watching him, he looked up. "Are ya alright, there?"

Anna could only nod.

"It's a bit hot yet," he said. "It'll cool as we walk. To the Claddagh, shall we?"

"Yes, let's." Anna followed him out the door, the brisk breeze a welcome change from the heavy air inside the fish and chip shop. She eyed the newsprint. Gray spots peppered the cone of paper as excess oil soaked through. While there was no denying the food looked delicious—and smelled even better—the paper cone unnerved Anna.

No wonder Father considers it peasant food. The thought arrested her. It was like a punch to the stomach, and she struggled to catch her breath at the realization that such ugly thoughts resided in her own heart. How many times had she inwardly railed at her father for his holier-than-thou view on those "below his station"? Even in her short time in this country, she had begun to see that perhaps her parents' views on the Irish were skewed—inaccurate. And yet here she stood, harboring such a hateful thought within her own soul. Hadn't she longed for adventure? To experience the "real" world beyond the confines of the court? This was her chance. Was she going to squander the opportunity simply because the new was slightly uncomfortable?

"No!"

Stephen spun round. "Pardon? Is everything alright?"

Anna's mouth fell open as she realized she'd shouted her thought aloud. Then a wide smile spread across her face. "Yes, it's fine. I just can't wait to give this a try!"

The pair walked in silence with the aroma of the freshly cooked fare wafting on the breeze until they reached a long grassy stretch on the north bank of the River Corrib. "Here we are," Stephen said.

Annabeth looked up at him and smiled before her clear blue eyes widened as she surveyed the surroundings. The Corrib ran swiftly around the bend on its journey southeast through the town before emptying here into the mouth of Galway Bay. Her gaze followed the river until it fell upon a pair of swans sunning themselves on the rock wall holding the wild Corrib in check. A giggle trickled from her lips. "It's beautiful."

"Aye, 'tis indeed." He allowed himself a moment to enjoy the scene as well. He'd seen this view every day of his life, yet he never tired of it. He would miss this part of life in Galway very much indeed. "This is the beginning of the Claddagh. That"—he pointed to a bridge crossing the water—"is Ballyknow Quay, spanning the River Corrib."

Annabeth nodded, then her eyes rounded once again, and an open-mouth grin spread across her face. "And what, pray tell, is that?" She pointed to a large, gray stone arch directly east of their position and headed for it without waiting for him.

Stephen had to jog a few paces to catch up with her. "That is the Spanish Arch. It is part of an extension of the city wall from premedieval times. Part of it was destroyed in the 1800s by a tidal wave." He pointed beyond the arch. "And behind it there are the barracks for the Brits." The words were like ash in his mouth, and his chest burned as he looked at the monstrosity of a building looming behind the landmark.

Absently handing her food to Stephen and seemingly unaware of the disdain in his tone, Annabeth placed the flats of her hands on the stones of the arch. "Incredible. If only these stones could talk." She closed her eyes and stood silent for several moments. Stephen wondered if she was truly trying to hear some cryptic voice from the past.

A gurgling rumble split the silence. Annabeth's eyes flew open, and her hands shot to her belly and then covered her mouth. Her cheeks flushed red. "Good gracious me!" she blurted. "I am so terribly sorry. Perhaps my appetite is greater than I'd realized." She dropped her gaze to her feet and rubbed her forehead with a gloved hand.

Stephen smiled in spite of his best efforts as he returned her food to her. So, she is, in fact, human. "Perhaps we'll make a proper Irish woman out o' ye, after all. Any decent Irish lass appreciates a good meal." Of course, they would when so many go hungry day after day. But he'd broach that subject another time. "Please, tuck in."

Grateful for the chance to finally enjoy the enticingly golden fish, Stephen took a bite and relished the crisp crackle of the batter. Flavor exploded in his mouth, and his hunger was all at once renewed and placated. "So?" he asked around another mouthful of fish. "What d'ye think?"

Annabeth's eyes were closed, and her head wagged back and forth slowly. One hand was raised with the palm facing him as she chewed. At length, she answered, "I . . . I've never had anything like that before in my life." She took a dainty bite of a chip, chewed, and swallowed. "It's absolutely magnificent. I can't imagine why Father—" She stopped short.

The magic of the moment broke. Stephen's mood darkened. "What about your father?"

Annabeth shook her head. "It's nothing. He just . . . he has very specific ideas about what's proper for a family of the court, that's all."

"Of course." Stephen bit his lip to keep all the angry thoughts from spilling out of his mouth. It would be just like an Englishman to look down his nose at something as simple as a meal of fish and potatoes. God forbid he learn to enjoy something not on a silver tray while sitting next to some faff about so-called gentleman with a meaningless title.

A hand on his forearm broke the line of his thoughts. He glanced down and found Annabeth's eyes boring into his. "I asked if you are alright. You've suddenly gone quite pale and quiet."

Stephen attempted a laugh, but it came out only as a strong snort from his nose. "Don't trouble yourself, lass. I'm fine."

"If you're certain." She dropped her hand to her side, the warmth leaving with it. "What's that there?" She pointed across the quay to a grouping of white, thatched cottages.

He stared at the buildings, letting the chill of the afternoon breeze soothe the ire threatening to break through his chest. "That's the heart of the Claddagh."

"Can we go there? I mean, if there's time. I've only seen your shop, the church, and the manor grounds. I want to see the real Ireland."

He looked at Annabeth from the corner of his eye. The real Ireland? Did she truly understand that her life in the manor was the furthest thing from what the Irish around her experienced every day? Did she really and truly want to see how the Irish lived—particularly here in the west? Was she *ready* to truly see? Aye, perhaps he would take her there. Let her see what her people's "rule" had done. He nodded. "We can walk while we eat. After you."

Her lips tipped up in the start of a smile. "Thank you."

CHAPTER

7

Anna's mind spun as they crossed the Corrib heading for the heart of the Claddagh. Stephen grew more confounding with each passing moment. One minute he was almost jolly, seemingly excited to share a part of his culture as simple as fish and chips with her, and the next he turned dark and bitter. And Anna seemed connected to the darkness somehow. She searched her mind for a way to pivot the mood.

"You said this area was named after the man who invented the Claddagh ring?" She kept her voice light and took another bite of the delectable fish, trying to ignore the grease on her gloves.

Stephen nodded. "That's right. He lived in this little village. Until he was kidnapped, that is."

Anna's eyes widened. "Kidnapped? By whom?"

Stephen stared straight ahead as he spoke, his voice flat. Tired. "Legend has it he was captured by Algerian ships, sold to a Moorish goldsmith, and worked as a slave. The goldsmith trained him until he was released from slavery in 1689."

Anna pressed a hand to her chest. "What a harrowing experience! And he returned to Galway after his release?"

"Aye." Stephen nodded and popped the last bite of fish in his mouth. "His captors begged him to stay. Some even say the goldsmith had grown so fond of him that he offered him half his wealth and his daughter's hand in marriage. But my ancestor was determined to come back."

A chilly gust blew in from the sea, sending a tendril of hair across Anna's eyes, before she tucked it away behind her ear. "Why? What drew him back after so much time away?"

Stephen cleared his throat and his jaw muscles tensed again. "Love." He ground out the word. Taking a deep breath, he continued, "He was kidnapped shortly before he was due to be married. While in captivity, he had a vision for the Claddagh symbol and created it into a ring as a token of his undying love for his fiancé and brought it back with him upon his return. As fate would have it, she had waited for him. So, he presented the ring to her when they married." Stephen shrugged and slipped his free hand into his pocket as they walked.

Anna gasped. "How romantic!"

"Right." Stephen scoffed, lifted his eyes to the sky, and returned his gaze forward.

Anna looked at him out of the corner of her eye. What on earth could have embittered him so to love? She decided to let it go for the moment and tried, instead, for levity. "Go ahead and roll your eyes if you like, Mister Scrooge. I think it's a perfectly lovely story."

He shook his head and muttered, "You and every lass who enters the shop."

Anna laughed. "And what of the symbols of the Claddagh design? Surely they must have strong meaning if he waited all that time dreaming of the day he'd see her again."

Stephen sighed and stopped walking. He held up his hands in a heart shape. "The heart stands for love. The crown, loyalty. And the hands . . ." He shifted his hands to hold an imaginary ball. "The hands stand for friendship."

Anna smiled and shook her head in admiration, picturing

the Claddagh on all the various pieces of jewelry in the shop. "Ingenious. Absolutely ingenious." She nudged him with her shoulder. "And it *is* romantic. I don't care what you say."

He merely responded with another sigh. Clearing his throat, Stephen swept his arm in an arc. "Welcome to the Claddagh."

A long, wide dirt path stretched before them, flanked on either side by low white buildings with thatched roofs. A barefoot woman, who looked to be at least the age of sixty, carried a basket slung over her forearm and walked past them, never meeting their gaze. A younger man stooped low to enter one of the cottages—though what Anna saw could hardly be categorized as such. Crude windows and doorways dotted the front of each home, and three or four at a time were connected in a row. Smoke curled from chimneys, and the clucking of chickens and braying of donkeys—along with their distinct scent—filled the air. In front of one of the open doorways, a group of five or six children sat around a large, overturned basket that served as a table. An empty table. They passed around a single cup, each taking a drink in turn. All of them to a one were barefoot, their faces smudged with dirt. While meager, the homes were all tidy and neat, some with wildflowers in boxes on the windowsills. But the sight of children with so little created an ache so deep in Anna's heart she feared she'd burst.

She smiled at the littlest one—a tiny girl of about three years of age with wispy blond hair. The girl eyed Anna's dress and smiled back.

"Hello there." Anna approached the children.

The eldest boy nodded. "Miss." He slid the little girl onto his lap and placed a protective arm across the table as though shielding the other children.

"That's a lovely dress you have on." Anna crouched down and ran her thumb over the hem of the girl's dress. Threadbare. The girl buried her face in her brother's shoulder.

"T'ank ye kindly, miss," the oldest boy replied for the girl.

Remembering the uneaten portion of chips in her hand, Anna smiled and offered them to the children. "Would you like some chips? I've had my fill, I assure you. But they're delicious."

Each of the children shook their heads almost violently. The eldest mumbled something in Irish, and they all scampered inside. He tipped his tattered cap before he disappeared inside, calling over his shoulder, "G'day, miss."

Anna's heart sank. She stared at the chips, now cold in the bottom of the soggy cone of newsprint. "They didn't want them." She wasn't sure if she was speaking to Stephen or merely to herself.

Stephen shrugged and nodded. "They're afraid."

In one motion she stood and spun on her heel to face him. "Afraid? Of me?"

Anna looked back at the doorway through which the children had disappeared. The door was now shut, protecting them. From her. "But why?"

Stephen slipped his hands in his pockets and said matter-of-factly, "They think you might be a souper."

Anna scowled, confusion swirling through her. "A super what?"

An unamused laugh escaped from Stephen's lips. "No, not super. *Souper.* I'll explain as we walk. We should return to the shop."

Anna nodded. Stephen started toward the city. Anna watched his back for a moment, wondering what he must think of her. "Alright." She fell into step beside him. "What's a souper?"

"Ye've heard about the Great Hunger, aye?" He continued walking, gaze straight ahead, voice low.

Anna searched her brain. She remembered learning about the famine in school. Could that be what he was referring to? "Do you mean the potato famine?"

Stephen nodded. "Aye. During the worst of it, people claiming to be missionaries came and set up soup kitchens."

Anna eyed him. She recalled conversations among various lords back in England, praising the efforts of certain houses to help during the famine. She herself had volunteered to feed wounded soldiers at the town hospital during the Great War, when things were desperate. She was honored to be able to help the greater effort in some small way, and she imagined that must've been how those who came to Ireland to help during the famine must've felt. "That . . . that doesn't sound so bad."

"You wouldn't think." He shook his head. "But they wouldn't just feed the people. They would only feed those who agreed to convert." He pursed his lips and adjusted his flatcap in apparent frustration.

The thought sent Anna reeling. How could people do such a thing? She would've never imagined anyone could be so heartless. So cruel. Images of Jesus feeding the five thousand, calling the children to Him, and commanding His followers to care for others flashed in her mind's eye. If it grieved Anna so, how much more must it grieve His heart for people to use faith—nae, religion—for such evil? "That . . . that's awful."

A sarcastic chortle rumbled in Stephen's chest, and he continued. "These people came from all over, but many were from England." He pinned her with a glare. "A souper is someone who claims to be here to help but really just wants compliance."

His accusation came like a slap to the face. Anna recoiled. "But I was doing no such thing. I only offered them some food—they looked starving."

"They probably are!" He gripped the back of his neck. "But look at you." He swiped a hand downward, gesturing to her dress. "You come here in your fancy clothes with your leftover food, thinking they'd be over the moon for your charity—for your *scraps*. And when you spoke? Your accent's a dead giveaway."

"But I only wanted to help!" She forced the words around the lump in her throat and willed the tears welling in her eyes not to fall. "And I wasn't offering them my scraps—the food is still good, and I wasn't going to eat it. I didn't want to waste it if someone else could use it. That's all!"

He pressed balled fists to his hips. "I'm sure you did want to help. But these people have been 'helped' to death by the English who come with their fancy goods and empty promises. Maybe you only wanted to feed them. But everything they've known their entire lives says you're a threat."

He took the wilting newsprint from her hands, balled it up, and quickened his pace toward the city before Anna could respond.

As she wiped the tears from her cheeks and hurried to catch up with Stephen, the muffled lilt of a tin whistle and the strong brogue of Ireland's native tongue flowed from one of the homes in a joyful reel.

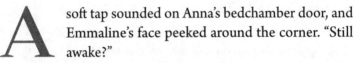

CHAPTER
8

A soft tap sounded on Anna's bedchamber door, and Emmaline's face peeked around the corner. "Still awake?"

Anna turned from the mirror and placed her hairbrush on the vanity. "Of course. Come in, dear."

Emmaline padded over and sat on the bed. Sitting there with her hair in a simple plait over her shoulder, legs crisscrossed under her, Emmaline suddenly looked every bit the sixteen-year-old she was rather than the distinguished young woman Anna had seen in town that afternoon.

"Well?" A girlish grin filled Emmaline's face.

After tying off her own braid with a ribbon, Anna joined her sister on the bed. "Well, what?"

Emmaline widened her eyes, mock incredulity painted on her face as she gave a playful push to Anna's shoulder. "You know very well *what*. How was lunch, silly?"

Heat seeped up Anna's cheeks. "Oh." She shifted to slide her feet under the duvet. "That."

"You cheeky thing." Emmaline crossed her arms. "The way you spoke about the younger Mister Jennings made him sound like a cranky old sourpuss."

Anna shrugged. "He is, in truth!" She couldn't help the laugh that bubbled from her chest.

Emmaline leveled a stern look at Anna. "That may be, but you failed to mention he was a devilishly *striking* sourpuss!" Mischief sparkled in her eyes as she fanned herself with her hand and blew a low whistle.

Her sweet sister, such a romantic. Suppressing an amused sigh, Anna smiled. Images of Stephen's arresting green eyes and dimple-accented smile filled her mind. Yes, he certainly was a handsome man, but their relationship—if one could even call it such—was purely professional. Emmaline, ever the dreamer, would never leave it be there.

"Don't you see?" Emmaline scooted closer and slid her own feet under the duvet next to Anna's. "If you can get Mister Jennings to marry you, you won't have to marry Lord Killjoy!"

Anna's heart sank. "Oh, Emmie." She'd nearly forgotten about Lord Corning's proposal. At sixty years of age, he was hardly the epitome of the romantic hero. Not to mention the fact that he managed to bully and belittle everyone who happened to cross him, no matter how miniscule the offense. When Father had first told Anna of the proposal, she'd burst into tears. He'd tried to convince her of the merit of the arrangement, once again using the fact that he had no son as an heir to drive the point home, once and for all, that her cooperation was needed. Nae, expected. But then came the blessed appointment to Ireland—a way out of a lifetime tethered to a man who carried the permanent facial expression of one having just eaten a lemon.

Lord Corning, however, had other ideas. *One year*, he had said. A year for Anna to help her family settle, to refine the ways of the woman of a house of the court, and then she was to either accept his offer, or reject it and live with the ire and public embarrassment that would follow. Though she was still seemingly trapped in the arrangement, in Anna's heart of hearts, a tiny flame of hope flickered that she might still be able to break free of it.

"You know Father would never allow such a thing. Could you imagine his face if I were to tell him I wanted to marry an Irishman?" Anna twisted the blanket in her hands. "Besides, I barely know Mister Jennings, let alone love him. And I get the distinct impression he doesn't care too much for my company."

Emmaline waved her hand and pulled the covers up higher. "You'll just have to work harder to earn his favor," she said, her eyes alight with intrigue. She clasped her hands under her chin, and her thoughts seemed to wander a mile away—most likely plotting ways for Anna to garner Stephen's affection.

Anna allowed herself a moment to consider Stephen. The mere thought of him set butterflies loose in her. Which, she admitted to herself, was utterly ridiculous given the incredibly short amount of time she'd known him, combined with the less-than-cordial attitude he carried toward her. Nevertheless, she couldn't deny that the idea of growing closer to him—and being embraced by him—warmed her to the core. Oh dear. She needed to guard herself. Settling a hand on her sister's knee, Anna willed her face to convey what her heart could not—that it could never be. And the sooner they both accepted it, the better off they'd be.

Emmaline dropped her hands to her lap, sadness filling her eyes. "What on earth would possess Father to agree to such an arrangement, anyway? Lord Killjoy could be your grandfather!" A pout filled her face, making her appear even younger.

"*Wsshhht!*" Anna shot a glance to the partially opened door. "Lord *Corning* is a good match . . . in theory, at least. Joining our two families would secure a place in society for our children's children." Anna forced a hopeful smile onto her face and hoped her sister would believe it. She must.

"That matters not, Anna, and you know it." Emmaline shook her head, a more serious demeanor settling over her. "As much as I wish to be part of courtier life, it should not come at such a cost. Father should be more concerned with his daughter's happiness than with bolstering his own position in society. Don't you want to marry for love?" She grasped Anna's hands, her eyes wide and imploring.

Anna squeezed Emmaline's hand gently. "Of course I do. But as the eldest, that is a luxury I may not be able to afford. Without any sons for Father to pass his legacy to, it's my responsibility to ensure our family survives."

"It's unfair." Emmaline huffed and played with the end of her braid with her free hand. "I could understand such a thing if Father's fortune weren't secure, God forbid. Or if our family were in trouble—but it's not! You shouldn't have to carry such a burdensome mantle."

"Sweet girl." Anna rested a hand on her sister's cheek. Had Anna carried such passion and conviction at that age? "I am a De Lacy—a name that I am proud to carry. It is an honor to do what I can to ensure our legacy's survival." Her gaze went to the window across the room. Darkness shrouded the trees and grounds beyond. Much like darkness seemed to shroud her future. "Even if it's impossibly difficult," she muttered under her breath.

Whether from the damp Irish night closing in, or the sinking sense that filled her heart, Anna shivered. "We'd best get to bed now." She leaned over and kissed the top of her sister's head. "Good night, love."

Emmaline turned and wrapped her arms around Anna's neck and held on. Light scents of lavender and rose wafted from her hair. "Sweet dreams, Annie."

◆ April 26 ◆

A satisfying sizzle rose from the cast-iron skillet as Stephen dropped two rashers of bacon onto it. Positioning the meat just so in the pan, he turned his attention to the steaming cup of tea awaiting him. He took a healthy sip, wincing as it scalded its way down his throat. He welcomed the heat, the sting. It matched his mood while also imparting the earthy, deep comfort only a properly brewed cuppa can. Things had been awkward at best with his new apprentice in the days since their lunchtime outing, and even now he couldn't shake it.

He flipped the rashers over and replayed last week's events at the Claddagh. What had the woman been thinking? What did she expect would happen if she approached those children? *How could she have known? You just wanted to watch her squirm.* He swatted the thought away and chased it down with another swig of tea. It served her right for having such a pious attitude.

"Ah, ye're a good man yerself." Seamus shuffled around the corner, his thinning white hair sticking out in all directions like unruly feathers. "Nothin' like starting a brisk morning with a bit o' bacon." He swiped his nose through the air and sat at the small rustic table that filled the center of the cozy kitchen.

Stephen set a cup of tea in front of his father. "Yeah, well, someone around here has to do the cookin'." He winked at Seamus and turned his attention back to the skillet. Just about perfect. He took it off the heat and placed a damper on the burner. The fire within the stove would burn all day, warming the flat that sat above their jewelry shop. He buttered two thick slices of brown bread, plated them with the bacon, and joined his father at the table.

Seamus devoured half the slice of bread in one bite. "How's it goin' with the lass?" he muttered around the food.

Stephen shook his head, blowing a sarcastic laugh from his

nose. "Just grand now, Da." He had to find a way to get out of this deal.

Seamus dropped his hands to the table and pierced his son with a stare. "What've ya done now?"

Just like his father to blame him first. "I've not done a thing apart from exactly what ye asked me to." He swiped his mouth with the back of his hand and downed the rest of his tea in a single gulp. "She's ridiculous, Da. She has absolutely no understanding of things here. Of Irish life. It's like she thinks she's God's gracious gift to *Éire*."

"Well, what do ya expect?" Seamus sawed a piece of rasher off and shoved it in his mouth. As he chewed, he poked his fork in the air toward Stephen. "The lass was born with a silver spoon in her mouth. She's been taught since the day she was born that her family was appointed by God to be in the position they're in. It's no wonder she sees her role as a blessing to Ireland."

Stephen stood with such force his chair tipped backward, nearly toppling over. He grabbed his plate and cup and carried them to the basin. "Thanks for makin' my point." He rested his hands on the edge of the counter and stared out the small, square window in front of him.

"What's got your knickers in such a twist about this, Stephen? It's not like I'm askin' ya to marry the girl!" The audible slurp that followed the statement sent a shudder up Stephen's spine.

He turned and leveled a glare at his father. "How could you invite her here—practically into our home? After what they did to Tommy? Ya do remember him, don't ya?" Stephen's gaze flitted to the floor and back up to Seamus. He crossed his arms.

"Don't." Seamus lifted a thick, crooked pointer finger. "I'll never forget your brother. Not a day goes by I don't mourn his loss, when I don't wish he was here with us. Just like you do." His voice trembled, and he steadied it with a swig of tea.

Stephen's shoulders fell, but he righted them. This was too

important. "Then I ask again—how could you bring her here?" he bellowed and instantly regretted raising his voice at his father. But the man simply didn't get it. He wasn't listening. How could he not understand? Stephen scratched his head and ran his hand down the back of his neck.

"Annabeth De Lacy didn't kill Tommy, Stephen." Seamus's voice swam in sadness. "Neither did Lord De Lacy, for that matter. What happened to him—"

"What happened to him was inexcusable!" Stephen swiped his hand through the air, accidentally knocking over his father's now-empty cup.

Seamus righted the cup, a sad sigh slipping from his lips. "Aye, it was. But it had nothing to do with that girl. And I won't let you pretend that it did." Seamus joined his son at the basin. "Tommy's death was a simple case of bein' in the wrong place at the wrong time, lad. He died at the hands of the British. But that doesn't mean every Englishman is to blame. As for Annabeth and what you've seen from her this week, she doesn't know any better. But I could tell from the moment I laid eyes on her—" Seamus's voice trailed off as he seemed instantly lost in thought or memory. "That's why I agreed to take her on as an apprentice."

Stephen searched his father's face for some clue as to what he could be talking about. He tossed his hands up in frustration. "What, Da? What could you tell?"

"*Och!* That this girl is different! She's not like the rest of the high-falutin' *Sasanach* who've sailed over here. She wants to learn. Haven't ya seen the way she looks at the world?" Seamus swung his arm in an arc. "The . . . the wonder that fills her eyes?"

A picture of Annabeth circling in awe the morning he'd met her outside the church last week materialized in Stephen's mind. All the questions she'd asked over the last several days. Many were about the jewelry, aye. But even more were about the Irish—their culture, language, history. Even how she'd reacted to the children in the Claddagh. He couldn't deny the fact that she was curious. But why? To what end? He folded his arms and leaned against the counter.

"So, she's curious. What difference does that make?" Stephen asked, an all-too-familiar ache filling his chest. In a flash he was back to that fateful day five years ago. That day when Marie revealed her true colors and abandoned Stephen. And took his heart with her. She, too, had been curious. What good had that done Stephen?

Seamus laid a hand on Stephen's shoulder. When he spoke, his voice was soft but full of conviction. "Hate is fueled by ignorance, son. The first step toward peace is the genuine desire to understand your so-called enemy. Don't punish her for the sins of her fathers. Let her learn. Teach her. Guide her. And maybe one day you'll see what I do. In both of you." He squeezed Stephen's shoulder and quit the room. Thunder rolled after him.

"Annabeth, will you come in here, please?"

Her father's call caught her as she headed down the hall to change and go to town. Perfect timing, as ever.

She entered his study where he received most of his guests—the majority of whom were other landlords, leaders in the British military, or dignitaries visiting the island. Mahogany bookshelves stretched from floor to ceiling and wrapped around three walls of the room. A fireplace divided the shelves on the center wall, and a massive oil painting of a deer hunt hung over it. Large windows stretched across the expanse of the front wall, offering sweeping views of the garden and woods flanking it on either side.

Her father, Lord William De Lacy, stood with his back to the door. His thin frame stretched tall, and he rested a hand on the spine of a book. His slicked-back salt-and-pepper hair glistened slightly in the firelight. While not a coarse man, he certainly did not give off an air of gentleness either.

"Yes, Father?" Annabeth dipped a shallow curtsy, a habit from when she was little.

He turned, revealing a pipe in the side of his mouth. He curled his lips around it in a tight smile. "Ah, there you are, my dear." He beckoned her to him and brushed a brief kiss on her cheek.

"How, ah, how fares the jewelry making?" He lowered himself into a high-backed chair near the fire and motioned for her to do the same.

Anna sat, crossed her feet at the ankles, and adjusted her skirt to cover them. "It goes well, Father. Thank you, again, for arranging it for me. I do so enjoy employing my creativity outside the manor." She laced her fingers together in her lap, resisting the urge to pick at her fingernails—a nervous habit that always earned her a stern reprimand.

He nodded. "And the Misters Jennings? They are treating you well?" Father puffed his pipe twice before placing it in the ashtray on the side table next to him.

"Yes, of course." Anna watched the flames dancing in the grate, her thoughts drifting to her conversation with Stephen in the Claddagh the week before. He'd been firm, yes. But had he been rude or treated her poorly? No, not one bit.

"Good. What do you two talk about all day?" He retrieved his pipe and the puffing continued as thunder rumbled overhead.

"Well." Anna searched her mind. "Mostly things to do with the shop—how they run it, how to make the different pieces of jewelry."

Her father shifted in his seat and nodded absently. "Anything else?"

Chewing her lip, Anna replayed the events of the last week in her mind before answering. "One day we took a tour of the part of town called the Claddagh. It's named after the Jenningses' ancestor who created the famed ring."

"Oh?" He focused on the bowl of his pipe while he took an inordinately long draw.

"Yes." She nodded. "It's really quite striking the difference in affluence in the various parts of the city. The people in the Claddagh . . . they live in little more than shacks. No shoes. No finery, merely the bare necessities. If they can even manage that."

"Indeed. *Hmm.*" Her father's gaze drifted to the window and he fixated on some unknown object beyond the confines of its glass. The ticking of the mantel clock filled the silence that stretched interminably between them until the slow tinkle of raindrops pattered on the windowpanes.

Anna glanced at the time and her pulse quickened. "Is there anything else, Father? I'm due at the shop in an hour."

His attention snapped back to her, and he tilted the corners of his lips in a slight smile. "Of course. But there is one thing." He removed his spectacles and polished them with a handkerchief. "I'd had a thought. As you know, things are quite tense these days, what with this war for independence nonsense and all."

Nonsense. Right. She nodded, willing her face to remain neutral.

"It occurred to me that you have a unique opportunity not usually afforded people of our station." He leaned forward, his face alight, a full grin now spread across his face.

Anna frowned. According to Father, her apprenticeship would be considered somewhat scandalous if it were done in England. What opportunity could this arrangement possibly offer?

"You see," he continued, "you are spending much of your days immersed in . . . in the common folk. It's these people who are the driving force of this . . . this 'war.'"

While she had heard troops marching past the shop every now and then, she'd seen no real activity to suggest that the local Irish were involved or even perpetuating the fighting. When she opened her mouth to respond, he lifted a hand, stopping her.

"It occurred to me your time there might provide more than just an enriching experience for you." He leaned back and retrieved his pipe, puffing with increased intensity. "It could prove invaluable for us—for *our* side of the issue—if you were to report back to me anything you might overhear." A loud crack of thunder shattered the air outside.

"Overhear?" Sweat pricked the back of her neck.

"Yes, my dear." He rose and circled around to his desk at the front of the room. "Anything you might hear of their plans. Times they are meeting. Days they are thinking of making a move. Anything like that."

Anna's jaw slackened and her head spun. "Father, I—"

"You owe it to your country, Annabeth." His voice took on a sudden sharpness. "These people think they are in the right, but they're not. They are threatening the very things we've built our lives upon. Don't you see?" he hissed.

Anna shook her head, searching for the right response. "Father, I have heard nothing of the kind. And I've seen nothing that would cause me to believe anyone I have been in contact with would be privy to such things." Anna's stomach clenched. Her father wanted her to spy on her hosts? How could he even suspect such things? Even if he was right, were the people so wrong to want equality, nae, independence?

Father straightened to his full height, and he assumed the countenance he used with his subordinates. "You will report anything you might hear, won't you, my dear?" It was a statement more than a question.

Unable to form words in her cotton-dry mouth, Anna managed a weak nod. Until she really understood what was happening—what the Irish were fighting for, what they wanted, what they needed, and what the English were really responsible for here—she couldn't take a stand for anything.

"There's a good girl. You'd best head off now, dear." He gave a conspiratorial wink. "You don't want to be late."

CHAPTER

9

Less than a half hour later, Anna peeked around the corner into the front hallway. The coast clear, she adjusted the waist of the trousers she'd borrowed from Katy. How odd it felt not to be wearing the layers of silk and fitted bodice of her usual dress. She wriggled and shrugged her shoulders within the button-front linen shirt. Yes, she could get used to this. Oh, she could never fully give up her frills and lace, but her current attire offered a freedom of movement such as she'd never experienced before. Straightening her posture, she made for the front door.

"To the shop, please, Owen," she called to the coachman as she bounded into the carriage before he could see her.

"Aye, lady. As you wish." With a snap of the reins, the rig jolted into motion. The motorcar had yet to arrive in this corner of the world and Anna relished the simplicity and charm of the horse and carriage.

Outside her window, the land rolled on in a patchwork of green and stone, ambling evermore to the bay below. Some said when the water was quiet, whales could be seen swimming in it on a side tour from their migrations. Today, however, the water seemed angry. Tumultuous waves pounded the shore with the vigor of a woman scorned. And it had been thus nearly every day she'd been in Ireland.

She gazed at the land across the bay, barely visible through the morning mist hanging in the air. On the water she could just make out the distinct red sails of a Galway Hooker boat. Built for such conditions, the vessel glided on the frothy white-caps with ease, rolling with the rhythm of the water rather than fighting against it. She wished her spirit would do the same. She wanted to chart a course through the storm she seemed to have sailed herself into rather than be tossed about by the ideas and opinions of those around her. *Lord, grant me wisdom.*

The rumble of cobblestone jolted Anna from her reverie as they turned off the coast road and headed into the heart of the city. The whitewashed walls lining the streets glowed in the diffused morning light, the mist a diamond curtain covering all the eye could see. Blessedly, the wind had yet to pick up, adding to the calm quiet of the spring morning.

"We're here, Lady Annabeth." Owen's muffled voice came through the window.

Anna clenched her teeth. Would no one save Emmaline call her Anna? "Thank you, Owen. I'll be finished around two o'clock." She stepped out of the carriage, noting again how much easier trousers made even that simple task. "Enjoy your day." She smiled at the driver.

He tipped his flatcap and urged the horses on. "Thank you, miss," he called over his shoulder before giving her a double take. His eyes narrowed as he looked at her and then widened before the slightest hint of a smile tugged at the corner of his mouth. He tipped his cap once more, turned, and snapped the reins.

A raspy voice drifted on the air. Anna entered the shop to find Seamus polishing the glass jewelry case as a jaunty fishing tune sprang from his lips. He finished with a flourish, head thrown back, arms stretched wide. Anna couldn't help the giggle that escaped.

Seamus spun to face her, eyes wide in surprise. "Och! I didna know ye were there, love! Welcome in, welcome in!" He shuffled over and placed a kiss on each of Anna's cheeks, his gray stubble scratching at her.

"Good morning, Mister Jennings." She offered a gentle smile, relishing the tenderness in his greeting.

"*Pfft*! I won't have ye callin' me that. Seamus, it is. Aye?" He pasted a stern look on his face, but the twinkle in his eyes belied his true meaning before a robust laugh broke the air.

"As you wish . . . Seamus." She removed her cape and hung it by the door.

Seamus blew a low whistle. "Look at ye! I'd say ye've come to work!" He clapped his beefy hands together.

Anna ran her hands down the front of her trousers. "Yes, I found my usual attire to be a bit cumbersome."

"I should think so." He shook his head and chuckled. "Yer fancy frocks looked lovely, but this new look suits ye. Now, come over here, Anna, and tell me what ye think."

Anna's step hitched, and a smile spread across her face. He'd called her Anna. It was all she could do to keep from running and wrapping him up in a bear hug.

"Now," he continued, apparently unaware of the effect he'd had on her with his simple gesture, "I've been thinkin' about adjusting things here in the shop. Sales have been down some, and I wonder if a bit o' change might be just the thing."

Anna joined him by the case facing the main entrance. Necklaces, brooches, and watches glinted in the lantern light. "You might be right. What are you thinking of doing?"

Seamus scratched at his jaw. "I'm not quite sure yet, Anna." He glanced at her from the corner of his eye. "Beggin' yer pardon, m'lady. I've a habit of leaving formality at the door." A wheezy chuckle fluttered from his lips.

Anna smiled. "Not at all. Please, do call me Anna."

Seamus nodded. "So, as I was sayin', I'm not entirely sure what to do. Sales have dipped, but I'm not certain as to why."

"I see." Anna chewed the inside of her lip and turned in a slow circle, taking stock of the inventory. An open case by the window caught her attention. Stepping to it, she ran her fingers over rows and rows of Claddagh rings set in velvet trenches. The same rings she'd admired the first day she came into the shop. An idea bloomed.

"Your store is renowned for the Claddagh ring, right?" she asked, her gaze fixed on the displays.

"Oh, aye." He crossed the floor and joined her. "The rings are by far our most popular item. We put them here by the window so they'd catch the light—as well as the eyes of those passing by."

"What if—" Anna chewed on her thumbnail. "What if you kept a small selection of rings here by the window—for the foot traffic, as you said—but then, moved most of them to the case by the door?" She turned to read his reaction.

Seamus lifted his brows and curved his mouth into an upside-down smile. "Hmm. Perhaps," he said slowly.

"My reasoning is this," she said, crossing back to the front case and spinning to face Seamus. "You know the majority of people who come in are already aware of your specialty—the rings. It's why they come, at least the first time. I'd wager most of your patronage comes from people like that rather than folks merely walking by and happening to glance in your window."

He nodded slowly. "That's true. We often get folk comin' in from all around Ireland, even the continent, because they've heard the legend." He scratched the whiskers lining his jaw again and stared at the display case.

Anna grinned. "What if you put the largest selection of your rings here, front and center? That way they are the first things people see when they enter. You said yourself most of them are here for the rings anyway. Why not capitalize on that and place them so that anyone who comes in has to see them before anything else?"

"*Tsk*. Ye're smart as a whip! I don't know why we didna think of that before." Seamus beamed and patted her hand while keeping his stare fixed on the case. Anna could almost see the wheels of thought turning in his mind. He stooped over and looked at the shelves inside the case, and then turned and studied the window display. He tapped his pointer finger on each finger of his other hand, as though counting. "We'll need more ring boxes, to be sure. I'll go fetch those. Ye can start moving them over from the window." Seamus headed for the stairs but stopped at the doorway and turned back. "You are a clever girl."

Anna warmed at his praise. She nodded and picked up a tray of rings.

Muffled voices drifted up the stairs. His father was talking with someone. Who, Stephen couldn't make out. Had the auld man opened the shop early again? Pulling his Aran-knit jumper over his head, he hurried downstairs, bumping into his father on the way. Murmuring apologies, he turned to watch the man amble up the steps. "Who were ya talkin' to, Da?"

Seamus paused on the stair and half turned back to Stephen. "There's ah . . . there's someone here to see ya." He winked and continued on his way.

Stephen scowled. What had the man done now?

Turning the corner into the back door of the shop, he found a woman in brown trousers and shirt standing behind the jewelry case by the main entrance. The case was open, and she was reaching inside. Panic seized him. What had his father been thinking leaving a customer unattended in the showroom? She could have robbed them blind if he hadn't come along!

"Oy! What are ye like?" In three long strides he was across the room. He grabbed the woman by the elbow and spun her around.

Clear blue eyes, wide in surprise, stared back at him. She blew out a breath and her hand flew to her neck. "Oh, Stephen, you gave me such a fright!"

Stephen blinked and fell back a step. Annabeth. His eyes swept over her from head to toe. While her hair was still coiled in an intricate braid, the trousers and shirt highlighted the curves her dresses, in the loose, boxy shape that was the latest fashion, previously left to the imagination. Heat crept up his neck and he forced his gaze to meet hers. "I beg your pardon, Annabeth. I didn't . . ." He swallowed hard. "I didn't recognize you." *Get ahold of yourself, man.*

Pink flooded her cheeks, and she absently patted her hair, then her pockets, before folding her hands in front of her. "Yes, well. After seeing what jewelry smithing actually entails, I thought it might be best if I wore something a bit more . . . forgiving."

Stephen cleared his throat. "Indeed." This attire would definitely afford more breathing room as they worked at the bench together. If only he could breathe. "I imagine your parents are wild about your new look."

The flush returned to her cheeks. "I may have found a way to leave this morning before they could notice." She grimaced and shrugged. "Mother simply wouldn't understand. It's not improper, I assure you. Women wear trousers all the time. Just not . . ."

"Just not courtiers," he finished for her.

She nodded.

A glint in the case caught Stephen's eye, and it was then he noticed the usual necklaces and brooches weren't in their places. He furrowed his brow and looked around the shop. "What're ye doin'?"

Annabeth's face lit up. "Oh! Your father and I came up with the most wonderful idea!" She explained their thoughts to rearrange the displays. Stephen's chest tightened and his jaw began to ache as he stared at the open jewelry case. The whole thing made perfect sense, of course. He and Seamus had just spoken at dinner the night before about the dipping profits. It was logical to think a change in display could be just the thing to reinvigorate sales. So why did it feel like the whole thing was slipping from his grasp?

This woman had been here barely a fortnight and already she was changing everything. From the moment she arrived, Stephen's life had spiraled out of his control. It was like his own personal British invasion, stripping him of all he'd known. Without even realizing it, she'd stolen his chance at starting over away from this place. Away from the legend that ever haunted him. And now that he was forced to stay here, she was changing everything about the shop that he'd built. The current layout had been of his own design. And it had worked fine—until she came along. He ran a frustrated hand down the back of his head when he realized she had stopped talking.

He tore his gaze from the case back to her face. Her countenance had fallen, and shadows replaced the light that had danced in her eyes moments ago. "Do you disagree?"

Stephen turned to the window and crossed his arms. Outside, rain splashed on the cobbled street. His side warmed as she came and stood next to him. "I don't know," he managed to say at length.

She placed a hand on his shoulder, and he fought the sense

that it belonged there. He shrugged and she removed it. "I meant no disrespect." Her voice was gentle, but not weak.

He kept his gaze focused out the window, the weather darkening along with his mood. "Things were working fine. Before," he said, knowing full well he sounded like a bellyaching schoolboy.

Annabeth circled around to face him. "I understand that change can be difficult. Take it from the new English girl in Galway." The corner of her mouth lifted slightly. "But I wonder if you might be so against the idea if it had come from your father instead of me?"

He turned his attention to her once more. In her eyes he found no judgment or anger. Only compassion. And intensity. When he didn't answer, she lifted another tray of rings from near the window and carried it across to the front case.

Heavenly thunder, the woman was stubborn. And, he feared, right.

"Just give it a try for a week or two. If it doesn't work, move things back." She headed toward the back door. "I'll go fetch the boxes from your father. Save his knees from the stairs," she said as she quit the room, leaving Stephen alone with his thoughts.

Blast it all, the woman had a point. When it came down to it, where the rings were displayed mattered not. It had mattered to him only that it had been her idea and not his—the idea that she might know better than he. He crossed to the front of the shop and was arranging the rings when the front door opened.

An older couple entered, looking road-weary, sluicing water from their sleeves and hats. "*Maidin mhaith, a mhác,*" the gentleman greeted Stephen.

"A good morning to yerself, sir." Stephen smiled. "Lovely weather, eh?"

"*Tá, cinnte.*" The man shook his head. "Certainly."

"'Tis absolutely lashing!" the woman added, shaking her

cloak. "Oh! See, Michael? They're right here." She hastened to the front case and gawked at the rings.

Stephen glanced at the ceiling where his father's and Annabeth's footsteps echoed.

Much as he hated to admit it, the lady had actually been right.

CHAPTER
10

Anna watched the deluge out the window before drawing the drapes. Lightning flashed, briefly lighting the front garden like midday. The rain, which Anna hadn't thought could get any worse, now came down in sheets, the roar almost deafening. Once she had the drapes securely fastened, she made her way to the blanketed safety of her bed.

Replaying the events of the day, she was grateful for the amiable afternoon working in the shop with Stephen and Seamus. After a bit of a rocky start that morning, things had calmed down and the trio settled into a comfortable routine and easy conversation the rest of the day. The worsening storm, however, rattled Anna's nerves.

Remembering the novel on her lap, she snuggled into the covers, and turned to the first page. Dickens always brought her comfort. Like a favorite pair of warm slippers, his words always soothed her soul in the hardest of times. But try as she might, her focus refused to rest on the pages as the wind grew to a gale outside. Thumps and crashes filled the space between lightning and thunderclaps. Anna whispered a prayer for the safety of those in less sturdy homes and extinguished the lantern.

Though she suspected sleep would be slow in coming, it was no use wasting the light if she wasn't going to read.

Birdsong stirred Anna from a dream. Stretching, she noted the absence of wind and thunder. She padded across the room and opened the drapes. Her jaw dropped at the sight. All manner of debris was strewn as far as the eye could see. Tree branches littered the garden. Pools of standing water staked claim along the front path and lawn. The clock chimed downstairs—eight o'clock. She was due at the shop by nine. "Please, let the roads be passable," she whispered.

After dressing and eating breakfast with haste, she summoned Owen and the carriage to take her into town. They bumped and splashed down the front drive, Owen unable to dodge the overlarge puddles creating a muddy, wet gauntlet for the rig.

Thankfully, the main road was fairly unobstructed, and they made it to Church Street without much delay. Owen opened the door to the carriage and helped Anna alight.

"Are ya sure ye can manage?" Owen turned a wary eye to the small road, the stones peeking through standing water. A thin path down the center remained mostly dry.

Anna eyed the path. While a steady arm to hold on to might be handy, she knew Owen was eager to get back and aid the cleanup efforts on the manor grounds . . . and at his own home, no doubt. "Yes, I believe I will be alright. Thank you, Owen."

Owen tugged on the brim of his cap. "As ye wish, m'lady. Until the usual time, then." His lack of argument confirmed his eagerness to depart.

"Good day." She smiled up at him as he lumbered back into his seat and then turned her attention to the street. Grateful she'd donned her borrowed trousers and boots, she set off for the shop.

Her heart clenched as she turned onto High Street. Front windows of shops were broken, branches were strewn hither and yon, and a grocer swept water out of his entryway. She approached him. "I am so terribly sorry, sir."

He nodded sadly and continued sweeping. "Thank ye, miss. Me and the missus is alright, thanks be to God. Things can be replaced." He frowned and glanced back into the shop. "Eventually."

"I am glad to hear you are both unharmed." Behind him, Anna could see inside the door of his store. Mud trickled across the threshold and shelves were toppled over, creating a maze of litter across the floor.

"'Sides," the man continued, "they fared far worse down the way—down by the Claddagh."

Anna's breath caught. The Jenningses . . . the shop. She set a brisk pace in their direction, calling over her shoulder, "Thank you. Good day!"

The journey to the Jenningses' shop passed impossibly slowly, time and distance seeming to stretch out longer the farther she went. All along the way, publicans and shopkeepers worked to clear the debris and mud from their stores. At last, the Claddagh shop came into view. Seamus stood outside, peering up at the roof.

"Seamus!" Anna called.

A weary smile lifted his countenance at her greeting. "Hello, my dear."

"Are you alright? Both of you?" She reached his side, breathless.

"Aye, God be praised." He gestured to the open door of the building. "Stephen's just checkin' the upper floors to ensure the roof didna leak."

Stephen's voice drifted from inside as faint footfalls padded down the stairs. "All clear, Da." Stephen stopped short when he stepped outside and saw Anna. "Mornin', Lady Annabeth. As you can see, there'll not be much business to do today. Da and I were headin' down to help clear the Claddagh. Ye can go on home."

Anna stepped closer to Stephen. "Was it hit hard? The Claddagh?"

"Aye." Stephen's lips drew into a thin line and he shifted his gaze to the Corrib. "It always is."

"The bay overflowed the barrier wall and flooded the whole of the Claddagh, all the way across to Salt Hill," Seamus said. "The streets ran like rivers. Nearly all the homes were flooded." He wiped his forehead and nose with a handkerchief.

"Those poor families." Anna thought of the one she'd seen on her tour with Stephen. The smudged faces of the children floated in her mind's eye and she wondered how they fared.

"We're goin' down to help in any way we can," Seamus added and grabbed the shovel and broom that leaned against the doorpost.

"May I come along? Please?" She looked at Stephen, her eyes pleading, her pulse quickening. How could she return home to drink tea and stitch needlepoint when she knew people were in such need?

"I'm not sure that's a good idea," he said, shaking his head.

"Lad," Seamus crooned under his breath.

"Oh please? You can't say I'm not dressed for it." She hoped her attempt at a joke didn't fall flat.

"Well, that is true," Seamus said with a laugh.

Anna laid a hand on Stephen's arm. "This is my home now. I want to do my part to help my community."

Stephen glanced down at his arm then back up to her face. His gaze searched hers, seemingly trying to judge her intentions. At length, he sighed. "Fine. They're going to need as many hands as can help."

Seamus clapped his hands together. "Grand, that settles it. Let's be off." He pressed the shovel and broom to Stephen's chest and started walking.

The trio joined the steady stream of locals winding their way down to the Claddagh and Salt Hill. Walking in silence, Anna took the opportunity to absorb it all. The people of Galway plodded together—men, women, and children—to go help their fellow community members. Clouds still dotted the sky, but the wind was calm and a musty saltiness filled the air.

Two women walked beside them. "Sure, I suppose they're lettin' just anyone join in," one said to the other.

"Aye. 'Tis bad enough for a blow-in to presume to be part of the locals, but for a Brit? *Tsk.* Shameless." The pair looked over their shoulders at Anna, their eyes shooting daggers at her.

A low rumble came from Seamus before he placed his hand to Anna's back, gently redirecting her. "Come this way," he said as he led her to the edge of the crowd. "Pay them no mind."

Anna nodded, but couldn't shake the sinking feeling that filled her. Had she made a mistake in trying to help? After all, the family she met in the Claddagh certainly didn't want any assistance from her. Would she be doing more harm than good? She glanced back toward the shop.

"Don' even think about it, dear. They're fools." Seamus waited for her to meet his gaze before giving her a friendly smile and decisive nod. "'Sides, there's only one way to prove them wrong." He shrugged and punctuated his point with a wink.

"Alright." She looped her arm through his and set her face forward.

Once they reached the end of Shop Street, the road muddied. Grateful for her boots, Anna sloshed through the muck, following Seamus and Stephen. After they crossed the bridge, some of the crowd split off to the right. Anna wondered where they were going.

"They're gonna work on the Prom and Salt Hill. Lots o' hotels and such down that way," Seamus said, as if reading her thoughts.

Anna's group followed the road around to the left, the puddles deepening as they approached the Claddagh. Anna's hand floated up to cover her mouth as her steps stilled. Mire and mud covered the streets. Trash and household goods lay half buried in the swampish mix. A cow dawdled off to one side, munching on a bunch of seaweed.

"God help them," she whispered.

"What do ya think *we're* here for?" Stephen scoffed.

Seamus sent a glare Stephen's way, then gently tugged Anna's elbow. "C'mon, lass, let's start over here."

CHAPTER
11

Stephen swiped the back of his hand across his forehead and replaced his cap. Despite the chilly day, heat shrouded him. He shoved his spade into the muck at his feet and tossed it into the wheelbarrow nearest him. Laughter floated on the breeze, and he lifted his eyes to find the source.

Annabeth and his father bantered back and forth as they scooped piles of seaweed and deposited them into a large bucket of water. The local women would wash and dry it for tea and medicinal poultices. Annabeth straightened, pressed her hands into the small of her back, and arched. Then she wiped her own forehead, smearing mud across it before returning to her work.

Stephen smiled in spite of himself at the sight of her—hair disheveled, face dirty, and her seemingly unaware. He couldn't deny she made a charming sight.

"Can I get a hand over here?" a woman at the end of the road called.

Stephen, Seamus, and Annabeth headed her direction. "What is it, Miss?" Stephen asked.

"The flood pushed all the mud into my front room. I need help sweepin' it out."

"I'd be happy to help," Annabeth said.

Stephen glanced at her from the corner of his eye.

"Much obliged, Miss. I'm Orla."

Stephen held his breath, wondering how Orla would welcome a lady of the British court into her humble Irish home.

"It's lovely to meet you. I'm Anna." Annabeth smiled and extended her hand. Orla reached out and shook it heartily.

"There's another *scuab* over there in the corner," Orla said and gestured to the broom leaning against the wall before turning her attention to Stephen and Seamus. "I'd say Anna and I have things well in hand, lads. T'anks."

Seamus caught Stephen's eye and inclined his head to the door. Stephen followed him back out to the road but not before glancing back at Annabeth to see her already at work sweeping the room.

Anna pushed the mud and filth from the corner of the room, slowly working it toward the door. Her back ached and her raw hands burned, but it felt so good to work. To have a real purpose that mattered. An unbidden smile tickled the corners of her lips.

"Ma! Ma!" A breathless boy, covered in dried mud, bounded into the small house. "Look wha' I found!"

Orla set her broom aside. "Settle down, lad. Calm yerself and show me yer finds."

"There's so much out there! It's like the whole of the Claddagh is my treasure chest!" He opened a grubby hand to display his cache.

Anna stepped closer to get a look. Seashells of all kinds filled his hand.

"Aren't they lovely, miss?" he asked Anna, face shining with excitement and pride.

"Lovely, indeed," Anna said. "May I?"

"Of course!" Delight sparkled in the boy's eyes.

Anna dug through the pile with her index finger, noting the rainbow of colors and myriad shapes. "A true testament to the ingenuity of the Creator, isn't it?"

The boy's head bobbed enthusiastically. "Oh, aye!"

"Very good, Cormac." Orla smiled down at her son. "Go put them in yer treasure box and head back out. I'm sure the men could use another nimble-bodied young man to help."

Cormac bussed his mother's cheek and scurried through the back door to an unseen room.

"He's a delightful young man," Anna said.

Orla stared after the boy, as if she could see him through the walls, tucking his loot away for safekeeping. "That he is. And he's been through so much."

Anna closed the distance between them. "Has he?"

"His da died when he was but a wee one. We lost his sister to the Spanish flu last year. He's the man o' the house now."

Anna squeezed Orla's hand. "I'm so terribly sorry."

Orla shrugged sadly. "Never mind. We've had it easy compared to other families in the Claddagh. Cormac works several odd jobs—delivering coal and milk, mucking out some stables, and such. I do a bit o' seamstress work when I can get it. We have enough to get by. That's more 'an most folk can say 'round here."

Anna struggled to keep shock from registering on her face. Cormac couldn't have been more than eight or nine years of age and already he had to work multiple jobs just to help them get by? Anna wondered what exactly it meant to "get by." By the looks of things, Orla and her son barely had enough to eat each day, let alone be satisfied. But after her experience offering food to one of Orla's neighbors that day with Stephen, Anna didn't want to risk another faux pas. "Sounds like he takes good care of you."

"Aye, that he does." Orla smiled and picked her broom back up and scanned the room. "I'd say we're almost done here."

"I'd say so." Anna returned the woman's smile, and the pair set back to work in amiable silence.

The light outside faded to a soft purple, and a river of folks passed by on the road. Seamus's form filled the doorframe.

He tipped his cap and said, "'Tis time to head back, m'lady."

"Oh, gettin' fancy now are we, Seamus?" Orla chuckled.

"Sure, 'tis how one addresses a lady. Do ye not know Lady Annabeth De Lacy?"

Orla's mouth dropped open, and heat crept up Anna's cheeks. What was Seamus up to?

"De Lacy?" Orla asked.

"Oh, aye! Her father's our new landlord." Seamus grinned and bobbed his head.

"Of course." Orla dipped a curtsy. "T'anks ever so much for yer help today, m'lady."

Anna waved a dismissive hand, annoyance at Seamus pulsing in her chest. "Nonsense. It was my honor." She shot a look to Seamus. "Now, it seems we'd best be off. I wish you and little Cormac all the best."

"Thank you, m'lady."

Anna slipped her arm through Seamus's offered elbow and squeezed. "What was that all about?" she asked under her breath. Of all people, Seamus didn't seem the kind to care about position and rank.

He beamed but kept his focus on the road ahead. "She was delightful while ye worked, aye?"

"Well, yes." They fell into step with the crowd snaking its way back to the city.

"That gave her the chance to get to know ye for who ye really are." He patted her hand that rested in the crook of his arm.

Anna studied his profile, ignoring the pain of the burning blisters on her palms. "Yes, but why reveal my title to her now and ruin the lovely encounter?"

"Did I ruin it?" He inclined his head to look at her. "She spent the afternoon learning what a hardworking, kind, helpful person ya are. And then she learned that ya *happened* to be the landlord's daughter. Perhaps the next time she encounters an Englishman, her view mightn't be so skewed."

Anna opened her mouth to reply but closed it just as quickly when no words formed on her tongue.

"And don't you think she won't be tellin' the whole of the Claddagh what ye did here today—helpin' yer fellow man. No tricks, no ulterior motive. It won't be lost on 'er that ye yerself didn't announce yer station. And she won't be quick in forgettin' it neither."

A slow smile spread across Anna's face. "You clever man, you."

CHAPTER

12

Y ou must maintain control of your county, Lord De Lacy." General Frederick George drained his glass of whiskey and set it firmly on the desk.

"You say that as if I mean not to." Lord De Lacy swallowed his ire with the remnants of his own drink. "There's been no trouble as of yet, General. I've got my people keeping a weather eye out at all times."

The general stared out the wall of windows that looked over the front garden as he puffed on his cigar. It would take weeks for the reek to leave the office. William preferred the softer aroma of the pipe. It was more civilized. Gentlemanly. He clasped his hands behind his back and rocked from his toes to his heels.

"Quite right." General George recovered his glass from the desk and helped himself to another dram. "As you know, the newest division of the Royal Irish Constabulary was deployed in January." He smacked his lips and turned his full attention to William.

"Of course." William crossed his arms over his chest and leaned against the edge of his large oak desk, blocking the decanter.

"We've had an entirely positive response, De Lacy. It's quite something. The numbers are growing by the day. Men are eager to fight for and protect their country, especially from a band of unruly insurgents." He examined his fingernail and picked at an errant fleck of skin, then took another long drag on his cigar before continuing. "We had hoped their presence would dampen the rebels' fervor. Alas, that has not been the case. Therefore, a unit of the RIC will be coming to the Galway barracks within a fortnight. It will be your duty to communicate with their commanding officer, Captain Roger Bradbury, and relay any pertinent issues or needs to me." He lifted the glass to his lips for another sip, only to discover it to be empty. Clearing his throat, he set the tumbler down with a hollow thud and settled in a chair near the door.

"Yes, sir." William moved a crystal ashtray from his desktop to the side table near the general, then extended his legs as he sat, crossing them at the ankles. General George scowled before mashing his cigar into the ashtray. The grotesque corpse of the cigar, and the news of the impending arrival of troops, irked William.

An increased presence of British troops could incite more violence than it deterred. However, having a unit of men in his county would give him the chance to show his superiors his true mettle. He couldn't afford another misstep. "What will be their primary objective?"

"These people made a right mess of things by declaring themselves an independent republic last year. As if they had the right to such a thing. That's why their *Dáil*—their so-called government—had to be outlawed in September." He sniffed in derision. "They don't know when to let go, so we must loosen their hands for them. The RIC will protect and uphold British rule of law. By any means necessary."

"Indeed." William swallowed hard. Though George rubbed him the wrong way, William couldn't let his own preferences and personal annoyances threaten his chances to secure his place in leadership for good. "Fear not, General. Galway is in very capable hands."

"Good man." The general stood and extended his hand to William, who shook it. "I'll be in touch by letter in a few days with more details on the timeline of the unit's arrival."

"Very good, sir." William moved to the door and opened it. "It was good of you to come."

General George took his hat from the stand and placed it on his head, gave a firm, single nod, and made for the front door.

As Anna came downstairs after changing from her muddy attire, she stopped short at the sight of General George. She watched from the corner of the hallway as he took his leave, the unmistakable stench of cigar following in his wake. She crinkled her nose. She hadn't meant to eavesdrop but couldn't help but overhear the general's baritone voice carry through the walls. Could it be true? More British troops coming to Galway? According to Stephen, the barracks were just behind the Spanish Arch, running along what they called the Long Walk down near the Claddagh. Near the shop. What could that mean for her? For the Jenningses?

When the Irish first declared independence last January, Anna remembered meeting after meeting with various military officials in her father's office in England. They weren't about to let Ireland go without a fight, she'd heard them declare. Endless grandiose ideas of how to deal with the Irish problem floated up the stairs to Anna's room many a night. At the time, she couldn't believe anyone would take issue with British rule of law. She was proud to be an Englishwoman—proud of her heritage and history. And she wouldn't abandon that stance lightly either.

However, after spending even just a little time here, seeing how they lived and how it seemed every effort had been made over the decades—nae, centuries—to squelch anything that made the people uniquely Irish, she had begun to see how they might want to govern themselves. To be independent. But did it take violence and war to accomplish that? Was there a peaceful way to accomplish such a thing? She didn't know.

As long as she'd been aware, the Irish had been at odds with the English. Going back just a few years to 1916 with the Easter Rising she'd heard about from her father and her tutors—a tantrum thrown by an infantile people, she'd been taught—the people of Ireland had voiced their desire for independence. She thought back even further to her lessons about the kings of old and wondered what those stories looked like from an Irish perspective. She thought of William the Conqueror, King Henry, and Sir Cromwell. What had those events been like on the Irish side of the story? And why hadn't she ever questioned it before? She'd always viewed Britain's conquests as righteous, but now she wasn't so sure. They all started out that way, she had no doubt, but over time, the motivation seemed to have shifted. But of one thing she was certain—this was an idea and issue that had been brewing for centuries, and it wasn't about to be solved in a hurry. And with more troops heading for her new home, it seemed it wasn't about to be solved peaceably anytime soon either.

Turning toward the kitchen for a cup of tea to soothe her anxious heart, she lifted a prayer. *Give my father wisdom as he leads,* she prayed. *And give the people justice where it's needed. And grace for everything else.*

The kitchen was quiet and dark, save for the crackling of the fire in the stove. The warmth enveloped her like a blanket, and she breathed deeply, replacing the sweet stench of the cigar with sage, rosemary, and thyme. She fetched the kettle and brewed a strong cuppa. Pouring the milk into the tea the way Katy had shown her, she watched as the two liquids danced and swirled together. First, the milk was held suspended in the tea. But as she stirred, the two became one. Two things so vastly different coming together, through friction, to make something altogether beautiful, soothing, and delicious.

Do that here too, Lord.

CHAPTER

13

The aroma of fresh brown bread and hot tea summoned Anna to the kitchen the next morning. It always came back to the tea. Pinning her final curl in place, she rounded the corner to find Katy at the stove, stirring a pot of porridge.

"Good morning, Katy." Anna lowered herself onto the bench at the table, which already held the steaming teapot surrounded by empty cups and saucers awaiting their owners. The frame hanging overhead, sporting pots and drying herbs, sent earth-scented wafts floating down anytime the air stirred. Anna wrapped one hand around the side of her teacup, savoring the warmth as the tea swirled into it. She then added the milk and hugged the vessel near her chest.

"Marnin', Lady Annabeth." Katy turned and placed a dish of piping hot porridge in front of Anna, who reprimanded her with just a look. "Beggin' yer pardon, m'lady. *Anna*," she corrected herself. "I see ye've adopted our way of mixin' yer tea."

Anna smeared a small pat of butter and a sprinkle of sugar on top of her porridge. How many others were starting their morning with such luxuries? The idea flitted into her mind and out again. "Yes, you're right. You wouldn't think the order of liquid would matter. But I do find I prefer it this way." She swallowed a bite of her breakfast. "For some reason."

The side of Katy's mouth tipped upward. "How're ye faring in the new togs?"

Anna hastily swallowed her mouthful of tea. She'd meant to express her gratitude to Katy, but she'd been in such a hurry to change yesterday, it had slipped her mind. "Oh! They're wonderful. Thank you again for letting me borrow them. I hope they aren't too cumbersome to launder. I tried to clean the mud off them as best I could."

Waving a dismissive hand, Katy turned her attention back to the stove. "Not a bother, miss. Anytime. It's lucky we are the same size."

Anna eyed the girl's back. Her gray maid's dress hung nearly to the floor, and the bright white ties of her apron accented her waist. "Very true! They made cleaning up after the storm so much more manageable!"

Katy puffed a sigh through her lips. "Can ye believe the state of things down the Claddagh? Desperate." She clucked her tongue and wagged her head.

"I've never seen anything like it," Anna said, her mind drifting back to Orla and Cormac.

"And good on ya for gettin' in there and gettin' yer hands dirty, m'lady. Not many courtiers would do that."

Anna's cheeks burned. She didn't deserve praise any more than anyone else who went down to help. "'Twas the least I could do."

"Well, I think it's grand, so." Katy went back to stirring the porridge.

Uncomfortable with the praise, Anna tried to steer the conversation back to safer ground. "Well, anyway, I appreciate the loan again. I had no idea trousers would afford so much freedom of movement. I'd wager women will be wearing them all the time in the future."

Katy's songbird laugh filled the air. "Can ye 'magine, m'lady? Yer mam runnin' around the bogs in trousers and a shirt?"

The image filled Anna's mind—her prim-and-proper British courtier mother donning trousers. And traipsing. Through a *bog*—she couldn't help but join Katy in laughter.

"What has you both so jovial this morning?" Mother glided into the kitchen looking as formal and dignified as ever.

Anna scooped her last bite of porridge into her mouth to stay her giggles. Katy spun back to the stove, tucking a stray shock of black hair back under her maid's cap.

"Oh nothing, Mother." Anna cleared her throat and rose from the table. "Just silly girl talk. I'm going out for a walk on the grounds." She bussed her mother's cheek, ignoring the perplexed look on the woman's face, and quit the room.

As she headed down the center hall toward the back garden, guilt niggled at her. She hadn't exactly lied to her mother about the clothes. But she hadn't been forthcoming about them either. She wasn't even sure why she felt the need to hide them, other than knowing her mother would have objected. She had objected to the whole arrangement with the Jenningses from the start. Not that there was anything that could be done about it now. Besides, Anna had already accepted the job, so she needed to do it properly. And that simply wasn't possible in her impractical gowns that were meant for dining at a fancy table, lounging, and embroidering.

As she stepped out into the clear late-spring morning, her heart lifted. Breathing deep the scents of grass, pine, and turf—a bouquet unique to Ireland—she eyed the expansive gardens. A gravel path framed a hedge maze that filled a large center rectangle. Beyond the footpath, on all sides, dense woods yawned as far as the eye could see. Choosing the path to her right, she set off on her walk. Pebbles crunched underfoot as she turned the corner to stroll parallel to the woods and maze. Birds twittered in the tall canopy and bright yellow daffodils and pink tulips dotted the edges of the walkway, dancing in the gentle morning breeze. All evidence of the storm was gone—not a twig or stone was out of place. Anna looked at her hands, still raw from the work she'd done in the Claddagh. And there was still more to do before those families could return to some semblance of normalcy. The chasm of disparity between her life and theirs seemed to stretch wider with each passing day. Or had the chasm always been thus and merely her awareness of it was growing? Anna chewed her lip as she pondered.

As she walked, Anna replayed the events of the past few weeks in her mind. Meeting Seamus and Stephen, making her first ring, sampling local fare, touring the Claddagh, and hearing the news of incoming British troops. A kaleidoscope of seemingly random events that Anna couldn't help but feel were part of something bigger. Like colored shards waiting to be joined in an artistic triumph of stained glass. Her part in this unfolding unknown was still unclear. What she did know was that she wanted to conduct herself with the utmost honesty and integrity. Starting with being honest with her parents. She couldn't expect to borrow Katy's clothes indefinitely. She would talk to her mother about her wardrobe when she returned to the house.

A twig snapped in the woods. Anna's head spun in the direction of the sound, but she saw nothing. Peering into the trees, she could see only a few feet beyond the edge. Darkness blanketed the interior of the woods. She turned to continue her walk when a louder crash ricocheted among the trees. Frozen, Anna squinted, straining to see into the thick forest. The sound of her own heartbeat in her ears drowned out everything else.

"Hullo?" Her shaky voice caught in her throat. She cleared it and spoke again with more strength. "Hello? Is anyone there?"

A rush of wind set the treetops dancing, scattering leaves and stirring up a haunting rustle around Anna. As the gust died down, the rustling continued. Whispers. Surely she didn't hear whispers among the trees?

Willing her feet to obey, she managed to break them free from where they seemed frozen to the ground and hastened toward the house. More cracks, snaps, and, yes, voices.

Suddenly two young men who could be no older than sixteen or seventeen bounded from the woods. They stumbled, hunched over, laughing before straightening and meeting Anna's gaze. "Mornin', miss," the taller one said.

The second young man shifted his feet and chuckled. "Marnin.'"

Anna's hand clasped her chest. "Good gracious me, you boys gave me a fright." She blew a long exhale. "Good morning."

The young men shared a glance, none-too-friendly smiles on their faces. "Beggin' yer pardon, miss."

Anna peered past them, back into the woods. "What were you gentlemen doing?"

Again, they grinned at one another before the taller one answered. "We must've lost our way, miss."

"Ye must be the new landlords, then, aye?" The shorter one stepped forward, surveying the land around them.

Anna swallowed hard and took a half step back. "My father is, yes. I am his daughter, Lady Annabeth De Lacy."

The taller lad lifted his cap and bowed from the waist, a look of mock impression plastered on his face. "Pleased to make yer acquaintance, m'lady. Ciaran O'Donnell at yer service. This here's my brother, Mickey." The corner of Mickey's lips curled, and mischief flickered in his eyes as he joined his brother in a bow.

Anna glanced back at the house. They weren't too far from it, which would hopefully deter these young men from any unwieldy behavior. Still, unease wound its way up her spine. Just what, exactly, were these gentlemen doing on their property, anyway?

She clasped her hands in front of her. "Is there something

you need? What brings you to Galway Manor . . . in the back garden?" She asked, eyeing the boys.

Mickey snorted and took a step toward her. "The woods 'round here are public land, miss—er—m'lady." He chuckled again and his brother elbowed him in the ribs. Mickey scowled at Ciaran before returning his smarmy smile toward Anna. "Or did they not tell ye that? We can be in there all we want, anytime we want."

Mickey started to step closer to Anna, but Ciaran put a hand on his brother's shoulder and mumbled something in Irish. Mickey looked at him and nodded, looking dejected.

"We were just out hunting fowl and got a wee bit turned around. We meant no harm, m'lady," Ciaran said, his voice sickeningly sweet.

Anna noticed neither one carried a gun or bow. An odd way to hunt fowl, to be sure, but she decided to keep the observation to herself. "I see." She forced a smile onto her face. "The woods may be public land, but this garden is not. I believe if you head east, you'll find yourself where you want to be. Good luck in your hunt. I hope you get what you're looking for."

The young men doffed their caps once more and turned back toward the trees. "Aye, Lady Annabeth. We always do." Their ominous farewell and caustic laughter met Anna's ears just before they disappeared into the shadows.

CHAPTER
14

Paddy watched as Ciaran drained his pint. Impatience swam in Paddy's gut, but he allowed the lad to finish his drink. Ciaran gulped the final swig, set his glass down with a thud, and swiped the back of his hand across his mouth. A satisfied "Ahh" snaked from his lips.

Paddy stared at him, waiting. When the lad failed to offer up a report, Paddy's patience wore thin. "Well?" he asked.

"Ye won't believe it." Ciaran released a belch and waved his hand in Paddy's direction. "The new landlord has his family in tow. A bonny lass with blond hair."

"Yeah," Mickey added. "And her hair's the worst part about her." He waggled his eyebrows, and a suggestive chuckle escaped his lips, which invited an elbow to the ribs from Ciaran.

"*Amadán*," Ciaran muttered.

Mickey rubbed his side and glared at his brother. "I'm no' an eejit."

Ciaran gave him a sidelong glance and rolled his eyes. "Anyhow, if worst comes to worst, I t'ink we can get to 'His Lordship' through his daughter." He nodded and looked from man to man around the table.

Satisfied murmurs and knowing grunts rippled through the group.

"We'll have ta draw straws. To make it fair, like," Molloy offered with a chuckle.

Another rumble of agreement. "I like the way you think, boyo." Old Man Burke wagged a crooked finger at Ciaran. "But we'd have to cover our tracks. Martin has that fishing shack out by Barnahallia Lake. We wouldn't even hafta do an'thing to her. Just take her out there. I bet His Lordship'd pay a pretty penny ta get her back."

The group nodded, clearly thinking about what Burke said.

Paddy's face twisted in thought. He'd met Annabeth De Lacy, and he couldn't deny she was lovely. But he also couldn't deny that the idea of using her to get to her father unnerved him. Much as he despised De Lacy's presence—all the Brits' presence—he couldn't shake the sense of unease at the thought of involving the girl. She didn't ask to be the daughter of a ne'er-do-well landlord. But he chose to keep his thoughts to himself. "Good work, lads."

Ciaran and Mickey shifted in their seats at his praise.

"Anything more about Lord De Lacy himself?" Paddy asked.

"Not yet. He wasn't to be seen this marnin'," Ciaran said, wagging his head. "But we'll keep on it."

Paddy took a sip of his pint and nodded. "Good. Now, I've come across a bit o' news that ye all should know."

The group of men gathered around the table leaned in. Paddy nodded at Molloy.

"Right." Molloy cleared his throat. "Rumor around the barracks is that a new lot of Black 'n Tans are on their way."

The group scoffed and Old Man Burke slapped his hand on the tabletop. "*Docreidte*," he muttered.

"Well, believe it." Molloy leveled his gaze at each man in turn. "But I've also heard that some of the dandy British bigwigs will be coming through town soon. And I've got an idea."

The group huddled closer, and Paddy glanced around, ensuring their privacy, before leaning in himself to hear the plan.

The words swam on the page and try as he might, William could not bring himself to concentrate on them.

"William? Are you listening to me?" Elizabeth's voice seeped into focus.

Closing the book with more force than he intended, William stood and faced his wife, who was standing at the drawing room fireplace, straightening a brass candlestick. "I'm sorry, dear. What did you say?"

Elizabeth huffed and dropped her hands to her sides. "Did you hear what Annabeth asked for this morning?"

William searched his mind. When wasn't that child asking for something outlandish? He shook his head. "What?"

Crossing the room, she clasped his hands in her own, her long ivory fingers wrapping around his wrists. "William, she's asked for—" Elizabeth grimaced as the words seemed to lodge in her throat. "She's asking for some trousers." She spat the last word as if it were poison, and her fingertips fluttered to her forehead as though she might faint.

William blinked hard, swallowing the chuckle that would most definitely rouse the ire of his bride. "Trousers? Whatever for?"

Releasing his other hand, Elizabeth paced in front of him. "For this jewelry nonsense." She waved her hand as if the arrangement were a bothersome insect. "She claims she needs them for working in the smithing room. Some drivel about how her gowns get in the way."

William thought back to what he'd seen in the back room of the jewelry shop when he'd first spoken with Seamus about the apprenticeship. Recalling the rough wood tables, stools, molten metal, and various tools, he could see how the fine gowns his wife and daughters wore could interfere. Or present a hazard. He crossed the room and placed tender hands on Elizabeth's shoulders. "What would you have her do? Risk getting her skirts caught in some jewelry-making tool? Or catch fire on the smelting pot? It seems to me trousers, while a bit unsophisticated, would be more . . . practical."

Elizabeth's eyes narrowed and she stepped free of his grip. "My daughter will not embarrass herself—and us—by wearing such things." Placing her hands on her slender hips, she resumed her pacing.

William lowered himself onto the settee by the fireplace. Goodness, he preferred the wingbacks in his office. "Would it really be such a crime, my love? I've seen that workplace. It's no place for—" He winced.

"For a lady. It's no place for a lady, William!" She spun and poked her finger in the air at him. "You should have never agreed to this in the first place." She tugged a dainty handkerchief from her sleeve and dabbed the corners of her eyes.

Rising and jamming his fists into his pockets, William stifled a frustrated sigh. "Elizabeth, we've been over this. Annabeth needs more than just . . . this." He yanked his hands back out of the pockets and held them wide. "She needs to be challenged, to create."

"You need her to, you mean." Elizabeth crossed her arms and turned her back to him. "You need her to be the son I could never give you." Her voice thickened and trailed off.

"What?" he hissed, not believing what he'd heard. "This has nothing to do with me. Or that. This is about our daughter." He strode to the drawing room window and looked out on the lawn. "There is no court here, no social calendar. How else is she to fill her time meaningfully?" A bird soared in the sky, riding the currents, seemingly unbothered by any care in the world.

William watched it and envied the creature. He longed to be so free. He shook the thought away as he reminded himself of the promise of reward that lay ahead of him.

"I was willing to go along with this apprenticeship," Elizabeth offered at length. "I know just as well as you how insufferable she gets when she's bored. So, even though it was unorthodox, I agreed. But trousers, William? Trousers?" Her voice raised an octave on the last word.

"What does it matter?" His hands flew out to the side like wings and fell back down.

In a flash her hand was on his arm, spinning him around to face her. Fire flickered in her eyes. "Someone could see her." She ground the words out through gritted teeth.

Confound the woman and her endless concerns with appearance. His eyes fell upon the copy of the British Military Manual on the table next to the high-backed chair he'd been sitting in earlier. The weight of what he'd been ordered to do by General George settled on him like a lead cloak. Couldn't his wife see he had more pressing matters to concern himself with?

Elizabeth sniffled. "If we were in Camberwick—"

"We aren't in Camberwick, Elizabeth!" His shout echoed in the rafters and his wife stepped back. "Hang it all, this is Ireland, woman! Ireland, *not* England! I have my hands full enough trying to keep order here—and keep our family safe—in the midst of an uncivilized war. What our daughter wears into a town of peasants to make jewelry is of no consequence to me." He pinched the bridge of his nose and pressed his lips into a firm line.

Elizabeth's eyes glassed over with unshed tears when she turned away from him once more. William couldn't remember the last time he'd raised his voice at his wife. Remorse filled his gut, but he didn't know any other way to make her see she was fussing over trivialities.

Frustration still simmered, but Elizabeth would never respond to that tack. He rolled his shoulders and took a slow, deep breath. Crossing the room, he stood behind his wife. He raised his hands to place them on her shoulders but lowered them to his sides. "Forgive me for shouting." He willed his voice soft.

Elizabeth remained motionless, her back straight and tall. "I'll summon the tailor in the morning." Her voice was barely audible.

William cleared his throat. "Alright." He wanted her to understand, to really grasp what they were facing. If things went ill with the war, all hope was lost. Not only hope . . . everything would be lost, and their livelihood with it. "Elizabeth—"

Elizabeth lifted a silent hand to her side, stopping his speech, then spun on her heel until she was nose to nose with him. "You are right about one thing, William De Lacy—this is *not* Camberwick. Or London. Or Bath. But isn't that the exact reason we are here? You would do well to bear that in mind regarding our daughters." She fled the room with angry, dignified steps in the way only a true lady of Britain could do, leaving William alone with an ache creeping up his shoulders into his head.

CHAPTER

15

◆ May 28 ◆

The last few weeks had passed in a flurry of work at the shop, returning to help clean up at the Claddagh, and family life obligations. Grateful for a few quiet moments, Anna sat at the counter of the shop. Pencil scratching at the paper, she was so engrossed in her sketch that she didn't hear the gentleman enter. He cleared his throat, and she jumped at the sound, flinging the pencil behind her.

"I'm terribly sorry," the robust man with rosy cheeks said with a pinched smile. "I didn't mean to startle ya, but I wasn't sure ya heard me come in."

Anna's cheeks flushed as she rushed to fetch the pencil, mortified at her clumsiness. "Mister McGinnty." Anna sighed and pressed her hand to her chest. "How lovely to see you again! And no, no, not at all. It's I who should apologize to you. You are the customer, after all." Returning to the counter, she slid the paper out of the way and gave the man her full attention. "Now, what can I help you with? Or are you here to see Ste— er—Mister Jennings?"

His eyes studied her for a moment, as though trying to decide how he wished to proceed. "Aye. Are the lads about?" he asked at length.

Anna looked to the ceiling, as though she could see Seamus and Stephen through it. "They're around somewhere, though I'm not sure how soon they'll be here in the shop."

Paddy turned toward the door, glanced at the clock, and turned back to Anna. "Hang it all," he said under his breath. He took a step nerarer. "I'm looking for . . ." He looked down into the glass display and pointed. "A ring, actually."

"You've come to the right place, indeed." Opening the back of the case, Anna lifted one of the velvet-covered ring trays and placed it on the countertop. "Is there a particular style or size you're looking for?"

"It must be a Claddagh, to be sure." He screwed up his face as he bent at the waist to examine the options more closely. "It's for my auld la—er—wife. It's our twentieth this year, and I promised her ages ago I'd do somethin' special. And I don't really know where to start." Panic flashed across his face before he lifted his eyes to meet Anna's in a silent plea for help.

The corners of Anna's mouth lifted, and her heart went out to the poor soul. Here was this large brute of a man—the kind no other gentleman would dream of crossing—reduced to tremors at the thought of disappointing his wife. She hadn't ever thought about the pressure a husband must feel making the decision about something his wife would wear for the rest of her life.

"Tell me more about her," Anna said.

The man's eyes stared a mile off and went glossy. "Oh." He sighed. "She's beautiful. But more than that, she's so kind and warm. She grew up working on her family's sheep farm—helpin' with the lambing and such, and then she knitted the wool into sweaters, scarves, and the like. Now, she helps me in the chipper." He jammed a thumb in the direction of his fish and chip shop. "But she still helps with her family's bits too."

"She sounds lovely."

"Aye, she is. Lovely and fair. And there's not a cruel bone in her body. Ye should see her with the wee lambs—so tender and gentle. But then she's a fiend on the spinning wheel."

Anna laughed and waited for him to continue.

"But the lass knows what she wants, and she's not afraid to tell ye." His eyes went wide, and he waved his hands in front of him. "But she's not demandin' neither. No, she has the perfect way of lettin' ye know where she stands and makin' ya feel like you can know yer own mind at the same time." He smiled and stooped to study the rings in the tray.

Anna grinned down at him, an idea brewing—but would he be receptive? "What does she like in terms of fashion?"

"She has simple tastes, but very good ones." He rubbed the back of his neck. "And expensive ones," he added with a grimace.

Anna chuckled. "I've an idea," she said, and watched him for a moment. "Does she already wear a wedding band?"

"Aye." His voice held a hint of a question.

"I was just thinking . . ." She chewed her lip. "What if you went with something other than a ring? Something . . . different?"

"Different?" He scratched at his jaw. "Different how?"

She stepped to another display case. "I was thinking perhaps a brooch. She could use it to fasten her scarves or wear on her blouses. She could pin it to a hat . . . There are countless ways she could wear it. And that way she wouldn't have to worry about catching it in the spinning wheel or dirtying it in the chip shop." She looked at him in anticipation.

Paddy crossed his arms over his broad chest. "Hmm." He shifted his weight. "A brooch, y'say?"

Anna nodded.

"Ye make a good point about her work. I'd hate for the ring to sit in the box because she was afraid to ruin it." He bent low and studied the selection of brooches in the case. "I suppose it could work. But it would have to be more . . . special . . . than any ye have here." He waved a finger at the display.

"I agree." Anna stepped closer. "And *special* is our specialty," she added with a smile.

After asking him a few more questions about his wife's style, color preferences, and fashion habits, she guided him to settle on a lovely brooch design of the Claddagh symbol surrounded by Celtic knots. They decided together to embed some small gemstones into a few of the knots.

"It's perfect," Paddy said, looping his thumbs through his suspenders. "Special, but not gaudy."

Anna matched his grin. "Perfect, indeed."

As they completed the transaction, Paddy paused and regarded her for a moment.

"So, tell me," he continued, "how'd ye—the daughter of a British landlord—come to be here, in the most Irish of jewelry shops?" No ill will shadowed his face. Only genuine curiosity.

Anna let a warm smile light her face as she considered what exactly to share with him. She settled on a simple version of the truth. "I have a keen interest in art and design. My father arranged this apprenticeship for me so I could learn from the best."

Seemingly satisfied with her answer, he nodded. "Ya came to the right place." He turned to go and then stopped and looked back. "And I'd say they made a right good decision in accepting ya. Ya certainly have a knack for it." He waggled the receipt in two fingers, then tucked it in his coat pocket and left.

"Thank you," Anna whispered.

Stephen leaned against the doorpost and crossed his arms over his chest as he watched the scene unfold from the smithing room. When he'd heard a customer enter the shop, his first instinct was to rush in and take over. But Seamus had had another idea.

"Leave her be, lad," he'd whispered as he placed a hand on Stephen's arm. "See how she does." Seamus had then conveniently excused himself upstairs.

The encounter had not started off very well, with Annabeth not even noticing the man enter. But as they interacted, the tension in Stephen's jaw relaxed and he watched in awe how naturally Annabeth dealt with Paddy.

She was entirely charming—even with managing to throw a pencil across the room. She knew just when to smile, laugh, and listen. And she'd asked questions Stephen had never thought to ask before. Without prying too much or being overly flirtatious, Annabeth had charmed the man into designing a pricier brooch—seeing that his original thought of a ring wasn't what he needed at all. And she'd done it without seeming like she was pushing a sale. It was one of the most genuine encounters he'd ever witnessed.

As Paddy left, Stephen watched her for another moment. She remained still and stared at the door for a long beat before returning to her sketch. "Well done," he said, breaking the silence as he stepped toward her, immediately ducking to dodge the pencil that flew his way.

Straightening, he swallowed a chuckle. Annabeth stood, both hands plastered over her mouth, eyes rounded, cheeks as red as cherries. "I am so terribly sorry." Her voice was muffled behind her fingers.

"Ye could kill someone doing that, ya know." His lips split in a grin he couldn't hold back. He bent to fetch the pencil, then held it out to her.

Annabeth approached him and lifted a hand toward his face but lowered it before touching him. "Are you alright?" She winced as her eyes roved his face and head.

"I'm grand. No harm done." He gestured for her to return to the stool in front of her sketching paper. "As I was saying, ya did a fine job helping Paddy."

She took the pencil from him and ducked her head, her lips tipping up bashfully. "Thank you. I was terribly nervous at first, but as I spoke with him, the nerves eased, and I found we just had a conversation. He's so smitten with his wife—even after so many years—and the little details he shared about her made me feel almost as if I knew her myself. That led me to suggest the brooch with gemstone design. And he loved it." She shrugged, a satisfied smile gracing her face.

There was no doubt Annabeth had a gift for conversation—a way of charming and disarming men with heartfelt questions. He'd seen it not only with the customer but with his own father as well. Deep down, however, Stephen wondered if she would be equally well received by the female customers. Of course, they were not nearly as common, but the occasional woman did come in on her own or with a sister to choose a special gift for her beau, or mam, or aunt. Making a mental note to observe Annabeth's interactions with the female customers, he turned his attention to the paper still sitting on the glass counter.

A few rough lines were scratched out, but the bulk of the image was hidden behind Annabeth. "What do ye have here?" Stephen pointed to the sketch.

Her cheeks reddened again, and she snatched the page and held it behind her back. "Oh, that's nothing. At least not yet." Bringing the paper in front of her, she folded it carefully and placed it in her apron pocket. "It's just an idea that came to me. But it's not finished."

"I see." Stephen stifled a sigh.

"What's on the plan for today?" Annabeth grabbed a rag and absently polished circles on the already spotless glass of the case.

Stephen described the pieces he wanted them to mold and

cast. As he finished laying out the plans, Seamus entered the room, his blue eyes sparkling.

"Hallo, Anna!" Seamus shuffled over and placed a kiss on her cheek.

Anna? When did Lady Annabeth and his father become so informal with one another? And how did he not notice it before? Better yet, why did it irk him so?

"Seamus! It's good to see you." She returned a brief peck on the auld man's cheek.

"Are ye excited?" Seamus looked back and forth between Annabeth and Stephen.

Annabeth glanced at Stephen, confusion painted on her face. "Excited? For what?"

Seamus swiped the flatcap off his head and swatted Stephen on the shoulder with it. "Did ye not tell her, ya scallywag?"

Stephen held his arms up over his face in mock defense. "I hadn't gotten 'round to it just yet, Da. But since ye're here, why don't *you* tell her?"

Seamus kept his gaze on Stephen's face, but he extended a hand toward Annabeth, expectation on his face. Clearly he wanted the news to come from Stephen.

Shuffling his weight to his other foot, Stephen cleared his throat. "There's a *seisiún* at Tigh Hughes this evening. Da said ye're interested in our music and he wants me to take ye. Would ye be interested?" He secretly hoped she'd say no, choosing to believe he'd enjoy the event much more on his own.

Annabeth pursed her lips as though she had to decipher what exactly Stephen had said. "A session? At Tee Hughes?"

The sound of Stephen's heart language on her lips filled him with a strange sensation. Her pronunciation left something to be desired, but he liked the sound of it, nonetheless.

"A seisiún," he repeated, and watched as she silently mouthed the correct pronunciation—seh-SHYOON. Forcing his gaze from her lips back to her eyes, he continued, "It's an afternoon of traditional Irish music played by locals. It's very informal. Tigh Hughes is the name of a pub just up the way."

Annabeth's eyes rounded and her face lit up. "Oh, yes, please! I'd love to go, thank you!" She clapped her hands.

Stephen forced himself to return her smile, trying to convince himself it wouldn't be so bad. "Grand. We'll leave here around four o'clock. Until then, there's work to do." He nodded at his father and made for the smithing room, watching over his shoulder for his apprentice to join him.

A quiet squeal eked from Annabeth's mouth. She squeezed Seamus's arm and followed Stephen.

CHAPTER

16

Though Anna thoroughly enjoyed practicing her new skills in the smithing room, the afternoon could not pass quickly enough for her taste. She had read about traditional Irish instruments and heard tell of the boisterous music but had yet to experience it for herself. At long last, the church bells clanged four of the clock. Yanking off her apron, thankful she had worn a simpler dress today rather than trousers, since her new pair was being laundered, she smoothed her hands over the robin's-egg blue skirt. Patting her hair to ensure all the coils were still in place, she forced herself to take a deep, calming breath.

Stephen rounded the corner sporting a cream-colored shirt, dark trousers, and a tweed waistcoat the color of emeralds and long-steeped tea. "Ready?" A less-than-relaxed smile lifted the corners of his mouth.

When he placed his flatcap on his head, his eyes came alive with color and Anna feared the pounding of her heart would reach his ears, even from across the room. Nodding, she wondered what Seamus had to do to convince Stephen to take her on this outing. Judging by the tension in Stephen's jaw, it must've taken quite an argument. Swallowing the twinge of disappointment at Stephen's stilted reaction, Anna tied her cape at her neck and determined to enjoy the seisiún.

She stepped out into the dimming afternoon light, a brisk breeze tickling the tendrils at her neck. A shiver wiggled up her spine and she pulled the cloak tighter around her shoulders.

The multicolored buildings stretched into an amber-painted sky. The scent of turf fires filled the air as lanterns flickered on in windows and streetlamps. Several other couples and a group of young women filtered onto the cobblestone streets. Like a stream winding lazily to a tide pool, the whole lot meandered in the direction of the pub.

Anna glanced up at Stephen, who looked straight ahead, his face devoid of any emotion. "Thank you," she said, breaking the silence, "for bringing me to the seisiún."

He turned his head slightly toward her, a hint of a smile appeared on his face, and he nodded. Anna studied his profile for a moment, and wondered once again what he was truly thinking as they walked toward the pub. When his jaw clenched, she then considered perhaps it was best she didn't know.

The pair continued in silence, the only sounds those of feet shuffling on the stone street and muffled conversations from the groups around them. As they approached an intersection, voices and spirited laughter spilled out of an open door on the corner. The late-afternoon light glowed from behind the pub, surrounding it in a golden halo that extended to the cobblestones below. People of all ages milled about just outside the building, while silhouettes roamed within.

Anna sucked in a breath at the sight and placed a hand on Stephen's arm. At her touch, he stopped short and from the corner of her eye she could see his face turn toward her. She, however, couldn't tear her eyes from the charm of the scene unfolding before them.

"Here we are." His voice was gravelly. "Tigh Hughes."

She turned her gaze to meet his at last, a grin spreading across her face. They stood for a moment and watched the patrons mingle. Anticipation welled up in her chest, and she bounced on her toes, grinning like a schoolgirl. "Can we go inside?"

A smile flashed in his eyes and he nodded, offering his elbow to her.

As she slipped her hand in the crook of his arm, warmth immediately enveloped it. He led her into the building and nodded in greeting to two gentlemen standing just inside the door. Anna couldn't help but notice conversations began to die down, and just moments after they entered, a blanket of silence fell over the crowd.

Stephen then nodded at a tall, gangly gentleman with a stout woman at his side. "Martin," he mumbled. The gentleman returned the nod, then pinned his stare on Anna, who repaid the attention with a shaky smile.

"A *Stíofán*!" The robust voice was followed by a solid hand clapping onto Stephen's shoulder.

"Paddy, how are ye?" Stephen grinned and shook the man's hand.

Anna smiled at the familiar face of Paddy McGinnty. "Good evening, Mister McGinnty."

Paddy shot a glance to Stephen and then around the room before taking Anna's hand and brushing a kiss across her knuckles. "Lady Annabeth."

"Please, call me Anna," she replied, but her words were swallowed up by a cacophony of instruments playing all at once. Paddy slipped to a corner of the room and disappeared behind a sea of faces.

"They're warming up," Stephen spoke in her ear. Goosebumps prickled her skin at his nearness. "We should find a seat."

Anna attempted to ignore the stares of the patrons already seated as she and Stephen made their way through the pub. As much as she tried, she couldn't overlook the women whispering behind their hands to their husbands, or the glares that greeted her whenever she managed to look someone in the eye.

Stephen gently tightened his elbow to his side, pulling Anna closer to him. A minute wave of relief washed over her at his small, but profound, gesture of protection. At least that's what she was choosing to believe it was.

He leaned closer to her and spoke low and clear. "Pay them no mind." His breath brushing against her neck as he spoke sent her heart racing. He led her to a small, round table at the front of the pub. It was joined with other tables that framed an empty space in front of a large bay window lined with benches. The musicians sat on the window benches, tuning their instruments. Stephen gestured for her to sit at one of the tables opposite them, and he followed suit in the chair next to hers.

"Maire there is playing the *uilinn* pipes." Stephen pointed to a red-haired woman inflating a leather pouch out of which came a shaft that looked like a whistle. A group of pipes extended out of the other side of the pouch. Once inflated, she positioned the pouch under her arm and pressed, extracting a sound similar to that of bagpipes, only the tone was mellower than its Scottish counterpart.

Stephen pointed out the rest of the musicians in turn. "Padhraig and Michael have the tin whistle, Deirbhle is playing the Irish flute, and Mona has the concertina."

Anna nodded and drank in every detail. A man on the corner of the bench opened a case and produced a shallow, round drum and small stick, thinned in the middle and bulbous on both ends. "Oh!" she exclaimed and pointed. "I recognize that. I read about it. That's a bow-der-awn, right?"

Stephen's head spun to look at her, dismay etched on his face. "Beg pardon?"

Anna beamed. "That drum. I read about it once. It's called a bow-der-awn, isn't it?"

Stephen exhaled quick and sharp, and Anna wasn't sure if it was a laugh or sign of derision. He lowered his voice and asked, "Do ya mean a *bodhrán*?"

Anna's hand flew to her mouth, eyes wide. "*That's* how you say it?"

Stephen pressed his lips together and bobbed his head, his shoulders shaking.

"Say it again." She dropped her hand onto his forearm. "Please."

He straightened his face and cleared his throat. "It's a bodhrán."

Anna worked to form her lips around the foreign sounds. "BOW-ron."

Stephen chuckled. "Close enough."

Anna pursed her lips and looked at him. "It's not at all how it's spelled, you know?"

"Oh, I know." He smiled in earnest, and Anna nearly melted. "That's because Irish was originally an oral language. It wasn't until about a hundred years ago that someone decided to write it down."

Anna shook her head in disbelief and untied the cape from her neck. The heat from the fire and the growing crowd pressing in had become nearly stifling. Her throat dry, she perked when a woman came by with a tray, setting drinks in front of each patron sitting at the tables. Anna smiled at the woman as she approached.

The waitress bent over until she was eye to eye with Stephen and winked. "Yer favorite for ya, love." Anna inwardly blanched at the woman's forwardness and feared she might present more than a drink to the crowd with as tight as her bodice was laced. The waitress set a glass in front of Stephen and proceeded to serve the rest of the patrons at the tables. Everyone except Anna.

Anna waved her hand. "Excuse me, miss."

The waitress looked Anna in the eye, narrowed her own, and walked away.

"Aoife!" Stephen shouted.

Aoife came trotting back, a sickly sweet smile plastered on her face. "Aye, love?"

Stephen gestured to Anna. "You forgot someone."

Aoife straightened and leveled a glare at Anna. "No, I dinna."

Anna dropped her gaze to her lap, trying to ignore the laughter that rippled through a few of the patrons surrounding them.

"Aoife." Stephen crossed his arms. "Ya don't have to be that way. She's my guest tonight, and ye'll treat her as such."

Aoife rattled off something in Irish, to which Stephen fired off an equally spirited reply. Behind them, a young man guffawed heartily at the exchange. Anna glanced back and recognized him as one of the boys who had met her in the back garden a few weeks before. Anna's chest tightened, and she righted herself in the seat. Finally, Aoife stomped off with a huff. When she returned with a drink in her hand, Stephen slid his glass over to Anna and took the new one from Aoife.

"Go raibh maith agat," he said.

Aoife scoffed. "Ye're welcome." Then she bent down again and, the sickly sweetness returning to her voice, added, "Let me know if there's anything else ya need." Another overly dramatic wink, and she turned to go.

As Aoife left, a lively reel kicked up from the musicians and the crowd cheered.

Stephen gave Anna a look that said, "I'm sorry."

Anna bit her lip to keep unbidden tears at bay. Perhaps her mother was right. Maybe this whole thing was a mistake.

Stephen's chest burned with anger. Never mind that he had some of the same feelings about Annabeth and her family, there was no need for Aoife to treat her that way.

As the music played on, Stephen eyed Annabeth. Her fingers

tapped on the table in rhythm with the jaunty jig, but sadness filled her eyes as she listened.

In the corner, a man stood and offered his hand to the blond woman sitting at the table with him. She accepted and the pair took off whirling and spinning around the dance floor. One by one, other couples joined the dance.

Sensing a presence behind him, Stephen turned to find Aoife looming over him, with Ciaran peering over her shoulder. As the jig died down, the leader of the musicians called out for any requests.

"Play somethin' that really kicks so Stephen here can give the lady a right Galway welcome!" Aoife winked at Ciaran.

Stephen gaped up at the waitress. A roguish gleam filled her eyes.

"What say you, a Stíofán?" Padhraig called from the front. "Will ya dance wit' yer lady?"

Stephen turned to look at Annabeth. All color had drained from her face, and her eyes pleaded silently with him for help. Clearly Aoife meant to humiliate Annabeth, but Stephen assumed the lady had been trained in dancing. He leaned over and whispered, "It'll only make it worse if you refuse."

He stood and offered his hand to her. "May I have this dance, m'lady?"

Annabeth nodded ever so slightly, her lips forming a shaky smile, and took his hand. At her touch, his very skin seemed to come alive. A rousing cheer exploded from the crowd, and the band played the intro to a high-tempo waltz.

All the other dancers cleared the floor as Stephen led Annabeth to the center of the room. "Ya know how to waltz, aye?" he whispered to her.

Annabeth nodded so slightly that Stephen almost missed it. "Yes. But never to something at this tempo."

"Right." Stephen tugged gently on her hand so that they faced each other, and his hand enveloped hers. Wrapping his other arm around her waist, his heart pounding in his ears, he pulled her closer to him. "Just follow my lead," he whispered into her ear.

The pair set into the waltz. Annabeth's steps were shaky, and when her ankle wobbled, Stephen tightened his hold on her. He glanced up and saw Aoife snickering into her hand. He turned his attention back to his dance partner and guided her through the quick-paced waltz. As they turned and moved, he used his hand on her back to guide her—gently curling his fingers into it to signal her to the right or pressing the heel of his hand into it to urge her to the left.

By the second chorus, they had fallen into a more comfortable rhythm. As they moved in time with the music, Stephen tried to ignore the scents of lavender and vanilla that wafted up from her hair. He closed his eyes and willed himself to calm.

As the dance went on, Annabeth relaxed in his arms and they began to move together naturally, as if they'd been partners for years. Stephen dared to look down at her, and she met his gaze, a radiant smile on her face. In spite of all his misgivings, he returned it with his own grin. Eventually, Paddy and his wife, Nora, joined them. Then the man and the blond woman from the jig. Slowly, more and more couples joined them on the dance floor, and as they waltzed, Stephen let himself be carried away by the music, the laughter, and the beautiful woman he held in his arms.

Stephen sank onto his back and folded his hands under his head. Staring through the blackness up toward the ceiling, he struggled to rein in his thoughts. What on earth had happened tonight?

His mind wandered back to the seisiún. To the feel of Annabeth in his arms, the electricity of her so near him, the scent of her hair, the heat of her breath on his chest as they spun around the dance floor. Stephen gritted his teeth and scolded himself for letting her draw him in. He hated that his arms felt empty without her in them. The ache that filled his chest to have her by his side made him feel weak. And a fool.

It's not real, he told himself. *None of it is real. Love isn't real.* He repeated the mantra over and over in his head. She's just a beautiful woman.

And beautiful she was, indeed. The image of her blue eyes, rosy lips, and blond curls floated into his mind. He could hear the music of her laughter through the darkness, and he smiled.

"No!" He chided himself, wadded up his pillow, and flopped onto his side. He had to find a way to distance himself. He wouldn't let this happen. Couldn't let it. Not again.

Rising, he crossed the room, poured some water into the basin, and splashed it on his face. The shocking cold jolted his senses. *Good, this is good.* He splashed again. Yanking the towel from the wardrobe, he dried his face and paced the length of his bed.

There is no way he could revoke the arrangement Lord De Lacy had made with his father. Snubbing the local landlord, while satisfying, was a bad idea under the best of circumstances. With the war ramping up, it was more vital than ever to stay within their good graces. No matter how much Stephen wished to be free of British rule, he had to protect his father from further violence. But the idea of being with Annabeth day in and day out was insufferable.

He envisioned them sitting side by side at the workbench, shoulders touching, her intoxicating scent wafting over him all day. His heart quickened as he imagined their fingers brushing as they both reached for the same chisel. A growl squeezed from his chest and he balled his hands into fists on his head. No, not possible. Unacceptable. He had to think of a way to separate them. To remind himself why it wouldn't work to be with her. In truth it was folly to be with any woman, but a British courtier? *Seafóid amach.* Absolutely absurd.

Racking his brain, he paced and thought until an idea began to brew. He scratched his stubbled chin, an impish grin lifting the corners of his mouth. The idea was too good. He fetched his money pouch and counted. There was more than enough. Yes, this could work. As he hatched his plan, fatigue settled over him.

He climbed back into bed and pulled on the woolen blanket, content in the assurance that he could keep himself safe from yet another heartbreak.

CHAPTER
17

The carriage wheels ground over cobbled streets, and Anna rocked to the rhythm as they rolled into the city. She gazed down at the sketch in her hands. Humming the tune of the waltz from the seisiún the night before, she traced with her eyes the rough figure she'd scratched out. The outline of a Celtic cross—a traditional cross shape with a circle slicing through the intersections of the two beams—filled the center of the page. At the bottom of the circle, she'd drawn the Claddagh symbol.

She smiled to herself as she anticipated explaining its inspiration and meaning to Stephen. Closing her eyes, she hummed the tune louder and let her mind drift back to the wonderful time she'd spent dancing in Stephen's arms. When that waitress first suggested it, sheer dread had sunk to the pit of Anna's stomach like an anchor. Clearly the woman had intended to embarrass Anna.

She'd felt like a newborn lamb on wobbly legs as she stepped onto the floor with Stephen. And the fact that every sense in her body came alive when he pulled her close unsettled her further. But he'd guided her beautifully and before she knew it, they had not only successfully navigated the trickiest waltz she'd ever seen, they'd continued on and jaunted through countless other jigs, reels, and group *ceilí* dances. Anna couldn't remember the last time she'd had as much fun. Or seen Stephen so joyful. The image of his dimple-punctuated smile was burned in her memory. She allowed a deep, satisfied sigh to fill the emptiness surrounding her in the carriage, saying what she couldn't verbalize to anyone.

The carriage slowed to a halt, and then rocked gently as Owen climbed down from his perch above. The door opened, and he helped Anna alight. "Enjoy your day, Lady Annabeth."

"Thank you, Owen. I'll be finished by four."

Tipping his cap, Owen clambered back to his seat and snapped the reins. Anna remembered the drawing in her hands and returned it carefully to its place in her pocket. The journey from Saint Nicolas' to the Jenningses' shop passed quickly, anticipation of seeing Stephen again propelling her. Anna entered, hung her cape on the hook, and hurried to the smithing room.

Stephen was standing at the workbench, his back to the doorway, arranging various tools. Anna warmed at the sight of him, and a wide smile spread across her face. "Good morning."

He stilled briefly at her voice, keeping his back to her. "Good morning, Lady Annabeth."

Anna chuckled. "So formal, good sir," she said, assuming her most posh accent playfully. She met him at the workbench and joined him in sorting the various implements scattered across the tabletop. When their hands brushed, Stephen flinched and stepped away.

"There's much to do today. I have ya set up to mind the shop for the morning. Then I have lunch arranged. After that, we will call it a day early." This coolness of his voice clenched Anna's stomach.

"Stephen—" She took a step toward him, but he turned and walked farther into the smithing room, away from her. The sudden change in his demeanor from the evening before was dizzying. Confusion swirled in Anna's mind, and she wrapped her arms around her middle as if that could bring the warmth back to his voice, the light back to his face when he looked upon her. If only he would look at her, but he'd yet to lift his head to meet her gaze. "Are you alright?"

"Yeah, I'm grand, so." He glanced at her briefly before turning his attention back to whatever he busied himself with. "Ye're needed in the shop. Be ready for lunch at one o'clock." He gathered a stack of papers from the corner desk then brushed past her and up the stairs.

Bewilderment clouded Anna's thoughts as Stephen's steps decrescendoed overhead. She racked her brain trying to make sense of the sudden change in Stephen's attitude. The memory of the music from yesterday evening evaporated like the morning mist in the wake of his callous retreat. Taking a slow, deep breath, Anna stepped into the shop. Going through the motions of opening the store for the day, she searched her memory for anything she might have said or done the day before that would have offended Stephen so deeply. But she could find nothing.

When the seisiún ended, Stephen had walked her to the corner where Owen awaited. How that had been arranged, she didn't know. But he'd opened the carriage door for her and when he took her hand to help her inside, he held it fast. They stood in the dark, eyes locked, for longer than Anna could tell. When Stephen's gaze moved to her lips, she wondered if he intended to kiss her. The strength of her desire for him to do so had almost frightened her. But he hadn't kissed her. Instead, he thanked her for the pleasure of her company, assisted her in, and closed the door. Whatever vexed him this day was beyond Anna's reckoning.

The morning passed without incident. Several customers came in, providing a welcome distraction to the deafening silence of the empty shop. She met and conversed with several locals who, despite seeming a bit distant at the beginning, warmed to her by the end of their interactions. She made three ring sales and took an order for a custom set for a wealthy landlord two counties away.

Stephen appeared just before the church bells tolled and ushered Anna outside. A slate sky hung low, bearing down on them, casting a gray pall over the city, muting colors and sounds. Beside her, Stephen walked with his hands clasped behind his back. His posture was straight and formal, his eyes fixed straight ahead. A strange smirk tilted his mouth.

Anna cleared her throat. "It was a good morning."

"Mmm?"

Repressing a sigh, she tried again. "I sold three rings."

His brows lifted, and he glanced at her from the side of his eye. "Very good." His countenance returned to stone.

She studied him for a beat before adding, "And Lord Arbury ordered a custom piece for his wife."

That got his attention. His head spun and he met her gaze. "Lord Arbury?"

Anna nodded. "Pieces, actually. He wants a matching set of brooch, earrings, and a ring. All inlaid with gems and a combination of gold and silver." She returned her own attention forward. "All the particulars are in the book at the shop. I told him we'd have it in a fortnight."

A puff of air forced its way out of Stephen's lips. He gawked at her for half a second before regaining his stoic composure. "Well done, Lady Annabeth."

"Anna." She stopped walking and faced him directly.

"Beg pardon?" He looked just beyond her.

"My name—" She pursed her lips as she chose her words and angled herself to put her face in front of his, forcing him to look at her. "I've asked you to call me Anna. Why won't you?"

His stature faltered slightly, and he cleared his throat. "It wouldn't be proper."

Anna pushed a sarcastic chortle from her chest. "I really don't understand you. From the moment we met, everything with you has been bucking the system, resisting the social code—particularly the British code." She crossed her arms. "And today, suddenly, you're concerned with protocol?"

"That's right, m'lady." He lifted his gaze until it rested above her head.

She rose up on her tiptoes. "Why won't you look at me?" The question came out louder than she'd intended and a grocer sweeping his stoop stopped and stared. Anna smiled and offered a timid wave in his direction before turning her attention back to Stephen.

"We're here." Stephen pointed to the building behind her.

Anna turned around. Emblazoned in gold letters on a black sign were the words THE KING'S RANSOM. Below the header, lattice windows, framed in bright yellow, stretched along either side of the main door. Overhead, a set of bay windows, also bright yellow, curved out over the doorpost. The rest of the building was bare gray stone stretching up three more stories.

Anna shielded her eyes as she gaped up at the structure towering over her. An enticing aroma wafted from the chimney spouts and drifted down on top of them, stirring Anna's appetite.

Stephen bent slightly at the waist and extended his hand toward the door. "After you."

They were welcomed as soon as they walked in. The steward seemed familiar with Stephen. "Yer table's all set for ye." He winked at Stephen and led them to a table in the corner near the fireplace. Tall-backed benches flanked two sides of the table, and Anna slid into the seat of the nearest one as she admired the vintage mantelpiece.

"This is one of the oldest and tallest buildings in Galway,

dating as far back as the mid-1600s," Stephen answered her unasked question.

"I believe it." Anna absently spread the cloth napkin on her lap as she drank in her surroundings. The interior of the pub was dark but cozy. They were the only patrons seated in the front room, but it appeared at least two more large rooms extended to the back beyond the kitchen. A middle-aged woman with kind but tired eyes scurried out and placed a bowl of vegetable soup in front of each of them. The fragrance of roasted carrots, onions, garlic, and parsnips curled up with the steam and set Anna's mouth watering. After whispering a prayer of thanks in her heart, she took a sip from her spoon. The rustic flavor delighted her senses and soothed her raw spirit on its way down. As she scooped up another bite, Stephen continued the history lesson.

"At one time, this was the house of the mayor of Galway. That accounts for its grand stature and outfitting." He slurped a spoonful of his own soup. "You can see over the fireplace the marriage stone sporting the family crests of three of the major tribes of Galway."

Anna craned her neck to observe the stone. The intricate carving was stunning in its detail.

"But then . . ." He set his spoon down and leaned in, intrigue filling his eyes. Anna did the same. "Then came the death of King Charles I in 1649, and that's where the real legend begins." His eyes danced in the dim light as he paused. Whether he was waiting for dramatic effect or the next course, Anna wasn't sure.

As if on cue, the woman returned with plates piled with lamb shanks, roasted potatoes, and boiled cabbage. Stephen muttered his thanks to her in Irish, all the while keeping his wide eyes fixed on Anna.

"Auld Cromwell was so cross, he sent garrisons over here to

assert his authority. He overran the city and ousted our honorable tribal mayor, God rest him."

Anna lowered her spoon, brows knit together. "And why was he cross with you? Or the Galwegians, rather."

He painted a look of mock surprise on his face. "Did ya not learn this in your history lessons, lass?"

She'd learned a version of it, yes. But she'd never heard the Irish side. Hadn't she just wondered about this very thing herself? "I'd like to hear your take on it," she said.

Seemingly satisfied with her answer, Stephen leaned against the back of the bench. "He was *feargach linn* because he suspected a Galwegian to be behind the assassination."

Okay, that lined up with what she'd learned. "Yes, I'd heard something to that effect."

Stephen nodded slowly. "Well, it's true!" His voice was an excited stage whisper, and he leaned closer, brows lifted. "When yer man the executioner in London refused to have an'thing to do with the execution of ole Charlie, the search was on for volunteers from Wales, Ireland, and Scotland. Cromwell knew there was no love lost between the doomed king and those lands. Well, Roger Store answered the call."

"Interesting." Anna dabbed the corners of her mouth with her napkin. Perhaps their side wasn't so different from what she'd learned. "The version I learned is very similar."

Stephen nodded. "But what ye don't know is *why* this establishment is called The King's Ransom." He leaned in once more, eyes hard, mouth slanted up in a smirk. "It's because we're proud o' that lad, m'lady. And we want to remember—and we want the throne to remember—that we've always wanted to be free of yer lot. And we will be. Soon." He shoveled a spoonful of potatoes in his mouth, sending gravy dripping down his chin. "Rid of ye for good," he muttered around his mouthful of food.

Anna sucked in a breath and fell back against the high-backed bench seat. There it was. "I see," she replied. Her appetite suddenly gone, she folded her napkin and placed it on her plate. That confirmed it. Clearly Anna would always just be a souper to Stephen. He saw her presence as a threat—nae, an insult—and he resented her for it. "Thank you for the meal. I must be going now. I can see myself home." She rose in silence, like a cork floating to the surface, and excused herself from the room, all the while sensing his gaze boring into her back.

Stephen watched her leave, almost giddy with himself for his grand performance. His history lesson, it would seem, had done the trick. He'd managed to distance himself from Annabeth De Lacy—or rather distance her from him. It hadn't been easy, to be sure, to remain in character while looking into her clear blue eyes. He was sure at any moment she would see through his ruse, but she hadn't.

He glanced out the window just in time to see her step onto the cobbled Shop Street. Her shoulders rose as though she was taking a deep breath, then slumped down in an image of defeat. Was she dabbing her eyes?

His glee melted and seeped through his insides before cooling into a weight like hardened lead, almost more than he could bear. Straightening, he reminded himself of why it had to be done—distancing himself from Annabeth De Lacy was a must for his survival. And he had accomplished his goal of driving a wedge between them. So why did he feel so wretched?

CHAPTER
18

◆ June 1 ◆

William bit back an oath and slammed the ledger shut. Rising, he raked shaky fingers through his hair and fled to the opposite side of the room. His eyes shifted to the ornate rug beneath his feet. It was a wonder a rutted path hadn't been worn in it with as much pacing as he'd done of late. Surely the numbers were wrong. There had to be a mistake.

He crossed the room again and reopened the book, flipping the pages roughly until they fell upon the most recent accounting. Bowing his head, he breathed deep and whispered a plea for a miracle. When he returned his attention to the seemingly unending lists of numbers, he sank into the chair. Running ink-stained fingers down column after column, he felt panic settle in his chest upon reaching the final tally.

Blast it all! How had it come to this? He'd sat at the gambling table with the other lords, sure. But he hadn't lost that much. Had he? He would have to tread very lightly in the coming weeks in order to keep up appearances. And with the war ramping up, along with the expectations placed upon him, there was no margin for error. Anxiety suffocated his spirit. He shoved a knuckle between his teeth to keep them from chattering. What could be done?

Yanking the crystal decanter from its place on his desk, he poured more of the amber liquid into his glass than was prudent. Downing it in one swig, he winced against the burn that trailed along his throat. He pressed his palms flat onto the desktop, racking his brain for any way to staunch the hemorrhage of money. A yellowed envelope caught his eye. He straightened slowly, a sense of hope rising in his chest—from the letter or the drink, he didn't know. Nor did he care.

Sliding the envelope toward him, he tethered his newfound hope to what he knew lay inside. He removed its contents, crossed to the fireplace, and eased himself into one of the tufted chairs before carefully unfolding the letter. As he reread the terms of Lord Corning's proposal, his head bobbed and a trembling grin split his face.

Of course! He'd held on to this ace in the hole as long as he could. Somewhere deep down, he'd hoped he wouldn't have to play it. But it was in Annabeth's best interests—and his own, of course. And now Annabeth would come to his rescue. She must. Often he bemoaned the fact that if she were a son, she could contribute more to the family fortune and secure a title of her own. Having only daughters made assuring his legacy all the more difficult. However, that mattered not now. The match with Corning secured his family's fortune and place in society, no matter what fate awaited them here in Ireland. Once they wed, it would make no difference whether or not he was able to recover the De Lacy fortune. They would be taken care of—all of them.

A knock at the door startled him out of his reverie. Carefully returning the letter to its place on his desk, he called out, "Enter!"

The door opened and a young man in uniform stepped into the office.

William stood and straightened his jacket. "Corporal Billings. To what do I owe the pleasure?"

"Sir." The young man saluted and clicked his heels. "I beg your pardon, sir, for the personal nature of my remarks, but I believe there's something you need to be aware of."

William gestured to the seat in front of his desk. "Sit, Corporal. What personal errand could have flustered you so?" He circled around and stood behind the desk.

Billings cleared his throat and shifted uncomfortably in the seat, unease registering in his eyes. "Begging your pardon. It's not personal for me." The slightest grimace wrinkled the corners of his eyes and he swallowed. "It's personal . . . for you, sir."

"Me?" William lowered himself into his desk chair. "How so?"

Billings paused and his gaze drifted to the window, then the floor. He shifted in his seat once more, then straightened his posture and looked William in the eye. "It's about your daughter."

Stephen swept the floor of the shop with a bit more gusto than necessary. Scraping at the wood planks over and over helped drown out the internal taunts that threatened to drive him mad.

Seamus sat on a stool in the corner fiddling with his pipe. "'Tis a mite quiet today." He stuck the pipe stem between his teeth and puffed.

"Is it?" Stephen kept his head down and continued sweeping.

"Don't tell me ya hadn't noticed. With just you and me rattlin' 'round the place, it's just a wee dreary, don't ya think?" Seamus puffed on his pipe once more, and Stephen could feel the man watching him.

Stephen sighed and rested a forearm on the top of the broom handle and looked at his father. The man looked right pleased with himself. Stephen had enjoyed the respite, truth be told. A couple of days had passed since she'd been at the shop, and the longer Annabeth stayed away, the easier it would be for him to keep the wedge between them—and give time for his own guilt about what he'd had to do to disperse.

"Look, lad—" The main door crashed open, stopping Seamus midthought. William De Lacy stood with one hand flattened on the door, the other balled in a fist at his side.

"Lord De Lacy," Seamus said. "Welcome in. What can we do for ye?"

De Lacy lifted a palm to the old man, keeping his eyes on Stephen. "Be still," he growled through ground teeth. Seamus returned the pipe to his lips and bobbed his head once.

The landlord stepped inside and slammed the door. "You." He jammed a finger toward the younger Jennings. Before Stephen could reply, De Lacy stomped across the floor until he was nose to nose with him. "I'm onto you." The stench of drink puffed into Stephen's face with every word.

Stephen grimaced and took a measured step back. "Beggin' yer pardon, sir?"

"It's Lord De Lacy to you. And did you think you could get away with it?" The nobleman's eyes were rimmed with red and swam with glossy, unshed tears. Or was that the effect of the drink?

Stephen raised his hands in front of his chest, palms facing out. "All due respect, Lord De Lacy, ye're confused. And to be quite honest, so am I."

De Lacy leaned farther forward, stumbling slightly. "You're right. I am confused." He poked his finger in the center of Stephen's chest. "I'm confused how you think apprenticing my daughter means stealing her honor!"

As if he was punched in the gut, all the air rushed from Stephen's lungs. "M'lord, I nev—"

"Did you or did you not take my daughter to some place called"—his eyes drifted to the side as he seemed to search for the word—"Tigh Hughes?" He said the name of the pub as if it were sour milk.

Relief washed over Stephen and he laughed. "Oh that? Sir, I assure you, everything was aboveboard."

"Did you or did you not take Lady Annabeth there?" De Lacy's shout reverberated in the small shop.

"Now, now, Lord De Lacy." Seamus stepped up next to the landlord. "Nothin' unseemly took place at Tigh Hughes. They were just enjoyin' the music, havin' a bit o' *craic*."

The lord ignored Seamus, keeping his gaze fastened on Stephen. "You have no idea what you've gotten yourself into, you . . . you dirty pillock. You've jeopardized everything!"

"My"—Stephen swallowed, angry heat creeping up his neck—"M'lord, I give you my word, I only accompanied your daughter there so she could hear the music and enjoy an evening of dancing."

De Lacy's lip curled in disgust. "So you admit it? How dare you deign to place your hands on my daughter? See to it nothing of that sort happens again." Straightening, he sniffed haughtily and smoothed his hair back. "Do not mistake my approval of my daughter's apprenticeship here to be an approval of *you*."

Stephen met his stare, clenching his jaw to keep from saying something he couldn't take back. He could say the same thing to the man—agreeing to apprentice the landlord's daughter did not mean agreement with the presence of the landlord. He chose, instead, to remain quiet. Though it pained him.

"She is a lady of the British court—a woman of means and impeccable upbringing. You," he snarled, "are nothing."

Seamus sent a warning look to Stephen. "Don't engage," his eyes read.

De Lacy mashed his finger into Stephen's chest again. "And don't you think for a minute I don't know what you're doing."

Stephen took a half step back and willed his voice calm. "And what is that?"

"Don't take me for a fool." De Lacy clasped his hands behind his back and walked a circle in the middle of the room. "I know word has reached you of the incoming reinforcements of the Royal Irish Constabulary. I also know you and your rabble of friends are plotting to advance your so-called war for independence in the west of Ireland." He looked at Stephen as if he were dung on the street.

Stephen's eyebrows pressed together, and confusion churned in his mind. After Tommy, Stephen had done whatever he could to distance himself from the front lines of the fight. He wanted an independent Ireland, to be sure, but he had no hand in the plans.

De Lacy came toe-to-toe with Stephen once more. "Furthermore, I know you plan to use our little arrangement to your advantage—to get whatever information you can from my daughter about our plans, movements, troop numbers, what have you."

Stephen stepped back again, bumping into the back counter. "M'lord, I'm afraid ye're mistaken." He lifted his palms to face the man. "Yer daughter is here at your bidding. We are merely abiding your request to teach her jewelry making."

"Nonsense!" De Lacy's face reddened, and the cords of his neck strained. "A true gentleman would never dream of using a woman's heart for political gain."

Stephen squinted, as though doing so would clarify the landlord's words. He had done no such thing—would never. The thought had never even occurred to him. He had enjoyed her company at the seisiún, yes. But not once had he thought to use her as some sort of pawn in the war. His mind drifted back to the night spent with Annabeth in his arms. His heart quickened at the memory.

De Lacy scanned Stephen's face and his brows lifted, his eyes alight. "Oh, don't tell me." He laughed. "You've grown fond of her!" He guffawed and wiped his mouth with his hand. "Don't tell me you actually hold some hope of her returning affections for you?"

Stephen's mouth bobbed, searching for a reply, but De Lacy continued before he could form one.

"So she hasn't told you?" The sense of decorum typical of a noble returned to De Lacy's stance, though he swayed slightly.

Stephen pushed his bottom lip up and shook his head. "Told me?"

De Lacy sniffed and straightened his cravat. "Ever the lady, even when faced with the sod of the earth, she still can't bring herself to do anything that would even smack of hurting one's feelings. She doesn't understand how you people work, anyway. What my dear daughter has failed to tell you"—an ugly smirk tipped his mouth to one side—"is that she's already promised. In marriage."

Stephen slumped against the counter. Promised? Betrothed? Of course she is. Utter sadness jockeyed for position with the rising sense of relief that he'd done the right thing pushing her away. Seamus laid his other hand absently on Stephen's shoulder. Stephen shrugged it off.

Rising to his full height, Stephen leveled his gaze to look De Lacy in the eyes. "She had not told me, but it matters not. Ye have misread the entire situation. I have no such intentions for yer daughter—politically or romantically. But if ya hold such a low opinion of me, remove her from our tutelage." Next to him, Seamus *tsked*.

A shadow flashed in De Lacy's eyes. "No. Much as I'd like to rid her of your influence, I've given her my word. Besides, she'd be insufferable were I to keep her home." He looked Stephen over from head to toe. "Just be sure your activities relate to jewelry work alone. No more, *ahem*, 'cultural experiences.'"

Stephen shared a glance with his father, whose face read the same confusion Stephen felt. He chose, however, to let the matter drop. The landlord held the upper hand. They always did. "As you wish, sir."

"Good. And you'll address me as 'my lord.' I am thus, you know, and you'd do well to remember it." De Lacy stared at Stephen for a long moment before spinning on his heel and making for the door. Before he exited, he stopped and added, "See to it you say nothing of this to her." He shut the door, leaving the odor of drink in his wake.

"He's a right delight, that one." Seamus puffed a sigh through his cheeks. "Cuppa?"

Stephen gaped at his father then declined. The auld man took his leave up the stairs.

Once alone, Stephen slumped onto the stool behind the display case. What would possess De Lacy to presume Stephen was using Annabeth as a proxy spy? If the man had done his research, he would know Stephen had no such ambitions. And he would know why. Even if he had such a goal, Stephen certainly wouldn't risk using the landlord's daughter to accomplish it.

And Annabeth. His thoughts swirled like the waltz they'd shared. Engaged? He dropped his head into his hands, his emotions warring within. Anger that she hadn't told him of her betrothal bubbled to the top only to be pushed down by smug satisfaction to have his view on love validated. Even so, an all-too-familiar ache settled in his chest, and he knocked the heel of a fist on the display case, as if that would bend his heart to his bidding.

CHAPTER
19

◆ June 2 ◆

Anna smoothed trembling fingers down the front of her dress. It wasn't often that Father officially summoned her to his study. And the look on the head maid's face when she presented the message had sent shivers of dread down Anna's spine. Checking her appearance in the looking glass once more, she headed downstairs.

"Enter," her father's muffled voice called through the door when she knocked.

Taking one more deep, calming breath, she obeyed. "Good morning, Father. Ciara said you wanted to see me?"

He was standing behind his desk with his head bent low over a yellowed document. He waited so long to reply, Anna wondered if he'd forgotten she was there. At length, he spoke.

"Come. Sit." He gestured to the chair opposite him in front of the desk. Not the high-back tufted chairs near the fireplace. That detail did not escape Anna's notice, but she did as he bade.

"Yes, Father?" She looked at him expectantly. He still studied the document. Lines framed his eyes and shadows hung below them, a stark contrast to the lack of color in his cheeks. Was he ill? He tossed back a swallow from his crystal tumbler and set it on the desk with a muted thud. *Ah. Of course.*

"I wanted to speak with you regarding Lord Corning's proposal." He sank into his desk chair and fastened his red, filmy eyes on her.

Anna straightened and pasted a doe-eyed look on her face. A sugar-sweet daughter was always the proper tack when he was in this state. "Alright." She forced a charming smile to lift the corners of her mouth.

"His Lordship initially gave you"—he referenced the page in front of him—"one year to give your answer." He paused, fixing her again with his stare.

Anna adjusted her skirts around her ankles. "That's right."

His gaze remained on her and neither spoke for a beat, then his brows shot up and he tossed his hands. "Well?"

Anna chewed her lip. "Begging your pardon, Father, but *well* what?"

A frustrated sigh puffed from his lips, the stink of stale whiskey floating on it. "Have you decided?"

Anna's mouth opened and closed twice while she searched for the words. They'd been in Ireland but a few months. She still had plenty of time before she was required to answer. "In truth, I have yet to reach a decision." Fire flashed in his eyes, so Anna hurried to continue. "I am still well within the year time frame. I—we—have time yet."

"Daughter." Her father spoke through gritted teeth. "You are not required to use the entire year. Imagine his delight were you to accept now. Don't you want to start your marriage in his good graces?"

He spoke as if she'd already accepted. "Were I to accept, yes, I'd want him to be as pleased as possible. But . . ." She swallowed. "I've yet to decide, Papa."

His expression softened at the use of her childhood name

for him. Rising, he rounded the desk and leaned back on the front of it. "Annabeth, you know I want nothing more than your greatest happiness. But there are some times in life in which we must learn to find happiness despite the circumstances. Titled life can be more burdensome than those outside of it could ever understand." He glanced out the window, and when he looked at her again, something akin to compassion shone on his face. Or was it pity?

Anna's brows drew together, discomfort swirling in her gut. "I give you my word, I will consider His Lordship's offer fully. You graciously told me that it was my decision. And he graciously offered me a full year to consider it. I don't want to rush a decision that will affect me for the rest of my life."

"You don't understand, girl!" His face hardened, and he pounded the edge of the desk. "You don't know what is at stake. You will give him an answer. Posthaste."

"Father, I—" she stammered, head spinning.

He bent at the waist until his eyes were level with hers. "Should you refuse him, it would fall to your sister to save him— and us—the humiliation."

Anna's jaw fell slack, and her stomach turned at the thought of her younger sister in the arms of that hateful old man. Yes, Emmaline always wanted the life of a nobleman's wife. But not like this. Not with him.

Her father nodded slowly, hardness filling his eyes. "That's right. Would you resign your sister to a fate you couldn't abide for yourself?" He straightened. "Or, perhaps, you would wish us ill."

Anna shot to her feet. "I would never!"

He waved his hand through the air as though swatting at an annoying pest. "Spare me the sentimental nonsense."

His words hit Anna like a fist to the stomach. What could have brought on such bitterness toward her? Anna had always known he'd wished for a son, but she'd felt they'd shared a special bond nonetheless.

He crossed his arms and turned to the window. "Tell me, what have you learned since we last spoke?"

Anna searched her memory for an anchor to his reference. "Learned?"

"Yes, daughter." He turned slowly on his heel. "I tasked you with reporting to me any information about these agitators' plans for this farce of a war."

Ah, that. "Truly, I've heard nothing."

A caustic laugh panted out of him. "Balderdash. You expect me to believe, after spending hours a day with these people, you've heard nary a word?"

Anna clasped her hands in front of her waist. "Yes, that's exactly right."

He crossed over to stand directly in front of her. He towered over her and seemed to relish it. "I don't believe it," he hissed.

Anna's breath caught and her heart quickened. How could she make him see? "The Misters Jennings—from everything I've observed—have no involvement in the rebellion."

His lip curled in a snarl. "And you've been able to observe much, haven't you, daughter?"

Anna blinked. "Pardon?"

He stepped even closer. The lines on his face and the stench of his breath magnified. "Perhaps, daughter, if you spent less time throwing yourself at him, you'd have more discerning vision."

The accusation was a blow, knocking Anna back a step. She shook her head, at a loss for words. "You misunderstand, Father."

"No, you misunderstand. Your first duty is to this family—to this title." He straightened and tugged his waistcoat back into place. "You will give your answer within the month. And see to it it's the right answer or your sister will suffer the consequences."

Tears stung Anna's eyes and she bit her lip to keep them from falling. Was there nothing she could do to convince him of the truth? Did he truly think so little of her, that she would deliberately sabotage her own family?

He turned his back and dismissed her with a flip of his hand. "That is all."

Anna stepped nearer. "Papa—"

He rounded his desk and sat down. "I said that is all." He busied himself shuffling the papers on the desktop.

Anna watched for a moment, then hugged her arms around her waist and slipped from the room.

"I simply cannot believe it." Emmaline slipped her arm through Anna's as they strolled along the path in the front garden.

"Believe it, dear sister." Anna sighed.

"He really said you had to accept and do it this month?" Emmaline pivoted her head to look at Anna.

Anna nodded and patted her sister's hand. Her gaze drifted to the sky. "He did, indeed. And he threatened to make you do it if I didn't."

"*Tsk!*" Emmaline wagged her head.

A cool breeze stirred tendrils of their hair as the sun warmed their backs. How could the weather be so pleasant at a time like this? Ireland seemed confused on the type of place it wanted to be sometimes.

Emmaline stopped, removed her hat, and turned her face toward the sun, eyes closed.

"Truly, sister? Sunbathing?" Anna chuckled. Did nothing ever rile the girl?

Emmaline smiled but her eyes remained shut. She inhaled deeply and sighed with satisfaction. "Do you not take strength from the sun, Annie? If the storm must rage inside our home, I shall soak up the beauty outside of it. 'Tis like a kiss of strength from heaven."

Anna watched her sister for a long moment. Though five years her junior, she often seemed far wiser. "Dear Emmie."

"You know I would." Emmaline straightened and met Anna's gaze. "Marry him in your stead." A flash of dread clouded Emmaline's eyes before retreating and allowing her trademark twinkle to return.

Anna sighed and took Emmaline's hand. "I know you would. And I love you for it." She pressed a kiss to the back of her sister's hand and let it go, shaking her head. "But I couldn't sentence you to such a fate."

"So you doom yourself to a life with him?" Emmaline freed her hand from Anna's arm and twisted her own fingers together. "If one of us must waste away with the old prune, it might as well be the one who wishes to have that life. It mightn't be so bad." She met Anna's gaze once more. "Would it?"

Anna cocked her head. "You don't wish to have *that* life. You wish the life of a grand, young courtier's wife." She grasped her sister's hand in hers again. "Hear me, Emmaline. A future with Lord Corning would be nothing like you've dreamed the life of a lady to be. 'Twoud be a life of relative servitude."

Emmaline's head drooped forward. Then she bent down to pluck a dandelion from the edge of the lawn.

"Plus," Anna added, "you'd have to kiss him."

Emmaline scrunched up her face and shuddered. "Revolting."

Anna chuckled. "Indeed." She shrugged. "I appreciate your willingness to fall on your sword for me. Truly, I do. I simply don't see any other way," she said around the tightness in her throat. "And I wouldn't dream of dooming you to such a future when it was in my power to avoid that for you."

Emmaline slipped her arm around Anna's elbow once more

and smiled. "There may yet be another way, sister. A way in which neither of us have to chain ourselves to such a bleak fate."

Anna pinned her sister with a look of incredulity.

Emmaline shrugged. "There may yet be. And we'll pray that 'tis so."

CHAPTER
20

P enny for yer thoughts, boyo?" Seamus squeezed Stephen's shoulder before sinking onto the chair next to him at the table in their flat. He slid the steaming pot of tea toward him, refilling Stephen's cup before filling his own.

Stephen watched the hot liquid, wishing it could soothe away all that ailed him. Closing the ledger, he pushed it to the far corner of the table. "Save yer pennies, Da. Just lookin' over the numbers."

Seamus took a gulp of tea, winced, and wiped his mouth with the back of his hand. His head bobbed up and down. "Aye, they look grand, so they do." Another drink, another grimace. Would the man ever learn not to burn himself with his *cupán tae*? "That wee Anna's brought new life to this auld shop," Seamus added.

Stephen looked at his father out of the corner of his eye. Things had picked up in recent weeks, to be sure. But could Annabeth really be credited with all that? "Oh?"

"Are ye so daft, lad?" The glint in Seamus's eye told Stephen the comment was good-natured, not scolding. "If ye'll take a good look at those numbers, ye'll see our best days are the ones she's in." He opened the book and poked a work-worn finger at various columns, a knowing spark in his eye.

Stephen met his father's gaze and found no jest in it. Stephen wondered what he meant by their "best days." Had he meant just the shop's best sales days, or was there some other meaning behind it? The thought vaporized as quickly as it entered Stephen's mind. "If ya say so, Da."

Seamus grabbed his cup and leaned back in his chair. "There's no say-so about it. And thanks be to God for it. 'Tweren't fer that lass, yer inheritance would be in danger."

Stephen's heart sank. His inheritance. No matter Annabeth's role in it, the fact was that they'd secured enough profit for Stephen to make the journey to the continent and begin his new life as an ironworks apprentice. He chided himself at the cowardice of his delay in telling his father. The only question remaining was the timing of it all—of telling his father, and of actually making the move.

"But no matter," Seamus continued, "the more pressing issue now is what to do about Lord De Lacy's latest call." He downed the rest of his tea and refilled his cup. A testament to the level at which De Lacy's accusations bothered him. On the surface, he seemed unbothered by the strange visit. But the fact that he'd downed three cups of tea in less than twenty minutes told otherwise. Some men turned to the bottle. Seamus Jennings turned to the cuppa. Stephen couldn't help but smile to himself.

"Aye." Stephen nodded. "Curious, that was. But I don't see there's much we can do. Save continue on as usual. To do an'thing else would risk retribution by 'His Lordship.'" He rolled his eyes at the title.

"That's not what I meant, lad." Seamus adjusted himself in the chair, keeping his eyes fixed on his son. "I mean, what are *ye* going to do about it?" He cringed as he swallowed another swig of the scalding liquid.

Stephen's brows pulled together. "I . . . I just told ye."

Seamus wagged his head. "Nae, man. I mean, what're ye gonna

do in here?" He tapped a pudgy finger on Stephen's chest over his heart.

Stephen sat back, words failing him. He absently rubbed the spot his father had poked. It was raw and sore from yesterday's encounter with De Lacy. Much like his own heart.

Seamus laid a tender hand on Stephen's forearm. "Son, ye've let the bitterness hold ye long enough. Ye can rant all ya want about the fallacy of love, but I've also seen the way ya look at Anna. I've seen the way ye are together. An' I saw the look in yer eyes when ya learned of her betrothal. Pile that on to Tommy—"

"*Seafóid.*" Stephen stood and crossed over to the basin.

"Call it nonsense if ya want, but deep down ya know I'm right." Seamus's chair scraped the wooden floor and footsteps scuffed toward the door.

Stephen hung his head over the basin, slowly wagging it back and forth. "Da."

Seamus released a long, slow breath. "Ya hafta get to the point where you decide if ye're going to let other people control whether or not you live a life of love."

Stephen gripped the edge of the basin, the rough wood pricking his skin, and pushed a sarcastic laugh through his lips.

"Compassion, then, if that word suits ye better." Seamus shuffled from the room, and called from the stairwell, "At some point ye have to choose—a life of bitterness and anger or one of peace and joy that runs deeper than yer circumstances."

As his father's steps retreated down the stairs, Stephen turned and swiped his arm across the table. The ledger, teapot, and remaining cup scattered across the room.

Clearly the auld man didn't understand. Peace? How could he expect Stephen to have peace after he'd been so wronged? First, Marie broke his heart. Then Tommy was stolen from them for no reason other than being an Irish lad. And now this. No. He couldn't abide it. Stomping across the room, he snatched the ledger from the floor and ripped a page from the back. Through blurred vision he hastily scrawled an acceptance letter to Roman Sánchez. That settled it. By the end of summer, Stephen would be basking in the Spanish sun, leaving all his troubles to mildew in the damp gloom of autumn in Ireland.

Icy silence stretched thin in the empty shop. It had been a busy morning, and business had boomed. Perhaps his father had been right last night when he went on about Annabeth's presence. Nevertheless, a more uncomfortable day in the store, Stephen couldn't recall. In the rare few moments when customers weren't bustling in and out, awkwardness had wedged itself between Stephen and Annabeth. When she'd arrived that morning, Stephen could hardly bring himself to look her in the eye. When he did, he saw only vague aloofness. A new development from Annabeth, and it was for the best that way. But it niggled at him anyway.

Stephen locked the front door and began wiping down the glass cases. Annabeth, her back to him, sat on a stool at the back counter, hunched over a piece of paper. Apparently now she was beyond helping close things down at the end of the day. Stephen watched her for several moments before frustrated curiosity got the best of him.

"So, Lady Annabeth, are ye going to help with this or just sit there while I do all the work?" He crossed the room until he was right behind her. "Then again, I suppose ye're used to that, aren't ya?"

Annabeth whirled around to face him, her cheeks reddening. "I beg your pardon, *Mister* Jennings. I was just finishing up." She huffed and spun back to the countertop.

Stephen leaned back, surprised at the speed and intensity of her response. Then, just past her shoulder, he caught a glimpse of the paper she'd been concentrating on. The outline of a Celtic cross caught his attention. He pointed to it. "What's that?"

She turned to look at him again, then slipped a hand behind her and rested it over the image. She blanched for a brief second before her stoic countenance returned. "Nothing. Rather, it's not ready yet."

At that moment, Seamus scuffled into the room, flatcap on his head. He tipped it and smiled at Annabeth. "I'm off to say ma prayers, just wanted to bid ye good night."

Stephen and Annabeth both nodded at him. "Good night," she replied.

"Good night, Da." Seamus tossed a look to his son that beckoned Stephen to join him. But Stephen looked away. "I'll see ya after."

Seamus's gaze drifted to the floor. When he lifted it, he seemed to notice the page Annabeth's hand attempted to cover. "Oh! Did ya show him?"

Annabeth's face flushed and she stammered. "Eh, no." She winced. "No, not yet."

Stephen planted his hands on his hips. Thick as thieves, these two were. "Show me? Show me what?"

Seamus waggled a hand in Annabeth's direction. "Ah, go on now! What're ye waitin' for?" He inclined his head toward her then swung it in Stephen's direction.

Bringing the sketch around in front of her, she gazed at it overlong before placing it facedown on her lap. She shook her head. "I'm not sure it's a good time."

"*Psh*! There's no time like the present! Now, I must dash. G'on and show 'im." Seamus turned his attention to Stephen. "Ye'll want to see this and hear what she has to say." With that, he doffed his cap once more and shuffled out the back door.

A great sigh welled up in Stephen's chest and he expelled it slowly. "Alright." He held out his hand, palm up, and curled his fingers inward a few times. "Let's have it."

She looked up at him through her lashes. But instead of coy and flirtatious, her eyes were somber. Sad. She slid another stool around so it was next to her. "Would you mind to sit?"

Suppressing another sigh, he did as she asked. But not before scooting the stool an inch farther away. "What have ye got there?"

She stared down at the back of the paper in her lap. "A couple of weeks ago, I was talking with your father. He was telling me how impressed he was with the speed at which I was learning the craft, my eye for seeing which pieces went with which personalities best, things of that nature." She paused, as though recalling the conversation again in her mind. "Well, he encouraged me to think about designing my own piece."

She glanced at him from the side of her eye. Design her own piece? The thought had never crossed Stephen's mind. She was good with the details, aye. But he'd never thought to have her attempt creating her own design. Part of him felt an almost jealous need to protect the Claddagh. To make sure an outsider didn't come in and distort it and—much as he'd tried to run from it—its legacy. Another part of him ached with curiosity. Truly, he'd never met anyone who looked at the world the way Annabeth did, and he could only imagine the unique spin she might put on a centuries-old design.

Stephen cleared his throat. "I see."

"I was overwhelmed by the idea at first," she admitted. "After all, the Claddagh is such a beloved image . . . particularly here in Galway. I was terrified I'd do something to ruin it. I refused at first. But your father wouldn't let it go. He said God gave me this gift of design, and He'd brought me here to your shop for a reason. To hide it under a bushel—to refuse to use it—would be a slap in His face. So, I, as your dad says, gave it a go."

Her respect for the art struck him. If he wasn't careful, Stephen was going to have to find a way to add even more distance between them. "And? What did you settle on?"

The corner of her mouth tucked in and she laid her hands gently on top of the paper. "Once I released the initial fear, an idea came to me almost immediately. I've been working on sketching it out since then. For weeks. Just trying to get it exactly right. It's still not perfect, but . . ." She closed her eyes and took a deep breath, then slowly turned the paper over and held it out to him.

Stephen's breath caught in his chest as he took in the image before him. It was the shape of a traditional Celtic cross—a Roman cross with a circle around the intersection of the beams. However, in Annabeth's design, the circle broke open at the bottom, forming hands holding the crown-laden heart. "It's . . . lovely." He inwardly cringed at the thickness of his voice.

"Thank you." Her gaze remained on her hands in her lap. Stephen resisted the urge to scoot closer to her. "Would you like to know what it means?"

He turned and looked at her profile. Was she joking? "I believe I'm familiar with the legend of the Claddagh." He kept his voice low and offered a hesitant smile. She looked so timid, he couldn't bring himself to be firmer . . . or more aloof . . . with her. Goodness, he was weak indeed.

Her shoulders bounced slightly. Was that a laugh? "Yes, I know. But this design has a deeper meaning." She finally lifted her gaze to meet his. Sincerity and urgency shone in her eyes. "I was so taken by your recounting of the legend and the symbolism of the elements—love, loyalty, and friendship." She pointed to the heart, crown, and hands in turn. "One night as I was praying, it struck me: What better way to express love, loyalty, and friendship than what our Lord did for us on the cross?"

Stephen blew out a breath and ran his hand over his head.

Her words struck him like a bright light in the middle of a pitch-black cave—bringing with it both revelation and pain. He met her gaze once more. She looked at him expectantly, hope filling her sky blue eyes. "Annabeth—er—Lady Annabeth, I don't know what to say."

Her face fell but she recovered with another smile. "Of course, I don't presume that this would get made. But the idea has stuck with me." She shrugged. "It's colored the way I look at things now. And filters the way I see the world . . . the way I see people. And I thought it might for you too."

The room was suddenly as hot as the bog in a drought. Looking back to the image, he fought the sense of . . . of . . . whatever he was feeling. Faith was supposed to uplift. Enlighten. Why did Annabeth's words weigh on him so?

"It's . . . it's very nice," he stammered and handed the page back to her. The truth of her words, of that image, seemed to almost stop his heart from beating. And yet . . . it quickened with hope at the same time. What was happening to him? He had to get out from under their weight—from under her ever-watchful eyes. "Well done. If you'll excuse me." He left the room, all the while sensing Annabeth's gaze following him.

CHAPTER
21

The door to the drawing room pushed open and Ciara came in bearing a tray laden with tea service.

"Set it there on the side table, please." Anna's mother gestured to the polished oak table near the settee. "Thank you, Ciara."

With the poise and ease of someone well seasoned in their job, Ciara set the tray down and dipped a curtsy. "An'thing else, Your Ladyship?"

Mother shook her head, her smile reaching her gray-blue eyes.

Remembering to serve it the "British way" in front of her mother, Anna added milk to the three cups and dropped a lump of sugar into her mother's, then poured the steaming tea. She handed a cup to Emmaline, who lifted her brows and angled her head toward their mother. Anna shook her head, but Emmaline only pinned her with a stare. She then shooed Anna toward their mother with her hand.

Anna flashed a playful glare at her sister and sighed. "Eh, Mother," she said. "Have you spoken with Father recently?"

"I speak with your father daily, dear," she said drolly. Flashing a playful look at Anna, her mother accepted the tea and sat down. "Are you referencing something specific?" She stirred her cup and gently tapped the spoon on the rim, then laid it on the saucer while lifting her eyes to meet her daughter's.

Anna ran her finger along the gilded edge of the delicate china, the words seeming lodged in her throat. Yet, her mother was her last bastion of hope. If anyone could help Father see reason, it would be her. She straightened her posture and steeled herself for whatever came next. "Lord Corning," she said.

"Ah." Mother dropped her gaze to her teacup, swirling it slightly.

Anna watched her, expectation and concern jockeying for top position. When she didn't offer further response, Anna returned the saucer to the tray. "So? Have you?"

"Oh, Annabeth, really." Mother sighed and took a dainty sip. "Don't be so dramatic."

"Dramatic?" Anna crossed the room and sat next to her mother. "Mama, he's going back on his word."

"He's done no such thing," Mother said quietly. She studied her lap. "Not technically, anyway," she added, her proper posture returning.

Could she be hearing this correctly? The rest of her life was being decided on a technicality? Anna cocked her head to the side, fighting to keep her voice even. "Father told me I had a year to decide. Beg pardon, but I was under the impression that making a decision implied a choice. But then in his study just over a week ago, Father all but commanded me to accept Lord Corning's proposal."

Mother set her cup down and angled toward Anna. "'Tis the responsibility of a noblewoman to protect her family—and their title. Your first duty is to that." She placed her hand on Anna's knee. If the gesture was meant to be a comfort, it was not.

"But Mama, don't you care about love? About my happiness?" Tears stung Anna's eyes, and she made no effort to contain them.

Mother softened and cupped Anna's cheek. "Oh, sweet girl. Of course, I want your happiness. More than anything." Her gaze flitted to the window and back to Anna. "But sometimes happiness is simply beyond our reach. No matter what name or title you hold."

Emmaline joined them on the settee. "Oh, Mother, I don't believe that. Nae, I cannot believe it. Is there truly nothing that can be done?" Such intensity and compassion shone on Emmaline's face, Anna feared she might crumble completely. What had she done to deserve such a gift of a sister?

"Really, girls." Mother looked at her daughters. "'Tisn't as bad as all that." She sighed, rose, and placed a kiss on each girl's head. "We're not living in a Jane Austen novel, you know. Real life isn't like the stories. Anna, you don't have to accept his offer this moment. But it should be soon. And when you do, it will all work out in time. You'll see."

Anna's mouth flopped open, but she closed it as quickly as it had fallen. "I see," she managed to say.

"Anna," her mother said, then sighed. "You must remember, this isn't only about you. Your family depends upon this arrangement."

Emmaline shot a confused look at Anna.

Mother laid a hand on Anna's shoulder and paused for a moment, then quit the room, her tea forgotten.

Anna sat in silence. Light filtered in through the sheer drapes and dappled the ornate rug spanning the center of the room. She'd never felt so trapped in her own home. Nae, in her own life. Girlhood dreams swirled in her mind before flitting away like a hummingbird. The pressure weighed on her chest, holding her breath at bay. Attempting to break its hold, she drew in a slow, deliberate breath.

Emmaline stood. "Anna—"

She held her palm out to her sister. Oh, the girl meant well, and she probably had some optimistic view on things. Some wise lesson no one would consider but Emmaline. Anna simply didn't have the stomach for it. She needed not to think about it for a while. She needed a task. A purpose. She rose and replaced the cups and saucers on the tray. She really should leave it for Katy or Ciara, but she couldn't. She needed to be useful. To *do* something. She lifted the tray and left the room, not looking to see what Emmaline did in her wake.

As she approached the kitchen, Annabeth could hear the maids' voices from the hallway.

"Are ya certain?" one asked.

"Aye, lass, I've seen it m'self," the other replied.

A pot clanked. "I just can't fathom it. Perhaps ya heard wrong."

"No, I'm tellin' ye, I've seen it. It's gone. And I heard him say as much hims—"

Anna rounded the corner and Ciara and Katy spun around, hands behind their backs. "Hello, ladies," Anna said. "I was passing this way, so I thought I'd bring this with me. Spare you the trip."

The maids curtsied.

"Thank you, Lady Annabeth. That's very kind," Ciara added.

Katy's eyes were round, her cheeks flushed. Ciara, however, was like a stone statue, no way to read her thoughts. Anna hadn't thought much of what she'd overheard, save a gentle curiosity. But their manner now gave her pause.

"So tell me," she said, keeping her voice light, "what's all gone?"

Katy's mouth bobbed open and closed like a fish. Ciara shot her an annoyed glance before plastering a shallow smile on her face. "Oh, nothing, m'lady. Just . . . we've run out of apples. And Katy here had planned on an apple tart for dessert."

Katy chewed her lip and dropped her head. Something was amiss, but Anna wasn't going to get anywhere this way. "Ah, very well. Perhaps bread pudding then?" Though Katy was the cook, Anna kept her eyes glued on Ciara.

"Very good, m'lady," Katy eked out then turned and rushed to the larder.

Ciara and Anna stared at one another for a long minute before Ciara broke the silence. "Is there an'thing else you'll be needin' then, m'lady?" The look on her face was one of pure innocence, but her eyes held an unsettling coldness.

"No, thank you. That is all." Anna waited for Ciara to drop into the customary curtsy before going back to the drawing room.

Despite the bright sunshine warming her skin, dread hung over Anna like a cloud as she walked along Shop Street the next morning. Her thoughts tumbled over how Stephen had reacted to her sketch. He hadn't dismissed her design out of hand. In fact, he'd seemed quite taken with it at first. But something had shifted as she had explained the inspiration behind it. He'd excused himself in such a hurry, Anna was left wondering which part of the conversation had vexed him most.

The shop came into view on the horizon and Anna's heart lurched. Her feet stopped moving for the briefest of seconds, as though in their own silent protest of what lay ahead. She was never certain which Stephen she would encounter each day. Some moments he was tender, open, and kind. Others he was distant and aloof. Still others he seemed almost antagonistic toward her. What would it be today?

Much as it pained her to admit, she couldn't help but think that perhaps aloof and distant was the best course. Because on his kind and tender days, she'd had to fight to keep her focus on the tasks at hand rather than his emerald eyes, his quick wit, and the dimple that punctuated the rare genuine smile. In those moments, it seemed impossible not to let her eyes drift from his dimple to his lips, and wonder what it might be like to feel them on her own. And given her most recent conversations with Father, continuing to fall for Stephen Jennings could only cause her further grief.

Releasing a sigh, she approached the shop. The door hung open, allowing the fresh June breeze to blow through. Raised voices caught her attention. Goodness, if she wasn't careful, eavesdropping would become her full-time profession. Only snippets of words were clear, among them were *Tommy* and *Brits*. Oh dear.

Anna stood frozen for a moment, unsure whether to simply enter or to knock and make her presence known first. Before she could decide, a couple breezed past her and went inside. She followed suit.

As Seamus greeted the patrons, Anna slipped to the back and hung up her reticule and donned her apron. She allowed herself a moment to take inventory of the smithing room, checking on the items they'd last finished and left to cool and harden. Satisfied with their progress, she gathered them up along with a polishing cloth and returned to the shop.

The couple had left, and Seamus's fiddling with the till told Anna they'd made the sale.

"Good morning," she called, infusing a singsong cheeriness in her voice.

Seamus beamed at her and scurried over to plant a kiss on both her cheeks. "Good morning, *a stór*." Anna's furrowed brow over her quizzical smile must've communicated her confusion. "A stór," he repeated. "It's like 'my dear.'"

Anna's smile deepened. "Ah, I see." She repeated the word, feeling and sounding every bit as clumsy as a toddler uttering her first words.

"Well done! Ye'll be learnin' the *Gaeilge* in no time!" He chuckled and shuffled back to the till.

Stephen muttered a greeting as he replaced the ring display in the case.

"So, what's on the docket for today, gentlemen?"

Seamus inclined his head toward Stephen. "That one's a bit narky this morn', so I'd steer clear for a wee while." He offered Anna a conspiratorial wink.

Anna stifled a giggle as she let her eyes drift over Stephen. His face was dark, his brows knotted, and his jaw muscle worked back and forth. Her heart ached for him. What must he have endured to carry such anger?

"Leave it, Da," Stephen murmured. Keeping his head down, focusing on cleaning the case, he said, "Lady Annabeth, those rings we made should be ready. Ye can get those and start polishing them up and add them to the display."

Anna waved the cloth in the air and lowered herself onto a stool. Stephen turned and nodded, seeing she had already begun that task. "When that's done, see me and we'll figure out what's next."

The rest of the morning passed in relative quiet as the three mainly kept to their own tasks in between caring for customers. As they worked, Anna's thoughts drifted back to what she'd heard as she came in that morning. This was the second time she'd overheard Stephen mention someone named Tommy. And both times, he'd mentioned something about England in the same breath—and anger usually seethed in his voice when he did. Curiosity filled Anna like water rushing into a breached hull. It had taken her all morning, but she had finally summoned the courage to ask who Tommy was when Seamus announced it was time for lunch.

CHAPTER

22

The trio sat around a small table in the smithing room, a simple but generous meal of bread, cold meats, and fruit spread before them.

"Thank you for lunch," Anna said.

"Not at all." Seamus grinned and handed the platter of bread to her. Stephen tilted his lips into a half smile and dropped his focus back to his plate.

After a few minutes of stilted small talk about the weather and the business, Anna couldn't hold it in any longer. She sliced a pat of butter and smeared it over her bread while she asked, "Who's Tommy?" trying her best to keep her voice light and nonchalant.

Stephen's utensils clattered to his plate. Seamus froze midbite, mouth hanging open around a slice of brown bread.

"What?" The chill in Stephen's voice raised goosebumps on Anna's skin.

Her confidence faltered, but she couldn't back down now. Anna cleared her throat and dabbed the corners of her mouth with her serviette. "Who is Tommy? I've overheard you speak of him on a few occasions."

Seamus shifted and looked as though he was about to answer,

but Stephen's hand on his arm stopped him. "What business is it of yours?"

"None, I suppose. At least, not directly." She placed her napkin next to her plate and folded her hands in her lap. "However, each time I've heard mention of him, it's been in conjunction with some hateful thing you have to say about the British. And seeing as how I am a representative of England, I figure it is my duty to know." She herself didn't quite believe that argument, but she hoped they might.

Stephen laughed, the sound laced with sarcasm. "And what would you, m'lady, know of duty?"

Seamus shot Stephen a look but said nothing.

Anna's heart quickened. Her father's demand that she accept Corning's proposal before month's end flashed in her mind. Stephen could never grasp the depths of her understanding. "I beg your pardon, but you have no idea the pressures and responsibilities of titled life."

Stephen shook his head. "Indeed, I don't."

Confidence rose and gave buoyancy to Anna's spirit. While she took no delight in arguing with Stephen, it seemed time he understood she'd received his message loud and clear. She straightened her posture, looked at him straight on, and said, "You've made no secret about your disdain for England and all things British—myself included." Next to her, Seamus hummed in agreement. "But despite what you may think," she continued, "I am not my father. And I am not the Crown. But as an Englishwoman who does represent her country—whether she wishes to or not—I think it would behoove you to be honest with me."

Stephen tossed his serviette in a wad onto the center of his plate and leaned forward. "Honesty? Don't speak ta' me of honesty, Lady Annabeth. Or were you never going to tell us about your engagement?"

Anna drew back and her hand flew to her chest. "I—how did—"

"That's right," Stephen interrupted. "We know. Even though ye had so conveniently left out that little detail."

Anna glanced at Seamus, who was staring at his son with a look Anna couldn't decipher. She turned her attention back to Stephen. "I fail to see how that is relevant to this situation."

A sad shadow flashed across Stephen's face, but was quickly replaced by one of bitterness. "Of course you don't."

"However, if you must know, I have not yet accepted Lord Corning's proposal. Much to my parents' dismay." She kept her posture tall and her eyes fixed on Stephen.

He inhaled and straightened, and Anna braced herself for whatever verbal barrage was to come her way, but Seamus lifted his hands. "That's enough outta the both o' ye. Ye're squabbling like a pair of angry geese. And for what purpose?"

Seamus leveled his gaze at them. "Ye're both fightin' one another as if ye are adversaries." He turned to Stephen. "Anna is not your enemy, son. Much as you might believe—or need— her to be."

Stephen crossed his arms and sank back in his chair.

Seamus turned to Anna, and his face softened, along with his voice. "And Anna, a stór, Stephen is not yer enemy either. Believe it or not, ye both have more in common in what ye're fighting for than ya realize." He gripped Anna's hand and reached over and squeezed Stephen's arm.

"Tommy," he continued, "was my son."

Stephen stood with such force that his chair tipped backward. Arms still folded across his chest, he walked to a shadowed corner of the room.

"He was my eldest son." Seamus's voice hitched and he wiped his eyes with his handkerchief. Clearing his throat, he continued, "He'd gone down to Dublin with a delivery for one of our more high-ranking customers. He got turned around and found himself in the wrong place at the wrong time. British guards mistook him for a rebel they'd been searching for and shot him."

Anna sucked in a breath and covered her mouth with her hand. "Oh, Seamus, I'm so very sorry." Instinctively, she placed her hand on his arm.

The corner of his mouth lifted slightly. "T'anks, *peata*. It was a simple case of mistaken identity."

"There was no mistake." Stephen's gravelly voice came from the shadows. "They were lookin' for someone else, aye. But the fact of the matter is, to them, the only good Irishman is a dead one. We're nothin'. It was no skin off their teeth to kill him. Or any other lad who might've happened down that road. 'Cause to Brits, to *your* people, we're not really men." His voice dripped with disgust. He turned farther into the dim corner, as though he could escape into the darkness.

"*Ach*, boyo. That's your anger talkin'." Seamus gave Anna an apologetic look.

A sense of defensiveness rose up in Anna, washing over her like a wave of injustice. How dare he! How unfair of him to lump her in with insensitive, prejudiced, hateful men such as those who killed his brother. Where did he get off? She opened her mouth to say as much to him but stopped short. As she considered their story, and the things she'd seen since she'd been in Ireland, she began to see a thread of truth to what he said. He was off the mark on many things, yes. But he was dead-on with many others—and all of a sudden, she understood his hurt, anger, and bitterness. Wouldn't she feel the same if she'd endured what he, and generations of his countrymen, had? Her defensiveness melted away into an overwhelming sadness.

She may not have held that view of the Irish herself. She certainly denounced such notions as wrong. Heinous to consider God's creation in such a way. And while she struggled to reconcile or believe men like her father might actively work to cultivate the kind of worldview Stephen suggested, she could also see how the actions of her own countrymen had—at the very least—done just that.

Rising, she crossed the room and stood next to Stephen. She lifted her hand but hesitated. Would he shrug it off? Would he continue to blame her? Like the spark of a candle in the corner of a blackened room, the idea kindled in her heart that she could no more control his reactions than she could the tides of Galway Bay. She could, however, control herself. She wouldn't let fear keep her from doing what she knew to be right any longer. She laid her hand on his arm. He stiffened, and she feared he'd walk away, but he remained still. She took a shaky breath. "I am so, very sorry," she whispered around the lump in her throat. "If I'd been through that, I'd be angry too."

He looked at her from the side of his eye. His brows were drawn tightly together and harsh lines etched his face, the shadows only hardening his appearance. Turning farther toward her, the lamplight reached his face. Tears stained his cheeks. Oh, how she longed to embrace him. To heal the wound between them. Their families. And, oh, would that she could bridge the divide even between their countries.

At length, the tension in his shoulders eased, and he released a long, low breath. Turning to face her more fully, he placed his hand over hers. He searched her eyes. His own seemed to be pleading for redemption. Freedom. Anna's hand tingled at his touch. She started to reach up with her other to wipe his tears but stopped short. Much as she might care for him, it wasn't fair to go down this road. Not fair to him. And not fair to her. "I pray you find your joy once more, dear Stephen."

Backing away with slow steps, Anna reluctantly slid her hand out from underneath his, the connection between them breaking as she did so. She couldn't stay here another moment. Not with Stephen's eyes boring into hers like that. Her resolve would crumble like shortcrust.

"Thank you for lunch." She placed a light kiss on Seamus's cheek and hurried outside. The June breeze was brisk, cooling her flushed cheeks. Grocers called out their wares, and women carried baskets of bread and fish on their hips, their children straggling behind them. How unfair. The world carried on as if Anna's hadn't just stopped, even for the briefest of moments. She couldn't go back inside, but she couldn't yet return home. So she turned south and headed for the only other place she knew—the Claddagh.

Anna stood in the shadow of the Spanish Arch and gazed at the water of the River Corrib. It swirled and spun this way and that, matching her thoughts. The salty air refreshed her lungs, but her heart felt as heavy as the fortress looming over her. Lowering herself down, she settled on the grass lining the wall that kept the river at bay, the damp coolness seeping through her new trousers. Still shaken by what Stephen had said, Anna combed her memories, dismayed to discover he had been right. Memories of conversations she'd overheard back in England, as well as several less-than-savory nicknames for the Irish, floated to the top of her memory like dross from silver.

She turned her thoughts inward to her own behavior and ideas. Surely she carried no such discrimination within her. However, her heart sank when she thought of her attitude upon first arriving. How she'd viewed her family's mission as one of saving the Irish—if not from themselves, then from not knowing any better. The Irish had room to grow and learn, to be sure. Just as any person, or people, did. Anna certainly did. It had never occurred to her that the people in her new community didn't really need her here . . . nor did many of them—or perhaps most—even want her here. And knowing what she did now, she could understand why.

And now that she saw, now that she knew, she simply could not carry on business as usual. She knew better, so now she must do better. She might have to marry Lord Corning and leave this land and the people she was growing to love, but so long as Anna was here and it was in her power to do so, she would treat every person the way they deserved—as one made in the image of God. She committed there, also, to carry that way of life, no matter where she lived. And if she must be tethered to a man such as Corning, she would use the influence afforded such a station to change the world around her—to help them see others the way God saw them.

The magnitude of such a commitment, such a responsibility, was daunting. *Oh Lord, bridge the divide.* The prayer whispered from her heart and took flight on the wings of the magpie that lifted off from the arch above her.

Anna shivered from the chill coming up through the grass and decided it best to head for home. McGinnty's Fish and Chips came into view just as a rumbling sound vibrated the stones beneath her feet.

Turning, she saw a regiment of the Royal Irish Constabulary marching in formation through the Spanish Arch. Understanding bloomed as to why some referred to them as Black and Tans. Their black military jackets hung low over their hips, covering the tops of their tan trousers bloused into tan socks. She'd forgotten their barracks were behind the arch. The unit pivoted in the direction of Shop Street. Stepping back to make sure she was fully out of their way, she eased into the shadow of McGinnty's. The door creaked open and Paddy McGinnty stepped onto the front stoop. His arms were crossed over his chest and his eyes mere slits. He jerked his head ever so slightly this way and that. Following his gaze, Anna noticed two young men in a doorway catty-corner from her. Another pair stood a few doors down on the same side of the road as the chipper. Yet another came up from the bridge near where Anna had been sitting.

The ground shook with each step the regiment took, the sound reverberating off the buildings in the narrow street, nearly deafening as so many booted feet struck the cobblestone in unison. Anna stifled a shudder. Once the regiment had passed, the lads Paddy had been looking at each moved off slowly in different directions, a pair at a time. *Odd.*

As the din of the marching faded, Anna became keenly aware she was standing alone with the large man. Feeling every bit the imposter, Anna couldn't stand the awkwardness of standing so near an acquaintance and not at least greeting him. "Hello, Mister McGinnty. How lovely to see you!"

Paddy jolted and looked at her with surprised eyes. Blinking, he extended his hand. "Lady Annabeth, beggin' yer pardon. I didn't see ya there. How do ye fare?"

"Very well, thank you." Taking a full breath for the first time in several minutes, she smiled. "Goodness, that was certainly a sight, wasn't it?" She gestured down the street in the direction the regiment had gone.

A shadow flitted through Paddy's eyes, and he turned his head away. He stared hard as though he could see through the buildings where the road turned to view the soldiers further. "Aye. 'Tis somethin', alright," he eventually mumbled.

Anna watched him carefully, wondering how he felt about the growing presence of the British military in his town. Though she was certain she had at least some idea.

As though he felt her looking at him, he met her gaze once more, his demeanor softening. "No bother. One o' these days, things'll be better."

Anna pressed her lips together and nodded, holding his stare for a long moment before answering, "God willing." She hoped he picked up on all that she intended in that statement.

Paddy chuckled. "Indeed. Now, tell me, when can we expect ye back in for some more fish 'n chips?" He grinned, brightening his whole face.

"Soon. Very soon, I hope."

"Brilliant. I look forward to it. And make sure ye take good care, aye?"

Anna nodded and matched his smile, then shook his hand once more and made her way back toward Church Street to meet Owen and the carriage. As she passed the Jenningses' shop, she avoided looking in the window but could almost feel eyes on her from within as she did so.

CHAPTER
23

Stephen hunched over the bar at Tigh Hughes, tracing the woodgrain with his finger. Never one to drown his sorrows with anything stronger than a cup of tea, he still indulged in a pint every now and then.

"Here ya go," the bartender said, sliding him a glass.

"Thanks, Martin." Stephen watched as the creamy foam settled and filtered down through the black liquid. Staunch believers claimed this famed Irish stout brought health, healing, and long life. While he didn't necessarily believe that, Stephen couldn't deny it offered a sense of comfort. An earthy tether of sorts, not entirely unlike that of a good cupán tae.

He took a sip, letting the bittersweet brew linger on his palate as his mind ran over Annabeth's reaction to Tommy's story at lunch. Recalling how the defensiveness in her eyes had melted into something else entirely, he took another drink of his ale rather than letting the stinging in his own eyes gain further ground. His gaze traveled to his arm, where Annabeth's hand had rested, the warmth of her touch almost returning at the memory. When she'd reached her other hand up, he thought she was going to stroke his face. And he'd ached at the desire that she would. In that moment, he'd wanted nothing more than to wrap his arms around her as he had when they'd danced, pull her to him, and—

Heaven help me. Keeping his heart distant from Annabeth De Lacy grew more difficult with every moment.

"So it's settled, then? Everyone knows his job?" The gruff voice came from over Stephen's shoulder, drawing his attention to a group of five men huddled around a booth in the corner.

"Aye. Yer man's supposed to be at the train station that night," one lad offered.

An older gentleman with an unkempt look about him nodded. "Good, good. And the other group's all set to be out at the man—eh, out west?"

A third man, somewhere between the ages of the first two, answered, "Aye. The auld codger'll never know what hit 'im." Coarse laughter rumbled from the cluster. "Right," the gruff-voiced apparent leader said. "Ye know yer tasks and the date. Now, we just bide our time." A round of affirmations murmured through the men as they rose and headed for the door.

Stephen's face twisted in suspicion as his stomach gripped. *I don't like the sound of that.* They could've been talking about anything, but a feeling niggled in Stephen's gut that he couldn't ignore. Draining his pint, he slapped his payment onto the counter and slipped outside to see if he could hear more.

Though mid-June, the night air held a damp, brisk chill that only added to the unease building in Stephen's chest. He lifted the collar of his coat and pulled the body of it tighter around his trunk. Squinting against the darkness, he glanced this way and that, looking for any sign of the group he'd seen inside. No use. The street was empty save for a cat trotting for home with his prized catch clutched between his teeth.

"Bother." Stephen tried to tell himself the lads could've been discussing anything—perhaps they'd been stiffed at the poker table or one of their sisters' virtues had been stolen by some rogue. But something told him it was much more than that. The Black 'n Tans' presence had certainly picked up of late, which was bound to stir the local militia. He made note to keep a watchful eye and open ear.

◆ June 15 ◆

Ciara put the finishing touches on Anna's hair, adding a decorative comb to the pile of curls woven at the nape of Anna's neck. How strange to share one lady's maid with Emmaline and Mother. Quite the change from their sprawling estate life in Camberwick, with a full and numerous service staff. Though, in truth, Anna wasn't sure she minded the change. There was something about this simpler way of life she found somewhat freeing.

"Thank you, Ciara." Anna smiled at her in the mirror.

"Of course, m'lady. They'll be expecting you downstairs." She curtsied and scurried from the room.

In the dining room, tall tapered candles cast a golden glow that bounced off the cutlery. Father, Mother, and Emmaline entered right behind her, and the family took their places at the table, which in the absence of any extra guests had been shortened slightly for the family of four. Though it still felt rather empty without any family or dignitaries to entertain.

A delicious aroma wafted from the direction of the servants' entrance, gleaming domed silver trays following quickly after it. A plate of braised salmon, topped with a sprig of dill, appeared before her. She inhaled deeply the heady scent of the fish, her thoughts immediately drifting back to the fish and chips she'd had with Stephen on the Claddagh. What Father and Mother would have to say about her adventures of late—Anna flitting about in trousers, eating peasant food from newsprint. She chuckled at the idea.

"I'm glad you find the situation amusing, Annabeth, dear." Her father's voice jolted her back to the present. He cocked an inquisitive brow at her while draping his serviette in his lap.

Anna's cheeks flushed, as though there was some danger of him being able to read her thoughts. "I beg pardon, Father. 'Twas just an errant memory."

He eyed her warily before slicing into his entrée. Anna smiled and tried to act every bit the lady he expected her to be as she took her first bite. A flash of sour lemon followed by the earthy dill burst on her tongue. Not quite the same as fish and chips but still delectable.

"Well?" Father wagged his fork in the air.

Anna looked around the table, waiting for someone to respond.

"Annabeth, dear, whatever has gotten into you?" Mother asked. "Your father's asked you a question." She patted her serviette to the corner of her mouth.

Good grief. If Anna wasn't careful, they'd lock her away, afraid she was losing her mind altogether. "I do apologize, Father. Might you repeat the question?"

An exasperated sigh puffed from his lips, and Emmaline came to Anna's rescue. "He'd inquired as to your decision regarding Lord Corning." Her face was the picture of propriety, but her eyes reflected kindness and empathy.

Anna's appetite suddenly diminished, and she poked her fork at her fish. "Oh." She willed a sweet smile to grace her face. "Not quite yet. I've a bit more time."

Father shot a look to Mother and he muttered, "Not as much as you might think."

"I'll decide soon. I promise."

His cutlery stilled, and his hardened stare froze Anna to her seat. "End of the month." The words were spoken slowly, and measured, one at a time, leaving absolutely no room for argument, question, or confusion.

The rest of dinner passed in a blur of uncomfortable small talk until, blessedly, the dessert was finished and the plates cleared. Rather than joining the family in the drawing room, Anna excused herself to her room. So weighed down by fatigue was she, even Ciara was relieved of her duties of helping Anna dress for bed.

Though getting from her dinner gown to her nightdress proved a little more challenging than she anticipated, she'd done it anyway and sat now in bed, leaning against the pillows, with a book open on her lap.

When a quiet tap sounded at the door, Anna stifled a moan. But before she could answer, the door opened, and Emmaline slipped inside.

"Oh." Anna sighed in relief. "It's you."

Emmaline smiled, her eyes kind but tired, and came to sit on the edge of the bed. "You poor dear."

Anna patted her sister's knee. "Oh, it's not so bad as all that."

"Isn't it?" She grasped Anna's hand. "Papa's going to make you marry that . . . that prune."

Anna laughed, in spite of the dread weighing down on her like a millstone. "If it's meant to be, it will be. I pray that another way might yet be found, God willing." She swallowed. "And if not, I must accept what He has for me."

Emmaline's shoulders drooped, and something akin to frustration flashed on her face. "So that's it, then? You're going to accept."

Tears stung Anna's eyes, but she willed her voice light. "I'm not ready to throw in the towel just yet." She thumbed the edges of the pages in her book. "But I'm not sure I see another way. And if I don't wish to accept him, I wouldn't dream of you having to do so in my stead." She shook her head.

Emmaline smoothed her hand over a wrinkle in the duvet. "You're kind. You've always tried to protect me—and I love you for it. But have you considered that I am more suited to that life?"

Anna's brow puckered, and she bade her sister continue.

Emmaline shifted to tuck her feet underneath her. "I only mean that I've always dreamt of life as a real lady, a countess or marchioness or some such title. But you . . . you're such a free spirit! I fear being forced to bind yourself to a man like Corning would snuff the spark of life from your eyes. And that is something I could not bear." Her eyes glistened and she swiped at her cheeks.

"And what of you?" Anna shot back. "Do you not see what that ogre would do to your spirit?"

Emmaline took a shuddered breath. "I am young, but I am not so naive. Of course I would prefer to marry for love—some handsome, young titled gentleman who would sweep me off my feet. But I see no such man darkening our door for me. And I see no possibility for one—particularly so long as we live here." She swept her arm toward the window then met her sister's gaze. "This is not an offer I make lightly, Anna. And what you don't see is that I would indeed be marrying for love. For true love—my love for you."

Anna's heart clenched with compassion, and she took both her sister's hands in her own. "Dear, sweet Emmie. So wise and kind beyond your years. Sometimes I think you were meant to be the firstborn. I adore you and your selflessness. And I wouldn't dream of doing anything to get in the way of your ambitions for a glamorous life in the court. If Corning were a truly noble man with a kind heart, I would be nothing but happy to stand aside. But the thought of you . . . with him? I cannot."

Emmaline smiled and wagged her head. "Well, my dear sister, 'tis clear we both love each other, which warms my heart, but we can't both be noble. *Someone* will have to accept him or our family may never recover from the social shame of it." Emmaline's eyes took on a new sheen.

Anna squeezed her hands. Stephen's eyes flashed in her mind. The memory of his arms around her threatened to smother her with desire and regret. In her heart and mind she whispered a goodbye to him. To what could never be. She scooted closer to Emmaline, straightened her spine, and said, "Then I shall. I will accept him."

"Oh, Annie." Damp tracks drifted down the young woman's cheeks.

Anna smiled, only to stop her chin quivering. "Only, let's not tell Papa," she said around the sharp lump in her throat. "Not yet."

Nodding, Emmaline said, "We've a couple of weeks yet until the end of the month." She pulled Anna into an embrace. The hall floor creaked and the girls shot their gaze to the door. Anna lifted a silent finger to her lips.

Emmaline bobbed her head. "I'd best be off," she whispered, barely audible even six inches away.

Anna nodded and dried her sister's cheeks with her sleeve before bussing her forehead. "Rest well, dear sister."

Molloy smoothed a map over the rough tabletop in the back room of Tigh Hughes. "Right, lads, take a look at this." He straightened and hooked his thumbs through his belt loops, his face awash with pride.

Paddy leaned over the paper and traced his finger along a line on the map that snaked through County Galway. Various markings denoted troops, their movements, and more. Eyes wide, he looked up at Molloy. "Well done, man." He dropped his gaze to the map again. "Well done, indeed."

The men gathered closer around the table and admired the map. "How did ye come upon this?" asked Old Man Burke.

"Never ye mind that," Molloy said, rocking on his toes. "But if this is correct, there will be a unit marching along the Tuam Road every night, starting at the weekend." He looked from one man to another. "We can take 'em out."

"Aw, class," Mickey said. "Count us in." He looked to his brother. "Right, Ciaran?"

Ciaran walked a slow circle around the table before pressing both palms onto the page. His eyes scoured the map, and he began to nod slowly. "Aye," he said at length. "We're in." His voice was low and heavy with hunger for a fight.

Paddy lowered himself onto the seat and studied the lines further, still amazed at the lad's find. "I . . . I think it'll work." He extended a hand to Molloy. Molloy grasped Paddy's arm just below the elbow and the pair grinned at one another.

"*Anois*," Old Man Burke said as he claimed the chair next to Paddy. "What of De Lacy?"

"Well," Ciaran said, keeping his volume just above a whisper. "I've heard the lads from Clairegalway are planning an ambush on some RIC bigwig coming up on the train from Dublin in a few weeks. And that got me thinkin'."

At that moment, the door creaked open, and Aoife, her dress laced far too tight, strolled in bearing a tray laden with fresh pints. Ciaran slipped the map off the table and onto his lap. "Ye're a doll, Aoife." He winked at her and she blushed and giggled. Paddy rolled his eyes.

"An' doncha forget it neither." Aoife set the drinks in front of the men and let her smile and gaze linger on Ciaran. She leaned over until there was barely a handbreadth between them. She tweaked his cheek with her finger, and he grasped her hand.

"That's enough outta you, Ciaran," Paddy said before Ciaran could pull her any closer to him. "Thanks, Aoife." She straightened and Paddy tossed a pound at her. She caught it, kissed it, and sauntered from the room, her hips swaying more than a lantern on a wagon. Ciaran stared after her like a lovesick puppy.

Paddy thumped his knee. "Ye were saying?"

Ciaran blew out a breath and shook his head as the door closed after Aoife. "Right, so. I got to thinkin' that the night the lads ambush the train might be the perfect night to finally hit the manor house."

Uneasiness rose in the back of Paddy's throat. "The house? What d'ye have in mind?"

"We need to send a message that they—the De Lacys and their whole lot—aren't welcome here. So, I say"—he paused and looked around the table—"we burn 'em out."

A sparkle flickered in Mickey's eye. He half grimaced, half smiled, looking smugly impressed. "Aye," he said, head bobbing. "Burn 'em out."

Old Man Burke nodded slowly. "That could work. 'Twould certainly send a message. An' with the Brits havin' sent him over so recently, and things kickin' up all o'er the country, it might make 'em think twice about sending another one to replace him."

Paddy's thoughts drifted to Anna. He hadn't known what to think when he first met her—especially with how she overstepped with paying for Stephen's lunch that first day. But, having worked with her to design a special piece of jewelry for Nora, he'd come to see that she was nothing like the Brits he'd known in the past. Not that he'd gotten to know any of them very well. But the thought of hurting her turned his stomach.

He couldn't very well say that to this lot though. "We need to send a message, *go cinnte*. Definitely," he said. "But . . . is fire the right one? Aren't we just hurtin' ourselves if we burn the estate?"

Ciaran scoffed. "Small price to pay, I say." He sniffed and his shoulders flopped in a shrug. "Grass an' land'll regrow." The group grunted their agreement.

"True enough. But are ya certain it's the right message though?" Paddy turned to the eldest among them. "Burke, doesn't your niece work at the manor house?"

The old man shifted in his seat. "Aye."

Paddy arched his brows and leaned closer, resting his arm around the back of the man's chair. "And ye're willing to risk her life to send this message?"

Old Man Burke rubbed his jaw. "Well . . ." He shifted again. "Maybe we could warn the help? There're several of our people that work there. We could tell them so they could get out ahead of time?"

Head's bobbed and faces scrunched as the men considered the idea.

"I dunno," Molloy said. "Seems risky." He scratched the back of his head.

"I think it'd work," Mickey said. "The whole idea of this t'ing is ta get rid o' them. Not our kind. Just tell 'em. It'll be grand, so."

"*Seafóid.*" Ciaran stood so quickly his chair nearly toppled over.

"Easy there, lad. Why do ya say it's nonsense?" Paddy asked.

"Don't tell me to take it easy. We're at war, or had ye not realized that?" Ciaran crossed his arms and stared Paddy down.

"Do you really want to have said that to me?" Paddy turned in his seat.

Ciaran only stared at him.

"No one is denyin' this is a war. We're all here for the same reason, *a mhac*. We're only tryin' to suss out the best way to accomplish our objective." Paddy leaned back in his chair. "I think Burke has the right idea. We let the help know what's comin', so they can get away safely. Then, if they choose to stay, that's their choice."

"*Humph*. Wha', and risk them tippin' off the family? No way." Ciaran tossed his arms in the air. "An' don't 'a mhac' me. I'm not yer son."

Old Man Burke patted the air in Ciaran's direction. "Now, now, boyo. Paddy's not yer enemy." He turned his attention back to Paddy. "Ciaran does have a point." Burke shrugged. "Mightn't it be a wee bit too risky? I was just thinkin' out loud, anyway."

"Perhaps," Paddy said. How could he get them to forget the idea of torching the house? Could they not target Lord De Lacy alone? "Alright, alright. So we wouldn't warn them. But I'm still not sure *fire* is the way to go. Do ye not find it a smidgen . . . predictable?" That ought to do it.

Ciaran stepped forward until his toes nearly touched Paddy's. Mickey joined him. "Ye're not losing yer nerve, are ye, auld man?"

Paddy stood as well and straightened to his full height—nearly a half foot taller than Ciaran. "Ye're one to talk at me about losing nerve, Ciaran O'Donnell. I seem to remember a night last year—"

"Enough!" Ciaran interrupted, his eyes wide. "Fine. We'll keep thinkin' on ways to get to De Lacy. Right, lads?"

"Aye," the group muttered.

Paddy thought he saw a look pass from Ciaran to the other men in the gang, but he couldn't be sure. Either way, Paddy would have to keep a close eye on the group. And on Annabeth.

Each man stood and shuffled toward the door. Behind Paddy, the whispers among Ciaran and some of the others deepened the unease already stirring in his gut. Surely they'd act as a unified group. Wouldn't they?

CHAPTER

25

Seamus's gravelly singing voice flowed from the open shop window and swirled about the street like a carefree dance. Anna's heart lifted at the sound of it. How many days had she been greeted in such manner as she arrived at the shop these last few months? It was one of her favorite things. The words of the song were completely foreign to her, but that mattered not. Seamus sang with such abandon. He seemed completely untouched by the disquiet—or was it discord—that had weighed on Anna and Stephen of late. In truth, the whole country seemed held captive by a pall of unrest. But not Seamus.

Just before she entered the shop, Anna noticed Paddy across the street, talking to a grocer. He smiled and waved. Anna returned the gesture.

After going inside, she hung her cape on the hook and peeked around the corner, taking care not to interrupt Seamus's ballad. He sat at the workbench, hunched over a wadding of wax, carving. His knee bounced in time with his tune.

In all the time she'd spent in the smithing room the last few months, she'd not seen Seamus carve a thing. Not once. She watched as his aged hands, though clearly not as nimble as a young man's, worked with dexterity and precision. She couldn't make out the carving itself, but the action, though small, seemed to bring him to life. The scene served only to endear him to her further.

She watched as long as she dared but finally ventured a greeting. "Good morning, Seamus."

The man's shoulders jerked, and he slipped the wax into a canvas bag before turning to face Anna. "Hello, a stór. How are ye?" He waddled over and bussed her cheeks.

"Just fine. And you?"

"Grand out, so I am." He smiled and shifted his weight back and forth.

"That was a lovely song. What was it?"

Seamus beamed. "It's just an auld ballad about love lost. I hadn't even gotten to the best part yet! D'ye wanna hear it?"

Anna nodded her head fervently. "Oh, yes, please! So very much." She settled onto a stool.

His chest puffed as he sucked in a deep breath. Then the tune burst forth from his lips with gusto. Though Anna could not decipher a single word, there was no mistaking the passion and drama on Seamus's face. The melody at first was fierce and strong... perhaps even angry. Or bitter. Then, it shifted to joyful, hopeful. As the chorus built to a crescendo, Seamus threw his head back and his arms out wide and finished with a flourish on a long-held note.

Anna rewarded him with a robust round of applause. Seamus's cheeks reddened, with pride more than embarrassment, it seemed.

"Wonderful, absolutely delightful!" Anna grinned. "What were you saying? In the song."

"Well, it's a bit hard to translate." He lowered himself back onto his stool. "But it's telling the story of my ancestor who created the Claddagh ring. It starts off mournful and dreary, because he's lost the love of his life. But he never gives up hope. In the end, he gets to come home, she's stayed faithful to him all along, and they get married." He shrugged. "It's the story of Ireland, really. It can seem bleak and doomed, ever under attack or oppression. But we must never give up hope on our happily ever after."

"Truly lovely, Seamus." The legend of the Claddagh really did seem to mirror the story of Ireland in many ways. So much heartache, sadness, and anger. And yet, underneath it all, a trickle of hope. "The way you keep hope alive in the midst of difficulty is admirable."

He shrugged. "What do you expect? I'm Irish."

Anna chuckled and her gaze drifted to the canvas bag on the workbench. She wrestled with whether to mention what she saw him doing, but her curiosity won out in the end. "What were you working on?" She gestured to the bench behind him.

He pasted a look of confusion on his face. "What? Working? Me? Nah." He flapped his hand. "I was just doin' a bit o' cleaning."

Anna didn't buy it for a moment. "You were carving something. I've not seen you do that. What was it? I'd love to see your style."

"*Psh!*" He batted his hand again. "That? That's nuthin'. Just keepin' my fingers nimble." He shrugged and scuffled back to his perch at the workbench.

"Alright then. Keep your secrets." Anna chuckled and donned her work apron and headed into the shop. After she polished the cases, shined the rings, and served several customers, Seamus dawdled in, balancing a tray on his arm.

"Cupán tae?"

"Oh, yes, please." Anna wiped her hands and joined him at the counter. "Shall I get a cup for Stephen?"

"Nah, the lad's tending to the horse in the stable. He went

for a long ride this morning, and the poor steed's knackered." He chuckled and they sat down together. Seamus handed her a cup and slid a plate of digestive biscuits her way.

They enjoyed their repast in comfortable silence. Anna tried to let her mind rest as well, but she couldn't help thinking about the last encounter she'd had with Stephen. The hurt in his eyes as Seamus relayed the tragic story of Tommy's untimely end had cut her to the quick. And something had seemed to shift between them when she'd laid her hand on his arm. Her heart certainly had shifted in that moment, so she'd fled. And she'd had precious little real contact with him since. It had been weeks.

"How is Stephen, by the way?" she asked at length.

Seamus brushed crumbs from his hands and sighed. "He's alright." He stared at his feet for a moment before lifting his gaze to meet Anna's. "Ye mustn't hold it against him. The way he's been wi' ye. He's come through a lot, and he's built a tough skin for himself. Not that that excuses his behavior. It doesna. But, he's built a wall 'round his heart, just the same."

"I can imagine. What happened to Tommy was such a tragedy. For both of you."

"Aye." His head bobbed. "But it's not just that. Before Tommy . . . long 'afore he passed, there was Marie."

Anna's heart lurched and she shifted on her stool. So much loss. "Marie? Was she your daughter?"

"No." Seamus looked all around before continuing. "She was Stephen's fiancée," he whispered—though it seemed his voice could carry to the back row of a theatre.

Anna's jaw fell open, but she closed it just as quickly. "Oh, I see."

"I don't tell ya this to just be tellin' stories. He'd be ragin' if he knew I was sayin' anything."

She could only imagine.

Seamus rested his forearms on the table and leaned on them. "But if ye're to understand his heart, ya hafta know."

Anna's pulse quickened. Oh, how she longed to understand his heart. Yet, how she also feared to. Drawing any nearer to him would only serve to cause her—and perhaps him—further pain. She couldn't bear the idea of hurting him. But when she tried to decline, to change the subject, she found herself nodding instead.

"Oh, they were in love, those two. Never seen a couple more googly-eyed." Seamus stared off as if he'd gone back in time, reliving the moments. "They were so verra young, but Stephen didn't care. He proposed, and of course, she accepted. But, not long 'afore the weddin', she left. Took everything. He'd set aside a nest egg—the poor lad had saved so long and worked so hard to put that money away. *Tsk.*" Seamus shook his head. "Well, she took it all when she left . . . the money, the ring, his heart . . . and his dignity."

"Oh, how awful."

"Oh, aye. 'Twas. An' don't you think this town didna have a heyday with it. Can ye 'magine? The heir of the Claddagh legend finds love, only to be jilted practically at the altar? Aye, that woman made a right mess of things for him." Seamus's face hardened for a beat, then softened.

"That's . . . that's terrible." How could someone do such a thing to another person? "Could he not file a complaint with the police to try and get his money back at least?"

"Nae, lass. The girl *left.*" He grasped her hand, his gaze boring into hers.

"Left?"

"Aye. As in . . . she fled. To England."

Anna's posture wilted. "Oh, goodness."

"She was half English, ya see? Once she crossed over, there was no findin' her."

Anna pressed a hand to her stomach, her mind spinning. No wonder Stephen held such disdain for her people. "I'm so sorry," she whispered.

"*Ach.* 'Twasn't yer fault, lass. But thank ye." He dabbed his eyes with his handkerchief. "He swore off love for good, then and there, and a seed of bitterness planted itself in his heart. Add then the war, and Tommy, and well . . ."

Anna could only nod.

"I've not given up hope for the lad yet though. And I don't want ye to either. But ya needed to know where he's comin' from in order to help him get where he needs to go."

Anna's eyes widened and she waved her hands in front of her. "Oh, I don't know how much help I could be to him. He won't even speak to me." She shook her head. "Besides, I don't know how much longer—never mind. Thank you so very much for sharing this with me."

Seamus smiled, joy radiating in his eyes despite the tears. "And I've not given up on ye"—he pointed at her—"either. The Lord moves in mysterious ways. And if bringin' a British lass to my shop to deal with my son isn't mysterious, I don't know what is."

A chuckle lifted from Anna's chest.

"Now, let's get back to work."

CHAPTER

26

I'm afraid the news isn't good, milord." Sergeant Townsend remained at attention in front of Lord De Lacy's desk.

"Go on. Out with it." William lit his pipe while warily eyeing the two men standing behind the sergeant. "And who are these gentlemen?"

"These are Captains Bainbridge and Livingston, milord." The captains saluted William, who responded with his own lackluster salute. "Sir, a rabble of Irish Republican Army activists ambushed an RIC patrol on the Tuam-Dunmore road last night."

William shot to his feet. "What?" he hissed. "How bad was it?"

Captain Bainbridge stepped forward. "I'm afraid two of our officers were killed. Livingston and I surren—er—were allowed to go."

William set the pipe down on his desk with more force than he intended. "Two officers killed, you say?"

"Yes, Lord De Lacy."

"Have you their names? I suppose it falls to me to write to their next of kin."

Bainbridge glanced at Livingston, who stepped forward and

handed William a slip of paper with the names of the fallen officers.

William studied the paper before sliding it into his ledger. "These republicanists are getting out of hand. Something must be done."

Livingston's mouth curled up in a smirk. "Don't worry. We've sent those rebels a message."

"Oh? How so?"

"We searched for the ambushers, but no trace of them could be found. However, as you say, we couldn't let the attack go unanswered. It only made sense that the attackers came from Tuam. They must've. So, I took a group of my reinforcements, and we made sure the townspeople understand what happens when you betray the Crown."

William's jaw ached and his chest tightened. "Speak plainly, boy! I need details!"

Bainbridge handed William a report of the events that took place in Tuam.

William scanned the page. His shoulders sank, and he squeezed the bridge of his nose. "Grenades? On civilians? Have you gone mad?"

"Quite the contrary, milord." Livingston's face shone with pride. "We did what needed to be done."

William read aloud from the page. "RIC soldiers fired into the streets. Burned the town hall. Rounded up suspected republicans and questioned them." His fingers curled around the paper, the report crinkling in his grip. "I don't suppose the questioning was done verbally alone?"

Livingston shrugged. "We only did what needed doing. To protect the honor of the Crown."

William rounded the desk, waving the report over his head. "Don't you realize what you've done?" His voice reverberated in the rafters. "Such a forceful response will only trigger further violence. Fools! If the ambushers could not be found, a proper investigation should've taken place to discover them. You've made a right mess of things, Captain."

"Have I?" Livingston's fingers closed and opened in fists. "Or perhaps Your Lordship has softened in his stance against the rebels?"

William's face burned. "How dare you!"

"Beg pardon, milord, but what else am I to think when your own daughter spends more time with Irishmen than her own family?" A nasty smirk lifted the corner of the captain's mouth and disgust sparked in his eyes.

Bainbridge placed a hand on Livingston's shoulder. "That's enough," he murmured.

"Quite enough!" William bellowed. "Out with you this instant! And when the whole county has devolved into chaos, we'll know who to blame."

Livingston frowned and shrugged Bainbridge's hand off his shoulder and placed his cover back on his head. The sneer then returned to his face in earnest as he said, "Indeed, we will."

William followed the three men to the door of his study and slammed it in their wake. How could they be so foolhardy? He paced the room. Fate certainly had a twisted sense of humor to send him here for a fresh start only to land him in the middle of a guerrilla war.

A knock sounded at the door.

"Enter," he growled.

"This came for you, m'lord."

"Thank you, Owen. That'll be all." William took the envelope from the coachman and went to sit at his desk. Judging by the script, Broadmor was finally sending word of his latest investment. At last, a piece of good news.

He sliced open the envelope with haste and unfolded the letter. His eyes flitted over the scrawled words and numbers.

No! This couldn't be. Words like *failed* and *lost* swirled on the page. The letter slipped from his hand and fluttered to the floor. Fingers shaking, he relit the bowl of his pipe and puffed feverishly.

That's it, then. The De Lacy legacy ruined. Not tarnished or besmirched. Ruined. Nonexistent. The only hope of redemption now was the match between Corning and Annabeth. He'd been more than generous with the girl regarding the arrangement, even extending his deadline past the end of June. How many daughters of lords had so much say in matters of marriage and prospects?

No. He'd given her the chance to do the right thing of her own accord. Undoubtedly spending so much time around the rebellious attitudes of the Jenningses and their ilk had tainted her view of family and duty. She'd shirked her responsibility to her family when given every opportunity to respond with honor. Clearly, she was incapable of recognizing that which was for her own good—both present and future. It was settled. She must accept Lord Corning. And she must do it now.

Drawing three long pulls on his pipe, his confidence growing with each one, he yanked the vessel from his mouth then straightened his jacket. "Elizabeth! Annabeth!"

CHAPTER
27

Anna sat in a tufted chair across from her mother in the study, her ankles crossed, sweat trickling down her spine. Her father paced in front of the fire. Must he have the room so stifling? Anna patted her forehead and looked at her mother. She willed her to see the question in her eyes: *What does he want?*

Mother lifted her brows and shook her head ever so slightly.

Father, his coat buttoned, hands clasped behind his back, finally quit pacing and faced the women head-on. "It's time we had a talk." He held them overlong with his silent gaze. "Annabeth, you will accept Lord Corning. And you will send word at once."

The fire forgotten, all heat drained from Anna and she shivered. "But, Father—"

He shook his head while lifting a finger and wagging it at her. "It's decided."

Anna looked at her mother, who only stared at the grate, unmoving, her eyes devoid of any emotion. "But . . . Papa, you said . . ."

Father huffed. "I know what I said, child. And I was wrong to say it. Never mind the fact that I've been more than generous with you. I told you to give me your answer by the end of last month, and here we are in the middle of July already!" He huffed and ran his hand over his head. "You should have accepted him from the very beginning. You could have married then and remained in England, where you belong."

Anna wrapped her arms around her middle. "It isn't fair! Why give the illusion of choice when you were only going to have me accept all along?"

Father frowned and glanced at the decanter on his desk. "There was no illusion. It just never dawned on me that you would be selfish enough to turn your back on your family."

Anna's jaw fell slack, and she gripped the arms of the chair. "I would never!"

He glared at her. "Wouldn't you?" His volume rose steadily with each word. "Haven't you already? You would rather spend your time outside these walls with . . . with *them*"—he swung his arm toward the windows and the world beyond, disgust painted on his face—"than here with your family—among proper people—where you belong." He returned his glare to Anna. When he spoke again, his voice was low, his words measured. "If you had any sense of loyalty, you wouldn't have had to even think about Lord Corning's proposal. You'd have accepted it straightaway. For the good of your family."

Tears filled Anna's eyes. "Papa"—her voice softened as she stood and placed her hand on his arm—"I've only ever wanted what is best for us. All of us. Besides, many ladies receive more than one offer of marriage. With our family's wealth and land, I assumed that . . . well, I did not think it necessary to accept the first proposal that came along . . . particularly not from someone like Lord Corning."

Father shrugged from her grip. "Don't you see?" He pinched the bridge of his nose, refusing to even look at her.

Anna blinked hard and glanced between her parents. "What?" She shook her head. "What don't I see?"

He covered his face with his palm and turned toward the fire. He stood still for a long moment before swinging back around and shouting, "That we're ruined!" When the echo of his exclamation died down, a wretched silence stretched long and merciless.

Anna stared at her father. His face had paled of late, and his eyes were sunken into shadowy pockets. Lines etched his forehead and gaunt cheeks. He turned his back to her and faced the fire once more.

"It's gone," he muttered.

Confusion swam in Anna's mind, clouding her thoughts. She waited for him to continue. When he did not, she ventured to speak. "Papa?"

"It's gone!" he shouted, his voice rattling the windows. "Don't you see? All of it! The money, everything. All we have left is this house."

Mother gasped. "William, you can't be serious."

The fiery countenance drained from his face as Father pulled a letter out of his coat pocket and handed it to Mother.

"What is that?" Anna asked.

Mother lifted a finger as she read. When she'd finished, she fell against the chair. "So that's it."

Father nodded, resignation clouding his eyes.

"What?" Anna wanted to sound eager, curious, but feared she sounded more like a whining child.

Her father sighed and lowered himself into the remaining empty chair. "I was sent here, as landlord of Galway Parish, not as an honor or promotion but as a punishment. I'd butted heads with the court one too many times, been too careless in my spending." His head lowered and he stared at his feet. "And gambling."

"William, no. You don't have to," Mother urged.

He sighed. "I do, Elizabeth. She has a right to know. Especially since"—his gaze drifted up to meet Anna's—"she's the only one who can save our family from utter ruin."

Mother nodded, relenting, and Anna struggled to swallow the sick feeling rising to the back of her throat.

Her father continued, "I'd thought the fresh start here would be good. And, at first, it was. But then, my past mistakes continued to haunt me. In a last-ditch effort, I invested everything we had left in a venture I'd heard about on the crossing. Some of the other gentries were involved, and it seemed like a sure thing."

"What was the venture?" Anna asked. It was all she could manage to say.

He waved a hand. "It matters not. I'd hoped to get word of a windfall soon. And today it came." He dropped his head again.

"But it wasn't a windfall," Mother said, defeat lacing her voice.

"No," he said. "Quite the opposite."

Mother turned to Anna. "You see, dear, your match with Lord Corning is the only option remaining to us. Even before this news of the failed investment . . . we were on shaky ground." She aimed an annoyed look at her husband. "If you don't accept him, Emmaline will have to."

Father's head remained low. "That's if he'd even accept Emmaline after suffering the humiliation of your refusal. Especially after such a long delay in answering."

"Please, my darling," Mother said, grasping Anna's hand. "'Tis the only way. You remember what I said in the drawing room? About the life of a lady?"

Of course Anna remembered. How could she forget such a conversation? Her mind spun. All this time her family had lied to her—to everyone—about their station. It was wrong. The lot of it. How unfair . . . how cruel . . . to expect Anna to be the one to clean up her father's mistakes. To sacrifice the rest of her life. No, she wouldn't do it. Couldn't.

She crossed the room to the wall of shelves, absently running her fingers over the wood. A framed photo caught her eye. Emmaline sat in a chair and Anna stood behind her, their backs stiff and straight, faces solemn. It was the first photograph they'd ever sat for. She remembered how their backs had ached as the cantankerous photographer manipulated their positions just so. The whole thing had been a miserable experience. The girls had laughed about it later, but oh what a wretched day that had been. She lifted the frame and studied her sister's face. A stoic, smileless countenance stared back at her, yet life and passion still sparkled in the young girl's eyes.

How could Anna put the mantle of responsibility on her sister's shoulders? To neglect her own obligation and thus pass it on to Emmaline? Wouldn't doing so make her just as bad as her father? She wouldn't dream of treating her beloved Emmie in such a way. There was no other choice. Her shoulders drooped. "For you, dear sister," she whispered and returned the photo.

She inhaled a shaky breath and straightened her shoulders. "So be it," she spoke to the wall.

The room itself seemed to suck in a gasp. "Beg pardon, daughter?" her father asked, his voice tentative. Hopeful. It churned Anna's stomach.

Mother came and placed a hand on Anna's shoulder.

Anna turned. "Alright. Since you were robbed of a son for an heir, I will do what I can to secure our family's station."

Mother cupped Anna's cheek, her own eyes wet with tears. "Dear girl."

Father puffed his pipe and nodded. "Good show."

Mother shot him a look.

He cleared his throat and shifted his weight. "Eh . . . thank you, daughter."

Anna nodded and lowered herself to sit behind his desk. She slid a piece of stationery to the center and scratched out her word of acceptance. When she finished, Father snatched it up, put it in an envelope, and addressed it.

"I'll have Owen take this to the post first thing." He tucked it into his coat pocket. It seemed as if he might break into a dance of joy at any moment. But he kept his voice level. "You're doing the right thing. Oh, and Annabeth? Don't utter a word of this to your sister. Especially about the money."

Anna stared at him blankly for a moment. "Of course," she mumbled and rose, numbness clouding her heart and mind. Suddenly overcome with fatigue, she excused herself and made for her room.

CHAPTER
28

Stephen set two plates of stew on the table and called for his father. Seamus shuffled in and lowered himself with a grunt.

"Stew, eh?"

Stephen murmured affirmation. As he sat, the letter in his pocket from Mister Sánchez jabbed his leg. The ironworks company had received his acceptance, and they eagerly awaited his arrival. With the increased traffic in the shop since Annabeth's coming, Stephen had been able to save enough to pay for his journey over, as well as set himself up fairly comfortably. He wouldn't be living like a king, by any means, but he would certainly be at least as comfortable as he was now. And with Annabeth progressing in her smithing skills, as well as her innate gift for connecting with people, Stephen finally felt comfortable enough leaving his father and his livelihood. At the thought of Annabeth, Stephen's mind drifted back to their last true encounter. His arm tingled where she'd laid her hand. He recalled the look in her eyes, and the tenderness toward her that had risen in his own heart. His pulse quickened as he pictured her face, her eyes, her lips. Yes, the sooner he started his new life, the better, as it seemed the only way he could keep himself distanced from the woman was to leave the country. The only hurdle remaining was to actually tell his auld man.

"Ye're a million miles away, lad." Seamus spooned a heaping bite of stew into his mouth.

Stephen chuckled. If only his father knew how right he was. "Da, there's something I need to tell ya."

His father swallowed hard and set down his spoon. "Oh? There must be somethin' in the water."

"What d'you mean?"

Seamus shook his head. "You first."

Stephen shifted in his seat, his heart clenching. He hadn't imagined breaking the news would be so difficult. Or perhaps he had, which is why he'd put it off for so long. He ran his hand up the back of his head and down his face. "Well, ya see, Da, I've had an offer."

Seamus's brows lifted, but he said nothing.

Stephen inhaled deeply and continued, "From an ironworks company. In Spain."

Seamus pushed his lower lip up and nodded. "Ironworks, ya say?"

"Aye." Stephen nodded. "And . . . I've accepted it."

The spark in Seamus's eye snuffed out for a moment before returning. "I see." He picked his spoon back up and scooped another bite of stew.

"I should've told ya sooner. But I didn't know how." Stephen stared at his untouched stew. "I'm sorry."

Silent, Seamus bobbed his head while still he ate. Confound it all, did nothing ruffle the man? Did Stephen's contributions mean nothing? Sure, he didn't want to fight about it, or see his father grovel and beg, but some sign that he would be missed would be nice.

"Well," Seamus said at length, "will that make ye happy?"

Stephen sat back in his chair. "Pardon?"

Seamus waved his spoon in the air. "This move, to the continent. Will it make ya happy?"

"Aye," Stephen said, sighing. "I believe it will." He shifted again and leaned forward on the table. "Da, ya know how I feel about love, about the 'legend of the ring.' And now with the Brits takin' over everything after Tommy . . . I can't stay. I simply can't."

"If ya say so," Seamus replied, his focus still on his bowl.

Stephen watched his father for a long moment. Finally, resigned to the fact that his father wasn't going to add any more to the conversation, Stephen turned his attention to his own meal.

The silence intolerable, Stephen found something else to say. "Did ye say there was somethin' ya needed to tell me?"

Seamus carried his bowl to the basin. "Aye. I wanted to let ye know that I told Anna."

Stephen twisted in his chair. "Told her what?"

Seamus met Stephen's gaze, his eyes moist and shining. "I told her about Marie."

"What? Why?" Stephen shot to his feet. "You had no right!"

Seamus shrugged. "Maybe. Maybe not. But she needed to know, and it was becoming clear that ya weren't gonna do it yerself."

Stephen gaped at his father, his voice refusing to cooperate. "Did you ever stop to think perhaps there was a reason for that, Da?" he finally asked.

"*Psh!* Seafóid!"

"No, it's not nonsense! What good did you think would come of tellin' Lady Annabeth about the most humiliating experience of my life? Huh?" Stephen crossed his arms over his chest.

Seamus looked at Stephen, compassion filling his eyes. "She needed to know why ye were pushin' her away." He spoke as though dealing with a spooked horse.

Stephen threw his hands in the air. "I pushed her away, because I *wanted* her away!"

Seamus wagged his head. "Nae, lad," he said, his voice calm, "ya pushed her away 'cause ya love her."

Stephen fell back as if he'd been socked in the gut. "Nope. Uh-uh. Ye're wrong. And I'll prove it." He yanked his coat from the hook on the wall. Jabbing a finger in the air toward his father, he added, "I'll put a stop to your cockamamie schemes right now."

"What're ya gettin' at, son?" Seamus's voice remained even.

"Before you can finagle any more fanciful ideas about my heart, I'll go tell that girl I'm leaving, closing any door you might believe is there for"—he flapped his hand and glowered as he growled out—"love."

Stephen stormed from the room, ignoring his father's calls behind him. He ran to the stable and saddled his horse. He pulled a sugar cube from a canister on the sill and held it up for the steed to see. "This is yours, Capall, if ya fly to the manor." The stallion snorted and stamped his foot. Stephen flung himself over the animal's side and into the saddle. At the slightest tap from Stephen's heels, Capall took off.

As they galloped through the night, Stephen swallowed against the burning in his throat. What was his father thinking? Him in love with Lady Annabeth? Preposterous! He didn't believe in love. He hated it. Hated that so many could be duped by the idea of it. He didn't love her. He couldn't wait to be rid of her! He would go now and tell her of his new job. Tell her that he was leaving.

Suddenly, Capall stopped short and reared up. Stephen had been so lost in thought, he nearly came off the horse. "*Tóg go bog é*, boy. Take it easy. What is it?" At that moment, the faintest whiff of smoke crossed his nose and an orange glow over the tree line caught his attention. How had he missed that? He looked to the road and his gaze followed it toward the light. That led the way to . . . *níl*!

Stephen urged Capall on and turned up the road to the manor house. The horse's hooves barely seemed to touch the gravel as they flew to the De Lacys' home. When they rounded the corner, Stephen's heart dropped. The whole house was engulfed in flames.

A mass of shadowy figures huddled around the fountain in the front garden. Owen ran by, tugging a horse behind him, all the while shouting orders to the stable lads. Stephen urged Capall in their direction.

"Mister Jennings!" Emmaline ran up to him, her hair in a loose braid over her shoulder, her dressing gown cinched around her waist. "Please help!"

He continued sweeping his gaze back and forth across the scene as he answered, "Of course. What can I do?"

She grasped his pant leg, desperation flooding her eyes. "It's Annabeth. We can't find her."

Stephen's attention shot to the blazing house, his breath catching in his chest. "Lady Annabeth!" he shouted into the night.

Lady De Lacy approached as Stephen jumped off Capall's back. Her face was smudged, clean tracks where tears had washed the soot away traced her cheeks. "Please, we can't find her anywhere."

Stephen removed his jacket and bolted toward the house, the screams of the family and servants echoing behind him. Ignoring their calls not to go in, he burst through the front door, the smoke immediately choking the breath from his lungs. He ripped the sleeve from his shirt and pressed it over his nose and mouth.

All was blackness, the deafening roar of the inferno surrounding him.

"Annabeth!" The thundering blaze swallowed his voice.

Unable to breathe, he lowered down and crept through the front hall. A loud crash sounded behind him. He glanced back. The ceiling had caved in, blocking the entrance.

"Annabeth!" he called again. He heard nothing but the fire. With every second she didn't respond, desperation and smoke threatened to choke his own life from his grasp.

When he got to the stairs, a thud from above caught his attention. It wasn't another cave-in. Someone was up there. He lifted his eyes to the ceiling and cupped his hands around his mouth. "Annabeth! Can you hear me?"

Cinders rained down and singed his scalp and arms as he climbed the steps. He slapped them out, but soon there were too many to deal with.

Once at the top, he stopped and listened. Another thud. A muffled cry. Running in the direction of the sounds, he whispered a prayer for a miracle. *Let her be here. Let her be alive.*

"Annabeth!" he called as he clambered down the hall. "Annabeth! Where are you?"

"Here!" The weak voice came from behind a door near the top of the stairs.

Stephen made his way back to the door, but when he tried to enter, it wouldn't open. "I'm here, Annabeth! I'm coming." Stephen barreled into the door with his shoulder. No movement.

"Stephen!" Annabeth called. "Help me! Please!"

"I'm here! But something is blocking the door. Can you get it?" A choking cough racked Stephen's chest after he hurtled himself at the door again. There wasn't much time now.

"It's an armoire." Annabeth's voice was closer. "It fell over." She sounded so weak. So very weak.

"Can you move it? Even just a little?"

She coughed. "I think so."

Another crash. The floor in the room behind him collapsed to the level below. "Hurry! We haven't much time!"

Muffled grunts came from behind the door. Then the screech of wood on wood. "That's . . . all . . . I . . . can . . . do."

Please let it be enough. "Stand back!" Stephen backed up as far as he could without the flames behind engulfing him. Then, with all the strength he could muster, he ran and slammed his body against the door once more. It, and the armoire behind, gave way just enough for Annabeth to crawl over and squeeze through the opening.

Stephen held his hands out to her.

"Oh, thank you! Thank God!" Annabeth's voice was hoarse as she scrambled over the charring wood. At last, she stood next to Stephen in the hall. The floor below them creaked. He grasped her hands, longing to make sure she was unharmed, but there wasn't time.

"We must hurry!" He scooped her up with one arm under her shoulders, the other under her knees.

With flames lapping at his legs and cinders dropping on their heads, he sprinted down the stairs. Annabeth's head lolled against his shoulder.

"My family," Annabeth said weakly. "They're out front by the fountain."

"No good." His lungs burned. "It's blocked. We have to go out the back."

Navigating a maze of furniture, beams, flames, and collapsed ceiling, he finally wound a path to the back door. He burst outside, the fresh air hitting them like ice on a summer's day. He continued sprinting until the blistering heat no longer threatened to snuff the very life from their bones.

Once he felt they were a safe distance away, he lowered her gently to her feet. He gripped her shoulders to steady her, while he looked over her hair, face, and hands, checking for burns.

Singed hair plastered her forehead and cheeks. He swept it away, taking care not to brush the blisters that were no doubt hiding underneath. Gently, he stroked his fingers over her cheeks, tracing her nose, her chin. "Are you alright?"

She nodded.

He wanted to shout his relief from the rooftop, but the jagged lump in his throat stole his words. Once more, he swept his hands over her hair, down her shoulders and arms, not yet convinced she'd escaped unscathed.

"Stephen—"

Her voice brought his gaze to match hers. He cupped her cheeks in his hands, his eyes searching her face, relief washing over him that she truly was going to be alright. "Anna."

He leaned down and brushed a kiss on her forehead. Then her cheek. Then touched his lips gently to hers.

Anna stood still for a moment before she wrapped her arms around his neck and melted into his kiss. Then their embrace deepened with such fervor it stole his breath.

When they pulled away, she smiled. "You called me Anna," she said.

The edges of his mouth turned up. "So I did."

She cupped his cheek, joy radiating from her face. Something in her eyes struck Stephen. As though waking from a dream, the fog seemed to lift from his mind, and he froze.

In that moment, he realized what he'd done. No. This can't be. It wasn't fair—not to her, or to him. "I . . . I'm sorry."

"Don't be." She gazed at him through lowered lashes, her cheeks a becoming shade of pink, even through the darkness and soot. She leaned up and slowly met his mouth with hers again.

Stephen hesitated, but the feel of her lips on his was too much to resist. He pulled her even closer yet, pressing further into her kiss, wishing time would stop, that he might be lost in this moment with her forever.

Another crash from the house jolted his mind back to the present. *Be strong, man. Let go. Don't do this to her—or to yourself.*

Though it pained him deeply, Stephen pushed her away gently, shook his head, and straightened his shoulders. "Nae, Lady Annabeth. I beg your pardon, truly," he said, breathless. "I want nothing more—we . . . I . . . can't—your family will be waiting for you."

He squeezed his eyes shut and swallowed hard. He then gestured to the path leading to the front of the house. "After you, m'lady."

She searched his eyes as a shadow of confusion swept across her face. When he looked away, she nodded and stepped past him.

CHAPTER
29

Anna touched her fingers to her smoke-lined lips, still tingling from Stephen's kiss. She had convinced herself such a moment would never come. Now that it had, she couldn't help the joy welling up in her chest. Nor could she help the longing she had to kiss him just one more time. But then his face had changed. Try as she might, Anna couldn't decipher the shadow that had fallen over him after he kissed her. Perhaps he was afraid of what Father would say or do. Perhaps he surprised even himself with the outburst. Whatever the reason, Anna couldn't shake the fear that slowly wound its fingers around her heart—that even though she'd already accepted Lord Corning, and a romance with Stephen would never be, she feared what he felt as they embraced had been instant regret. As they walked, Anna watched Stephen from the corner of her eye. His posture was impeccable and his gaze forward, jaw set—just as composed and stoic as the day they met. Would that Anna could rein in her own emotions so easily.

As they rounded the corner, Mother's voice caught Anna's ear. "Oh, Annabeth! Thank heavens!" Then she ran—this woman

Anna had never seen move faster than a brisk walk—and swept Anna into her arms. Sobs shook her mother's body as she muttered her thanks over and over in Anna's ear.

"I'm alright, Mother." Anna returned her mother's embrace, relishing the warm contact she'd lacked growing up. "Thanks to Mister Jennings here."

Releasing Anna, Mother turned to Stephen. "Mister Jennings." She grabbed his hand and shook it vigorously. "How can we ever thank you enough for saving our Annabeth?"

Emmaline, Father, and the rest of the household staff joined them. Shouts of joy rippled through the group as they approached Anna. Katy stepped up, eyes glistening, and grabbed Anna's hand, squeezing it before retreating to the back of the group with the rest of the staff.

"Indeed." Father extended his own hand. "Very good of you." His eyes were red and glistening, and white tracks snaked their way through the soot on his cheeks. Was he crying? Anna had not once in her life seen her father cry.

In the distance, the wail of the fire brigade grew louder. Stephen bowed shallowly from the waist. "It was my honor, Lord and Lady De Lacy. I am glad Lady Annabeth was found safe. I must now take my leave."

Anna's jaw dipped open, and she gripped his elbow. "Must you? So soon?"

"Yes, I'm afraid I must. Thanks be to God the family is safe." Stephen glanced at her and then the house. "I only wish I could say the same for your home."

The family turned in unison to face the manor—or what used to be the manor. The flames, while still strong, were dying down. The roof had crumbled in on itself, and black stains licked the outer walls above the shattered windows. Then, for the first time, the reality of what they'd lost hit Anna. She lifted a hand to her mouth. An arm slipped around her shoulder, and another around her waist—Mother and Emmaline. "Oh, Mother. Whatever shall we do?"

Mother sniffled and dabbed at her eyes. Father stepped up in line with them. "There's a smaller cottage farther up the property," he said, defeat lacing his voice. "We can stay there."

The pounding of hooves and the shrill whine of the siren jolted the group's attention from the burning manor house. It was then Anna noticed Stephen had gone. She had no right to love him, nor to expect his love in return. In a few short hours, her acceptance of Lord Corning's proposal would be hastening to England. She was all but spoken for now. And yet, she couldn't help but feel she'd lost her home and her heart in one horrible moment.

Chaos had erupted in the city. Policemen and RIC soldiers scurried through the streets. Bells clanged, shouts echoed through the cobbled city, and gunfire ricocheted in the distance. Surely this wasn't all because of the fire? Stephen struggled to guide Capall through the melee. Just before reaching the stables, a man called out to him.

Stephen turned. "Paddy! Are ya alright?"

Paddy lumbered over. "Aye, for the most part. The chipper's a bit worse for wear, but nothin' what can't be fixed." His eyes widened as he took in the sight of Stephen. "What happened to ye?"

Stephen explained about the fire, but impatience niggled in his belly. He needed to get home.

Paddy's mouth flopped open. "What? They burned it?" Anger clouded his face, and he ground a fist into the palm of his other hand.

"'Tis a right shame." Stephen adjusted the reins in his hands. "I'm sorry, Paddy, I must go."

Paddy waved him off. Stephen couldn't be sure, but he thought he heard the man mutter, "They're going to pay."

Urging Capall onward, they eventually made their way back to the stables, grateful to find them intact and unharmed. Usually Stephen would see to the steed's water and food himself, but concern for his father trumped routine. He slipped a pound to the stable boy and rushed home.

As he burst into the flat, relief washed over him to find his father pacing in the kitchen.

"*Buíochas le Dia!*" Seamus pulled Stephen into a firm embrace. "Thanks be to God, lad. Are ye alright?"

Stephen winced, noticing for the first time how his shoulder ached where he'd rammed it to free Anna. "I am. Ye? What's going on?"

"Aye, I'm fine. Ya won't believe it." Seamus's eyes widened as he looked fully at his son for the first time. "What happened? Where were ya?"

Stephen looked at his soot-covered hands and clothes, assuming his face looked just as bad. "Galway Manor. It burned."

"*Ó, a mhac go deo!* Man alive!" Seamus's hand flew to his forehead. "And Anna? Is she alright?"

Stephen nodded. "Aye." He swallowed hard, still trying to recover his breath. "I had gone out there to tell her my news. About the job. When I got there, the whole place was ablaze. Lady De Lacy came to me and said they couldn't find Annabeth. So . . ."

Seamus's mouth pulled into a circle. "And ye went in after her?"

"I did. She was trapped upstairs. It was touch-and-go fer a bit, but I got her out."

"Oh, God be praised." Seamus sank into a chair. "And the rest of the household?"

"All safe and unharmed, thankfully." Stephen went to the basin and cleaned the soot and ash from his hands.

Behind him, Seamus asked, "What're ya not telling me, lad?" Stephen could almost hear the twinkle in the man's eye in his voice.

His first response was to hide what had happened. But he was tired. Tired of lies and half truths. Tired of the constant wedge between him and his father. And much as he hated to admit it, his father had been right about Anna—and he was tired of fighting that too. Drying his hands, he joined his father at the table.

Stephen scratched at a stain on the table while he gathered the gumption to tell the truth. "I . . . I kissed her." His cheeks warmed—from embarrassment as well as the memory itself—and he shrugged. "After I got her out of the house. Once I could see she was alright, I was so relieved that . . . I kissed her. I couldn't help myself."

Seamus hooted and slapped his knee. "Ya don't say! Well, ya know what I say to that?" He leaned forward, his eyes sparkling with delight. "It's about time!"

Stephen couldn't help but laugh. He also couldn't help but concede to himself that his father was right. Having Anna in his arms, and being in hers, felt like coming home. She fit just perfectly in his embrace, as if she were made to be there.

Seamus's eyebrows danced. "And? What did Anna say?"

Stephen's cheeks flushed again, and he couldn't stop his mouth slipping up to the side. "She kissed me back." *Boy, had she ever.*

Seamus beamed and gave Stephen's shoulder a congratulatory slap, sending a shock of pain through him. "Well, I don't want to say I told ya so, but . . ."

"Yeah, yeah. Steady now, auld man." Stephen waved his hand, then gripped his own shoulder. He rolled it a few times, hoping to ease the discomfort. His grin retreated as he replayed in his mind what had happened next.

Seamus's smile faded, and he crossed his arms over his chest.

"Oh, lad. What did you do?" The tone of his voice was reminiscent of Stephen's childhood, when he'd committed some egregious gaffe.

"I left!" He stood and paced the room. "What hope could I have with a woman like her? She's a lady and I'm . . . Irish!"

"*Psh*! The world's changin', boyo. And them royal types are more open to such things. For goodness' sake, the man let his daughter spend all her days with you, if you recall."

Stephen shrugged. His father had a point. But doubt still plagued him. Gnawed at him. How could he be certain she felt the same way?

"What're ya so afraid of?" Seamus joined him on his feet.

"I never thought I'd love again. I don't believe in love, Da."

Seamus laughed. "Don't ya?"

"No, I don't! At least . . . I didn't."

Seamus pursed his lips and sighed. "Alright, then. I'll ask again. What're ya so afraid of?"

Stephen turned to look at his father. His eyes glued him to his place, searching, waiting for an answer. He wouldn't understand even if Stephen told him.

When Stephen's answer was long in coming, Seamus lifted his brows, urging a response.

Though certain the auld man wouldn't understand, what good would it do not to try and explain? His father had been more right than Stephen could've ever guessed thus far. Perhaps he could help now too. "How can I be sure?"

"Sure? About what?"

Stephen huffed and tossed his hands. "How can I be sure that she meant it? What if she was just swept up in the relief of the moment? Or . . . didn't know how to refuse my advances?"

"Oh, my dear boy." Seamus rounded the table and placed his hand on Stephen's shoulder. "What did she do after ya kissed her?"

Stephen thought back to the moment. He could almost feel her arms around his neck, her lips pressed to his. He recalled the look in her eyes then lifted his gaze to meet his father's. "She smiled."

A slow grin spread across Seamus's face. "Well, there ya go! No woman smiles after she kisses a man by mistake." He tightened his grip on Stephen's shoulder and shook him lightly. "Did she do or say an'thing else?"

"Well . . ." Stephen couldn't help the smile that deepened on his face. "She . . . she kissed me again."

Seamus's mouth fell open and a guttural laugh bubbled out. "Now, d'ye need any more convincing than that?" His eyes were wide, and his hands splayed in front of him, palms up.

Stephen ran his hand over his head, ignoring the sore and singed places along his scalp. "I s'pose ye're right."

"O'course I am." His grin widened. "I'm yer da."

The pair shared a laugh as Seamus put the kettle on for tea and Stephen excused himself to go clean up. As he traversed the steps to his room, he slipped his hand into his pocket. A folded paper poked his hand. As he pulled it from his pocket, his heart sank.

Stephen sank onto his bed, not caring that his clothes were still covered in ash and soot. He turned the still-folded paper over and over in his hands. How could he have been so daft?

Moments later, Seamus's voice floated up the stairwell, summoning Stephen to tea. Numbly, he washed and put on a clean set of clothes. Before returning to the flat, he slipped the paper back into his pocket. He slunk down the stairs, each step like a weight around his neck.

"We'll have to think carefully how we approach His Lordship," Seamus was saying when Stephen re-entered the kitchen.

Stephen lowered himself into a chair and dropped his head into his hands. When Seamus turned to the table, he stopped short. "Oh, what is it now, lad?"

Stephen slipped the folded paper from his pocket and slid it across the table to his father.

Seamus took the page, opened it, and sank into his seat as he read. "Right. The job." He lowered the letter and lifted a sympathetic gaze to Stephen.

"How could I be such a daft fool?" Stephen rocked his head side to side in his hands.

"Ye're no daft fool, lad. Ye're in love." He leaned closer to Stephen. "Aren't ye?"

A low groan rumbled from Stephen's throat. "Aye."

Seamus poured the tea, and when Stephen looked up at him, he could almost see the wheels of thought turning.

"So, you love Anna." He took a sip of tea. "And it seems Anna loves you"—another slurp—"or, at least, she liked kissin' ya." He winked.

Stephen chuckled and shook his head.

"And it seems ye've already accepted the position in Spain?"

"Aye." He let his head slip from his hands to rest on the table itself.

"Hmm." Seamus scratched his jaw. "And . . . if ye were to stay here—which I know ye're not—but *if* ya did, ye'd want to marry Anna?"

Stephen puffed a breath. How had he gone from keeping the woman at arm's length to thinking of marriage in the matter of a few hours? If he was honest with himself, though, it had been much longer than that.

Of course, Lord De Lacy would never allow his daughter to marry a lowly Irish tradesman. And even if he did, Stephen had already accepted the apprenticeship in Spain. It was all set, except his departure date—which was looking to be sooner rather than later. Never mind the fact that the idea of making himself vulnerable again to the kind of rejection Marie had given him was nauseating. He shook the thought from his head. No, Anna was not Marie. That much was abundantly clear. The truth was, if De Lacy would allow it, and Anna would have him, he wanted nothing more than to spend his life with her.

"Aye," he said at length. "I would want to marry her."

"So marry her!" Seamus stared at Stephen, grinning like his cat'd just had kittens.

"Da, yer not lis—"

"Nae, lad, it's ye who won't listen. So ya have this new job an' ya have a woman ye love. Ye don't have to just settle for one." He shrugged. "Ask Anna to go with ya." He said it so matter-of-factly. As though it was a simple thing.

Could Stephen really do that? Would it work? They'd have to marry first, of course. Would there be time for that? What if De Lacy refused? Stephen laid all his questions bare for his father.

"Land sakes, no wonder ye're so cranky all the time, what with yer mind going a mile a minute like that." His father blew out a breath and rubbed his hand over his face. Then he chuckled and shook his head. "Look, if De Lacy refuses you, at least then you'll know. And if Anna wants you badly enough, she may even break with tradition and marry ye anyway. But ye'll never know if ya don't ask. And ya don't want to spend the rest of your life wonderin' and regrettin' if you don't."

Stephen let his father's words sink in. Had the man always been so wise in ways of love? Of course, he was right. What was the worst that could happen? That Anna or her father would refuse him. If that happened, he could still take the new job and start a new life like he'd always planned. But if they agreed . . . oh, he could hardly let himself hope they would. But if they did, he would start a life he never dreamed he would have. "Alright."

"Attaboy." Seamus grinned and refilled his tea.

A clatter outside drew Stephen's attention. He rushed to the window just in time to see two RIC soldiers dragging a man off, his cart overturned in their wake.

"What on earth's going on out there?" Stephen jabbed a thumb in the direction of the street.

"Och! Wait 'til I tell ya!" Seamus joined Stephen at the window and flipped the drapes closed. "Auld Constable Edward Krumm—y'know, that Black 'n Tan who tossed McGee's store a fortnight ago. He lost his mind and went amok at the train station. He started firing his revolver in all directions. A bunch o' lads tried to stop him, but several were shot in the process. Poor Mulvoy was killed."

Stephen craned his neck to look at his father. "*Ceard*? What? Where did you hear this from?"

"Father Dowd told me hi'self! Rumor has it there was an IRA man on the train bringing munitions for an attack on one of the RIC barracks."

Stephen spun on his heel and headed for the door.

Seamus grabbed his arm. "Stay, lad," he crooned. "They're not aimin' for Galway City. Somewhere else in the county. 'Sides, they're already investigatin' the claims. But they're sayin' that's what made Krumm fit to be tied. He was apparently trying to cut them off at the pass but just went mad instead."

Stephen's mind spun, trying to make sense of all that had happened. There had been other attacks and scuffles of late, and they certainly seemed to be increasing in frequency and intensity. The conversation Stephen had overheard among the men at the pub that night a few weeks back floated to the front of his mind. Was that the "bigwig" they'd referenced? The timing of it all made a little too much sense. And hadn't they started to say something that sounded like "manor," before stopping short and changing to "out west"? There were too many connections for it to be a simple coincidence. He held little doubt now that the fire at the De Lacys' had been part of it all. Indignation burned in his chest. He rubbed his head, wincing as he disturbed the fresh blisters dappling his scalp. And he whispered a prayer for the strength not to do something stupid in return.

CHAPTER
30

William stared at Sergeant Townsend, who was once again standing before him at attention. How often would his visits be? Just over a week since the fire, it seemed the sergeant now arrived almost daily with more disturbing news.

"What is it now, Townsend?" He set his glass down on the desk and gestured for the man to stand at ease.

"Sir." Townsend removed his cover and relaxed his stance to the customary position. He then cleared his throat, obviously uneasy with whatever message he carried. "More attacks, Your Lordship."

William waited for the rest of the report. When Townsend failed to continue, William sighed and placed his hands on his hips. "On which side?" Must he pry every piece of information from the man?

"Both, milord. The RIC and IRA are in a battle of retaliation, it would seem. And ever since Krumm was killed, and then the fi—" His voice trailed off.

"And then my family was attacked, and our home destroyed." William ground his teeth, desperate for the dull ache to leave the base of his neck. It had plagued him ever since that dastardly assault on his family.

Townsend shifted. "Exactly, milord. Since that dreadful night, things have been picking up in both number of occurrences and ferocity. In the city it is still fairly quiet . . . other than the incident at the train station, of course." He hesitated. "But villages like Tuam, Spiddal, and others are seeing . . . daily occurrences. And, begging your pardon, but it shows no signs of slowing down."

William pursed his lips. He wanted to throttle the man, but that would do no good. It wasn't as though Townsend himself had committed the attacks. "You have the report, I presume?" he said, keeping his voice taut but cool.

"Yes, Your Lordship." Townsend produced the papers and held them out to William.

"Very well. Leave it with me." He gestured to his desk. "You may go."

Townsend clicked his heels, did as instructed, saluted, and quit the room.

William circled around and sat. He stared at the report then shoved it aside. All thoughts of the war were clouded by his desperate financial situation. Whether the fighting would help or hurt his prospects was yet unknown. Therefore, it held less priority for him at present. Though, if he failed to get things with the attacks under control, it was bound to be the final nail in his proverbial coffin.

He drummed his fingers on the desktop, itching to cradle the precious numbers of his ledger. Tracing the numbers, seeing the tidy rows, and knowing it all arrived at the correct sum brought him comfort. A sense of control. Never mind that the money was already gone, but now the ledger itself was gone. *Everything* was gone. And precious little was left with which to hearten himself.

Arching his back, he shifted in the foreign chair. The room

now serving as his office was much smaller and mustier than the one he'd had in Galway Manor. Though a pleasant enough house, De Lacy Place, as it was now called, was certainly not outfitted as nicely—or comfortably—as he was accustomed to. But it would get the job done. It had to.

Like his previous study, windows made up the bulk of the front wall. The view from this room, while still scenic, was not near as grand. Like everything, it would seem. He'd always assumed his life—and his family—would get grander as time went on. And once he'd been given the land in Ireland, he'd hoped he'd find a way to turn things around and finally achieve that grand dream. He'd never been more wrong.

He swept his gaze around the room. A crystal decanter caught his eye. *At least this place has whiskey.* Pouring himself a large glass, he settled in front of the fire. The first long draw imbued him with courage as it drained from his lips down to his stomach. The warmth radiated in his belly, and an idea bloomed right along with it.

"Perhaps," he said aloud, "this is all a blessing in disguise." Yes, this might work. The ledger was gone, true. But the record book's destruction meant all evidence of his failures was gone as well. Sure, the banks would catch up with him sooner or later, but without written proof that the money was gone, he might have enough time to find a scheme to earn it back. At least some of it, anyway.

A grin spread across his face as the idea took root. Downing the last of his drink, and eager to scratch out his thoughts before they left him, he retrieved paper and pen from his desk and set to work.

Light dappled the floor of the small sitting room in De Lacy Place. Anna repeatedly wound and unwound a string from the fringe of a scatter cushion around her finger. She'd removed the small decorative pillow from the settee in order to free a place to sit down but found comfort in hugging it close, so she kept it on her lap. From the corner of her eye, she could see Mother pretending to read a book.

"It's easier to read if you actually look at the words." She lifted her eyes and allowed a coy smile to turn her lips.

Sighing, her mother crossed the room and joined Anna on the settee. "Are you sure you're alright, my dear?" She touched a tender finger to a blister hiding at Anna's hairline.

"I'm fine, Mother." Ignoring the continued stinging in her throat and chest, she gently grasped her mother's hand and lowered it. "Please stop fretting."

"I'm not fretting. But when I think what might've happened to you had Mister Jennings not showed up . . ." She pulled a handkerchief from her sleeve and held it to her mouth.

Anna's heart hitched. Her mother had been more tender and caring toward her in the days since that fateful night than she'd been Anna's whole life. She nodded and said, "I've had the same thoughts." Many nights of late, sleep had eluded her as she turned that exact scenario over and over in her mind.

"It's quite the miracle he arrived when he did. Did he ever say why he was coming out this way? We certainly weren't expecting him."

Anna furrowed her brow. "Come to think of it, no, he didn't."

"'Tis a shame he had to take his leave so quickly. We were all in such a state of shock, we weren't able to thank him properly."

Anna's mind wandered back to the kisses they'd shared. *I think he knows of my gratitude.* Her face warmed at the thought.

"Perhaps . . ." Mother paused, her lips forming a thin line. "It might take some convincing for your father to come around, but . . . perhaps we can invite Mister Jennings for tea. That way we might express our gratitude accordingly."

Anna's heart lifted at the proposal. "What a wonderful idea! Do you really think Father would be against it?"

Mother sighed. "It's difficult to say, really. Under normal circumstances, I wouldn't dream of even approaching him about it."

"But saving his eldest daughter's life is hardly a normal circumstance."

Mother met Anna's gaze with a smile. "Precisely."

Anna tried to imagine what it would be like to have Stephen in their house, even this one of lesser grandeur. It had seemed so natural when she'd sat at his table for tea. She'd seen and learned so much about him and his community. Somehow, though, it was a very different thing to imagine him in her world. And Galway Estate felt very much like a different world, indeed, from the one that lay beyond its borders.

"I only wish we didn't have to entertain him *here*." Mother grimaced and waved her hand in an arc.

Anna resisted the urge to roll her eyes, thinking about the small flat Stephen shared with his father. Not to mention the rustic homes she'd seen in the Claddagh. "He won't feel this house is beneath anyone, Mother, I assure you."

"I suppose so." She sighed again and thumbed the pages of her book. "Leave your father to me. I'll see to it he agrees to let the man come just this once. That will give us time to find suitable attire for such an occasion."

Anna smiled and set the cushion aside. She took her mother's hand. "Thank you for thinking of inviting him. It's very kind of you."

"It's not every day your firstborn is saved from the clutches of a fiery, certain death." She bussed Anna's cheek and rose. "You just get some rest. I know Doctor White said you'll be alright, but it's still been only days since the incident and your lungs need time to recover."

Anna couldn't deny the burning that still plagued her insides, even several days after the fire. She didn't cough all the day long anymore, but she certainly tired more easily than before. She adjusted herself on the settee and rested her head back. Closing her eyes, she tried to drift off to sleep. But all she could think about was Stephen's kiss.

CHAPTER
31

Seamus's whistling entered the room long before he did. Stephen chuckled and shook his head as he finished polishing the latest ring they'd created.

"Well, boyo, ye're in the big time now," Seamus declared as he came in and tossed his hat onto the peg.

Stephen kept his gaze on the rag and ring in his hand. "Oh?"

Seamus thrust an envelope in Stephen's face. Intricate cursive writing flowed across it. Frowning, Stephen set the ring down and opened the letter. He'd hardly read the greeting when his father began pestering him.

"Well?" Seamus asked, impatience flooding his voice. "What do they want wi' ya?"

Stephen considered stalling just to toy with his father. But his own excitement trumped his desire to tease the man. "They—the De Lacys, that is—request the honor of my presence the day after tomorrow for tea at De Lacy Place." He glanced at his father. "That's where they are staying now that the manor is destroyed. Her Ladyship writes that they wish to thank me 'for the service of rescuing Lady Annabeth.'"

225

Seamus blew a low whistle. "Well, well, well, looks like some-one's gotten himself in their good graces." He offered an overly emphasized wink and clapped Stephen on the back.

"So it would seem." Stephen absently rubbed his sore shoulder and let his thoughts drift to Anna. He wondered, for the thou-sandth time, how she was getting on. Were her burns healing? Did her energy return? Did she regret everything that happened that night? It seemed ages since he'd seen her. Even longer since they'd worked together in the shop. They'd both done a fine job of avoiding one another the past month or so. The thought of her both endeared and disconcerted him. How would he ever deserve her?

"So, are ya gonna use this opportunity to ask Lord De Lacy for his blessin'?" Seamus's question shattered Stephen's thoughts.

He dropped the letter to the table and shot his gaze to his father's. "Wha—I dunno." He stared down at the document again, his stomach flopping.

"Seems the perfect time, ya know. What with them fallin' over themselves to thank you for savin' their wee girl." Seamus waggled his eyebrows at Stephen.

"True." He scratched his head when he suddenly remembered what Anna had said. "Aw, sugar!"

"What, lad?"

"It's no use, Da. She's *geallta*, remember? Promised to some high-falutin' lord in England." Stephen dropped his hands to his sides.

Seamus puffed a sigh as he thought over what Stephen said. Suddenly, his eyes lit up and a grin split his face. "She said she had been *offered* a proposal."

Had his father not listened to anything he just said? "Right, exactly."

"But she didn't say she'd accepted it." He tapped a finger to the side of his nose. "In fact, if I remember correctly, she specifically said that she hadn't."

Stephen clapped a hand to his forehead. "Bless me, ye're right! She did say that." He walked a circle around the room before returning to the table. Retrieving the letter, he reread every word. Could it really be possible? He had seen respect shining in Lady De Lacy's eyes when he returned Anna to her side. But would that be enough given the current state of affairs between Ireland and Britain? Not to mention Stephen's station—or lack thereof.

"Do ya think I really have a shot?" He turned hopeful eyes back to his father, all the while doubts whispered in his mind.

Seamus shrugged. "What have ya got to lose? The worst they can do is say no. And if that be the case, ye're just back on the original path ye'd set for yerself." He smiled. "And ye'll never know if ya don't ask."

"Annabeth, dear, don't pick at your nails. It's so unladylike." Mother waggled her hand toward Anna's, her face the image of disapproval.

"Sorry, Mother." Anna dropped her hands to her sides and surveyed the mess of fabric swatches, ribbons, and sample menus strewn about the sideboard in the drawing room. She picked up a swatch of coral silk and turned it over in her hands.

"That one is a bit gauche, don't you think?" Mother sidled up to her and slipped the fabric into her own grasp.

Anna sighed. "I suppose."

"This one is much prettier." She handed Anna a square of blue tulle.

Anna scanned the heap of wedding paraphernalia once more. "Is all of this really necessary?" She swept her hand over the fabrics.

"*Tsk*! Of course it is! It's the wedding of Lady Annabeth to the grand Lord Corning, fourth Earl of Camberwick! Everything must be perfection."

"But the wedding won't even be here in Ireland. Why bother choosing all this now? Besides," Anna said, lowering her voice to a whisper, "can we afford it?"

Mother's shoulders sank for a brief moment before returning to their proud, stiff position. "That matters not. Lord Corning will foot the bulk of the bill. And until then, we need only keep up appearances."

Is that all that mattered in the House of Lords? Appearances? Would they truly prefer to spend their family into utter ruin, and pretend they didn't, simply to save face among the gentry?

Anna sighed. The more time she spent away from the court and all its trappings, the more tiresome that lifestyle and its expectations grew on her. It hadn't been so wearisome when she believed in the purpose of it. But now, especially after the fire and what she'd seen around Galway, she struggled to see what purpose it really served. And she was ashamed to have ever put so much stock in such trivial things.

Clearly unaware of the war raging in Anna's heart and mind, Mother held two swatches of fabric up to the light. "I think we should do the blue tulle with yellow silk accents for the tables. Don't you agree, dear?"

Anna swallowed a scream. There was no denying marrying Lord Corning was the only way to save her family from certain financial and social ruin. But after getting even the briefest taste of what love could be like, the longer things went on, the more trapped she felt. Galway Estate felt less a sprawling oasis and more a prison with each passing day.

The image of Stephen's face floated across her mind's eye. She could almost feel his arms around her, his hand stroking her cheek, concern and relief filling his eyes. Anna shook her head and brushed her hands over her arms to rid them of the memory of his touch. It would do no one any good to dwell on what could never be. No matter what feelings she held for him, it simply would never be possible for Anna to pursue a relationship with him. She had to find a way to put Stephen out of her mind. Out of her heart. The sooner she not only accepted her marriage to Lord Corning but anticipated it as her lot, her responsibility, the sooner she could be free of the shackles of her love for Stephen. Filling her still-healing lungs with a resigning, cleansing breath, she turned her attention fully to the plans at hand.

"Quite right, Mother. Good choice. What about the menu?"

Stephen sat hunched over the workbench, the dim, flickering light tricking his eyes as he carved the intricate design. They ached as he strained to focus on the wax that was covered in a weave of Celtic knots, which appeared to dance in his hands along with the candlelight. He straightened and stretched. He could really stand to light the lamps but couldn't risk attracting attention to himself. Nae, to his project.

It was bad enough his father had seen through him. He couldn't give the auld man the satisfaction of knowing what he was up to. He bent over the wax once more, examining the knots he'd scraped out with care. Now, he moved to the crown, then the hands. The heart he carved more deeply, in order to have room to seat the gem.

Once the design was finished, he molded the clay around it, taking care not to distort his handiwork. Setting the clay in the fire to dry, Stephen pressed the heels of his hands to his eyes. Thank goodness it was almost done. Too much more work in the dark like this would ruin his sight for good. He poured himself a fresh cup of tea, knowing from years of experience that by the time he was half done, he could pull the clay from the heat.

And by the time his cup was drained, it would be cool enough to handle and pour the metal into.

Following his plan, he carefully poured the molten silver into the mold, his heart quickening as he thought of the finished product. Of what it meant. As the metal cooled, he turned his attention to the gem. Polishing it and shaping it to just the right specifications, he worked long into the night.

At last, just when the metal was almost cool, but still pliable, he gently lifted the heart-shaped diamond with tweezers, set it in place, and bent the prongs down to hold it. He dunked it in the cold water, dried it, wrapped it in a soft cloth, and hid it away, knowing this night his dreams would be filled with visions of the moment he at last presented the ring to its rightful owner.

CHAPTER
32

◆ July 29 ◆

A pewter sky hung low over the city as Anna made her way to the Jenningses' shop. How much time had passed since she'd been to see them? To work? The damp air weighed on her shoulders, much as her apprehension weighed on her soul. She'd not seen Stephen since the night of the fire. She absently touched the now flattened but still tender blister at her hairline. Would the thought of that night always conjure such a muddle of emotions? The horror of seeing her new home destroyed tempered by the joy of discovering Stephen's feelings for her. Uncertainty over the sincerity of his feelings balanced with the sheer delight of his kiss.

Now, she found herself nearing Shop Street and the place where she'd fallen in love with this country, with these people. With Stephen. Would she be able to keep him at arm's length? She'd settled in her heart that it was her duty and destiny to marry Lord Corning—and she felt more and more resigned to that decision with each passing day. But now, as Stephen's shop came into view, her confidence faltered.

Straightening her shoulders and bolstering her courage with a deep breath, she whispered a prayer for strength. She entered and found Stephen in the smithing room, his back to her, reading a letter. "Good morning."

Stephen spun to face her, his eyes bright. "Anna," he said.

Heavens, he was even more handsome than she remembered. Dark stubble speckled his jawline, the dimple returning in earnest as he smiled at her. His steely eyes bore into hers, and her resolve threatened to crumble under his intense gaze. "Good morning," she repeated, at a loss of what else to say.

"Are you well?" He approached her and dabbed the mist from her face with his handkerchief.

Anna closed her eyes at his touch, even through the fabric as it was. *Steady.* Unable to find her voice, she nodded.

"I'm glad to hear it," he uttered, voice thick with emotion. He stepped back and retrieved the letter from the table, all the while never breaking his stare.

"What's that?" Anna's voice returned. Only just.

"I'm glad you asked. There's something I've been meaning to tell you." He handed her the paper and shifted nervously as her eyes scanned the page.

Confusion knotted her stomach. "I don't understand."

His grin deepened. "You see, I've been offered an apprenticeship in Spain. And I've accepted it."

Anna fell back a step. "I see. That's quite the boon for you." She forced a shaky smile on her lips.

"Yes, well, it's a grand opportunity. And it's a very prestigious company. A chance fer me to really expand my skills." He stepped closer to her, warmth radiating from his presence.

"Of course. You'll do very well, I'm sure." She couldn't lift her gaze from the page, the words on it swimming through the tears that threatened to spill from her eyes. He stepped closer still, the distinct scent of musk and leather washing over Anna.

Her skin chilled to be so near him. She managed to glance up at him briefly. He smiled down at her, his eyes alight.

Why would he be treating her thus if he was only going to leave? Was he relieved to no longer have to endure her presence? Or perhaps he was thankful for a way out of an impossible love, just like she was. Though she'd not expected such news, and it pained her to think of his absence, of course it was for the best. They both had their paths set before them. With Stephen—and his eyes . . . and lips—so far away, it would be all the easier to move on with her new life as Lady Corning.

"What's the matter? Are ya not happy for me?" He placed his hand over hers.

Anna's skin came alive at his touch. She willed her voice steady and forced her eyes to meet his. "I am, of course. Truly. Congratulations."

He lifted the corner of his mouth and then opened it as if to speak when Seamus bounded into the room.

"Ah, Anna, I didn't hear you come in!" He gestured to the letter in her hand and Stephen dropped his. "So, he's told ya, has he?"

Anna nodded. "It's lovely news."

"I'd say it is! Though, I must say, ya look like someone's killed yer dog." He chuckled before adding, "Have ya given yer answer yet, lass?"

Stephen gripped his father's arm. "I've told her about my new job, Da." He pinned his father with a look. "That's all," he added under his breath.

Curious. What could that be about?

Seamus scowled at his son. "Oh? Nothing else?"

Stephen shook his head. Father and son looked at one another, seemingly having an entire conversation with their eyes.

"Stephen's told me about his opportunity to study ironworks in Spain. It's wonderful for him," Anna interjected.

Seamus sighed. "Yes, yes, it is. Very well, then." Wagging his head, he shuffled toward the shop. "C'mon, ye two, there's work to be done," he called over his shoulder.

Anna and Stephen stood in silence. Anna searched his face, unsure what she saw there. Stephen closed the gap between them until there was but a handbreadth separating them. His gaze traveled from her eyes to her hair to her lips.

"Are ya sure you're alright?" Concern clouded his eyes, but they remained tender and kind. So unlike the hardness she'd seen there just a few months ago.

Anna nodded. To have him so near unnerved her in the most glorious way. It took all her strength not to lay her head on his chest and ask him how things were ever going to be well with her. To beg him to whisk her away from the life that lay before her—a life she had never wanted but had no choice but to enter into. Alas, that could never happen. She had to be strong. For her family's sake. For Emmaline's future, if not her own.

She took a measured step back and cleared her throat. "Will we see you tomorrow for tea?"

Stephen kept his eyes fixed on hers. "Aye. Ye will." His cheeks pinked, and the corners of his mouth lifted slightly. "Please express my gratitude to yer mother for the invitation."

Anna nodded and Stephen gestured to the door, suggesting they should follow Seamus into the shop. He turned back at the doorway and sent her a playful wink. Goodness, it was going to be a long day.

CHAPTER
33

The sunlight scattered on the bay like so many diamonds on blue velvet as Stephen, astride Capall, made his way to Galway Manor the following day. Or De Lacy Place, more like. Breathing in the fresh, salty air, Stephen made no attempt to stop the grin that spread across his face. For the first time in recent memory, his heart was as light as the lambs that gamboled in the patchwork fields studding the landscape. Though the uncertainty of how Lord De Lacy—and even Anna, for that matter—would react to his proposal churned within, the weightiness of the grudges and bitterness he'd carried for so long was beginning to wane. Coming out of the fog of such misery, he wondered now why he'd chosen to hold on so long to something that all but poisoned him, leaving him the shell of the man he was meant to be.

As he turned up the road to where the manor once stood, he couldn't help but sober at the sight. The sad pile of rubble sat alone in the shadows of the surrounding wood—it mirrored the way his spirit had been the past several years. A new sense of gratefulness welled up in him for the redemption that was just beginning to renew his heart. Whispering a prayer for such redemption for the De Lacy family, he continued past the charred remains, eyeing the corner where he'd stood with Anna. Where the wall around his heart finally cracked and he embraced what he'd been fighting by embracing the woman he'd grown to love. Smiling at the memory, he slipped his fingers into his waistcoat pocket and let them linger on the cool silver hiding within. Drawing in a deep breath to bolster his nerves—and his courage—he urged Capall on.

Cresting a small hill, he caught sight of the cottage. Stephen pulled the reins, slowing his steed to a halt. Rolling hills and knolls ambled before him as far as the eye could see, flanked by dense woods. Sheep roamed freely, some grazing the sun-warmed grass, others bedded down in the deep shade of the trees. In the center of the valley stood De Lacy Place. Stephen couldn't help but laugh. The so-called small cottage still looked to him every bit a palace. Though not nearly as grand as Galway Manor, the almost-mansion still had two floors, and likely a basement or cellar. Large windows stretched tall on each floor, and a pillared portico greeted guests in style.

A flight of doubt winged through Stephen's heart. He could never provide such a life for Anna, no matter how successful he became in either jewelry making or ironworks. Slipping his fingers inside his pocket once more, he let the cool metal ground him—to remind him of all he'd been brought through to get to this point. He'd let doubt and skepticism rule his life for far too long. In order to make a new start, he had to make new choices. And he chose in that moment to refuse to let the sense of inadequacy take root, and instead to hope, to trust, that if he was meant to be with Anna, it would be so.

As Stephen approached, Owen met him out front and greeted him.

"Welcome, Mister Jennings." He took the lead rope from Stephen.

"Hello, Owen. It's good to see you."

Owen tipped his hat. "And ye. Ciara will show you inside." He nodded to the open front door. Then he took the reins from Stephen. "And I'll see to your horse."

Ciara appeared in the doorway and ushered Stephen inside. He removed his flatcap and squinted against the darkness of the interior. They didn't have to walk long before Ciara turned and opened a door. "Lord and Lady De Lacy, Mister Jennings." She gestured for Stephen to enter.

The ornately outfitted room stretched tall with papered walls adorned with all manner of portraiture. In the center of the room, a small table, draped in an intricate white cloth, was set for tea. A tiered silver tray laden with sandwiches was flanked with smaller dishes of tiny cakes and biscuits.

"Mister Jennings." Lord De Lacy approached him, hand outstretched. The men shook hands. "You remember Lady De Lacy and Lady Emmaline. And, of course, Lady Annabeth."

"Of course." Stephen bowed shallowly from the waist. "Thank you so much for the invitation."

"Not at all," Lady De Lacy said, a warm smile gracing her face. "Do come in. Katy will be in shortly with the tea."

Stephen thanked her again and approached Anna. "Lady Annabeth." He ventured a quick wink, relishing the way her cheeks pinked when he did.

"Mister Jennings." Anna dipped her head. "'Tis good of you to come."

"If you'll excuse me for a moment, Mister Jennings." Lord De Lacy angled toward the doorway, the shadow of someone behind it darkening the opening.

"Yes, of course." Stephen nodded.

"I'll just call Katy for the tea," Lady De Lacy said. Emmaline busied herself adjusting a large arrangement of flowers in the far corner of the room.

For all intents and purposes, Stephen and Anna were alone.

He had intended to say more to Anna when she read the letter yesterday, but he lost his nerve. It had done his heart good to see she seemed upset at the idea of his leaving. And it spoke to her own goodness that she efforted to be happy for him. But he had to know. For all the love that had grown in his heart for Anna, doubt still plagued him. He didn't want to risk asking her father's blessing if she had no interest in what he proposed. Resting his hand lightly on her elbow, he guided her toward the window.

"Anna," he kept his voice low, "there's something I wanted to ask you."

Her brows lifted. "Oh?"

"Yes." He cleared his throat. "And I'd like to try to do so while we're alone." His gaze flitted to Emmaline, still busy with the flowers. "Well, mostly alone."

She looked at him, curiosity filling her eyes.

"As you know, I've accepted the job in Spain. But there's more to it."

"Go on," she said.

Stephen's heart pounded in his chest. His ears thrummed and sweat prickled his palms. He steadied his nerves with a breath. "You see, I want you to come with me." He dropped his gaze to his feet before bringing it back up to meet her eyes. He searched them for a beat before swallowing hard and adding, "As my wife."

Anna's eyes grew as wide as saucers, and her jaw fell open as she sucked in a breath. Blinking, she seemed at a loss for words. "Stephen, I—"

"Sorry about that," De Lacy's voice boomed as he swept into the room in grand fashion. "I'd forgotten a document I needed to get in the afternoon post." He sauntered to the table as Lady De Lacy and a housemaid carrying a tray of tea things followed him. "Now, Jennings, do sit."

Stephen shot a look at Anna. Could she give him no indication of her answer? Her cheeks were flushed and she laced and unlaced her fingers, her gaze set on the floor. When she said nothing, he forced his attention back to her father. "Thank you, sir—er, m'lord," he managed to say.

The group arranged themselves around the table. Katy poured tea for each one, starting with Stephen, then brought the dishes of food around before retreating to stand against a wall as though trying to disappear into it.

"So, Jennings, how goes things in the jewelry business?" Lord De Lacy asked.

"Very well, thank you. Your daughter has learned—and con-tributed—a great deal." He smiled at Anna, who studied her plate. "Which reminds me, Lady Annabeth. Paddy McGinnty was in yesterday and asked me to send his regards. Nora loved the brooch."

"Oh, I'm very glad to hear that," she said, and took a sip of tea, seeming careful to avert her gaze from ever fully meeting his.

After several minutes of small talk about the weather and the cucumber sandwiches, Lady De Lacy turned her attention to Stephen.

"Mister Jennings, we cannot say enough how grateful we are to you for Lady Annabeth's rescue." She took a sip of her tea, added another lump of sugar, and stirred.

Lord De Lacy murmured an affirmation, his eyes fixed on his teacake.

"It was an honor, Lady De Lacy." Stephen looked at Anna, his heart quickening. "I'm glad I was able to get to her in time." *More glad than you could possibly know.*

"Yes, quite," Emmaline added. "Do regale us with the tale of how it happened. Everything was so chaotic that night, and all our recollections seem so muddled."

The four De Lacys ceased eating and turned their full at-tention to him. Taking a sip of tea to soothe his suddenly dry throat, he worked to compose his thoughts. "Well, it's quite straightforward, really. I was on my way to Galway Manor, but when I arrived, I found it ablaze." He went on to recount how Her Ladyship had informed him Anna was missing, and how he'd run inside to find her. When he reached the point of the story when he realized where Anna was, his voice caught. He coughed, hoping to convince his listeners it was a stray crumb rather than emotion that wedged in his throat. He looked at Anna, who glanced away when his gaze met hers.

"The door was blocked," he continued, "so, with Lady Annabeth working on her side, and me ramming the door repeatedly, we were able to free it enough for her to escape. She was understandably weak, and it was unclear at the time if she was injured in any way, so I carried her down the stairs and out the back door since the ceiling cave-in had blocked the front." He looked at her again, his stomach flipping. She met his gaze now and time seemed to stand still. He wondered if she was reliving that moment after they escaped. He most certainly was. The edges of her mouth lifted slightly, and her eyes flitted back toward her parents. Stephen blinked to try and shake the memory, then cleared his throat. "And that was it. I brought her back to you."

Emmaline erupted into applause, the sound muted by her gloved hands. "Bravo, Mister Jennings." She looked to Anna and lifted her brows, a wide smile stretching across her face.

"Yes, jolly good," De Lacy offered, returning to his tea.

"Quite," Lady De Lacy added, a single brow floating up. "Only, one question remains unanswered."

Stephen's collar suddenly felt tight, and he resisted the urge to tug at it. What else could they want to know? Surely Anna hadn't told them about their kiss? "Yes, m'lady?"

"You never said why you were coming this way to begin with. We weren't expecting you." She looked at him intently, brows lifted, though no judgment clouded her eyes.

Should he divulge the real reason? He'd been coming, of

course, to tell Anna he was leaving, with no intention of asking her to join him. He'd ridden out in anger. He still intended to inform them of his leaving. Only now he wished to take their daughter with him. Was the time right? With the tea and sandwiches nearly extinguished, likely little time remained beyond now.

He wiped his serviette across his mouth and set it on his now-empty plate. Shifting in his seat, he turned his full attention to her. "Actually, m'lady, it's curious you should ask. I was hoping to bring it up to ye today."

De Lacy set his teacup down heavily, looking Stephen in the eye. Did he suspect what Stephen meant to say next?

"You see, Your Lordship, Your Ladyship, I've been offered an apprenticeship at a prestigious ironworks company in Spain, and I've accepted it."

"Well done, you," Lady De Lacy said. Emmaline hummed in agreeance.

"Thanks, m'lady." He shifted in his seat and took a sip of tepid tea. *Quit stalling, man.* "I was hoping . . . well, that is, I'd like to bring An—er, Lady Annabeth—with me."

A collective gasp rose from Lady De Lacy and Emmaline. Smile lines creased Emmaline's face behind her hand. No such smile graced Lady De Lacy. "I see," she said coolly.

Lord De Lacy balled up his napkin and tossed it on his plate. "You can't be serious, man."

"I am, m'lord."

"If you think," De Lacy said, rising to his feet, "that I am going to allow my daughter to flit off with some . . . some . . . Irishman and tarnish her impeccable reputation, you are sorely mistaken."

"Father, please." Anna's voice was small and meek.

De Lacy lifted a finger to silence his daughter but kept his stare fixed on Stephen. "No."

Wishing he'd made his true intention more clear, he tried

again. "I understand, m'lord. I don't want anything improper. I'd like to bring her along . . . as my wife."

"Your wife?" De Lacy exploded. "Have you gone mad? Do you mean to tell me you don't see anything improper about that prospect?"

Stephen looked to Anna, his heart swelling. "Perhaps I have gone mad. But the fact remains that I love your daughter, and I want to marry her. I see nothing 'tall improper about it. In fact, just the opposite." Stephen stood and looked De Lacy in the eye. "And I'd like to ask for your blessing."

De Lacy's face reddened, and his cheeks trembled. "You shant have it!" He rounded the table. "You shant! Don't you know, Lady Annabeth is—"

"Papa, please." Anna rose and circled around to her father, placing her hand on his arm. "Please. Let me speak with him."

De Lacy's flushed face beaded with sweat as he breathed heavily through his nose. He leaned closer to Stephen, his jaw clenched.

"Papa." Anna maneuvered to put her face in front of her father's. "Please."

De Lacy looked to his wife, who nodded once. "Very well," he spoke through gritted teeth. "So long as you know, you will *never* have my blessing for *anything* except to leave my family, and Lady Annabeth, alone for good."

Stephen fought to keep his own temper under control. "Understood." He swallowed. "M'lord."

De Lacy stared Stephen down another long moment before sniffing haughtily and turning on his heel. "Katy, stay!" He barked as he marched out of the room and beckoned Lady De Lacy and Emmaline to follow.

Anna touched Stephen's sleeve and gestured for them to sit on a settee on the far side of the room.

As they settled, Stephen angled to see her eyes. Red and shimmering with unshed tears, they undid him. "Oh, Anna. I'm sorry to have upset you."

She shook her head and dabbed at her tears with a handkerchief. "'Tis not you."

Stephen looked to the door where De Lacy had taken his leave. "I must say, yer father took it even worse than I was expectin.'"

She closed her eyes. "No," she said, her voice cracking. "It's not that either."

"What is it then, darling?" He shifted closer to her, but she only scooted away from him. Confusion bore down on him, stifling his breath.

Anna was quiet for a long moment, choosing her words or composing herself, Stephen couldn't tell. Eternity seemed to yawn between them until, at length, she sniffled and lifted her gaze to meet his. "Do you remember what I told you? About Lord Corning?"

Stephen's gut twisted. "Aye. You said he'd proposed, but you hadn't responded."

She looked at him, searching his face. "Stephen . . ."

The way she said his name was like a punch in the stomach, and all the air left him. The room spinning, all the pieces began to fall into place in his mind. "You've accepted."

Her face crumpled and she nodded. Pressing the handkerchief to her nose once more, her head fell forward. Her shoulders shook as silent sobs racked her body.

The sight of her weeping cut him to the quick, and he warred between the urge to sweep her into his arms and console her and the anger and hurt that roiled at her rejection. Had he misread her—both the night of the fire and at his news yesterday?

"Oh, Stephen," she uttered finally. She reached for his hand, but he couldn't allow himself to hold on, not even for another moment. He recoiled from her touch, and her face buckled again, silent tears rolling down her face.

"I should go." The words barely eked from his throat. He stood.

"Don't you see?" She grabbed his hand now and looked up at him, eyes pleading. "I don't have a choice."

He kept his gaze on the door and yanked his hand free. "There's always a choice."

CHAPTER
34

Capall couldn't gallop fast enough for Stephen's taste. The sun beat down on his back, heating him to the core, stoking the pain that smoldered there. The sea that had lifted his spirits so on the journey out now taunted him with its serene beauty. So like a woman was the sea, luring a man with her beauty and charm only to unleash the devils swimming deep within.

How could he be so daft? A woman like Anna couldn't love him. And if she did, she wouldn't stoop to the level of marrying such a man as he. No, he'd been duped yet again, only affirming his earlier convictions. Love was a farce. A fallacy contrived to control weak men and deceive lonely women. Perhaps he should be grateful to Anna for revealing this to him before it was too late. 'Twas his own fault, really, for not learning from Marie. Marie, Anna, it mattered not now. It was all the same, all folly and foolishness. But the nature of it was enough to send a man "back the way," as his father oft said of those driven to the asylum by age or addled mind. He rode far past the road that led to home. For hours he urged Capall to fly.

At length, the sun dipped into its watery bed. Both man and beast exhausted, Stephen turned his horse back toward the city. Reaching down and offering Capall an extra, coveted sugar cube, he enticed the animal to fly once more. Not bothering to rein in his steed as he entered the city, Stephen and Capall sped through the cobbled streets, the animal's hooves pounding, matching the striding of his own heart. He guided the steed down to the Claddagh. Shrouded in the dark and mist of an Irish night, the place was empty save for him. He tugged the reins and Capall slowed to a trot. The horse shone with sweat, and his breathing was still heavy. Stephen slid off before the animal could stop. He pulled the ring he'd crafted from his pocket, the silver and diamond twinkling in the mist. He balled his fist around it and hoisted his arm back to throw it into the bay. But he stopped short. Three times he tried to heft the cursed ring into the water, and thrice he couldn't bring himself to follow through. He gripped it so hard the prongs and facets dug into his skin. He gritted his teeth and dropped his hand to his side. Was he so weak that he couldn't even rid himself of such a token? A daft fool he was, and a daft fool it seemed he would remain.

He heaved himself back into the saddle and bade the beast to gallop. Paying no heed to late-night strollers or pub-crawlers, he hurried to the stables. A hastier cooling down of a horse had never before been seen. Once Capall was seen to, more or less, Stephen made his way home. Bursting into the shop and bounding up the stairs to their flat, two at a time, Stephen scarcely knew what to do with himself once he got to the kitchen. Opening a cupboard, he looked for nothing in particular, and then slammed it shut. He stomped a circle in the room, kicking the leg of the table as he passed. Blast it all.

"Oy! I don' know who's there, but ye best be makin' yer way out 'afore I call the *gardaí*!" Seamus rounded the corner brandishing a cane and a collapsed umbrella as both weapon and shield.

Stephen growled. "Easy, Da. Don't call the police. It's only me."

Seamus lowered his makeshift weapons. "Stephen! What're ye like?"

Stephen stopped in front of the window, crossing his arms, huffing and puffing from his tirade.

"Things went . . . not well, I'd wager?" Seamus joined his son at the window.

Stephen shot him a look from the corner of his eye.

He lifted his hands in mock surrender. "Alright, boyo, don't take it out on yer auld man. Why don't ye tell me what happened?"

Stephen hung his head. Heaving a sigh, he said, "She said yes."

A hoot rang through the rafters as Seamus clapped his meaty hands together. "She said yes! So what's got ye stompin' 'round here like a bull in a china shop?"

Stephen turned to look at his father over his shoulder. "She said yes to *him*," he ground out through clenched teeth.

"Oh." Seamus wrapped an arm around Stephen's shoulder. "My dear boy, *tá brón orm.*"

The tender gesture and Seamus's attempt at comforting words in their mother tongue softened him. "I'm sorry too."

"Did she say why? I thought she was sweet on ye?"

Stephen forced a sarcastic laugh from his lips. "Ya thought wrong, Da." His head sank low again, along with his voice. "We both did."

Instinctively, Seamus shuffled to the kitchen and put the kettle on to boil. "She didna say why?"

Stephen shook his head. "Anyway, De Lacy wasn't havin' it."

"*Psh!* Ya knew he wouldn't. Not right away, anyway. It was up to Anna, and her mother . . . or that sister of hers . . . to help convince him." The kettle whistled and Seamus poured it into the teapot. "But she wouldn't, eh?"

Stephen shrugged and scratched his head.

"Och, lad." Seamus crossed his arms. "Ya lost yer head, didn't ya?"

Stephen's remorseful gaze met his father's and he grimaced.

Seamus quirked his mouth and angled his head to the side. "Ya didn't give out to the poor girl, did ya?"

Stephen huffed. "No, Da."

"But ya didn't stick around long enough to hear her side of it?" He jammed his arms folded across his chest.

Stephen scoffed. "Side? What side? Her side is she chose *him*, not me."

"Did she though?"

"O'course she did! She told me herself, 'I've accepted,'" he mimicked a feminine voice and tossed his hands in the air. *Well*, he thought, *she'd practically said it.* What was so difficult for the auld man to understand?

Seamus kept his gaze fixed on Stephen's face. "From where I stand, acceptin' something is far different than choosin' it."

"Och! There's no point in splittin' hairs."

Seamus shrugged and poured the tea. "If ya say so, son. Just . . . give it a wee bit more time. Ye're not leavin' for a coupla weeks yet. Things may turn around." He set a single steaming cup of tea in front of Stephen and left the room.

Anna rolled to her other side, willing her tears to cease. How much longer would they flow? Apparently a week since Stephen's visit still wasn't long enough to stay her grief. When her tears refused to comply, she gave in to them and her body rocked with sobs. She mourned so much—the life she thought she was coming here for, the idyllic worldview she'd once held, and the love she carried for a man she never thought would return it and now could never hope to have anyway. She mourned the idea of a life tethered to a hateful, vindictive old man, fearing she herself would succumb to the bitter clutches of regret and anger.

A quiet knock sounded on the door. Anna rushed to dry her face, but before she could bid the person enter, the door opened and Emmaline slipped inside.

"Oh, my dear sister, I thought I heard crying." Emmaline hurried to the bedside and placed the back of her hand on Anna's forehead. "Are you ill?"

"No." Anna sniffled. The tears welled up again, and despite her attempts to stop them, her face crumpled. "And yes." She clapped a hand over her mouth to keep from wailing.

"I do wish you'd open up to me. You've not been the same since Mister Jennings came to tea."

Sweet Emmie, so naive. Had she truly not noticed Anna's state until now?

Emmaline smoothed a shock of hair from Anna's forehead. "In truth, you've not been the same since the fire. Then again, none of us have. Such a dreadful thing."

At the mention of the fire, the memory of being in Stephen's arms flooded Anna, and she collapsed into another fit of tears. "I'm . . . I'm sorry," she said between sobs.

"Oh, sweet Annie, please don't apologize. I'd like to help." She handed Anna a handkerchief.

"If only you could." Anna dabbed her eyes and blew her nose. "'Tis no use now."

The pair sat for several minutes in relative silence, broken only by Anna's sniffling every few seconds. Then, Emmaline placed a hand on Anna's knee. She worked her mouth as though trying to find just the right words. Finally, she said, "Does . . . does it have anything to do with Stephen's proposing?" Her eyes shone with compassion and curiosity. Did the girl truly not know? Anna only stared back at her but couldn't answer. Emmaline continued, "I must admit that it came as quite a shock for Father ... for all of us, really."

"Quite the shock for me too," Anna said. "I had no idea that's what he intended." Her gaze drifted to the candle on the bedside table as the events replayed in her mind. "I do wish Father hadn't reacted so strongly. Poor Stephe—Mister Jennings."

Emmaline regarded Anna again. "What did you say to him after, when we all left the room?"

Anna shrugged. "I simply told him about Lord Corning."

Emmaline cocked her head. "But I thought he already knew."

"He did." Anna paused. "That is ... he knew Corning had proposed." She grimaced. "But at the time, I made quite a big deal of the fact that I hadn't accepted."

Emmaline's eyes rounded. "Anna, why did you do that?"

"Because it was true then." Her shoulder lifted and lowered. "And he'd accused me of being dishonest. I felt he should know the truth." She shifted her feet under the covers. "And then, once I'd accepted Corning, there was no indication of Stephen's feelings for me. In fact, he went to great lengths to push me away. At least, it felt like he did. So, I saw no reason to inform him of the change."

Emmaline nodded. "But why did you tell him in the beginning? When you and I spoke of him before, it was clear you found him attractive. But when you accepted Corning, I assumed you'd put Stephen aside. Besides, you don't owe him anything."

"Don't I?" Anna searched her sister's face. "He opened his home to me, let me in to his livelihood. He spent his time teaching me his family's trade when I had no real right to know such things."

"Goodness." Emmaline rocked back and tucked her feet underneath her. "I didn't realize it was quite so ... involved."

How could she help her sister understand all that her time there had meant—what they had done for her? "The Misters Jennings saved me from boredom and opened my eyes to a whole new world." She looked to the draped window, as though she could see the Claddagh from here. "Emma, the Irish people are some of the warmest, kindest, most creative people I've ever met. Working with the Jenningses revealed to me a new way of life—one built around community and relationship rather than position and title."

"Well, when you put it like that." Emmaline shifted, her kind eyes meeting Anna's. "Is that what vexes you so? It's been days since he came for tea, and your melancholy has only grown in that time."

Anna looked to the door, ensuring it was closed. Scooting closer to her sister, she lowered her voice and admitted, "He kissed me."

Emmaline's jaw dropped, her eyes widened, and a giggle escaped her lips. "He did? When?"

Anna let her mind drift back to that night. She tingled at the memory of his lips on hers. "The night of the fire."

Emmaline sucked in a breath. "Truly?"

Anna nodded. "After he rescued me, he brought me outside. At that point neither one of us was certain if I was injured or not. When we confirmed I was not, he seemed awash with relief. And"—she dropped her head, heat rising up her face once more—"he kissed me."

Emmaline giggled again and covered her mouth with her hand. "And?" she whispered. "Did you kiss him back?"

Anna tilted her head, new tears stinging her eyes. She touched her fingertips to her lips, and her lids drifted closed. An ache filled her chest as she nodded.

"Oh, sister. Do you love him?"

At the question, the reality of the depth of Anna's love for Stephen washed over her, and she crumpled again. Emmaline wrapped her arms around her.

"Shh, shh," she crooned. "My dear, sweet Annie. No wonder you're so upset."

Anna righted herself and shook her head, steadying her tears with a deep, raggedy breath. "I have no right to love him."

Emmaline's posture slumped, and she cocked her head. "Do you not?"

"How could I? Father would never agree to it, even if I weren't promised to Lord Corning."

"Have you told Father how you feel?"

Anna shook her head. "What would be the point? You saw his reaction when Stephen asked for his blessing. It wouldn't matter."

"I don't know," Emmaline said as she stood and circled the room. "That was before he knew your heart. All he saw was a chancer looking to break the social ceiling and get his hands on the fortune of a lord."

Anna's heart sank. She'd forgotten about the fortune. It was the whole reason she was marrying Lord Corning to begin with. Clearly Emmaline still didn't know, and Anna couldn't bring herself to shatter her sister's world along with her own. "I appreciate the thought, Emmaline. But it won't work."

Emmaline flopped down to sit on the bed again. "Were you at least able to explain to Mister Jennings why you couldn't marry him?"

"I told him I had accepted Lord Corning's proposal, but he doesn't know the full reason I accepted." *And neither do you, dear sister.* "Anyhow, he's leaving."

"Ah." Emmaline lifted a finger. "But has he left yet?"

"I'm not sure, to be honest. He didn't tell me his exact departure date. I just know it was soon."

Emmaline crawled over to join Anna under the covers. She snuggled close and whispered, "Go to him. Explain why you're marrying Corning."

Sweet girl, ever the romantic, could never understand. And how could she without all the facts? "Emma—"

Emmaline lifted a hand. "Hear me out. Tell him why you're

marrying Corning. Then explain that you are going to withdraw your acceptance, because I will be marrying Corning instead."

Anna clutched a hand to her chest. "No, Emma. I couldn't let you. We've been over this."

Emmaline shook her head. "I couldn't let *you*, dear sister, walk away from a marriage of love for a marriage of duty. Not when I am willing to enter into that world. The life I've always dreamed of—courtier life with its titles, land, social calendar."

"Titles aren't everything, Emma." Anna looked to the door. "And it can all disappear in an instant."

Emmaline sighed. "I don't mean to sound so shallow. It's not about my pride. I believe there to be purpose behind it all . . . and I see how I can live out my purpose through it. Most of all, I don't love anyone else and I have no other prospects. You do."

"Well, I can't argue with that," Anna said. "And you're very kind. I know you want a life in that world, but I cannot in good conscience thrust you into it with a man like Corning. I've given my word. At any rate, Father will never allow it."

"He dotes on you, Anna." Emmaline angled so she could take her sister's hand.

Anna shook her head. "He wishes I were a son."

Emmaline pursed her lips. "Perhaps, in a way. But I don't believe he truly does. He's smitten with you, which is why he's allowed things like this apprenticeship. What other lord would allow such a thing for his daughter?"

Anna mulled it over. "Maybe. But what if Lord Corning refuses you? It would be no small humiliation to him for me to withdraw my acceptance . . . especially in order to marry an Irishman."

"That's a risk we have to take." She shrugged. "Besides, if he refuses me, then we will finally be free of him."

Anna took her sister's hands in her own and squeezed them. If only she knew. Their family would never survive if Corning severed himself from them. If only Emmaline could know the whole truth. But it wasn't Anna's place to share her family's dire circumstances. Not when Father had forbidden it. She purposed in her mind to agree to Emmaline's plan but never bring it to Father, and then tell her sister that Stephen refused to accept it. Her conscience niggled at her at the thought of lying, but in this case, it was in everyone's best interest. A bending of the truth wouldn't be so bad to protect the people she loved, would it?

CHAPTER

35

The world seemed dampened of late. All the things that brought Anna joy now held not even a sparkle of interest to her. Even the steaming cup of tea before her lacked taste and its usual comfort. Despite Katy's best culinary efforts, the breakfast held no appeal for Anna, but she ate it dutifully anyway. The satisfied sounds coming from her family around her spoke to the shrouded senses Anna now endured. Was this what love felt like? Or was it merely love lost?

Having taken as much food as she could stomach, she excused herself to her room. As she walked absently down the hallway, Katy came rushing to her.

"Beggin' yer pardon, m'lady. Might I have a word?"

Concern flooded Anna. Katy, while a welcome member of the household staff, rarely ventured to the private quarters. "What is it, Katy? Is everything alright?"

Katy glanced up and down the hall before pulling Anna into a rarely used room. "Beggin' yer pardon, m'lady."

Impatience flowed through Anna. Desperate to hear whatever news Katy held, she fought annoyance at the girl's delay for the sake of airs. Anna efforted to keep her tone neutral. "So you said. What is it?"

"I've just heard that Mister Jennings is leaving," Katy said, breathless.

Anna released a sigh. Was that all? "Yes, that's true. He's taken a new job on the continent. To Spain, I believe."

Katy shook her head and grasped Anna's hands. "No, m'lady. I mean, he's leavin' *now*. Today."

Anna recoiled. "What? How do you know?"

Katy closed the gap between them, her voice low. "I had to run into the city this morning to fetch somethin' fer dinner tonight, and I saw the ship. Then I saw Mister Jennings stacking trunks outside his shop."

Alarm coursed through Anna. Today? How could he be leaving today? She wrestled back and forth with surprise that he hadn't already left and sadness that he was leaving so soon—and without saying goodbye. Even as the thought had formed, she knew it foolish to hope he would have. The pair hadn't spoken in the two weeks since his visit.

Katy continued. "I know he proposed—I was standing by in the room, if ya remember. In case I needed to serve another round o' tea." She shrugged, a sheepish look on her face. "And I've heard ye cryin' these last weeks. I thought you might want to know in case you wanted to say goodbye"—she leaned closer and looked Anna in the eye—"or convince him to stay."

Heat flooded Anna's cheeks. Was it so obvious to the world how she felt about Stephen? Equal parts mortified that her heartbreak would be so evident and grateful that Katy had made sure to share this news, Anna remembered her plan to pretend that she'd presented Emmaline's arrangement to Stephen. Now, though, faced with the reality of Stephen's departure, the dam burst in Anna's heart, and it seemed impossible not to go to him. Emmaline's plan was a bit far-fetched, but not so much so that it was guaranteed to fail. She had to give it a try. She'd hasten to the city, explain the situation to Stephen, and accept his proposal—if he'd have her. Anna thanked the girl and rushed back downstairs.

Popping her head into the drawing room, she called out a breathless, "I'm headed to the city," then burst outside and instructed Owen where to take her.

Stephen counted his trunks and cases. Everything seemed to be in order and in its place.

"Have everything?" A smile played on Seamus's face, but his eyes seemed heavy. Sad.

Stephen nodded. "Aye." He sighed. "And I've spoken with Tadhg and Billy from the stables, as you and I had discussed. They'll be by a couple times a week to help ye with cleanin' the shop and the like."

Seamus gave his son's shoulder a squeeze. "I'll be fine. I already told ya a hundred times over."

"I know. But I want to make sure ye're cared for."

"I know ya do. Ye're a good lad." Seamus swiped at his nose and squeezed Stephen's shoulder once more. "I've looked after meself for a dog's age, boyo. I'll be right as rain. G'on now and have yer adventure. I'll just go check one last time to make sure ya didn't miss anything." He turned and shuffled back inside.

Stephen lifted his gaze to the horizon, squinting against the midmorning sun. The world around him carried on in a blur of activity and commotion, as though Stephen's heart wasn't breathing its last on the cobbled streets he'd called home the whole of his life.

One moment, grief weighed him down, threatening to drag him to the bottom of the bay, and in the next, relief flooded him to be leaving these shores—and all that remained on them. Forever? He wasn't sure if he wanted it to be or not. He'd spent the bulk of his adult life hoping, praying, and planning for this day. Now that it was here, the depth of pain he felt at the idea of leaving shocked him. Was he doing the right thing? No matter now. He'd given his word, paid his steerage fare, and packed all his worldly belongings. Besides, he reminded himself, nothing but heartache and regret remained for him here. Time for a fresh start. A new life.

"Stephen!"

Anna's voice jolted him like a shock of lightning. He turned to see her, skirts in hand, running toward him. Was it proper for a lady to run in public? Or ever? He tipped his cap. "Lady Annabeth."

She stopped short in front of him. Tendrils of hair curled wildly in the damp air. Her cheeks were flushed from exertion. "Is it true?" she asked in short puffs. "Do you leave today?"

He cocked an eyebrow, glanced at the pile of trunks and cases next to him, and bit back a sarcastic answer. "Aye." He shifted his weight and looked back to her.

Her blue eyes, devoid of their usual spark, turned down as she nodded. She laced her fingers together and unlaced them. Then lifted her thumb to her mouth, as though to bite her nail, but dropped her hand when her glove touched her lip. Something he'd seen her do many times when nervous or uncertain. "Might I have a word?" she finally managed to say.

Stephen sank his hands into his pockets. His heart squeezed at the sight of her. Unshed tears shimmered in her eyes as she looked at him expectantly. He bit his lip to bring himself back to reality. He couldn't allow himself to be swept away by her again. She'd already played tug-of-war with his heart enough. He couldn't bear to be drawn in by her only to be cast aside once more. Yet, perhaps a last word would be good. To put the final nail into a relationship that could never be, once and for all. He gestured to a bench nearby.

"Thank you," she whispered.

Stephen bobbed his head and stepped over to the bench.

"I wanted to explain," she began as they sat. "About Lord Corning."

Stephen started to protest—to say that she owed him no explanation. Part of him didn't want to know. Didn't care—or so he told himself over and over. However, the truth was he needed to know. He had to hear directly from her what exactly it was the old man possessed that Stephen lacked. He nodded for her to continue.

"When I first told you of his proposal, it was true that I had not accepted. Nor did I want to." Her voice trailed off and she looked away.

"Then why did you?" He couldn't help the sharpness in his voice.

She smoothed her hands over her lap. "Because things . . . changed. For my family. If I don't marry him, we will be lost. Ruined." She lifted her gaze to meet his, her eyes imploring him to comprehend.

He wagged his head and he shrugged. "I don't understand."

She inhaled and released a deep breath, as though searching for what to say. "I cannot divulge every detail. Out of respect for Father." She angled herself to face Stephen more directly. She lifted her hand as though she was going to reach for his, but she placed it back in her lap. "But suffice it to say that without Lord Corning's estates and fortune, my family would not be able to continue on. We'd be destitute. It was . . . nae, *is* my duty as firstborn to ensure the continuance of the De Lacy legacy. And it is for duty alone that I accepted him."

So there it was. Stephen's heart lightened to hear it was not for love of another that she had jilted him. Perhaps she truly didn't want to marry the English lord. Yet a part of him couldn't be sure he could believe her.

She looked at him now with such intensity that he crossed his arms over his chest to keep from pulling her into an embrace. It was a marriage of duty, of survival. And at the same time, she made no attempts to profess her desire to marry someone— anyone—else. The old familiar ache of rejection settled in his gut. The door to his heart Annabeth De Lacy had spent months prying open slid shut in a silent, final realization. Love for Stephen was never meant to be. And never would be. "Thank you for tellin' me." He looked to the harbor. "I should get goin.'"

She placed a hand on his arm. "Wait. Please, just another moment."

He stilled at her touch. It still warmed him as much as he remembered. He fixed his stare at the water, for if he looked on her face, he feared he'd give in and pull her into his arms. She was a siren that lured him and his heart to certain death. But the harbor? The harbor called to him with the promise of escape—of freedom from this tormented life. And yet the feel of her hand paralyzed him. When he said nothing, she continued.

"My sister, Emmaline . . . well, she discovered . . ." Anna heaved a sigh before continuing. "She figured out how I feel about you. She knows court life has never appealed to me like it does her. And she knows I . . ." Anna's voice faded.

Stephen still looked to the harbor. "She knows you what?"

Anna's grip on his arm tightened. "Stephen, she knows I love you."

Stephen held his breath and looked at her from the corner of his eye. Was she in earnest? Anna's cheeks flushed anew, but not, he suspected, from physical exertion this time.

Anna grasped his hand with her free one. "She's offered to take my place. To accept Lord Corning's proposal."

Stephen shifted to face her. "What?" The word oozed out slowly like molasses on a cold day. Anna pulled her hand back, as though she hadn't realized she'd reached out to take his.

Her gaze drifted to her lap. "She has offered to marry Lord

Corning in my stead. Freeing me to be with you." Her gaze floated up to meet his, and he could see she swallowed hard. "That is, if you will still have me," she added, her voice a mere whisper.

The world around him spun, stealing his breath and setting his heart ablaze. The corner of his mouth tipped up, and he lifted a hand to stroke her cheek and dry the tear that had slipped down it. But he stopped short. How could he be certain this was the truth? He could not, he feared, recover from another romantic blow. If he accepted her offer and De Lacy blocked it—or Anna changed her mind some weeks hence—he wouldn't survive it. He had to protect what was left of his heart, and his sanity.

"That is very kind," he ventured at length, "but I cannot. I am sorry."

Anna sucked in a breath as though she'd been struck. "Oh. I see." A shaky, watery smile lifted the corners of her mouth slightly. "Is there no changing your mind?"

He tore his gaze from hers and turned it to the water once more. His resolve wouldn't hold under the intensity of her attentions. "I . . . I'm afraid not. I wish ye all the best, Lady Annabeth." He stood and stalked back to the shop. As he closed the door behind him, her soft cries followed him like a ghost.

CHAPTER

36

Stephen leaned his head back against the closed door. His jaw clenched and he squeezed his eyes shut, a dull ache taking up residence in the base of his neck.

"Ye're a daft fool of a boy!"

Stephen jumped at his father's voice. He could count on one hand the number of times Seamus had truly raised his voice in his lifetime.

"Da?"

Seamus stormed across the room, pointing toward the door, as though he could see through it to Anna sitting on the bench. "Are ya really going to refuse that woman?"

Stephen's jaw fell slack. The auld man couldn't hear a whisper across the room, but that conversation he heard? Figures. "Aye, Da. I am."

A swift hand boxed the back of Stephen's head. "Fool."

Stephen flinched and rubbed his hand on the spot of the blow. "Ow! What was tha' for?"

"You know what!" Seamus paced the entryway. "Do ye have any idea what it took for that girl to come do what she just did? What she risked with her family?" Seamus shook his head and huffed a deep sigh.

"I do. Truly. It's just . . ." Stephen rubbed both hands over his face.

"Just what?" Seamus tossed his hands in the air.

"I just . . . can't."

Seamus folded his arms. "And why not?"

"Because!" Now Stephen's voice was the one raised. "What if it fails? What if she leaves me? Rejects me again? What if her father refuses to allow it?" He waved his hands back and forth in front of him. "No! I cannot. I wouldn't survive it."

"Seafóid!" Seamus took a slow, deep breath. When he spoke again, his voice was calm and measured. "Come. Sit with me, lad. I want to show ya somethin.'"

The pair shuffled up the stairs to the kitchen table. They sat in silence for a long moment. Just as Stephen was about to break the silence, Seamus pulled something from his pocket and handed it to his son.

Stephen examined the silver Claddagh ring. "What's this?" He joggled it between his thumb and forefinger.

Seamus rewarded him with a blank stare. "It's a Claddagh ring."

Stephen scoffed. "I know that. What did ya give it to me for?"

"Tell me," Seamus said. "The meaning."

"You know the meaning," Stephen said, growling. He dropped the ring onto the table and fell back in his chair.

Seamus shrugged. "Humor an auld man."

Sighing, Stephen straightened and reclaimed the band. "Centuries ago, a man was kidnapped and sold into slavery."

"Skip ahead." Seamus flapped his hand. "What does the *ring* mean? And save me the theatrics."

Stephen examined the pattern so familiar he could carve it in his sleep. "The crown represents loyalty, the hands friendship." He gulped at the next phrase. "And the heart represents love." He dropped it onto the table once more.

Seamus's head bobbed. "Aye. Verra good. Now, look at this one." He handed Stephen a cloth parcel.

Stephen unwrapped it, curiosity snaking its way through him. When the material fell away, a necklace in the shape of a Celtic cross, with the circle forming the Claddagh symbol, sparkled up at him. He lowered his brows and traced the circle with his thumb. "Anna's design?"

"Aye." Seamus pointed a knotted finger at the pendant. "And do ye recall why she wanted to put the Claddagh on the cross?"

Seamus looked at Stephen so intently it unsettled him. He'd never seen his father so resolute. Stephen regarded the man again, who merely gestured to the cross in his hands.

Stephen's mind drifted back to the night Anna had explained her sketch to him. He remembered how tenderly she'd spoken of it. He recalled how impressed he had been by her attention to detail as well as her respect for the craft—and the people who created it.

"I remember." Stephen's voice was thick with emotion, and he inwardly chided himself for it.

"Tell me." Seamus leaned forward and rested his elbows on the table.

"She said . . ." Stephen cleared his throat, wishing he could swallow the lump choking him. "She said she wanted to place the Claddagh on the cross because she could think of no better display of love, loyalty, and friendship than what our Lord did for us there." He clinched his eyes closed, not willing to release the tears that threatened to fall.

"Mmhmm." Seamus nodded and slid back in his seat. "Let that sink in, boyo."

Stephen opened his eyes and ran his thumb over the design once more, its smooth edges and clean lines blurring in his vision.

"Think back to all the times Anna has shown you—and others—such things. Love. Loyalty. Friendship."

Like moving pictures in the cinema he'd been to as a boy, images of Anna rolled through his mind: Anna talking with the busker boys the morning they met on the street. Anna caring for his father—making sure he ate and rested when he needed—or running errands hither and yon to save his father's legs and energy. Anna reaching out to help a hungry family in the Claddagh. The kind and attentive way she helped each and every customer, taking the time to listen to their stories and get to know them in a real way. Helping the families of the Claddagh restore their homes after the flood. Lending a compassionate ear and an open heart as he spoke of Tommy. Her attentiveness and genuine desire to learn more when he taught her the rough and rugged history of this beloved city. And with all the times he'd been gruff, aloof, or rude to her, she'd only ever responded with kindness and compassion—yet she wasn't afraid to push back and stand up for truth.

Stephen ran his hand over his mouth. He finally understood. In the few short months she'd been in his life, Annabeth De Lacy had been one of the clearest examples of God's love Stephen had ever encountered, aside from his father. All these years, he believed those professing to be in love were blind. It turned out, it was he who was visionless. Looking back at Anna's life and example since she'd arrived, it was so clear. How could he not have seen?

Stephen slowly lifted his face to look at his father. His eyes round, mouth slack, he knew his expression registered the realization he'd come to in his own heart. "I am a daft fool."

Seamus pulled his lips into a thin line and nodded. "Aye. That you are. But ye're not alone. Every last one o' us has been one. But ya don't hafta remain one, ya know." He rose, rounded the table, and placed a hand on Stephen's shoulder. "The Good Book says that a fool walks away from a mirror and forgets his own reflection. Ye've seen your reflection now, boyo. What're ye going to do about it?"

Stephen shook his head. "I dunno. I don't even know where to begin with myself, let alone Anna. I've been so cold to her. She'd never take me back now."

"Won't she? She knew what ye were like when she came here this morn. Do ya think her heart is so easily changed?"

How did his father know so much about matters of the heart? Or was this just another facet of Stephen's reflection—the failure to see his father had known better than Stephen realized all along? "What do you think I should do?"

Seamus pulled in a deep breath and twitched his head to the side. "It's hard to know, exactly." He returned to his chair. "But one thing is quite clear—ya need to go ask for her forgiveness. Nothin' will be right with anythin' until you do that. Then, profess yer undyin' love."

Stephen puffed a breath through his lips. "Is that all?" He chuckled.

Seamus didn't miss a beat. "If she'll have ye, then ye can tackle the issue of her father later."

Stephen nodded gently, his fingers slipping into his waistcoat pocket and winding around the familiar silver band. How often had he held it thus? And how often had he tried to dispose of it, only to return it to its place there in his pocket. Perhaps . . . perhaps he might just make use of it, after all. "Thanks, Da."

"Ye're welcome. Just see to it ya get yer own heart right first."

"I will." He bobbed his head. "And, Da?"

"Yes, m'boy?"

Stephen stood and placed his hand on his dad's shoulder. "I'm sorry. For everything."

A slow smile spread across Seamus's face and his eyes moistened. "All's forgiven, a mhac."

Coarse sand crunched beneath Anna's and Emmaline's shoes as they strolled along the beach. It was the hottest day since they'd been in Ireland, and the coastline teemed with people in the midday sun. Big burly men sat along rock walls, licking ice cream cones while kids skittered up and down the strand. Despite the throng, a shroud of loneliness surrounded Anna, hiding her heart from the world and threatening to suffocate her.

Finding an empty spot, the girls sat, slipped off their shoes, and buried their toes in the sun-warmed sand. Anna scooped up a handful of grains and let them slip through her fingers. *Just like my life is slipping away from me.*

A long, thin shell the width of her finger remained. Turning it over in her hand, she admired the iridescent colors as they swirled in the afternoon light.

Footsteps ran up behind her. "Oooh, miss, ye found the devil's toenail!"

Anna craned her neck to discover Cormac, the boy whose home she'd helped clean up the first morning after the storm, standing behind her, a wide grin splitting his face. She curled the corners of her mouth up. "So I did." She held the shell out to him. "Would you like it?"

His smile widened. "Gee, t'anks!" Taking the shell, he spun and stumbled through the sand, waving his treasure over his head. "Look, Ma, she let me have it!"

Anna smiled after the boy before turning her attention to the waterline.

"I take it things didn't go as you'd hoped this morning?" Emmaline asked, kindness lacing her voice.

Anna shook her head.

"Oh, sweet Anna." Emmaline slipped her arm around Anna's shoulders and squeezed. "Did he say why?"

"No." Anna picked up a stone and scratched at it with her fingernail. "And his ship leaves for the continent today—it likely already has." She swallowed around the knot in her throat.

"Oh, dear. I am sorry."

Anna shrugged. "No matter. 'Tis done now." She let her gaze drift out to the horizon, watching the red-sailed hooker boats gliding like geese on the water. How at peace they seemed. Unlike her heart.

"Lady Annabeth?"

Anna spun in her seat and squinted up to see who beckoned her. Her jaw slackened, and she scrambled to her feet, absently brushing the coral sand from her skirts. "Lord Arbury," she said and shook his hand. She turned to the woman at his side. "Lady Arbury, I presume. It's lovely to make your acquaintance."

She nodded. "And you."

"I've been meaning to stop into the shop," the salt-and-pepper-haired gentleman said, his eyes kind. "But since you're here—"

"I hope everything is in order?"

"Oh yes, of course!" He guided his wife forward and held up her hand. "I've been meaning to stop by and thank you for your impeccable craftsmanship. Lady Arbury adores the set you created—in fact, I can scarcely get her to remove them."

Lady Arbury lazily waved a lace fan with her other hand and giggled. "'Tis true. And all my friends are positively green with envy! Their beaus will be in to see you in no time, I'd wager."

Anna smiled. "I'm so happy to hear it! And we will welcome them with open arms." Behind her, Emmaline cleared her throat. "Good gracious, I'm terribly sorry. May I present my sister, Lady Emmaline De Lacy."

Emmaline stepped forward and dipped a shallow curtsy before shaking the lord's and lady's hands in turn. "It's lovely to meet you both."

"Indeed," Lord Arbury said. "And may I present our son, Master Goodwin Arbury."

A young man stepped forward and swept his hat in a low arc, revealing a shock of sandy blond hair. He shook Anna's hand gently, then turned his attention to Emmaline. "How do you do, Lady Emmaline?" He bent and pressed a gentle kiss on her fingers.

Emmaline's cheeks flushed. "Very well, thank you, Master Arbury."

Anna watched the unfolding with a spark of delight and a twinge of sadness. Her sister might yet find love, after all—though it would be foolish to think it would happen today with a man she just met.

"Are you in town long?" Emmaline asked the elder Arburys, but not before her gaze flicked to Goodwin and back.

"*Mmm.*" Lady Arbury's brows arched, and she nodded. "We're on holiday for the summer. We're staying at a delightful place down in Salt Hill. We must have your family out for dinner or drinks one evening."

"We'd be delighted," Anna answered.

"Indeed, that would be lovely," Emmaline said, her gaze fixed on Goodwin. She smiled coyly before flicking her own fan open and hiding all but her sparkling eyes behind it.

"That settles it," Lady Arbury said. "We'll have our man set it up. We'll be in touch." Then she took her husband's elbow and they turned to stroll back whence they came.

"Brilliant." Anna smiled, all the while attempting to shrug off the sinking feeling settling in her spirit.

"I look forward to it," Goodwin said, as he lifted Emmaline's hand to his lips once more.

"Come, son," Lord Arbury called over his shoulder. "We must away."

"Lady Annabeth, Lady Emmaline," Goodwin said with a final tip of his hat. He then turned and joined his parents as they moseyed back toward Salt Hill.

Anna and Emmaline watched their backs for a moment before turning to one another, laughter erupting from them both.

CHAPTER

37

William leveled a glare at the messenger who'd brought the missive. "Is this some sort of joke?"

The lad, a young civilian dressed in clean but ragged clothes, frowned and shifted his feet nervously. "No, m'lord."

William looked over the message once more. The scrawling writing looked official enough. And the royal seal at the top bore all the trademarks of authenticity. Still, deep down, he hoped it was a sick prank. Another attempt from the locals to oust the family from the area.

The rabble who set his home on fire had been caught and thrown in prison. Some local lads—a name something like Ciaran and some other bloke—seemed to be the ringleaders. Ire burned in William's belly at the thought of how close he'd come to losing his family because of a petty fight over so-called independence. How could it have all come to this?

The messenger cleared his throat. "Is that all, m'lord?"

William startled. He'd forgotten the lad was there. "Yes, yes, of course." He flicked his wrist toward the door.

The messenger didn't move. He cleared his throat once more.

William growled. "What is it, boy?"

"Beggin' yer pardon, m'lord. It's just the small matter of . . . eh . . ." He held out a shaky hand.

Of course. It all came down to money. Always did. "Oh, for heaven's sake." He dug in his pocket and tossed a few pence at the boy. "Off with you, now."

"Yes, m'lord." The boy jammed his hat onto his head and scurried out.

Elizabeth floated into the room as on a cloud. Despite the family's dire circumstances, she looked every bit the part of a lady—her ornate dress flowing in her wake. "What was that about, dear?"

William stared at her for a long moment. Gone were the days of showering her with finery and fluff. He wanted to soak in this moment—her, a vision in lavender taffeta, blissfully unaware of the latest blow to befall the De Lacy family. His throat burned.

"William?" She stepped nearer. "What is it?"

He extended his hand to her and she took it. "Well, my darling, I regret to announce that this is the end." He drew her closer and brushed a kiss onto her cheek.

Her flawless brow furrowed. "William?"

He handed her the royal decree, unable to bring himself to voice the depths of his failures.

Elizabeth stepped closer to the fire and angled the message toward its light and read aloud.

By Royal Decree:

Let it be known henceforth that William De Lacy is hereby stripped of his title. For displaying a lack of discernment and financial wisdom so prudent to a lord of the British Court, and for failing to protect the interests and assets of the Kingdom in Ireland by allowing the destruction of royal property, and a complete absence of military control. You must vacate the premises of the Galway estate forthwith and surrender any and all rights and privileges afforded to a member of the House of Earls.

Elizabeth dropped her hands and looked at him with such sadness in her eyes, it made William squirm. "Oh, William! They can't be serious!"

He winced and turned away from her piercing gaze. "I'm afraid they are, my dear. I'm afraid they are."

He felt her warmth before he caught sight of her joining him at the window. She placed a tender hand on his shoulder, and with it, the full weight and reality of his failings settled upon him. He swung his head side to side. "Oh, my darling Elizabeth. I'm so sorry. I've failed you. I've failed us all."

He collapsed onto his knees, his head in his hands. There was no point now in keeping up appearances. He was no longer a lord of the court of Britain. There was no point to decorum and propriety. He sobbed and shook like a leaf in a gale, letting his wife see the true broken shell of a man that he was.

Elizabeth sank down next to him. "Shh, my love," she crooned in his ear as she wrapped her arms around his shaking shoulders and laid her head on his. "We'll get through this. Somehow we will."

William almost believed her, until one of her tears fell and slid down his own cheek.

When Anna and Emmaline entered the front door that afternoon, both refreshed and worn out from their long walk on the beach, the sound of crying met their ears. The girls shared a glance and hurried to the study.

As they rounded the corner to the doorway, they both stopped short. Their parents sat hunched on the floor, sobbing.

"Mama, Papa, whatever is the matter?" Emmaline reached them first.

"Has someone died?" Anna joined them.

"No." Mother sniffled and shook her head. Her face, wet with tears, was dappled with red splotches and her eyes were puffy. The sight of their prim-and-proper mother in such a state was unsettling, to say the least.

"But at the same time, yes." Father straightened and looked from one daughter to the next. The state of his own face matched their mother's. This must be very serious, indeed. "Sit down, girls," he said.

Once they were settled by the fire, Father swiped his eyes with a handkerchief and stood before them. "I'm afraid I have some bad news. Dreadful, really." He gazed out the window, and he seemed lost in thought for a stretched-out moment. "Following the loss of the manor house and the growing unrest with the locals, adding to that our recent financial distress, the Crown has seen fit to . . . to—" He swallowed hard and hung his head. "To strip me of my titles and anything else that remained of my land and fortune."

Emmaline clasped her hands over her mouth. "Oh, Father."

Anna's gaze flew to their mother. She stared at the floor, hankie pressed to her mouth. "That's . . . that's terrible." Mother nodded. Anna grasped her hand.

Emmaline looked at each of them in turn. "Forgive me, Father, but . . . I don't understand."

"Did I not speak plainly enough, daughter? Another item to add to my list of shortcomings." He turned his back to the family.

"'Tis not what I meant." Emmaline stood and placed her hand on his shoulder. "I'm only confused as to what you meant by financial distress." She turned and looked to Anna. Heat flushed to Anna's cheeks, so she dropped her gaze to the floor.

"I'd presumed your sister had told you," Father replied, his voice devoid of any emotion.

"Told me?" She turned to face Anna fully. "Told me what?"

Anna met her stare. "I am sorry, Emma." Anna stood now as well. "'Twasn't my story to tell." She looked to their father, who leaned against the mantel, head in his hands. "But I'll tell it now."

Anna took her sister by the hand and led her back to their chairs. As they sat, Anna angled herself to face Emmaline.

"Apparently," Anna began, "our financial situation has been precarious for quite some time. So much so that Father's appointment here was a last-ditch effort to get him back on track—and not the honor we'd originally believed."

Emmaline released a breath. "Goodness. Truly?"

Anna rolled her lips between her teeth and nodded. "Father has been trying to rectify it, but the damage was already too great. When his last investment failed, that sealed it."

Emmaline slumped in the chair, her gaze drifting to the fire in the grate. "How frightful."

"'Tis, indeed." Father pushed away from the mantel and paced before them. "And if that wasn't bad enough, I'm afraid we must vacate De Lacy Place. At once."

Both girls gasped. "Where will we go?" Emmaline asked.

"We'll find somewhere," Mother said, finally finding her voice.

"I am sorry, my dears." William's voice caught. "'Tis not the life I wanted for you girls. Any of you." He looked at his family. "I never wanted to leave you destitute with no money, no land, no title. Alas, that is to be my legacy."

Hope dawned in Anna's heart. "All may not yet be lost," she said, rising. "There is still Lord Corning."

Her father scoffed, swatting a hand.

"No, truly, Papa." She stepped closer and placed a hand on his arm. "I admit, I was loath to accept his proposal. And had even considered giving my heart to . . . another."

At the hint of Stephen, her father scowled.

"But I see now," she continued, "that it was for this reason Lord Corning proposed to begin with. Of course, he couldn't have known you'd lose your fortune. But, as far as he knows, I've accepted his offer and we plan to wed in the fall. We need only get by until then."

"Dear sister." Emmaline blinked back fresh tears. "You mustn't. Remember our agreement."

Anna crossed near to Emmaline and took her hand. "No, I must, Emmie. 'Tis the only way." She shook her head. "I couldn't risk losing his support asking for a transfer of his proposal to you."

"What's this?" Father's gaze flew to meet Anna's.

Anna held her palm out. "It's nothing. At least . . . not any longer." She offered him a shaky smile. "Take heart, Papa. There is yet hope."

CHAPTER
38

Katy appeared in the study doorway, breathless. "M'lord, ye must come. Hurry!" She gestured to the hall. "Come the back way."

Anna and her family looked at one another, their faces painted with the same confusion that swirled within Anna, before scurrying down the hall to the modest wing housing the servants' quarters.

Katy thrust clothing at each of them. "Ye must dress in haste. We haven't much time."

Father scowled at the common work clothes she held out to him. "What's all this about, Katy?" he demanded. "Speak quickly."

Katy's eyes were wide, almost wild. "They're comin', m'lord. They've come for ye." She pointed a shaky finger at him.

"Coming? Who?" he barked.

Katy cringed and motioned for him to lower his voice. "Everyone, m'lord." She spun a glance around the room. "Everyone what was involved in that fire. They're cross wi' ye that Ciaran and Mickey are in the clink. They aim to make ye pay." She stepped closer, and her voice dropped even lower. "And I don' mean money."

"Oh, good heavens." All color drained from Mother's face and she wavered. Father steadied her with an arm around the back of her waist. Mother laid a hand on her chest and fanned herself with the other.

Katy thrust the clothes at Father once more. "I can get yas out, but ya must hurry." Outside, the muffled din of a mob grew louder. Katy's gaze flew to the drape-covered window and she took two steps backward toward the door. "I'll leave ye to change. But don't dawdle."

She fled from the room, closing the door in her wake. Through the walls, the De Lacys could hear harsh whispered Gaelic floating to the other help, who by the sound of it awaited her orders.

The family each retreated to a corner of the room to dress. Anna's fingers shook so violently, she could hardly loosen the ties of the brown peasant dress Katy had given her. Once dressed and tied, she tugged the maid's cap over her locks, tucked them in, and turned. Her heart clenched to see her family adorned in the clothes of commoners—not because it seemed beneath them, but because it reflected the finality of what they'd lost. What her father had wasted.

Father rolled his shoulders and nodded. "Let's go."

The family rushed into the hallway to find Katy and Owen waiting for them. Owen held a rake, shovel, and *hurley*. "Right," he began. "Ye'll need to head out the back and make immediately for the woods. Make sure ye get deep enough in the trees that ye canna be seen from the lawn."

"Follow the tree line south," Katy added, "until ye're well past the mob. Then, make yer way to the main road. Owen'll meet yas there with the wagon."

"Not the carriage?" Father asked.

Owen shook his head. "Nae. Too conspicuous. 'Sides"—he swallowed and a pained look came over his face—"it don't officially belong to ye anymore."

Father's face blanched. "Right."

Owen handed Anna, Emmaline, and Father the tools. "If anyone should stop ye, pretend ye're part of the mob and say ya got separated from the group." He looked at each of them in turn. "If that happens, pretend to be angry. But keep yer words few—so yer accent doesn't give ye away."

The group nodded collectively. "That shouldn't prove too difficult," Father said.

"Indeed." Owen nodded.

"Now off wi' ye. Quick," Katy said. "And stay quiet! Owen'll go prepare the wagon, an' I'll hold them off at the door as long as I can." The two shared an indiscernible glance and each took a deep breath.

Anna turned to follow her family outside but stopped and pulled Katy into a firm embrace. "Thank you, Katy." She pulled back to look the girl in the eye. "I owe you. We all do."

Katy offered a watery smile. "'Tis an honor, m'lady. I know ye don't play hurling, but this isn't a game." A sad chuckle lifted from her chest, and she pressed the hurley in Anna's hands toward her. "Now go."

After one last glance behind her, Anna hurried to meet her family in the woods. She squinted at the shadowy darkness threatening to smother her under the trees, the afternoon sun nowhere to be found within the thick wood. Willing her feet to carry her faster than they ever had before, she felt twigs snag at her dress and cap. Casting glances over her shoulder, she wove between and around the dense trees, straining to find the out-lines of her family. Her mind spun and so, apparently, did the trees. Anna suddenly had no idea which way was which. She wheeled this way and that, trying to gain her bearings.

"Anna," a voice ahead of her whispered.

She squinted. "Father?" Her voice squeaked, barely audible.

"Over here."

Anna crept toward the sound, praying she was heading into the arms of her awaiting family and not a member of the lawless rabble seeking her destruction.

She breathed a sigh of relief when Emmaline and her parents appeared from behind a large pine. They hugged each other briefly.

"Which way?" Anna whispered.

"That way's south, I believe." Father pointed.

"Yes, that seems right," Emmaline agreed.

The family made their way as quickly and quietly as they could. Anna twisted the hurley—a wooden stick used in the ancient Celtic game of hurling—in her hand. Though not overly heavy, it certainly sported some heft, and she imagined its flat, round end could do a good bit of damage to a human body. She wondered if she'd truly be able to wield it as a weapon if it came to that. She shuddered at the thought.

A shout drew their attention, and they scooted as close to the edge of the woods as they dared. The front of De Lacy Place came into view. Anna absently questioned in her mind what it would be called now that it was no longer under De Lacy care. The thought, however, evaporated when she noticed the mob pressing in on the front of the house. Far larger than any of them could have anticipated, the crowd shouted and jeered. She spotted Paddy in heated discussion with those at the front of the throng. Katy was right beside him in the dooway. Paddy gestured to the northeast, where he pointed in the opposite direction the De Lacys had gone. One faction of the crowd split off and followed where he pointed.

Why was he there? Anna narrowed her gaze as she stared at the spectacle before her. Was he trying to help her family escape?

Someone threw a rock, shattering one of the upstairs windows. Paddy shoved Katy into the safety of the house and closed the door before assuming a defensive stance, fists raised. "No!" Anna gasped and lunged toward the house.

Father's hand gripped her elbow and pulled her back. "That's exactly what that rabble wants. Sadly, Owen, Katy, and the rest of the staff must fend for themselves." He looked to the house once more. "We don't want to waste this gift of an opportunity they've given us."

Anna grimaced and looked back at the home. The mob surrounded it now, the sickening crash of glass breaking and of clubs on the door echoing among the trees. Paddy was no longer in sight, and she prayed he'd escaped.

"Besides," Emmaline offered in a breathless whisper, "it seems they've found their own way out." She gestured toward the back of the house. Owen and Katy sprinted into the woods, heading northwest.

Anna breathed a sigh of relief.

"We must press on," Mother pleaded.

"Aye," Father added. "We must keep going. Owen will be waiting for us with the wagon." He turned and hastened away.

They slipped farther into the wooded shadows, snaking their way south. The only sounds to be heard were the muted rustle of leaves quivering overhead and their huffed breaths. More leaves crackled beneath their feet, and a loud snap sounded behind them.

"What was that?" Mother's breathless, whispered voice was strained.

The group huddled together and peered back into the obscurity. Only the black trunks of trees could be seen in the inky dark. Another crack. This one closer.

"Oy!" a man's voice called. "I know ye're out here!"

"Quickly," Father hissed. "Go!"

They turned and sped through the maze of trees and shrubs as quickly as they could. Anna's toe caught on a root, and she skidded onto her stomach, her hands splayed across the carpet of leaves. In the distance behind her, branches cracked. Emmaline grabbed her by the elbow and pulled her up.

"Are you hurt?" she asked.

Anna shook her head even as she continued running.

The four ran for what felt like hours. Anna's palms stung, and her cheek burned where a wayward branch had scratched her as she fell. She dabbed at the wound with her sleeve.

"Look there," Father said, his breaths coming in labored puffs. Up ahead, through the tree line, daylight glimmered.

"The road," Mother added, hope buoying her voice.

"Let's rest a moment and catch our breath," Father said. "If anyone but Owen spots us, we want to seem like we're part of the search party, rather than the ones being hunted."

The De Lacy women nodded, and they all stood in shrouded quiet. Slowly, their breaths came easier. The pounding of Anna's heart left her ears, and she felt she could speak normally now if need be. The crashes and creaks of their follower had also diminished. Anna hoped he'd given up or headed along a wrong course.

Once sufficiently rested, they emerged onto the main roadside, hands shielding their faces at the brightness of the sun still hanging in the sky.

A low rumble rattled from the west. "Quick," Father whispered, "to the trees." The women slunk back into the woods. Father craned his neck, feet poised to rush back to the cover of darkness. The rumbling drew nearer. His stance relaxed, and he waved them out from their hiding place. "'Tis Owen."

Breathing a collective sigh of relief, Anna, Emmaline, and their mother emerged from the woods once more.

Owen tugged the reins, bringing the workhorse to a halt. "Climb in the back. Hunker down so yer faces can't be seen."

The group did as he bade. Anna lumbered into the wagon

and crawled to the very rear. Resting her back against the wall, she tucked her knees up and bent her head so only her maid's cap could be seen over the edge of the wagon. The rest of her family followed suit.

Owen urged the horse onward and the rig rumbled into motion. Minutes stretched on like hours as the journey passed in relative silence until hoofbeats approached from the east.

"Down," Owen grunted. "Someone's comin.'"

"Owen, how are ya?"

The wagon slowed to a stop. *Whatever could Owen be thinking?* Anna thought. Could he not simply nod a greeting to his acquaintance and move on? Their lives hung in the balance and he stopped to make conversation?

"Just fine indeed, t'anks," Owen answered. "How d'ye fare, Mister Jennings?"

CHAPTER
39

I t was odd to see Owen away from the De Lacy Estate at the helm of a wagon instead of their grand carriage. In fact, Stephen had never seen him driving the work wagon before. That task typically fell to the farmhands or stable lads. Stephen noticed the beads of sweat pooling on Owen's forehead when a creak drew his attention to the wagon bed.

A man and three women sat hunched in the back. They had the look of household workers about them, but something seemed off.

"Grand out, now," Stephen answered Owen's question. He cast another wary glance at the passengers. "Are ya sure ye're alright? I don't often see you with this rig."

The maid's cap on one of the women in the back turned, and a pair of striking blue eyes peeked over the edge of the wagon bed. He knew those eyes, and they looked very surprised to see him indeed. Anna? Frowning, Stephen urged Capall toward the woman.

"Anna?" Stephen looked at the rest of the group. "Lord and Lady De Lacy?"

Slowly, the De Lacys lifted their eyes to meet his. Hair disheveled, faces smeared with dirt, clothes snagged. Stephen's jaw fell slack. Then his gaze fell back to Anna's. A large scrape tore across her cheek, and when she smoothed a shock of hair from her forehead, she revealed bloodied hands.

"What's happened?"

Anna opened her mouth to speak, but it was Owen's voice that answered.

"Beggin' yer pardon, Mister Jennings, but we must away. I can fill ye in later." Owen's head swiveled in all directions. "'Tisn't safe here."

Stephen nodded, determination painted on his face. "Right. Take them to my shop," he said, keeping his voice low. "Tell Da I sent ye. I'll continue down the road a bit before I turn back. Then I'll meet ye there in a wee while."

Owen nodded and snapped the reins, jerking the wagon into motion. "*Slán.*"

Stephen tipped his flatcap. "Slán."

Leading Capall farther west on the road toward Spiddal, Stephen's mind spun. As he passed the turnoff to the De Lacy Estate, a large group headed his direction, angry shouts filling the air.

"Oy!" an older man called. "Have ya seen the man?" he asked Stephen in Gaelic, jamming a thumb behind him toward the old manor house. Stephen recognized him as the gruff-voiced ringleader he'd overheard at the pub.

"*Ní fhaca mé iad,*" he lied. "I haven't seen them. But if I do, I'll be sure to let ye know." Stephen struggled to keep the disdain from showing on his face.

"*An-mhaith,*" the man replied. "Very good," he repeated, then informed Stephen where he could be found within the hour.

As Stephen continued down the road, he could hear the man calling orders for the group to split up, commanding some to hide out in the woods by the estate and the others to go back north and continue the search there. He ordered a third group to head to McGinty's chipper, and Stephen wondered how Paddy was mixed up in all this.

The road snaked along the coast, and Stephen tried to slow the merry-go-round of thoughts swirling in his mind. What could've ignited such an attack? Had there been another RIC offensive? Why were the De Lacys dressed as household staff? Could Owen truly be trusted?

Stephen rounded the bend and crossed into the village of Barna. He made a quick stop in one of the shops there and chatted with the shopkeep to give his story some truth should anyone ask. Then he hurled himself astride Capall and urged the steed home as quickly as his hooves could carry them.

Anna's heartbeat matched the incessant rumble of the wagon wheels on the cobblestones as they crossed into the Galway City Centre. She huddled tighter with her parents and sister, hoping and praying they wouldn't be discovered. How does one hide without the appearance of hiding?

The wagon slowed and eventually rolled to a stop. "We're here," Owen said, his voice barely above a whisper. Anna glanced up at him, and he looked around as though he were simply waiting for someone. "Don't alight just yet," he said. "I'll tell ye when it's clear."

The telltale pounding of soldiers' boots rumbled in the distance. No, no. Not now. Mother tensed and Father slid his arm around her.

"There, there, my dear," he whispered. "They wouldn't be looking for us." He had no way of knowing. The Crown had all but disowned them. They could be on the hunt to ensure the De Lacys had departed, removing their stain of failure from the kingdom's assets. However, his soothing words seemed to do the trick and Mother settled into the crook of his arm.

The wagon rocked as Owen climbed down. "I'll let Seamus know we're here," he said, speaking from the side of his mouth.

The creak of the door reached their ears, along with Seamus's trademark spirited greeting. "Owen! What brings ye here?"

Owen's voice, filled with urgency, rumbled low so that only Seamus could make out the words.

"Oh, *mhaidean*. My goodness," Seamus said. "Bring 'em in, bring 'em in."

As Owen appeared around the back of the wagon bed, Seamus called out louder than truly necessary, "Yes, I'll show ye the designs right in here. I think ye'll find I have just the thing."

The group slid from the wagon and hurried inside and Seamus ushered them upstairs to the flat.

Once safely inside, Anna breathed fully for the first time since the ordeal began. Mother pressed a handkerchief to her mouth and broke down sobbing.

"Aw, there, there, m'lady," Seamus crooned. "Have a seat here." He guided her by the elbow and eased her to sit in a chair at the table before shuffling over to remove the whistling kettle from the stove. "Perfect timin', eh?" He chuckled.

"Now," Seamus continued, "first things first. Are ye alright? Is anyone hurt?" He tenderly dabbed a damp cloth on Anna's cheek before handing her the rag. Anna's heart clenched at his kindness. She smiled her thanks.

"We're fine," she said, her throat dry. "Physically, anyway." She winced as she pulled the cloth from her cheek.

"Wha's happened, if ye don' mind me askin'?" Seamus poured tea for the lot before joining them at the table.

Before anyone could answer, the door downstairs thudded, causing the group to jump. Seamus lifted a finger to his lips, urging them to silence. He slipped down the stairs and opened the door. Muffled voices wafted up to them. Emmaline grimaced and Mother's tears returned, though she pressed her fingers to her mouth to stay any sound.

Anna gripped her sister's hand and chewed her lip. Had someone followed them here? Footsteps pounded up the stairs, Anna's heartbeat matching each one.

Stephen rounded the corner. "Buíochas le Dia," he said. "Thanks be to God yas are alright." His gaze fell to Anna's, and her stomach flipped at the look of concern and relief that swam in his eyes. Whatever was he still doing here? Hadn't he left? He placed a tender hand on her shoulder for a far too brief moment.

Seamus absently handed his son a cup of tea. Stephen took it and leaned against the counter. "What's happened?"

"It's all my fault." Father stood and paced the room. "I've failed in my duties."

Seamus and Stephen shared a quick glance before Stephen nodded to Father to continue.

Father pinched the bridge of his nose between two fingers, lines etching his face. Anna's heart squeezed to see her father so vexed. Might his love for her and Emmaline run deeper than it seemed?

Father took a long draw of his tea and gave a quick shake of his head. Anna wondered if he wished it were something stronger. "After the fire, word got back to the Crown," he said at length. "It would seem that act was enough to condemn me as unfit for the title of lord." He turned his back to the group. That wasn't the whole reason, but Anna understood why he chose not to divulge everything. At least not right now.

Eager to ease his suffering, though it made no logical sense that she would want to, Anna rose to continue their tale. "We've been ordered to evacuate the estate at once. We no longer have a title, land, or money."

"Uafásach," Seamus mumbled. "How terrible!"

"Indeed," Stephen said. He pushed himself to stand and rounded to the basin. He stared out the window. "I met your, ah, welcoming committee on the road after I left ye," he added. He turned and faced the group again.

"Yes," Anna said. "Just as we got word of our eviction, Katy came and warned us that a mob was on its way, angered about the imprisonment of the men who set fire to Galway Manor."

"Amadán." Stephen huffed and dragged his hand through his hair. "They're fools to think they had a right to do such a despicable thing. And fools to believe they could get away with it unpunished." He shook his head, retrieved his cup, and poured himself more tea.

"Thankfully, Owen and Katy hatched a plan to get us to safety," Father said, rejoining the conversation. "I owe them a great deal. Everything, really."

The group murmured agreement.

Father lowered his head. "Not that I have anything to repay them with," he added under his breath.

After that, relative silence settled over the room, and they drank their tea that way for a long while.

Seamus slammed a meaty hand on the table, startling them all. "That settles it," he said. "Ye must stay here until we figure out what's next."

Father waved his hands in protest. "No, no, it's far too much." He looked around the humble flat. "You don't want us taking over your home. You haven't the space for it."

"*Psh*! Nonsense!" Seamus drained the rest of his tea in a gulp. Then he pinned them each with a focused gaze. "'Sides, where else do ye have to stay that's safe?"

Father sucked in a breath as if to protest, but then his shoulders slumped in defeat. Anna and Emmaline looked to one another, speaking volumes between them with their eyes as only sisters can do. They then turned their attention to their mother, who, seemingly calmed by the tea and set at ease by Seamus's good nature, laid a hand on their father's arm and nodded slightly.

Father heaved a resigned sigh. "Very well, then," he said quietly. "We're much obliged to you both."

Anna met Stephen's gaze. A curious smile played on the corner of his lips. She nodded her thanks, and he responded in kind.

CHAPTER

40

Stephen and Seamus laid out blankets on the shop floor where they would be sleeping for the forseeable future. "So, what of it, lad?" Seamus whispered, his voice gravelly and hoarse.

Stephen pursed his lips. "It's a twist, to be sure," he replied. "I never would've dreamed Lord—er—Mister De Lacy would be stripped of his land and title because of the troubles here."

Seamus's head bobbed. "Aye, that is a shocker. Though, I'd wager there's more to that story than we've been told." He shook his head. "But I wasna talkin' about that. I was talking about Miss Anna."

Stephen dropped his arms to his sides, slapping his legs. "Will it never end with you?" He laughed. "The poor thing has just lost everything she's ever known."

"And?" Seamus spread his hands and wagged his head. "When ye headed out that way earlier today, ya had a very specific mission in mind, if I'm not mistaken. What are ya gonna do now?"

Stephen let his mind drift to the conversation he'd had with his father. Had that been just this morning? The fact remained that he loved Anna and wanted nothing more than to marry the girl. The fact also remained that she had accepted Lord Corning's proposal. And given the day's turn of events, it would stand to reason the De Lacys couldn't risk turning him down and offering Emmaline's hand instead, as Anna had suggested.

The irony that this British family had been evicted from Irish land by the Brits was not lost on Stephen. And chances were, they needed Anna's marriage to Lord Corning now more than ever. But seeing her in his home tonight, battered and scared, only further cemented his love for her—and his desire to protect her. He crossed the room and slid the small canvas bag that held the necklace Anna designed from a drawer.

He unwrapped it and turned the pendant over in his hand. His mind wandered back to the night she explained the meaning of the Claddagh on the cross. He remembered all the times he'd watched her sacrifice her time, energy, and strength to serve and love those around her—whether man, woman, Irish, or Brit. A verse drifted across his heart and mind. Though he couldn't remember the exact verbiage, the idea of it held him fast: There's no greater or better way to show love to someone than to lay your life down for them.

Stephen opened another drawer and pulled a leather pouch from it. He tugged it open and poured the contents into his hand, coins jingling.

Seamus sidled up behind him and peered over his shoulder. He blew out a puff of breath. "Yer nest egg, eh?"

Stephen nodded and eyed the money for a long moment before laying it out on the countertop. Though he knew the exact sum by heart, he counted it again anyway.

"What's on yer mind, boyo?" Seamus crossed his arms and leaned against the counter.

Stephen turned and leaned his hip on the counter as well, looking his father in the eyes. "There's enough here to set the De Lacys up in a new, safer place." He scooped up the coins and notes and returned them to the pouch. "Until Anna can wed Lord Corning."

"Och, lad." Seamus gripped Stephen's shoulder and squeezed as a tear slid down the old man's cheek. "I've never been more proud o' ye than I am in this moment."

Anna and Emmaline lay next to one another in Stephen's room. Father and Mother resided in Seamus's, and the Jennings men took up residence in the shop downstairs.

"That was quite the gesture for Mister Jennings to open his home to us," Emmaline whispered to the ceiling.

"'Twas, indeed." Anna let her gaze drift around the foreign room. Though tidy and neat, the distinct scents of musk and leather mingled with that of the heather mattress, marking the space as distinctly Stephen's. Anna tried in vain to ignore the idea that she was in the exact spot Stephen laid each night. She flattened her palm next to her head on the pillow, imagining him doing the same. The simple act connecting them through an impossible situation and inaccessible love.

"He missed his boat," she spoke into the night air.

Emmaline raised up on her elbows. "Holy buckets, you're right." She turned her face to Anna, a wide grin lighting it even in the darkness. "What an unexpected blessing!"

"Blessing? How?" Clearly her sister didn't understand. "Don't you see? I've once again stepped in and interrupted his plans— destroyed his hopes."

"*Tsk, tsk.* Sweet Annie," Emmaline crooned. "Do *you* not see?"

Anna shook her head in the dark, the straw pillow rustling her response for her.

"Perhaps this is the way things were meant to go?" Emmaline shifted to lie on her side, facing her sister, supporting her head in the palm of her hand.

Anna turned to look at her.

"'Tis a blessing of extra time." Emmaline stretched the last word long. "The Lord moves in mysterious ways, they say."

"Hmm." Anna returned her gaze to the ceiling, hidden by darkness. "Perhaps." Her heart remained unconvinced. Besides, there was no way she could refuse Corning now. She'd have to marry him—a decision she'd made with conviction and clarity only days ago. But to see Stephen now, to be in his home—in his bed—muddled her resolve.

"How will we ever afford the crossing?" she muttered.

"The crossing?" Confusion cracked Emmaline's voice.

"For the wedding," Anna whispered, unshed tears threatening to steal her words.

Emmaline groaned. "Well, if there is to be a crossing, perchance the Misters Jennings could start paying you for your time worked in the shop." She paused, as though in thought. "If things continue to go well in that way, as they have done so far, you should have the money you need in no time. Even if Father and Mother must stay here."

Anna knew she could not risk being seen in the shop. Not after the day's events. She chose, however, not to dismiss her sister's offer of hope. "Perhaps." Anna found her sister's hand in the inky blackness and squeezed. The idea of marrying Lord Corning weighed on her chest. The idea of having to do it alone threatened to suffocate her altogether.

CHAPTER
41

Anna stared through the glass case at the countless rows of Claddagh rings as rain pelted the windows the next morning. She traced the outline of the crown, hands, and heart of one ring with her finger. Grief and fatigue weighed her down like a millstone. Her faith had always been a source of strength and light to her. But now it seemed the source of her distress, which pained her to admit. The weight of responsibility she felt to carry her family pinned her where she stood. The conviction of doing what she knew to be right and the deepest desire of her heart had never before been so opposed. Her desires and the things her faith led her to do had always aligned. Until this moment.

Now, they threatened to tear her asunder. She drew a shaky breath, finding no strength in the action. Warmth spread up her back, and she glanced over her shoulder to find Stephen behind her.

"Can we talk?"

Anna dropped her head. "Of course."

Stephen gently tugged her shoulder so she faced him. His eyes searched hers. Oh, how she'd missed that sight. Anna looked away before she could get lost in the depths of his green gaze.

He hooked a finger under her chin and tenderly lifted her face to meet his. "I'm so terribly sorry for yer family." He swallowed. "Fer what ye've been through."

"Thank you, Stephen." She dropped her gaze once more. "Truly."

"Ye've been dealt a terrible blow, havin' yer home and all ye know ripped away," he continued. "And I want ya to know that ye—all o' ye—are welcome to stay here as long as ya need." The tenderness in his voice, and the generosity of his offer, melted her.

Anna wagged her head and swallowed around the lump in her throat. "You're far too kind." She glanced at his face, anxious for what she had to do next. "Especially given what I'm about to ask you."

He stepped closer. So near their toes nearly touched. Heat radiated from him, and Anna drew a deep breath to steady her nerves. She clamped her eyes shut before continuing. "I hate to even ask this, given how generous you and your father have already been to me, but might it be possible for me to"—she swallowed—"to start drawing wages for my work? I don't want to endanger you and your father by being seen in the shop. But perhaps I can continue creating pieces in the smithing room? I wouldn't ask only . . . only I need to earn fare . . ." She lifted her eyes to meet his. "For the crossing," she whispered.

Stephen reached forward and took her hand in his—his long, calloused fingers wrapping around hers. His thumb rubbed circles on the back of her hand. Anna's eyes closed at his touch. Before she could further get lost in it, he turned her hand over and placed something in her palm.

Anna opened her eyes and lifted the leather pouch. It jingled softly and her eyes widened. The heft of the small bag bespoke the extent of the sum inside. She frowned and met Stephen's gaze. "What's this?"

"'Tis enough for your family to settle someplace safe." He enveloped her hands in his once more, closed her fingers around the pouch, and pressed it toward her. "Until you can make the crossing."

Anna shook her head. "I couldn't." She extended the pouch back toward him. "I can't accept this. It's too much."

"Let me do this. Please." He held his palms up, refusing to take it from her.

"Stephen, I—" Her voice caught. "I've already cost you too much. You missed your ship, though I don't know why. Now, you'll be late reporting to your new job. If I take this, you won't be able to afford to go start your new life." She sucked in a jagged breath. "You deserve a fresh start," she said on a sob.

He slipped his hands in his pockets. "Anna." When he didn't continue, she looked at him. "I've already turned down the job." His eyes held her gaze with intensity and earnestness.

Anna's hand flew to her chest. "You what? Why? When?"

Stephen's stare dropped to his feet for a moment before meeting her gaze once more. He slid a hand from his pocket and cupped her cheek. His thumb stroked in tender arcs and Anna nearly buckled. "Anna," he placed a second hand on her other cheek. "I love you."

A breath puffed from Anna's chest. Her heart pounded in her ears, and her head spun at the magnitude of his declaration. She searched his face and the truth of his love that reflected back undid her. Fresh tears spilled down her cheeks. "Stephen—" She placed her hands over his. "Oh, Stephen, I love you too." She squeezed her eyes closed, unable to bear looking at him when she uttered what must be said. "But I . . . I can't."

Stephen lifted her hands to his mouth, brushing his lips on the back of one, and held long. She relished the nearness of him, the feel of his lips on her skin. At length, he skimmed two quick kisses to her other hand and straightened. When he looked at her anew, his eyes shone with unshed tears. "I know." His voice was thick. Longing and emotion seemed to be vying for control. "And it's because I love you that I want you to have this. I want what's best for you, Anna. I know your family needs you." He tenderly kissed her hands once more before releasing them. "So, please, take this. Settle your family somewhere safe. Outside of Galway." He swallowed hard and offered her a sad smile. "And then cross over, marry Lord Corning, and save your family."

A quiet sob escaped Anna. "Oh, Stephen. It's too much." She clutched the pouch to her bosom.

"Aye, 'tis." He nodded. "I thought I knew what love was before. And then I thought I knew what it wasn't. But it wasn't until you that I truly understood. You showed me what love really is. And I can say with absolute certainty that I have never loved anyone the way I love you. And I never will again." He turned his head and looked out the window for a long moment before returning his gaze to hers. "And it's because of that love that I must free you to do what you need to do."

He reached into his pocket once more and produced a velvet packet and held it out to her. He tenderly unwrapped it and held it up to reveal a necklace.

Anna gasped when she recognized her own design. She slipped her hand behind the pendant and ran her fingers over the cross, the image blurring as a new spate of tears filled her eyes.

"You've had it right all along," Stephen said. "I thought you coming here was the worst thing to ever happen to me. Turns out I was wrong. So horribly wrong. Ye've changed everything, Anna—my life, my heart . . . me." He unclasped the chain and gestured for her to turn around.

She did and his hands slipped around her as he placed the necklace about her neck. He clasped it and she sensed him draw nearer. He gripped her shoulders with tenderness. "Wear it," he whispered, his lips brushing her ear. "Wear it and remember.

Know that you go with my blessing. And my heart." He pressed a slow kiss to her cheek. Her neck. Her shoulder.

Anna's breath stilled, fighting the urge to spin and meet his lips with her own. Instead, she grasped the cross around her neck and smiled, even as her heart broke. Maybe it wasn't too late. Perhaps there was some way they hadn't thought of. There had to be. "Stephen—"

"Shh. There's nothin' more to say. I'm sorry, Anna, I must go now. Paddy's in need of help." He gently squeezed her shoulders and slipped away.

She turned around just in time to see him disappear through the doorway. The door to the shop clicked shut, the cold breeze wafting after him, freezing her heart and quelling the fire he'd lit within it.

CHAPTER
42

A knock sounded on the door downstairs. Mother jumped at the sound and shot a helpless look to Father. The De Lacys were gathered around the Jenningses' table. Stephen had been gone ever since his encounter with Anna in the showroom a few days before.

Seamus gestured for everyone to be quiet. "I'll see to it," he whispered. "I'm comin', I'm comin'," Seamus called as he ambled down the stairs.

"Who could it be?" Mother whispered.

"Could be anyone," Anna replied. "'Tis a busy shop, and Seamus and Stephen are well known about town." She shrugged one shoulder.

"*Shh!*" Father hissed and moved to the door. "I want to listen," he mouthed. He inched toward the open doorway and inclined his ear near the opening. Voices carried up the stairs, but the words were indiscernible.

"This way," Seamus called before the door thudded closed. It seemed to take ages for him to ascend the stairs again, the De Lacys holding their breath all the while. When he came around the corner with an armful of packages and a woman and young man appeared from behind him, the family released a collective sigh of relief.

"Oh, you poor dears!" the woman exclaimed when she laid eyes on the family in their borrowed togs.

"Lady Arbury." Emmaline rose to her feet. "What brings you here?"

"Word is out all over town what happened to your place—the mob and all." She pressed a hand over her heart. "Dreadful mess, really."

"A dreadful mess is right," Seamus said. "They even tossed McGinnty's chipper."

Anna gasped. "What? Whatever for?"

Seamus shrugged. "Turns out, he's the one who turned in the lads that started the fire at yer place."

"So that's why Stephen needed to go help," Anna replied, almost to herself.

Seamus nodded and the uncomfortable silence of a group helpless to act filled the room.

Goodwin stepped around his mother, a smile splitting his face and concern clouding his eyes as he fixed them on Emmaline. "Are you alright?"

"Goodwin—er—Master Arbury." Emmaline turned to her parents. "Father, Mother, you remember the Arburys? They own the estate down in Clare."

Father shook Goodwin's hand. "Yes, of course. How do you do?"

Goodwin nodded. "When we heard the news, we sent word to your man, Owen. He brought what spare clothes he could scrounge from De Lacy Place to us. It draws less attention for us to come into the shop than it would if Owen did."

"God bless that man." Emmaline sighed, grasping Anna's hand.

"Indeed. Jolly good show," Father agreed. "Quite admirable. Especially for an Irish—er—" He stopped short, and his eyes darted around the room.

Seamus laughed. "For an Irishman, ya mean? I'd have to agree." Laughter bubbled out of him, his face reddening with delight. "Ye're comin' 'round, Mister De Lacy, so ya are. Though it'll take some gettin' used to for ye, I'd wager."

Father slipped a finger between his neck and collar and tugged. "Indeed." He cleared his throat and busied himself with untying the parcel Seamus had handed him.

"It was so very kind of Katy to lend us these garments," Mother added while smoothing her hands down the borrowed maid's uniform. "But I will admit, it will feel so nice to slip into a fresh set of clothes." Anna and Emmaline nodded and hummed their assent. After several days in the same attire, they were eager to freshen up properly.

"And we'll let you do just that." Lady Arbury squeezed Mother's hand. "If there's anything else at all you need, please send word. We'll help in any way we can." She gazed kindly at the group, compassion shining in her eyes. She then turned her attention to Father. "In fact, we've a smaller estate in West Clare that needs a manager. I'll have His Lordship contact you with the details, Lord—eh—Mister De Lacy." She offered an apologetic smile.

Mother's mouth dropped into a round chasm before her decorum returned. Father seemed stunned silent as well, until Mother elbowed him in the ribs.

"Much obliged," he stammered, rubbing the offended spot. The realization of what the lady was truly offering dawned on his face and he added, "You and His Lordship are far too generous. We thank you. Deeply."

"We'll be in touch." Goodwin shook the men's hands all around, tipped his hat at the ladies, and offered a warm smile in Emmaline's direction.

She blushed and ducked her head coyly in response.

The group murmured farewells as the pair took their leave. Then each of the De Lacys examined what had been salvaged for them. Anna smiled as she unwrapped the simple day dress she'd worn the afternoon Stephen took her to Tigh Hughes. She ran her fingers over the light blue fabric, the music from that night almost materializing in the room.

"Oh, I almost fergot." Seamus clapped a hand to his forehead. "This came fer ye as well." He slipped an envelope from his waistcoat pocket. "It's addressed to you, Anna."

Anna rose and accepted the letter. At the swirling lettering scrawled across the page, her heart sank. She would recognize the script anywhere. Lord Corning. She steeled herself to learn of the travel arrangements he'd made to get her across for the wedding. She broke the seal and read the letter aloud:

My Dear Miss Annabeth De Lacy,

Word has reached me of your family's unfortunate demise—your father's financial indiscretions and lack of leadership are disappointing to hear. Learning of the stripping of his title, land, and such was quite distressing indeed.

Word has also reached me of your most hapless endeavors, as well as what seems to be your regrettable change in loyalties while in your new home. It falls to me, therefore, to formally withdraw my offer of marriage and all the benefits and betterments entailed within it. I cannot allow the shame your family has brought upon the Crown and Kingdom to any further tarnish my own good standing.

Sincerely, Lord Corning,
Fourth Earl of Camberwick

"Oh, William." Mother collapsed into a fresh spate of tears, burying her face in Father's chest. "'Tis finished, then. No hope yet remains for our family," she spoke through sobs into his shirt.

"Dear Annie." Emmaline placed a sympathetic hand on her sister's shoulder. "I—I don't know what to say."

Relief and despair engaged in a tug-of-war in Anna's heart. Knowing that she would no longer be required to spend her life as the wife of that man allowed her to take a full breath for the first time in weeks. But knowing there was now no hope of saving her family's future stole it right back. "Oh, Father, I am so very sorry." Anna wiped her eyes and shook her head. "I . . . I should've accepted him sooner. Married him earlier. Then we would've already been bound, and he'd have had no choice but to take us in."

Father wagged his own head. He released Mother and stepped over and wrapped his arms around his daughter. "'Tis not your doing, Annabeth. 'Tis mine and mine alone."

Anna sank into his embrace, allowing his confession to lift some of the weight from her shoulders.

"William, whatever shall we do?" Mother whined.

"I have an idea," a voice spoke from the doorway.

All heads spun toward the source. Anna's breath caught in her chest. "Stephen!"

He crossed the room and took her hands in his. "Annabeth De Lacy," he said, then released one of his hands and slipped it into his pocket. "Ye've shown me the truth of unconditional love. And like my great ancestor, I've been through the gauntlet waiting for the love of my life. And now ye're here." He sank to one knee and held up a ring—an intricate design of Celtic knots surrounding the Claddagh. In the center, a heart-shaped diamond sparkled in the candlelight. "Anna, will you marry me?"

The room itself seemed to hold its breath. Anna sank down until she was eye to eye with Stephen. She opened her mouth to speak, but no words would come.

"What d'ye say, love? Will ya have me?" His eyes searched hers, pleading, questioning.

Anna looked to her parents, whose eyes glistened. Shaky smiles graced their faces. Her father nodded. Anna squeezed Stephen's hand and she bobbed her head vigorously. At last, an enthusiastic "Yes!" eked from her lips.

"Yeow!" Seamus howled and slapped his leg. "I'll put the kettle on!" Anna and Stephen laughed.

Stephen took Anna's left hand, her fingers shaking, and slipped the ring on her finger—the tip of the heart pointing toward her. "That's it now, my love. Ye're spoken for."

"Thanks be to God." She laughed again and ran her fingers over his stubbled jaw. He grasped her face and brought her gently toward him.

"I love you, Anna." He whispered just before his lips met hers with such tenderness, her breath caught. When she slid her hand around the back of his neck, the kiss deepened, and Emmaline clapped her hands.

"I love you too, Stephen," she uttered when the kiss broke off.

A wide grin spread across his face. Anna leaned in and planted a kiss on the dimple that had appeared in earnest for the first time in far too long.

EPILOGUE

Stephen stood at the back door of the showroom, watching the scene unfold.

"T'anks ever so much," a glassy-eyed young man said to Anna, though he gazed at the woman next to him. Stephen smiled.

"You're quite welcome. And congratulations."

The couple shared a kiss, smiled at Anna once more, and left the shop. Anna pressed a hand to her lower back and turned, her rounded belly protruding more than it had even yesterday.

Stephen frowned. "Are ya alright, love?"

Anna ran a hand down her belly, a grin tipping her mouth. "Never better. Just a little tired."

Stephen crossed the room and slipped his arms around his wife. Just as he was about to kiss her, a ruckus bounded into the shop.

"*Mamaí!*"

"There's my boy." Anna stooped down. "How was your day with *Mamó* and *Daideo*, Seamus?"

"Grand, so! Daideo De Lacy let me steer the wagon!"

Anna looked up with wide eyes at her father, who was now standing in the back door. "Did he indeed?"

William's shoulders rose and fell, delight sparking in his eyes. "I needed to carry a load of sheep's milk and cheese down to The King's Ransom. The lad did a very good job."

"That sounds grand, so. Thanks for lookin' after him." Stephen smiled and shook his father-in-law's hand. "And it seems farm life still agrees with ye?"

William nodded and straightened his cap. "Oh, indeed! You know, when Lord Arbury mentioned it was a sheep farm that needed managing, I was quite skeptical as to how we'd get on." He crossed his arms over his chest and added under his breath, "Particularly Elizabeth."

"Oh?" Stephen chuckled.

"Well, she's always been a bit of an indoor girl." The pair laughed.

"That's an understatement if I ever heard one," Anna said, joining in the conversation.

William shook his head, shoulders still bobbing. "Quite right. But it turns out, we're quite well suited for this lifestyle. And Elizabeth adores the lambs. She's even taken to learning how to spin wool!"

"Well, if that doesn't beat—"

"I'm hungry, Daideo," wee Seamus interrupted, tugging on William's coat hem.

"Well, we can't have that. Let's go find you something to eat." He scooped the four-year-old up and onto his back and galloped up the stairs to the flat.

Stephen wrapped his arms around Anna once more. "Da woulda been so proud." Emotion thickened Stephen's voice.

"Yes, he would have." Anna brushed Stephen's cheek with a kiss, and he smiled, still gazing after William and little Seamus. Anna's grin spread at the confirmation that even after all these years, she could still warm him with just a kiss. "I'll never forget his face when he saw his namesake," she added.

A sad smile tilted the corner of Stephen's mouth. "Aye. The auld man looked on him with such awe. I'll always be grateful for those few days we had with him and wee Seamus before Da passed."

Anna nodded and laid her head on his shoulder, both in silent reverence of the moment.

At length, Stephen sighed and turned his attention from the doorway to his wife. He studied her face for a long moment before brushing his lips against her forehead. He then puffed out a chuckle and shook his head.

"What is it?" Anna asked, looking up at him, absently rubbing her belly.

He brushed a stray hair from her face. "Oh, just thinkin' about what I could've missed out on." He leaned down and placed a gentle but earnest kiss on her lips. "Y'know, since I don't believe in love." He winked at her and they laughed as they followed their son and his grandpa up the stairs.

AUTHOR'S NOTE

Oh, dear reader, thank you so much for joining me on this journey to Galway. I hope you've loved Stephen and Annabeth's story as much as I have. Just like my first book, *A Dance in Donegal*, this book is a love letter to Ireland and her people. I had the privilege of living in County Galway—about a thirty-minute drive west of Galway City—for four years. In fact, our son was born in Galway City! So this place holds a very special piece of my heart. I wanted to bring the charm and authenticity of Galway and her people to the pages of this book. Therefore, many real places appear in it. Others are of my own making, with strong influences from actual establishments or areas.

The Jenningses' shop is based on the real Claddagh Jewellers shop, located on Shop Street in Galway City Centre. The legend that Stephen recounts is true. However, in order to be able to take creative license, I have changed the name of the family, as well as some details about the shop itself. The Claddagh ring was originally created by a man named Richard Joyce, and his ancestors run the store to this day. I chose the name Jennings for its similarity to Joyce, as well as it being an authentic surname to that region. You can read the original legend, as well as learn more about the authentic shop, at www.thecladdagh.com.

The area of town called the Claddagh is real, and it truly does flood quite often. In fact, just before we moved there, the road flooded and there really was a cow in the road after the waters receded, munching on seaweed!

McGinnty's Fish and Chips is fashioned after the very best fish and chips in the whole of Ireland—McDonagh's. Paddy McGinnty is entirely fictitious, but his delectable food is the real deal. Even people who don't like fish have sung the praises of McDonagh's fare. And if fish really isn't your cup of tea, they offer chicken and sausage that are just as melt-in-your-mouth. And their garlic dipping sauce? Forget about it.

The King's Ransom Pub was inspired by The Kings Head, located on High Street in Galway City Centre. I borrowed many of the details for The King's Ransom from the real pub, including its look and much of the history that Stephen used to distance himself from Anna that fateful day at lunch. If you ever have the chance to visit, I highly recommend the mussels—delicious!

Tigh Hughes is an amalgam of countless pubs dotting the streets of Galway. Many offer weekly, or sometimes nightly, "sessions" where you can sit and listen to local musicians play traditional Irish music. Dancing will often break out at these, much like it did for Stephen and Anna.

Galway Manor was inspired by St. Cleran's Manor, which you can find in Craughwell, Loughrea, County Galway. To my knowledge, it was never used to house landlords, but it was the perfect image for where the De Lacy family lived. The De Lacy Estate is entirely fictitious. The road Anna follows to get there in the carriage is authentic, but were you to journey there now, you'd discover only a wooded area and a squash club.

The Irish War for Independence was really going on during this time. While to my knowledge St. Cleran's was never set on fire, other landlords—typically the harsh ones—suffered the same fate over the decades of struggle. The attack on the Tuam Road did happen, though reports are conflicting about who was actually responsible. Constable Edward Krumm actually did open fire at the Galway train station and was there on that night, though I played with the timeline on this to fit my narrative. That event occurred on September 8, 1920. If you research it, you'll find it nearly impossible to discover the true story of what took place, which made it the perfect event to include in this story, adding to the chaos that was being unleashed during this difficult time in Ireland's history.

I wrote the bulk of this story during the summer of 2020. To say civil unrest roiled in the United States at that time would be an understatement. I had always planned to build this story around the Irish struggle for independence, so I feel the timing is nothing short of God's orchestration. Stephen and Annabeth's story takes place as the Irish War for Independence was beginning to gain ground. Though Ireland wouldn't officially gain independence until 1937, things were already in motion in 1920. The era of the British landlord in Ireland was swiftly coming to an end, and tensions between the two countries were high. Even to this day, there are strong, deeply entrenched beliefs about where Ireland belongs. Some want it to remain as it is, with the Republic an independent nation and Northern Ireland under the UK banner. Many others wish to see a unified Ireland, all under the British Crown. And still many others wish for an entirely united and independent Ireland that merges the Republic and Northern Ireland into one fully independent state.

It is a centuries-old argument that will not be solved in a hurry—if ever. However, I hoped to show the disparity between the beliefs held on both sides of the aisle and reality. Just as Stephen and Annabeth began to see the things they'd been taught about the "other side" were more often than not downright false,

I pray that we would each examine our own hearts for any shreds or whiffs of prejudice, ageism, or sexism. The struggle between England and Ireland in 1920 is mirrored in so many ways by the struggle we find in the United States in 2021 and beyond. This is in no way a bid for any certain political ideology. On the contrary, my prayer is that this story would open your eyes to see that all are created in the image of God, therefore, all are valuable and hold purpose. And when we see injustice, it is our responsibility—inasmuch as we are able—to live at peace with everyone and stand up for the vulnerable, as well as those being ostracized.

I love this story—and these characters—so very much, and I hope you do as well. If you'd like to experience more of Galway, the Claddagh, and the legend surrounding it all, check out my inspiration board on Pinterest. You can find it here: https://pin .it/2QgRFAN.

Thank you, again, for journeying along with me to the enchanted Emerald Isle. *Beannachtaí Dé ort, a chara.* God's blessings upon you, friend.

ACKNOWLEDGMENTS

It might seem ironic that I would be at a loss for words, given that I write books. However, when it comes to expressing my appreciation for everyone who made this book possible, I find I fail miserably every time. The words *thank you* don't feel strong enough to fully communicate the depth of my gratitude.

First and foremost, to God my Father. Thank You, Lord, not only for the opportunity to share these stories with the world but also for Your gracious kindness in helping me do so. May the words on these pages bring glory and honor to You and You alone.

And to my ultimate love, friend, and partner, Seth. There is no way on earth I'd be able to do these things without you and your support. Not only for the tangible ways you help keep our household running smoothly—even as I was writing this book and we were miserable with COVID, you still managed to take care of us all—but also for all the intangible ways you lift me up. Your support, encouragement, and unending belief in me mean more than I could ever fully articulate. I will always be grateful to God for the gift of getting to be your wife.

Hannah, Cailyn, and Isaac, my fellow bibliophiles and my

three favorite shamrocks. Your excitement about my books, your willingness to talk through story ideas, and your consistent enthusiasm swell my heart with gratitude. Thank you for stepping up and taking care of our family when Daddy and I were sick, and for cooking more dinners—both then and while I was writing—than I know you wanted to. I love you so very much.

Mom and Dad, what can I even say? Thank you for your amazing, endless, enthusiastic support. Mom, thank you for reading every chapter as it was written, for sharing your honest thoughts, and for being willing to read them again once I changed them. I'm so grateful for you and your influence—and for the crocheted Grogus.

To my mother-in-law, Cheryl Deibel. Your prayers have carried me through countless seasons and scenarios. Your shared excitement along my publishing journey has been such a blessing. I am so grateful to get to share life—and your son—with you.

To Cynthia Ruchti, my incredible agent. Thank you for all the late-night chats, for your invaluable wisdom and insight into this story, and for sharing that one piece that finally opened the floodgates and allowed me to finish this tale. Your help and guidance took this story from one I loved to one I absolutely adore.

To my Panera Girls Writing Group—Liz Johnson, Lindsay Harrell, Sara Carrington, Ruth Douthitt, Erin McFarland, Tari Faris, Rhea Adley, and Sarah Popovich. Your friendship, support, encouragement, insight, and laughter have been a blessing and an answer to prayer for the last four and a half years. I thank God all the time for bringing us together.

Go raibh míle maith agaibh to my Irish friends. Debra and Brian Ó Ghibne, Linda and Donal O'Donnell, Mart O'Donnell, J-Me Peaker, Rick Russell—ye all are members of our extended family. My understanding and love of Ireland, her culture, and her people would not be nearly as rich without you. We love and miss you all desperately.

To my real-life friends and family—Charity Verlander, Stacy Dyck, Tiffany Kilcoyne, Donna Carlson, April Maxey, Andrea Williams, Lori Palmer, Tim and Melissa Palmer, Ron and June Palmer (all separate families, ha!), Terri Logelin, Judy Albakry, Sara Walton, Nancy Patton. You all keep me sane. Thank you for being listening ears and for giving me the occasional kick in the pants I needed!

Writing can often feel like a very lonely journey. It is easy to believe you are alone in the struggle, and imposter syndrome sets in something fierce. Jaime Jo Wright, Sarah Sundin, Courtney Walsh, Jocelyn Green, Natalie Walters—Thank you all for investing in me, sharing your hearts, and coming alongside me in this journey.

To my Highland Lakes family, specifically my leadership—Mark Anderson and Danielle Ware. Thank you for your unwavering support and understanding as I balanced writing, teaching, online teaching, teaching with COVID. I am so grateful for the servant leadership you provide to me and the whole HLS family. To my teammates Matt and Brittany Verlei and Paris Johnson. Your shared enthusiasm for my writing gives me strength and energy to put my booty in a chair and write, even when I'm worn out from long school days and endless grading. And to the rest of the staff—I was blown away by your support and enthusiasm when my first book released in 2020. The way you would go out of your way to ask me how things were going, the way you cheered me on, and the way you ordered the book blessed my heart more deeply than I could say. Thank you, I love you all.

And finally, but in no way least, huge, massive thanks to my editors, Rachel McRae and Robin Turici. Thank you for loving these characters as much as I do and taking my mess of a draft and turning it into something beautiful. To Brianne Dekker, Karen Steele, and the rest of the most amazing team at Revell, you all are truly magical. I am in awe of your creativity, tenacity, and the impeccable quality of everything you do. Thank you, thank you, thank you.

GLOSSARY OF TERMS

anois—[eh-NISH]—now; can be used as a measurement of time, or a filler in conversation

a Stíofán—[uh SHTIFF-ahn]—Stephen, in direct address

a stór—[uh SHTOHR]—my dear

a mhác—[uh WAHCK]—son, when addressing directly

an-mhaith—[AHN-wah]—very good

bodhrán—[BOW-rahn]—a traditional Irish drum

Buíochas le Dia—[BWEE-huhs leh JEE-uh]—Thanks be to God

ceard—[KYAIRD]—what?

ceart go leor—[KART guh LORR]—alright?

ceilí—[KAY-lee]—a party with music, dancing, and often storytelling

Cén chaoi a bhfuil tú?—[KAY KWEE uh WILL TOO]—How are you?

Claddagh—[CLAH-duh]—the name of a type of ring design, as well as an area within Galway City

comhghairdeas—[koh-GAR-juhs]—congratulations

craic—[CRACK]—fun, good times; often, but not always, involving music

cupán tae—[KUH-pahn TAY]—cup of tea

Daideo—[DAH-joh]—Grandpa

Dáil—[DAHL]—the first parliament of Ireland

dhá phláta—[ghah FLAH-tuh]—two plates

feargach linn—[FARR-gack LYNN]—angry with us

iontach—[EEN-tahk]—excellent

Gaeilge—[GAY-lih-guh]—Gaelic/Irish

gardaí—[garr-DEE]—police

go cinnte—[guh KINN-chuh]—certainly, for certain

go maith—[guh MAH]—good, well

hurley—the stick used in the game of hurling; the Irish word for it is *caman*

Óró Sé Do Bheatha Bhaile—[OH-roh SHAY duh VAH-huh WALL-uh]—the name of a traditional Irish song

go raibh míle maith agat—[GO ROH MEE-luh MAH uh-GUT]—thanks a million

Maidin mhaith—[MAH-jeen WAH]—Good morning

Mamaí—[MAH-mee]—Mommy

Mamó—[mah-MOH]—Grandma

ní fhaca mé iad—[NEE AH-kuh MAY EE-uhd]—I haven't seen them

níl—[NEEL]—No

Ó, a mhac go deo!—[OH uh WAHK guh JOE]—Oh, man alive!

scuab—[SKOO-uhb]—broom

seafóid—[SHAH-fooj]—nonsense

seafóid amach—[SHAH-fooj uh-MAHK]—utter nonsense

seisiún—[seh-SHYOON]—an informal gathering for traditional Irish music, song, and dance

slán—[SLAHN]—goodbye; literally translated means safety/health

tá brón orm—[taw brone OR-uhm]—I'm sorry

tá, cinnte—[taw KINN-chuh]—Yes, indeed/certainly

tóg go bog é—[TUG guh BUG uh]—take it easy

uafásach—[OOH-fuh-sack]—terrible/horrible

uilleann pipes—[UHL-uhn PIPES]—the Irish form of bagpipes, played by pumping a bag using one's elbow rather than blowing into a mouthpiece

Loved this book?

Turn the page to read the first chapter of another sweeping Irish romance from Jennifer Deibel!

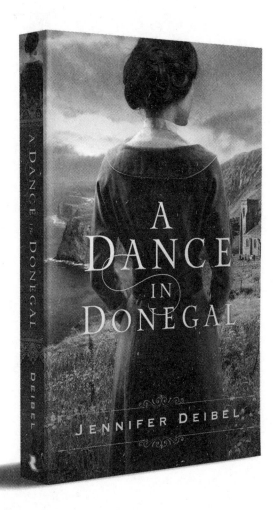

CHAPTER 1

Boston
October 1920

The grandfather clock downstairs chimed the hour, its clangs all too reminiscent of the funeral bells presiding over Mother's service just yesterday morning. Silent tears slipped down Moira Doherty's cheeks—each one punctuated by the unforgiving *clang, clang, clang.*

I never did care for that clock.

Moira's gaze fell on the street below, though she truly saw nothing more than blurry figures and blotches scurrying in the rain. Her burlap travel bag lay forgotten on the bed, surrounded by all the trappings of her impending overseas voyage. Moira feared if she returned to packing, she would find herself hurling each item in anger, rather than carefully rolling and placing them in the bag for her journey—a journey she was no longer sure she wanted to take.

How had it come to this? Only weeks ago life was simple and good. Moira, having just graduated from Boston Normal

School, was set to begin her teaching career not far from the brownstone where she grew up. Her mother was alive and well, and Moira was content to daydream about someday embarking on a grand adventure to see her mother's homeland. Today, life was drastically different.

Thunder rumbled across the sky, sending a chill down Moira's spine. Hugging her shawl tighter around her shoulders, she turned to the bed and travel trappings strewn across it. Heaviness weighed her down like an anchor. Neither able to continue packing nor clear the bed for sleep, she shuffled to the tufted chair near the fireplace and slumped into the seat.

The flames danced hypnotically in the grate, drawing Moira into their spell. No thoughts flitted through her mind as she absently watched the fire. Time released any grip on sense or logic, and she gave herself over to the trance as the flames slowly died. Her eyelids growing heavy, Moira rested her head on the quilted back of the chair and let her lids fall closed.

"Goodbye, Mother," she whispered into the darkness.

The explosion rocked the building, and Moira shot up in her seat, gripping the armrests so firmly she feared the fabric would tear. Beads of sweat dotted her forehead and dropped in dark stains on her shawl. She struggled to catch her breath, and she clutched one hand to her chest to quell the pounding underneath.

Rain pelted the windows, lightning split the sky, and another peal of thunder shook the room.

"Not an explosion," she spoke to the room and gulped. "Thunder."

Falling back in the seat, she wiped her brow with the hem of her shawl. Chills crept up her neck as the details of the dream floated to the forefront of her mind.

Mother.

The door to her bedroom squeaked open, and dusky-haired Leona entered. "Are you alright, Miss? I thought I heard you cry out."

Leona looked at Moira with an expression of sadness and sympathy. A look Moira had grown to hate in the short days since Mother's passing.

"Yes, Leona." She pasted on her most authentic-looking smile. "I'm fine. Thanks for looking in on me though."

"Of course, Miss." She bobbed her head before scurrying to the window to draw the drapes. "It's a frightfully awful storm tonight, if I say so. I've not seen one like this in years."

Moira straightened her shawl once more and poked at the embers in the grate. "Goodness, it sure is."

Leona finished her task, then came to rest a hand on Moira's shoulder. "Are you sure you're alright? You're as pale as a white rose, and despite the chill in the air, I can't help but notice the perspiration on your face."

Sighing, Moira measured the loyal housekeeper. Leona had proven to be an invaluable help and comfort these last weeks. She, more than most, would likely understand. "It was a dream," Moira began at last.

"A dream?" Leona's brow furrowed.

Moira motioned to the stool across from her, and the woman sat down.

"I saw a far green country with hills rolling on for eternity. Waters crashed upon the shore, and when the sun shone on the hills, they glistened like emeralds."

"Ireland." A small smile dawned on Leona's face.

Moira nodded. "I can only assume so. It was breathtaking—like nothing I'd ever seen before. It felt so familiar, yet I know I've never been to this place."

Leona knitted her brows together and leaned over to place more coal on the grate. "Interesting."

"Indeed," Moira continued. "But then, out of nowhere, pewter clouds darkened the sky and fog as thick as I've seen closed in around me. In the distance, I could just make out the figure of a woman standing on a hillside. I squinted to try and make out her face, but it was too dark, and the fog too thick. But I could see her skirts blowing in the wind."

"That sounds . . . eerie."

"It was, and yet I felt compelled to press on. In a flash, the scene swept forward and I found myself standing right behind her."

Leona scooted forward on the stool, her eyes as wide as saucers.

Taking the cue of Leona's interest, Moira continued. "I extended a trembling hand to tap the woman on the shoulder, but before I could touch her, she turned around." Moira squeezed her eyes shut and took in a slow, steady breath. Her heart already quickening, she could feel the sweat pricking the back of her neck.

"Well, who was it?"

"It"—Moira paused—"It was Mother."

"*Tsk!*" Leona wagged her head. "Oh, you poor dear. That must have been shocking."

"Yes, truly, it was. But more than that, it was the look in her eyes." Moira turned her own gaze back to the fire, searching for the best way to describe the haunting look she'd seen on her mother's face. "She looked . . . terrified. And sad."

"Goodness, I wonder what that could be about?"

Moira slowly raised her eyes to meet Leona's. "That's not the worst of it." Her throat tightened, and she suddenly wished she hadn't shared the dream. Not because she worried about Leona's reaction but because she wasn't sure she could get through the rest of the telling.

"Oh, sweet Moira." Leona rested a hand on Moira's knee. "It

might ease your heart to share the burden." She offered a kind smile, and compassion shone in her eyes.

Moira sighed and rubbed her palms up and down her skirt, drying and warming them at the same time. "She looked me square in the face and said, 'Save me, Moira. Come to Ireland and save me!'"

Leona's jaw fell open. "But—"

"I know." Moira shrugged.

"It's as if she was trying to tell you—" Leona stopped short and shot her eyes to meet Moira's. "Never mind."

Moira furrowed her brow but, eager to be done sharing her dream, chose not to question what Leona was referring to. "Before I could ask her what she meant, she disappeared. And that's when I woke up."

"No wonder you were so upset when I came in."

The two sat in silence for several minutes before Leona turned her attention to the window. "It seems quieter out there." She stood and made her way across the room to the window. On the way, she kept her eyes on Moira's clothes and travel bag on the bed. "So, you've decided to go?"

Moira's shoulders rose and fell. "Maybe. I don't know."

Jennifer Deibel is a middle school teacher and coffee lover. She believes no one should be alone on their faith journey, and through her writing she aims to redefine home through the lens of culture, history, and family. After nearly a decade of living in Ireland and Austria, Jennifer now lives in Arizona with her husband and their three children.

Meet *Jennifer*

Find Jennifer online at
JENNIFERDEIBEL.COM

and sign up for her newsletter to get the latest news and special updates delivered directly to your inbox.

Follow Jennifer on social media!

 JenniferDeibelAuthor    ThisGalsJourney    JenniferDeibel_Author